Moon Cursers

Moon Cursers

John Swantek

A Novel

Eagle Crest Publishing

Eagle Crest Publishing

Author's Revised Edition.
Copyright 2016 by John Swantek

ISBN 13: 978-0-9729996-1-8
Library of Congress Number: 00-192667

For John and Mike
My two best buddies from Day One.
Thanks for being such great kids and such fine men.

"History is written by the victors."
Winston Churchill

Prologue

The hangman smeared the soot-blackened lard over his face and neck. The tissue-thin veneer of society's good intentions demanded a killer remain anonymous. Silly custom, he thought, rolling up the sleeves of his black shirt so as not to soil it. The whole damned city knows who the hell I am. Bet Old Jack Ketch never had to be so discreet. Nevertheless this was 18th century New York and the man who pulled the lever sending another man to Elysium or Erebus, Avalon or Abaddon, or whatever version of paradise or oblivion one professed, could not be allowed to take pride nor pleasure nor even claim the deed as his own.

He scooped another handful of the foul-smelling mess out of the wooden bucket and rubbed it under his ears and on his cheeks and carefully around his eyes. It was barely 10 o'clock in the morning but the early summer heat wave of the past three days continued and the hangman felt sweat trying to burst through the black-crusted coating at the back of his neck. By the time it came to do the real work of this morning, he would feel like potato pulp baking inside a fire-hardened skin. He had been through these preparations many times. He dragged his fingers over the lip of the bucket to scrape off the excess and wiped his fingers on the wooden posts holding the crosspiece of the gallows platform trying to get rid of the greasiness. He daubed at the sweat forming under his nose and then quickly drew his hand away, the odor making his stomach do a small flip. He wiped his hands on a rag. Satisfied he could get a solid grip on the trip mechanism, he tested it. He pulled sharply on the lever. The four-foot-square panel fell quickly away from the platform deck. He climbed down, reset the panel and tried the mechanism again. Once again, it fell away with single-minded finality. He reset the mechanism and waited.

The gallows had been erected two days before, a day before the military tribunal had even confirmed the death sentence. A mere formality. This was no common murderer. This was not merely an enterprising printer turning out a good version of counterfeit scrip. No recidivistic thief. No common highway thug masquerading as the personal guardian of the King's interests. This was a man trusted with the very protection of His Excellency George Washington himself. A man who had betrayed his adopted country in the very throes of its birth pangs. A man involved in a far-reaching plot so heinous it threatened the entire patriotic cause. No, there was no doubt about the verdict. And, no doubt that the people of New York were anxious to get a glimpse of this grub that had crawled out into the daylight of discovery once the rock of conspiracy had been ripped up out of the ground.

This ghostly city could still muster a sizeable crowd. The noise had grown steadily during the past hour despite the palpable humidity that already hung over the field near the Bowery Lane like pipe smoke in a tavern. Now, the brigades of Generals Scott, Spencer, Heath and Lord Sterling were marching into place. His Excellency George Washington had sent out the order that every soldier not on duty or otherwise officially excused must attend. The commander-in-chief, it was said, wanted to make certain his men got the message. The large field, just off the Broad Way between the camps of Colonels McDougall and Huntington, was already crawling with several thousand residents laughing and bantering, joking about the hangman, whispering about their own personal knowledge of the Grand Conspiracy, always looking side to side so as to be sure they were among those of like persuasion. No Tories here. Were there? No, indeed. Except, perhaps, you, or, maybe, me. As the soldiers marched into the field, the crowd pushed in closer to the gallows not wanting to give up their vantage point. Most of the city residents who remained were here. That is, those who hadn't fled to the north or to the Long Island. Young and old. Unspoken Tory and silent Patriot. Dock workers and shopkeepers. Cooks and chimney sweeps. There was a sizeable contingent from "The Holy Ground," that steamy, forbidden nest of sailors' brothels and rum joints that the guest of honor at this party had been known to frequent. One elderly gent, who only minutes before had left the thick tobacco haze and malt-scented coolness of the Hog's Head Tavern, remarked to a companion that it seemed as if the entire population of 25,000 had turned out for the event, although, not counting the troops, there couldn't be but half of that number still remaining in the city.

"And why not?" asked his companion, a skinny, pale little man with one tooth in his lower jaw stabbing the air. "Everybody wants to see Kip, the moon curser swing."

His friend, sporting a stained grey vest over a frayed shirt, expelled a high cackling laugh at the use of the latest slang for the city's low life.

"A sight for sure, Zeke. Truly a sight not to be missed," he said pushing his way through the crowd to get closer to the gallows.

As he pushed on, creating a crevice into which the skinny man slipped before it closed behind him, he incurred the wrath of a large woman in a soiled brown frock who had staked out her spot for a clear view of the proceedings, hands on hips and two small girls in tow.

"Watch where you're steppin' or I'll be dragging you up

there and slippin' that rope around the necks of both of ya,"
she said to the two ale-soaked newcomers while tilting her
head toward the gallows. She knitted her brow and forced a
narrow mouth, which didn't quite cover the smile. The men
laughed and offered exaggerated pardons, bowling and making broad sweeping motions with their hands. They continued pushing forward, however, drawing similar comments
all along the way.

The woman, her frock straining against her ample breasts
and exploding outward on all sides, quickly forgot about the
rude old gents and looked around to make certain her two
girls were in place. The youngsters, each of them inheriting
ample girths, were hopping on one leg. Their small piscine
mouths lost in the round bulk of their faces were working in
unison, chanting singsong:

"Tories with their brats and wives should pack and run to
save their lives."

The woman laughed a deep mucousy laugh that ended in
a sharp cough. She bent over, hands on her thighs, and saw
the cough through to the finish. Then she cuffed the little
girl in the green dress for making her cough and once again
directed her attention to the platform where the hangman
was now standing with his hands on his hips.

The two old gents, after earning a few halfhearted swipes
of a hat, a poke with a cane, and an earful of choice words
from those whose feet they trampled or whose pleasant small
talk had been interrupted by a jolt to the back, reached the
front of the crowd and stood directly in front of the gallows.
They whooped and cheered as loud as anyone when the
troops marched into place, all the while exchanging knowing glances and whispering to each other.

"Hope they keep marching straight into Hudson's River," said the man with the gray vest.

"Me, too," hissed his cadaverous drinking companion.
"Between the patriots and the lobsterbacks, they'll send this

city straight to hell."

Similar sentiments played out across the field as the troops slowly moved into position to witness what would be the first military execution of the struggle with Mother England.

The old men were too filled with ale and the excitement of the impending show to notice the young woman with the smooth cinnamon skin staring at the gallows. Tears flowed steadily from her large dark eyes, coursed down her flushed cheeks and splashed on her breasts swelling out of the open bodice of her dress. She made no attempt to wipe them away. She stared at the gallows, narrowing her eyes, trying to focus as if myopia kept her from seeing what she really wanted to see. In her mind's eye, however, she saw all too clearly.

New York in 1776 was a city whistling in the dark. A city torn between the promise of a new order and the familiarity of the way things used to be. Praying for change and in the next breath praying from their deepest hearts that nothing would change. They knew that change was coming and that it could destroy them. New York was a child walking the rail of a picket fence. On one side was the thick, sharp, irritating thorn bushes of the British; on the other was the bottomless pit of unknown freedom. Pick a side. Falling straight down on the pickets of status quo was not an option. It was quickly becoming time to choose.

***

Just a mile away, the centerpiece of this grim garden party sat in a guarded room. Thomas Hickey could not see the crowd gathered to watch him die but he could hear the hum, the expectant buzz of tens of thousands of New Yorkers eager to see him hang.

Hickey sat on a rough-hewn wooden bench, his back against the wall facing the only door to the dry goods storage room of the mercantile building just off Bowery Lane. A single window high up in the wall overhead allowed in the insistent hum of the crowd. He repeatedly rubbed the back of his thick right hand alongside his left jaw, a mannerism he had exhibited most of his adult life when he was uncertain what to do next, though, as he got older, such instances were less frequent. He brushed wavy black hair from his eyes, caught himself rubbing and quickly looked at the door. Every few minutes an armed guard would look through the door to be certain the prisoner was still contained within and Hickey did not want the guard or anyone to see his concern. What had gone wrong? Large parts of the puzzle were still missing. He had helped uncover a counterfeiting ring, not to mention a conspiracy. He had, he was certain, saved the life of that pompous Virginian ass Washington and, in so doing, probably saved the cause of independence. Whatever that was worth. Truth be known, it was "His Goddamned Excellency" the rich southern planter who should be sitting on this hard wooden bench.

He chastised himself. "I'm not going over it all again. I did what I had to do. Washington will do likewise."

The events of the past year played themselves out in his mind again, despite his protestations. Each time when he got to the present, there was a different ending. Word will come, he thought, and they'll let me ride out of the city. The grand event of the day will be postponed. They'll tell everyone there is new evidence. His role in the conspiracy would eventually come to light and it would make everything clear. Or, perhaps, Phoebe would convince Washington of the only reasonable decision. Maybe, he thought, they'll say I escaped. The word will go out that I took Phoebe hostage. They'll say I went up to Canada but Washington will know I went west. That is, we went west. He owes me that much.

Phoebe. A spasmodic gulp of air belied his false calm and he again glanced at the door. What does she believe?

What does she know? The thought of never seeing her again twisted his gut and wrenched the breath from his lungs. His chest tightened over his thumping heart until he thought for certain it would burst through the skin. He stood and walked to the opposite wall, his muscular back pressed against the wall, which contained the door. He bent at the waist, hands on his knees and gasped for air, his heart racing. The thought of never touching her again was nearly too much. He had to clench his fists to keep from screaming. Her coffee-colored breasts. The glow of her skin. He would be with her again. He had to be with her again. Doubt got a foothold once again.

Emotions careened through his head like a 12-pound navy gun loose in a storm. First anger slammed into one bulkhead. Then fear slid across the deck of his mind. Phoebe's face crashed into him, then moved away. He was angry, bewildered, frustrated and scared. Yes, for one of the few times in his life, he was very scared.

Why? He was good at his job. Perhaps, too good. He should never have taken the job in the first place. Never have given in to the temptations of the promises. Never trusted the rich owners and manipulators of the world. They always win. He had gone against his own principles. Anger again. They talk of honesty and loyalty. That's what I gave them. They go on and on about liberty, and freedom. They know nothing about truth and liberty and all of that political nonsense they spout about. Fear exploded into terror. He was going to die. Was there any way out? Thousands of people were waiting to watch him die. Maybe they were waiting for someone else. No. No use playing with that kind of trickery. It was his death they wanted. Someone had to tell them the truth. Why was that so important right now? Because he just might die. In fact, in an instant of clarity, he was certain there was no stopping that now. At least Phoebe and others who mattered should know what really happened. He clung to this thought.

"No!"

He gave himself an order, which he immediately disobeyed. He started through the scenes of the past year again, rubbing his jaw.

He was going to die. He was powerless. They had all of the power. They always did. Always would. What could he do? Action was better than just sitting and waiting. He took several deep breaths, straightened up to his full five-foot six-inch height, swiped his left jaw resolutely and called for the guard.

"Bring me pen and paper. I want to write a letter," Hickey said, surprising himself in the steadiness and clarity of his demand.

"Traitors are in no position to demand anything," said the private wearing the distinctive sash of the general's Life Guard to which Hickey himself had belonged in what seemed a lifetime ago. The private was startled by the forcefulness of the prisoner.

"Private," said Hickey, his voice controlled. Softer now, realizing the soldier was just doing his job. "Can't you see your way to do this thing for me? I'm going to my death. The Almighty will be doing the judging soon enough. For now, can you give a fellow soldier a chance to set down his last respects?" Hickey's smile had carried him away from danger and from bed to bed for years. It had been like a magic light. It worked yet again.

The private stared hard at Hickey, thought for a second, and walked away. He returned a few minutes later with a pen with a worn nib, a spot of ink and some paper. Hickey snatched them like food offered a starving man. He walked to the wall with the high window, straddled the bench and began writing.

"My dearest Phoebe. I know by now you will have heard many things but you must believe me when I say that what

I tell you here is the truth of it all. These last few months in New York have been the best of my miserable life. Because of you. But also because I had the slight taste of what it is like to have a purpose, a meaning other than one's own self-ish pleasures and survival. Now, it seems, I am at an end. It is not so bad. The dying that is. I have only to think of you and the brief time we had together to know I've had what few men have ever had. What is hard, what sticks in my throat like a chicken bone, is that the lies they have told and are telling may somehow work their way into your heart. The court martial was a farce. I could not believe what was said. I did not take it serious. But, surely they knew the truth before it ever began. At least as much as I did. Surely Mr. Washington has told them. Told them all that I have already told you. The truth. I thought I was being loyal in not telling the others. It was what I had to do. It doesn't really matter now. I am just one man. It doesn't really matter to me if anyone else knows the truth. But I have to know that you believe what I told you. That you believed me when I told you just how all of this happened."

Hickey wrote furiously, splashing ink on paper and bench. After several minutes, he stopped, put his hands over his eyes and remembered a night that now seemed a lifetime in the past. It couldn't have been only a single year since that night. He could feel the cool breeze and the splash of the river. And the moon. It had never been brighter nor more to be cursed.

Part I

Chapter One
Charles River, Cambridge
10 p.m., Tuesday, June 13, 1775

Thomas Hickey crisply stroked the oars through the smooth dark green surface of the Charles River. A light coating of sweat on his thick forearms caught the bright moonlight and made them glow. With each stroke, his wide, muscular back tested the fabric of his dark green shirt and the sling boat surged forward. Though only five feet six inches tall, Hickey was thick and powerful. He loved nights like this. It had been a steamy day but a slight breeze sweeping the small waves of the night water made it just about perfect. Though not a full moon, the white light was nearly as bright as a Hunter's Moon. Hickey could clearly see the marshy shore of the Boston Neck a half mile away. Cap's sunken face was cast in white jowls and dark shadows as if he were standing under a lantern. His eyes bulged in terror as he expected the devil himself. He wasn't contributing much to the forward progress of the craft but it was a two-person job and Cap had been available.

"Enjoying the voyage, Cap?"

"Voyage? This ain't no voyage. This is suicide you crazy bastard. Know what I would enjoy? Shoving this oar up yer arse. God damned moon. The redbacks can see us. I know they can. And they'll be coming to hang us. And you sit there with that stupid grin on your face. Why didn't we wait for a cloudy night? This stuff will keep. Why tonight?"

"Best night to see where you're going," said Hickey, delighting in the nervousness of his cadaverous smuggling companion. "This ain't nothing, Cap. I remember a few years ago, in fact, just about three years ago tonight, when I had my first taste of the trade." Hickey settled comfortably into the oars making smooth, powerful strokes and delighting in the storytelling.

"I'm not needing any tales from you just right now, Tom," said Cap, his voice stumbling over a large lump in his throat while his eyes shifted excitedly left to right.

"I was hired by a gent down in Providence," continued Hickey ignoring the protests as if telling a story to a child, more to entertain himself than his audience. "He tells me all I need do is board and ride this sloop into port and help her unload and I'll have three dollars continental. Sure it'd be easy money. 'Course no one told me about King George's Gaspee. An armed schooner, it was. Just waiting to sink the sloop, along with me and the rum we was carrying. The rum, of course, not bearing all the proper customs stamps and other such official muck and mire. It was bright that night, too. Men were cursing at the moon like wolves with burrs in their backsides. Just like you. The Gaspee came right at us and we were making pretty good headway. They were almost on top of us but, in the end, we didn't have much to worry about. The lobsterbacks ran the schooner right up onto Namquit Point. We escaped, unloaded the sloop. Fact is, Cap, we went back later in a crowd of small boats to try and torch'em. They saw us and began firing. So we fired back. Will you believe it? We took over the schooner. Tied up the crew and walked them ashore and then set fire to the Gaspee. Talk about bright! Now that was bright. Greatest bonfire I ever saw," said Hickey, flashing a smile that made even Cap ease up for an instant. Hickey's smile was like a mother's open arms. It was as honest as a dog's wagging tail. There was no solicitation. Nothing due for the receiving. It was offered freely. There were no hidden costs.

"Yer crazier than a wharf dog, Hickey," said Cap, still casting his eyes about waiting to be discovered.

"Maybe, Cap. Maybe. For me, that's what life is all about. I do what I want as often as I can. I try to stay out of another man's way but if he gets in mine, then we go to it. A couple of ales, a dram of rum and a small woman with large white breasts with large, pink nipples makes for a perfect night. That's just what I'm going to be looking for later on when we get rid of this load." And, again, he smiled.

"If we get to unload," said Cap, his voice cracking, "Sam Pigge tells me the King's men have been patrolling the river every night since Lexington. He says they already shot a dozen or so and just left 'em right in the river. He says the Sons of Liberty are preparing for a fight and that...."

"Sam's like a prissy little schoolgirl," said Hickey interrupting, "He sees his own shadow, he jumps straight up in the air. I've been doing this twice a week for two months. Haven't had a problem yet. The damn lobsterbacks are the ones that want this stuff anyway. They like the Virginia tobacco better than the rotten weeds they're gettin' from the King and the rum is cheaper. Why this tobacco here probably came right from the Virginia manor of old Colonel Shoot'em Up Washington himself. They're all getting rich off this. It's all a game, Cap. Rebel or redcoat. They're all the same to you or me. I'd just like to get my fair share. I personally don't care who wins or what they think they won as long as they leave me alone."

"What about martial law? Sam make that up? You tellin' me there really ain't no Gen. Gage? I s'pose Boston is free as the wind. No, those ain't lobsterback soldiers walkin' up and down each street day and night. No, sir. Nothing to worry about even if we make it across this damned river."

"That proclamation is cow dung, Cap. I read it. 'The high almighty crown won't slaughter any more of you nasty rebels if you just give up and swear allegiance to Georgie Three.' Except, of course, Sam Adams and Hancock. No slackened rope for them. I read it to a few boys at the tavern and they just about jumped up right and ran out and got them a soldier or two to hang from the Liberty Tree. It's been almost seven years since the King's men came to this city. People are tired of it. They're up to here with it," said Hickey, cracking his fingers into his forehead in a rough salute. "What they don't understand though is that Hancock and Adams and all the rest won't give'em any more'n they got right now under the king. It's men like you and me that pay and keep paying. You gotta take what you can when you can."

The sling boat, loaded with contraband, neared the midway point between the Cambridge and Boston shores. The boat rode low in the center, weighed down by the barrels of rum and sacks of tobacco along with some fresh fruits and a few silver items specially ordered by a British captain. Smuggling had been Thomas Hickey's main occupation since his desertion from the British Army ten years earlier. An Irishman from the Province of Connaught, he had been tricked into joining the army by a British sergeant charged with filling a new ship headed for the conflict in North America.

As it turned out, he hadn't minded the adventure at first. It was better than farming the small plot of dying land, all that was left of the family farm. Originally owners of a choice plot of land in Munster, Hickey's grandfather had been banished to Connaught after Cromwell and his successors swept through the island. In the early 1600s, the Flight of the Wild Goose had sent most Roman Catholics fleeing to France or Spain or even Germany. The political fate of the Hickeys and other Roman Catholics rose and fell for a century until the Treaty of Limerick had finally given them some legitimacy.

By then, however, Catholics owned only five percent of the land whereas a hundred years earlier, it had been nearly 90 percent. Hickey's father had stayed. He didn't know much about politics and was too busy earning a living to be much of a rabble rouser. In the end, it didn't matter. He died at the age of 41 from body-breaking hard work and dead dreams. Young Thomas was 13, the oldest of five children, two boys and three girls. He began to do the man's work. He tried. He really tried. He worked until his developing 13-year-old body literally fell to the ground. He worked for two years. But, there was nothing to show for it. They got further and further behind in payments for everything. They were broke, in debt, and hungry most of the time. They sold the land and moved to the city.

He was 15 when he got a job on the docks. Three years later, he heard about the need for soldiers to go to America. His brother and sisters were able to work now and could take care of his mother. The older dockworkers talked of America, of sailing the ocean. A grand adventure. He knew he would die right here on the docks if he didn't get away. He had been thinking about signing up when word got to a local recruiting sergeant. That very day, Hickey had been "enlisted" by the acceptance of a shilling offered as a gift to a hard working boy. He didn't mind the trickery at all. Barely two weeks later, he was shipped to the colonies as part of the "protective force" the crown thought necessary to protect its colonial interests after the war with the French and heathens.

From the start, military life did not agree with him. There were constant orders. Don't do that. Do this. Stand here. Turn this way. Don't look at that. The penalty for not doing so was public lashing, ordered by white-faced, women-like little officers who wouldn't last half a second on the wharves in a fair fight. Hickey had several lash scars on his back to prove he had not always done what he was told. The sting of a lash was enough to make a man renounce the Pope himself at the time. But the sting went away quickly and the scars were a good conversation piece with women. They'd want to see his back and he would trade for a look at theirs. He'd often thought and now, in hindsight, firmly believed, that the officers had been particularly diligent in their lashings knowing that he was, as they said, a Papist; an Irish Catholic who actually believed Pope Clement XIV and now Pope Pius VI were God's chosen representatives on earth.

After he had served a little more than four years, things got worse. The pettiness of the military and the strict discipline were bad but tolerable. However, at about this time, the British became more and more afraid that Catholic soldiers were French spies, that they were all papists and would turn on them. Hand and hand with these feelings was Freemasonry. The Freemasonry rot was particularly hard to take. Every regiment, it seemed, had its own "temple" where the porcelain-skinned, girlish heathens would give each other secret signs and plot how they'd make the scum of the rank and file pay for being what they were. Especially the Catholics. Military life became unbearable. There was no way to survive in the ranks. So, one morning he walked away. Simply put on some civilian clothes and walked down the road, just as hundreds had done before.

Hickey had not been to Mass since leaving Ireland but he wasn't a pagan. His mother had taught him to pray and to believe. He had hammered out a nice, workable agreement with the Lord. He would do the best he could. Never start a fight. Never abuse a woman. Try and be honest. Talking up a woman didn't count, of course, they expected it. Loved it. Making love to a woman, especially the way he did, slow and easy, couldn't be a sin. It brought them too much pleasure. In return, the Lord would look the other way if Hickey didn't go to Mass or partake of the other more formal rituals of the church. This special Hickey Sect of Catholicism worked well.

The Freemasons claimed to be Christians or at least didn't deny they were. For all Hickey knew, they were, but the fact that they didn't want real Christians — Catholics — to know their business had always left Hickey with a burning knot in his stomach. It didn't matter anyhow. Just so much smoke. The commandments were all a man needed. Treat others as you wanted to be treated. But, never forget an eye for an eye if the need arose.

Now, with the Sons of Liberty kicking up new troubles in her colonies, the King's troops had taken over Boston. The red-backed soldiers and their local Tory sympathizers, continued to hold their Masonic rituals in Boston. What was bewildering to Hickey was that many of the Sons of Liberty themselves continued to hold Masonic rites. Benjamin Franklin and others had carried the Freemasonry fad to the colonies. Surely that would end with the latest tensions. But, it didn't. The Sons of Liberty themselves would move from the Liberty Tree right into the Masonic Hall for a ritual meeting.

The talk of the rum houses was that the Tories and Sons of Liberty were arsehole compatriots cause they were all Masons. Mr. Franklin was a Mason and proud of it. Who else? Adams. Revere. Hancock? Hancock for certain. But it was Hancock who had provided Hickey's livelihood for the past few years. Hickey had never actually met him but knew that the goods he carried on these night trips belonged to Hancock's enterprises. It was a laugh actually. The very pillar of liberty, continued to make his fortune by avoiding the King's tariffs. After all, they said that's the way his Uncle Tom put together the largest fortune in the colony. And now they were all after something called liberty or freedom from taxes or something. But, that didn't matter much to men like Hickey. As far as he could tell, they were just after more money and not having to pay taxes.

"Cap? You believe in this liberty shit, anyway?"

"Ain't thought much about it," said Cap, slightly more relaxed for the moment. "Never had much of what you might call liberty to speak of. Started working at the mill when I was 12. Married Gert at 18. No liberty for me. Wouldn't know what to do with it if I had it, I guess."

"I know what you mean. I don't need anybody to tell me I'm free. I am. Don't need anybody fighting for me either. I can ..."

Hickey's philosophizing was cut short by a sharp noise from in front of the boat. He had been so busy telling his story he hadn't noticed a small patrol boat which had slipped in ahead of them from the north and was now just a few hundred yards away and closing.

There was another hollow blip, like a fish surfacing and quickly diving. For an instant, Hickey thought that might be what it was but that idea evaporated with the sharp crack that reached his ears. Several more cracks followed with puffs of water dancing around the small boat.

"Oh, shit!" said Hickey. "Some arsehole is shooting at us."

Cap dropped the oars and began to shake violently.

"Cap! Grab those oars. You hear me, Cap. Grab those fucking oars and row. You hear me?! Row or I'll kill you myself."

Cap looked quizzically at Hickey, the terror of the British patrol evenly offset by the terror of Hickey's threats. It was a standoff. He shook off the uncertainty and grabbed the oars and flailed them like the arms of a drowning man, water splashed over him, dripping from his brow and chin.

"Hey, whoa, Cap. C'mon now," Hickey said, his voice calm now and firm, realizing he had sent Cap into even more of a panic, "I need you now. We'll row to the east, along the Roxbury Flats. If we pull, we can be out of range until we hit the shoreline. They're just firing crazy. They can't aim from there. Probably got the muzzle up like this." Hickey held an imaginary rifle with the end pointing up at a 45 degree angle. "C'mon now. Stroke it. Stroke it, Cap."

Hickey knew better. The British patrol would probably have four oarsmen. They could be on them in minutes. Only shit luck would help them. He thought about dumping his cargo but that might not sit too well with the customers he knew would be waiting. It might be the end of a good thing. And, the end of something even more important. He set his back into his own oars and the small boat, even with its overweight cargo, began to glide through the water. Cap was actually helping now.

As their small sling boat turned east, the British guard yelled something inaudible. There were two more shots about 30 seconds apart. The first slapped into the water off Cap's right hand. The second punched loudly into the cargo, behind Cap's head. He jumped, letting go of the oar. It swiftly floated back away from the boat out of reach.

"Shit, Thomas, oh, shit," said Cap, standing up in the boat, making it roll to the right. "They gonna kill us. For a few shillings. I shoulda never said yes to you. Good Jesus, Gert. I ain't ever gunna see ya agin." Cap was looking back over his shoulder toward the patrol boat. His eyes were wide. His mouth opening and closing like a fish tossed up on a dock.

Hickey knew he had to shake Cap out of it. They had to make it to shore or there would be no chance. The lobsters might shoot them on the spot and take the haul or, if they felt particularly forthright this night, they would arrest them and lock them up in the Boston jail. Neither choice was particularly agreeable. Hickey reached under the tarp covering the load and brought out a pistol. He stood up in the stern of the sling, facing the British patrol and screamed. "C'mon you fuckin' King Charlie lovers. We got a dozen of us sons of

God's liberty waitin' for you. We got you outmanned and outgunned." With that he held the gun up for a lofty trajectory, aiming in the direction of the patrol and fired. He quickly reloaded and fired again.

"Tom, what the...," Cap had snapped out of his terror by the sheer idiocy of Hickey's actions.

"What's a matter, Cap. Ain't you havin' fun? Where's your yen for adventure?" Hickey yelled at him, his eyes blazing. "The redbacks are always popping at us. Why can't we take a pop at them every now and again?" Hickey was grinning, his near perfect white teeth gleaming, making Cap shudder like he was watchin' the devil do a dance.

Hickey grabbed the oar and tossed it to Cap, telling him to row like it was the only thing that mattered in the world. Cap did just that. Hickey reloaded the pistol and fired. Twice. Then, ripping a board from the top crate, plopped down into the stern seat, and paddled like a mad man.

Oar and board slapped the water furiously. Water splashed into the boat, soaking them both. Their arms ached and the air was too thin to satisfy the craving in their lungs. But, they were only 50 yards from the shore. Hickey stopped paddling first. He listened, trying to hear above the frenetic splashing of Cap's oar.

"Whoa, Cap. Wait. Listen."

"Row, Tom. Row! Please...."

"Cap. Stop. Listen to me."

"What?"

"Hear anything?"

"No, wha...I don't....," said Cap not wanting to hear anything.

"They turned back, Cap. They're gone."

"What?" Cap stopped the frantic splashing and listened. There was only the rhythmic wash of the river on the shore. No shouts. No gun fire.

"Maybe I got lucky and hit one of 'em," said Hickey.

"Minute you fight back, they go runnin'. Knew they would. By the way, Cap, are ya havin' fun yet?"

"Yer far too crazy a bastard for me, Thomas," Cap said, but the terror had gone from his voice.

"Right you are, Cap. Right you are. Now, we'll stay close to the shore. We'll be fine. Almost there. Another few minutes or so. Right around the knob here. There's a little inlet just before Fox Hill. It's about 500 yards from where Frogg Lane comes to an end. Our customers should be waiting in the tall grass and scrub just at the end of the lane."

It was nearly midnight when Hickey guided the sling into a small cove where a natural silt deposit formed a narrow beach among the small trees and thick scrub of the river bank. Hickey jumped out of the boat in knee-high water and pulled the boat up onto the beach. A foot-thick section of a newly-felled tree had been set on the beach and Hickey was able to securely tie the boat. Cap stood up, his legs still a little weak from the crossing and the gunshot. He spread his feet, steadied himself and jumped off the starboard side into the water, his hands guiding the boat into the beach. Hickey took a lantern from under the tarp and climbed to the crest of the hill. He lit it and waved it back in forth for half a minute. He then doused the lantern, climbed back down the hill and stretched out on the beach.

Within minutes, they could hear the clomp of horses and the wheels of a wagon crushing through the night-moist grass. The rude noises stopped and a more subtle sound of footsteps followed.

"Tom?" inquired a voice with a heavy British accent.

"Right here, general," said Hickey, mocking the sergeant's rank.

"I'll give you general, Thomas Hickey. I'll give you a general going over. Perhaps, then you'll learn some respect for the King's soldiers," said the man with a laugh. He walked down the slope and held out his hand to Hickey.

They shook hands and Hickey introduced Cap to Sgt. William Oliver of the Royal Light Infantry. Oliver introduced the blond young soldier with him only as Sutherland.

"Heard shots," said Sgt. Oliver, "Any trouble?"

"None. Just some large fish trying to jump into my boat. They can't resist me, general. No one can resist me." Hickey smiled.

Introductions and small talk out of the way, they got to work. It took about an hour to unload the boat and haul the cargo up the small embankment and load it on the wagon.

"Want a ride, Tom? Cap?" said Oliver, climbing into the wagon seat. 'Where you going, Hickey? Probably to the bed of somebody's woman, no doubt. Better not be mine. On second thought, maybe you ought to take care of her tonight as I'm going to be a little busy." He laughed.

"Not a bad idea, general," said Hickey. "Take me home. To your home."

"I'll take you to town. That's as close as you're getting to my Peggy."

"How about you, Cap?" said Oliver.

"I had my fill of excitement for one night. For a year of nights. Drop me off out at Orange Street? I'll make my way out the Neck and home."

Hickey and Cap climbed into the the wagon. For Cap, it was almost over. Just hop off the wagon at Orange. No one would ever know he had anything to do with anything. He had a dollar in his pocket. That would be put to good use. He would make his away west and north. It was only about five miles. He'd play drunk if stopped by the guards at the fortification the British had built across the neck. Probably the same guards that fired at them. He shivered at the thought, though they had all worked up a thick sweat loading the wagon. For Hickey, the real work of the evening had not yet begun. This particular boat trip was only a cover. The tricky part, the night's real work, lay ahead.

Chapter Two
Philadelphia
11 p.m., Tuesday, June 13, 1775

"A marvelous affair, simply marvelous. Don't you agree, Colonel Washington?" squealed the Chevalier Jean Pierre Maurat de Bonvalier, waving a lace-edged kerchief in front of his face to stir up a breeze. The Chevalier, having been in Philadelphia for several years, spoke English with the pursed-lipped correctness of the educated French.

George Washington, delegate from Virginia to the Second Continental Congress, resplendent in the blue and scarlet Virginia militia uniform of a colonel, which he had taken to wearing daily, nodded and smiled politely. His eyes were fixed on the Chevalier's attractive young wife who met his gaze for a second and quickly turned away, a slight blush in her cheeks.

"Such a civilized city, is Philadelphia," said Maurat, "an oasis in a maelstrom as it were. My country much admires what the gentlemen of your Congress are attempting to do. One must hold tightly to one's dignity but one must also be certain not to visit Madame du Guillotine in the process."

Washington's thin lips spread ever so slightly, a painful half smile. It was difficult, he thought, to determine whom was more effeminate, the Chevalier or his lovely wife. But he could not afford to be rude. The Chevalier was one of a score of influential Frenchmen who were thriving in Philadelphia by making deals with Pennsylvania businessmen for a variety of goods produced in the colony. Some, and it was often difficult to know which ones, were quietly engaged in politicking; brokering the French government's assistance in the colonial struggle against France's longtime enemy England. On either account, Washington could not afford to alienate the Chevalier. In spite of the effeminate facade, which the rich French seemed to cultivate, the Chevalier's reputation as a tough, shrewd bargainer was widely known. One never knew when a man like this could be useful.

"Chevalier," said Washington, "would you grant me the pleasure of a dance with your charming bride? My dear Martha has remained in Virginia and I have all that I can do to keep my feet still. The music is much too fine to be ignored."

Maurat, his head and eyes fixed on his wife, considered the request and, not looking at Washington, said: "Indeed, colonel. I am certain Marie would consider it a pleasure. The colonel's reputation on the dance floor is widely known." The Chevalier did not ask his wife. He simply gestured for her to join Washington. She did so without remark or question.

Washington was grateful the orchestra had decided to play a waltz. It was a welcome change from the programme dances that had become the rage of cosmopolitan Philadelphia. They were, he felt, stiff, contrived dances with silly names such as "The Campaign Success" and "Burgoyne's Defeat." Besides, he much preferred to hold the Chevalier's wife closer than those new fancy prancings allowed. Her hand was delicate and warm and lost in his large mitts. At six feet two inches, Washington's chin took the measure of Marie's full height. Despite nearing 200 pounds at age 43, inflated by 20 pounds or so since his war years, he was straight-backed, solid and extremely light on his large shoes. And, as attested to by the more private campaigns of recent years, he was still quite attractive to women, younger and older than he.

Marie said nothing but gracefully followed Washington's lead. She stared ahead not unaware of the admiring glances from the other women and also not ignorant of the southern colonel's reputation. As one wife of a congressional delegate had told her: "Colonel Washington is impertinent with the ladies. The kind of attentive impertinence we all desire but so seldom receive."

Washington, too, held his head high, his lips in a polite, closemouthed smile but his gaze strayed to the soft curve of the young woman's breasts. The bodice of her evening gown was cut in the latest fashion, low from the shoulders and curving around the front of her light pink cleavage. His eyes slowly rose from her breasts to the soft, infant-like down of her high cheekbones, a wisp of golden Mt. Vernon grain catching the sun of a summer morning in Virginia. Her ear was of such delicate curve and curl as to be a sculpture. He had an urge to place his lips on the curves of this ear. To whisper into it. But, of course, he did not. It had been six weeks since he had left Martha and recognized this urge for what it was; a desire for female pleasures that was continuing unabated into his mid-century mark. Discretion was important here in Pennsylvania.

"Are you enjoying America, madame?" said Washington, in a slow, pleasant but dull, almost disconnected voice, once again in control of his emotions. He spoke slowly, uncertain of the young lady's prowess with English.

"Why yes I am, colonel," said Marie Maurat de Bonvalier in clear unaccented, native Pennsylvanian English. There was a tinge of playful mockery in her voice as she drew her breasts away from his chest and cast her light green eyes up at him playfully.

"I see," said Washington, skillfully playing along.

"Are you enjoying America, colonel?" Marie asked with a coy tilt of her head.

"I am, madam, enjoying it extremely much at the present moment," he said, his blue-gray eyes fixed on hers.

She gave in first, pink blush filling her cheeks and a smile revealing small, even white teeth. A rarity these days. By the time most young women got to this age, they already had several gaping holes where decayed teeth had been pulled from their mouths. Those with the means, such as the women at the ball, filled the gaps with roughly carved false teeth made from ivory or animal teeth. Marie's bright white smile made Washington think of what a joy it would be to be blessed with such a mouthful of natural teeth. He lost his first tooth when he was 22 and they had been falling out steadily ever since. Gum disease said the experts. Now, he seldom opened his mouth to smile and there was constant pain, ache, irritation or inflammation of some kind or other from the current set of ivory false teeth held together by metal springs. And he was certain they clacked as he spoke. So, he had trained himself to speak slowly and deliberately.

The dance ended and Washington, holding Marie's hand like a delicate small bird perched on his fingers, escorted her back to her seat.

"Chevalier," said Washington, bowing his head slightly, "thank you for the delight of dancing with your lovely wife. It has been the highlight of my evening."

"Our pleasure, colonel," said the Chevalier, "my dear Marie is, indeed, a treasure."

The Maurats sat in the straight-backed velvet cushioned chairs along the east wall of the ballroom. They whispered and giggled like sisters. Washington continued standing. He had not sat throughout the ball. He felt it was important that his uniform be seen tall and crisp and its occupant seen as a man of strength and military bearing. Dr. Benjamin Church had arrived in the city from Boston almost two weeks ago. Church, a confidant of the Bay Colony's staunchest supporters of liberty since the very beginning, arrived with a request from the Massachusetts Provincial Congress. They posed two questions: Should the colony take control of the provincial congress? And should the Continental Congress be in charge of the military forces around Boston? With little debate, Washington and the other delegates had created an Army Pay Department, although they hadn't yet voted on taking control of the Boston troops. That was a major step. To form a Continental Army would mean they were ready for war with the King's troops. Many delegates were still not ready to take that step. Appeasement and reconciliation measures were proposed daily, attempting to find a graceful way out. Washington sensed this was impossible. On June 3, Washington, Philip Schuyler, Silas Deane, Thomas Cushing and Joseph Hewes had been named to a committee to determine just how much money was necessary to provide an army. It was only a matter of days. And when the army was created, they would need a commander in chief.

For weeks, he graciously would demure in private conversations with fellow delegates when asked if he would accept the command. It was a major task, he would allow. Perhaps, at his age, he wasn't up to it. He cultivated a sense of quiet humility, fertilized with an iron resignation that he would have to do what the cause wanted him to do. He was committed to the end. He wore his militia uniform at all times in public. He said little during the congressional sessions. What he did say, he said simply, directly. He applied himself to committee work. In his heart, he knew it was his destiny to lead an army of the colonies. And, despite his outward countenance, he wanted the job more than he had wanted anything for a long, long time.

He had dreamed of leading a grand military force since he was a boy. His mother had almost ended the dream by denying him permission to go to sea at 14. Mother. Still a thorn. Constant demands. Send this. Send that. 'You treat me like a stranger, George,' she had written in a recent letter. She still swears allegiance to the king. The king! He had daydreamed about fighting grand battles for the king. Many a school day was taken up by such crusades. He never cared much for school, having ended his formal education in the seventh grade. He did like math and for most of his life kept meticulous records, counting everything from cattle to the number of windows in Mt. Vernon. But, a few years later, at 21 he had undertaken his first adventure to the Ohio River Valley. Gov. Dinwiddie of Virginia had sent a messenger west to the Ohio Valley to sound out the French on their intentions. The governor and 19 other gentlemen had staked a claim to 500,000 acres of land that the French now claimed as their own. The messenger returned without having delivered the message. The brutal wilderness and Indians had turned him back. The young George Washington fascinated by the military life, had, through connections and perseverance, attained the office of adjutant of one of Virginia's four military districts. It wasn't a very demanding job but it did carry the rank of major.

So, in November of 1753, at 21, Major Washington set out to deliver the message to the French. On the return to Williamsburg in January 1754, it had snowed so hard that the horses had to be left behind. The Indians kept up a constant barrage on the Washington party. Every step was an adventure. A raft they constructed to cross the Monongahela overturned and they swam to shore in the frigid water. But, in the end, he had delivered the message. Throughout, Major Washington remained calm and collected. He had found his true occupation, his calling.

Later that spring, dressed in the red coat and three-cornered hat of a Virginia militia officer, he led two companies of men west to protect the colony's interests against the French. Along with him as an interpreter was Jacob van Braam, a Dutchman who had been in Virginia barely two years. He made his living teaching French and fencing. He and Washington had joined the Masonic Lodge at Fredericksburg earlier that year. He talked with van Braam. He trusted him. His relationship with his troops, however, was much different. A military officer had to remain at a distance to maintain discipline. God knows, he thought, this rabble needs discipline.

Early in the morning of May 28, Washington caught 30 Frenchmen at breakfast. There was a brief exchange of gunfire. Ten Frenchmen were killed. Only one of Washington's men was killed. He was exhilarated. "I heard the bullets whistle," he wrote in a journal, "and, believe me, there is something charming in the sound." During the war that followed, he would again experience the whistle of bullets, several plowing through his hat and coat. He was never scratched, though often riding at the head of his troops. He knew he was destined to lead.

The young Major Washington had ordered the first shots of the French and Indian War.

As it turned out, the French party was on a diplomatic mission and not prepared for battle. Nevertheless, Washington was promoted to colonel on the spot. The British military back in England had begun equating the name of Washington with sophomoric, colonial incompetency. Washington's journal had found its way to King George III. When he heard about the young military officer bragging about whistling bullets, he said: "He would not say so had he heard many." The head of the royal forces openly criticized Washington's performance and he was demoted to captain. He resigned. He would pay his own way into another engagement but, at age 23, his military career had come to a close. The British regulars reported they found the young officer cold, overly ambitious and, just barely competent.

Now, after twenty years of domestic life on the plantation, there was another chance. An opportunity to lead a full army with a cause. Of course, it didn't hurt at all that the cause happened to be against the arrogant British military that had dismissed him as a young man.

"Colonel Washington!" The voice was loud and excited. Washington knew the voice instantly.

"Mr. Hancock, I didn't know you were here," said Washington, smiling as broad a smile as he dared without showing the full appliance crammed into his mouth. He didn't care much for John Hancock. He was loud, carping, demanding, and ostentatious. Hancock was so full of himself, Washington had heard, that when he and friends dined around Philadelphia, they didn't bother to pay the bill. Why pay? Wasn't it, after all, a privilege just to host the great Hancock and entourage. Washington, however, was generally alone amongst the southern delegates in his feelings about Hancock. Most of them identified with and enjoyed his patrician attitude. There was no doubt that he had great power among the delegates. There was certainly no mistaking his commitment. He was gambling the greatest fortune in Massachusetts, perhaps, in the entire colonies, on this cause. It was understood by Washington and others of means that Hancock was also enlarging his fortune as a result of the conflict. There was money to be made in providing goods untaxed. Washington knew this quite well from his own endeavors.

Word had arrived only this morning of a new proclamation by General Gage offering amnesty to any rebel reaffirming allegiance to the crown. There were two exceptions — Sam Adams and John Hancock. These two, Gage had said, were too criminal to be pardoned. They must be tried and punished. Washington respected this courage. It, for him, made up for the package in which it was contained.

"Just arrived, George," said Hancock, going right to the backslapping familiar first-name basis which rankled Washington. "Have to make the rounds, you know. I have my admirers to please." He laughed a hardy, disarming laugh and gulped another mouthful of madeira.

Hancock did not bother to introduce the cadre of six men who were with him. Washington recognized two as prominent local businessmen. All seemed jovial and enjoying Hancock's company. He smiled a tight-lipped greeting and nodded slightly.

"Did you hear of our reception in New York, George?" asked Hancock.

"No. Nothing," answered Washington, not quite truthfully but not able to resist a display of disinterest in Hancock's comings and goings.

"It was truly overwhelming. Three miles from the city, we were met by thousands. Thousands! An entire company of grenadiers, a militia regiment. Men in carriages and horseback. People walking. Just to see me, er, us. They went along with us, laughing and telling us of their loyalty and admiration. Then, and I must say I protested loudly, some of the men insisted on freeing the horses from my phaeton and pulling the carriage the last mile by hand! Remarkable. A remarkable display of the people's support for our cause."

"I should say it was," replied Washington, not confronting Hancock with the facts as he had heard them from another of the Massachusetts delegates. All four others had protested the display. Hancock, the source said, was ecstatic at having a score of men pull his chariot into New York like a roman emperor. It was Sam Adams who had forcefully put a stop to the undemocratic spectacle. He would not have his fellow citizens acting like animals, degrading themselves.

"You look quite impressive in that uniform, George," said Hancock.

"Thank you," said Washington quietly wanting to comment on the glittery coaches with full complement of footmen that Hancock had been using to get around the city. He decided that would not be a politically intelligent thing to do.

"Any of these Philadelphian bobtails enough to make a little Virginia foot soldier come to attention?" He winked and the entourage exploded in wicked laughter.

"Well, John," said Washington, smiling and looking down into Hancock's eyes, "I confess I do not know a great deal about my colonial brothers from Massachusetts but in

Virginia we have only generals at our disposal ready to come to attention at our least call. You are aware, I am certain, that generals command much more attention than those 'little foot soldiers'."

Hancock and crew laughed, though somewhat less heartily than before.

There was a moment of oppressive silence and then Hancock and crew excused themselves and moved on around the room. Loud laughing and joking trailed back to where Washington stood as they made their way.

Before moving on, Hancock had stepped closer to Washington, his lips within inches of Washington's left ear. "Will you be attending the lodge meeting on Monday, George?" said Hancock in a whisper. Before Washington could speak or gesture, Hancock continued. "We have had some interesting information come to us. We thought we'd talk about it after the meeting." Washington indicated he would be there.

It was nearly midnight. The music stopped and the musicians set aside their instruments, stood up and stretched. A few minutes later, a butler rang a single bell. It was time for the food. Washington was starved. He had not eaten dinner. In fact, he hadn't eaten since breakfast. And, if there was one good thing — besides dancing — at these balls, it was the food. If his dentures would refrain from chaffing, he would enjoy the offerings. There was meat and seafood, including turtle. Twenty kinds of sweetmeats. Curds and jellies and creams. Finely piled displays of tarts, fools, trifles, flummery and mounds of whipped sillabubs filled an entire table. The finishing touches included parmesan cheese, almonds, fruits of all kinds and plenty of wine — claret, madeira, and burgundy. Or, if you preferred, punch, porter, and beer. It was a good teeth night. Washington managed to work through a bit of everything.

An hour or so later, he drained the last bit of madeira, offered his thanks and gracious good-byes to the host. It was after 1 a.m. Congress was scheduled to open at 9 a.m.

Chapter Three

New York City
3 p.m., Tuesday, June 13, 1775

Henry Dawkins, oblivious to the besieged citizenry of Hickey's Boston or the delicacies of Washington's Philadelphia diplomacy, had his own worries. The 10-foot-square cell smelled like a cesspool. The rough hewn stone walls were covered with a damp green mess of growth of some kind of vile moss, lichen or similar variety of oily, weepy plant life. He had been here a week now. His sentence was seven months. If he didn't take the initiative to make some improvements, he would not survive. The city officials felt no special responsibility to provide regular meals, clothing or bedding to its jail inmates. If you were locked up, you had to rely on the care and generosity of your friends and family to survive your sentence. Without this care, you might get a bit of bread or a bowl of unidentifiable mush every few days. But, when the winter came, you might freeze or come down with an ague. Nearing 50, and always wanting for flesh on his bones, it was all the more important for Henry Dawkins to be attentive to his own health.

Henry Dawkins, in America 20 years and lately of Philadelphia, had no friends, nor relatives in New York. His wife of 18 years, Priscilla, and their seven children, were still in Philadelphia. He would have to rely on his own devices, which, in Henry's case, could be quite impressive when he put his mind to it.

Nothing in Henry Dawkins' first two decades in the colonies indicated a future in crime. He was an accomplished engraver, specializing in copper. For years, he earned a respectable, in fact, modestly prosperous, income. He designed and drew etchings for bookplates, caricatures, maps, coats of arms, rings and seals for the many wealthy families of Philadelphia. His work was exquisite. In 1769, he drew and engraved an elaborate plate illustrating the 1769 transit of Venus for an astronomical article in a major publication. It received many compliments and his reputation grew.

Somewhere, however, in the convoluted lumps and hollows of the artist's mind, the combination of constant dealing with the gentry, envying their privileged lives, and his own evaluation of his work and its true value, resulted in a brainstorm. It would be much more profitable to use his considerable God-given skills to produce wonderful likenesses of the Pennsylvania currency. This enterprise had caused his flight from Philadelphia.

In New York City only a few months and, again, making a respectable living with his talent, the get-rich-quick urge again took over. He began to engrave and print ingenious forgeries of importation document stamps.

A month ago, an anonymous tipster had turned in Dawkins. He surmised a competitor was the rat. The sentence: seven months in city jail. Counterfeiting was rampant in the colonies and had been for decades. With so many varieties of legal tender in each city and each colony, it was relatively easy to produce some passable scrip of your own. The offense was so prevalent that, unless you persisted time and again, you were usually punished by a year or so in jail and then booted out of the city.

His stomach hollow and his eyes squinting not only from the dim light but also in an attempt to close out the palpable odor, Dawkins knew he had to do something.

"Guard," he called in his deep, normally resonant voice

now hoarse from the dampness and filth, "come here, please."
There was no response. No footsteps.

Generally, there were only two or three guards on duty at
any one time. There wasn't much for them to do. Meals, or
actually bits of food, were served irregularly. Once the door
was locked, a prisoner might remain unvisited for days or
weeks without ever being let out for food or exercise. The
job of a guard consisted mainly of providing a modicum of
security and in escorting visitors to cells. Bribes and escapes
were common practice.

Dawkins waited an hour or so and, when he heard noise
in the walkway, yelled again. "Guard!"

A young red-haired man with a gap-toothed grin and dull
green, lizard-like eyes walked to Dawkins' cell. "What?"

"You like the ladies?" said Dawkins with a wink and las-
civious grin.

"What're yer up to?" said the guard in a nasally whine
that was almost too comical to bear with a straight face. He
pulled away from the cell door.

"Nothing. Asked a simple question is all I did. You like
women?"

"Sure, what man don't?" said the guard, absently, his
voice seeing to come right out the end of his crooked nose.
He was in no mood for this prisoner's foolishness. He wanted to get back to the dice game where he was having an
unusual run of good luck.

"How do you like them?" said Dawkins, pressing his
face to the bars and capturing the guard with his dark eyes.
These were the eyes of a hawk circling a field. They belonged in the face of a much handsomer, much younger man.
Not in this stretched, gaunt white, pointy-nosed mask.

"What do you mean?" said the guard, slightly more interested.

"I mean what do you like them to do for you," said Dawkins, winking and grinning, sensing the young man had
probably not had many if any women of the kind Dawkins

had cultivated in recent years.

"Huh?" said the guard, brow furrowed.

"Do you like women with big breasts and their cunnys spread wide open?"

The guard wet his lips, he thought for an instant that he should censure the prisoner but decided he wanted to hear more first. "Sure. Ain't a man who don't?"

"Bring me paper and quill and I'll show you the woman of your dreams."

"What the hell you talking about? Prisoners ain't allowed no paper or nothing."

"Prisoners ain't allowed a lot of things but a lot of them have them anyway. Now, why is that?" said Dawkins in a voice dripping with soppy, sing-song sincerity, grinning and wide-eyed.

"We have to live too, don't you know. A shilling or two for treatin' a prisoner like a human being ain't wrong."

"Bring me the paper and pen and I'll show you something worth more than a shilling or two."

"Maybe. We'll see. If I can find any, I might." The guard walked away.

Dawkins was confident he would get what he asked for.

Later that evening, the guard returned with eight pieces of good-sized paper and an old pen and ink vial. Dawkins, making use of the late summer sun, quickly sketched out an almost real likeness of a woman with her skirts hiked around her waist and a finger plunged into her private parts. It was the work of a talented artist, despite its decidedly bawdy theme. The guard stood at the door straining to make out the lines on the paper across the room.

"There," said Dawkins, "finished. A masterpiece." He held the drawing to the bars of the cell. The guard's mouth opened and he let out a low grunt. He reached in to take the drawing but Dawkins pulled it back.

"You like her?" said Dawkins pleasantly.

The guard could only manage a nod.

"She's yours," he said, holding it out and then pulling it back once again. "But, first, I'm awful hungry. I don't think I could draw much more on an empty stomach."

"I've got some bread and cheese I brought with me. I'll go get it."

Dawkins laughed to himself. The power of a female crotch was amazing. The guard could have opened the door and taken the drawing by force. He was so mesmerized by the lewd rendering that it had dulled his senses. Dawkins admired the work once again. It had turned out quite nicely for a quick sketch. Given time, he could produce even more realistic works of pornography. He felt certain he could survive the fall and winter in relative comfort and with a full belly.

Chapter Four

Boston Common
1 a.m., Wednesday, June 14, 1775

Perhaps, Cap was right about the moon, thought Hickey. It lit up the Common nearly as bright as a cloudy winter day. Rows of tents filled with British Regulars covered most of the Common. He was close enough for the slightly pungent but pleasant smell of dying campfires to reach his nostrils. Guards were walking their posts. He could hear an occasional laugh and a loud reply as the soldiers settled in for the night, though he could not make out what they were saying. Hickey was prone under a large oak tree on a ridge to the southeast of the open or common area near Beacon Hill. His "customers" had let him off the wagon at Frogg Lane, near where Orange becomes Newbury Street. He had walked along Newbury to West, turning north near the school. Sgt. Oliver had reminded him to stay away from his beloved Peggy. Hickey wished that a warm bed and a warmer woman were the goal of the evening. That would be far easier and the outcome far more predictable. The streets were dark and he was able to make his way to the southwest corner of the Common unseen. Most of the gentlemen farmers who had not fled the city were sound asleep in their Tory beds. From his slightly elevated viewpoint, he could see the full expanse of the Common and also the few mansions on

the hill to the north. The old Powder House and the smaller
Watch House were still visible in the center of the Common.
The Liberty Tree was thriving despite the presence of the
King's men. Hickey felt a kinship with the bloated old tree.
It didn't matter by what name you called the rulers of the
moment. One had to keep getting on with life. Keep living.
A day at a time.

The large house, which from this vantage point was just
to the left of the beacon, was the Hancock house. The real
job of the evening was to get into that house and get back
out with a leather pouch, the pouch and, of course, his good
health. But now he was questioning whether this was a
good idea. It seemed next to impossible. Since Hancock,
along with Sam Adams, had been forced to flee the city as
the King's men marched on Lexington a couple months before, the luxurious Hancock mansion had been occupied by
several of the British officers. Hancock had left his home to
attend a session of the Provincial Congress, fully expecting
to return a few days later. So, he took nothing but his ne-
cessities and a few papers. All else was left for his return.
Now, it seemed, that return could be months or years away.
In fact, though none of the rebels liked to think about it, he
might never return. It didn't much matter to Hickey. Mr.
John Hancock or Lord High Royal Twaddlebottom. There's
rich and there's poor. As long as Hancock kept paying in
silver, he'd keep providing his services. But this job was the
trickiest yet. Hancock had promised a large bonus in gold if
he succeeded. He had a gut feeling about this one. He would
earn every pence on this one.

Hancock and Adams, Hickey was told, had moved from
Lexington to Woburn, from Woburn to Connecticut, and
then on to New York City and finally Philadelphia where
they were meeting with leaders from all over the colonies.
Hickey, at first, had been concerned for his livelihood. He
had, after all, built up a good working relationship with the
Hancock businesses. From the routine smuggling of a few

years ago, to the present smuggle-to-order and special jobs, he had amassed a comfortable nest egg thanks to Mr. Hancock and company. Lately, the constant carping about the endless rationing forced on the British soldiers had made business better and better. Then, the martial law of the past few days made the demand go sky high. He had proven himself to be an enterprising agent. Tough enough to handle the seamier jobs, like the odd customer who refused to pay, and yet trustworthy. He never held back. Never tried to skim a few extra shillings.

Tonight's mission, however, was anything but routine. That had been evident from the minute Adam Hopkins, Hancock's agent in Cambridge with whom Hickey usually dealt, had suggested a "more dangerous assignment." He had danced around the issue never saying what was afoot. "Perhaps, this is not for you, Tom," he'd said without having even told Hickey what it was that was not for him. "For, if I lost you in this," he said, "I'd be losing my best regular run man."

Finally, Hickey had to throw up his hands, frame Hopkins face with his large mitts and settle him down. "Jesus' mother, Adam! Tell me what it is you want done. You know me. If I don't want to do it, I'll tell you. Have out with it!"

Hopkins needed someone to go back into the Hancock mansion and retrieve a hidden leather pouch filled with 'very important papers.'

"These papers are extremely important to Mr. Hancock, Tom. Even so, I fear it may be impossible to get to them. The lobsterbacks have moved right in and made themselves at home. Officers. Every room. For all we know, they may have already searched the house. It's unlikely they found this pouch but they might have. They'd hang you on the spot, Tom. If anybody can do it, you can. Mr. Hancock wants those papers. It's important to the cause. I know you don't care much about that but you do care about this...." He reached into his pocket and pulled out a small purse. He dumped the contents on the table. There were ten Portuguese gold Johannes worth about 25 Pounds Sterling. Ten times as much as he had been paid for any other job. More than a year's wages at a good job. Hickey accepted without hesitation.

"They'd hang you on the spot, Tom....." Hopkins' words echoed in Hickey's mind. He could see himself hanging from the Liberty Tree where so many others had been hung in effigy. The image was well defined. The thick rope had cocked his head at a sickening angle and his eyes bulged from their sockets. But, the image of the gold coins was even sharper. He would be a long way toward his goal with that kind of coinage. He agreed to do the job.

He had been planning the route subconsciously as he lay in the soft grass. He got to his feet and shifted to the east a few paces so that he was fully protected by the darkness of the trees. The trees separated the school on Common Street from the mall of the Common itself. He made his way steadily northeastward through the trees. It was about a quarter of a mile to the far edge of the stand of trees. As he neared the end of the protection of the trees, he could see a road and a fence in the bright moonlight. He pressed his back against the last tree searching for his next objective. The fence enclosed a small cemetery in sort of a flattened square at the corner of Common Street. It was about 80 yards from tree to fence. He slid around to the front of the tree, still protected by the overhanging darkness but feeling naked and exposed, as if the entire regiment was being called from their sleep to look at him. There were no tents, nor guards within 200 yards. He took a breath, crouched himself as low to the ground as possible and ran for the fence. There was no call to alarm. He was up and over the low fence in a second and darted behind a white stone tablet, shielding him from the troops. The stone was cool against his back. But the cold seemed to make his innards even more hollow and the banging of his heart louder. He wanted to stay here. Go to sleep.

Forget this craziness. They'd find him in the morning, just another drunk wandering the roads. He got to his haunches before the idea could take hold. He slipped past rows of thin headstones each with sullen, dead eyes watching his every move. Within minutes, he was up and out of the burial ground. Now, the full width of the cemetery protected him from the troops but the more difficult problem was ahead. Beacon Street had seen sort of a building boom a few years back, before the British occupation had begun in earnest. The Hancock house was high up on the road and stood alone on a healthy expanse of land. Here at the lower end of Beacon Hill, however, the houses were more tightly packed. He would have to pass by more than a dozen residences before even nearing the Hancock property.

He sat and thought for a minute. Then he got to his feet and walked briskly toward the back of the house nearest him, fronting on Beacon. He slipped quietly through the yard and out into the middle of the street. The house he had just passed alongside was one of five built close to one another. Across Beacon Street, there were three homes but these were spread out, each with side yards. Once he made it through this gauntlet of residences, he had about 400 yards of clear road, past the beacon itself, before reaching the Hancock House.

He drew in a deep breath and began to sing at the top of his lungs.

"Yankee Doodle went to town a ridin' on a pony. Stuck a feather in his hat and called it macaroni." He used the derisive Tory words to the tune, which had been around since the French and Indian War. The Sons of Liberty, of course, had their own version but that wouldn't do here. He warbled and hooted and sang, attempting to convert the edges of his Irish accent into more of a British sound. As he sang his head bobbed and he drunkenly staggered from one side of the road to the other. "Long live King Georgie," he slurred, lifting an imaginary rum bottle to a toast. The act had the desired effect. A man stuck his head out of the upper window in the third house along.

"Quiet!" he yelled in a deep, husky, sleep-filled voice. Hickey could hear him still complaining to his wife or whoever was sharing his bed. "Damn soldiers. Wish they'd keep'em in line. Night after night ... " The voice faded as the man walked away from the window and went back to his bed.

The charade had accomplished its aim. Hickey was able now to stagger straight up the road without raising any further suspicions. If they hadn't heard him singing, they surely had heard the man yelling at him. The uncommitted middle-of-the-road inhabitants were right now sinking back into their deep dreams having scratched a somnolent check mark next to the drunken soldier singing his way back to camp.

Beacon Street ran roughly east and west past the hill where the beacon had sat for more than a hundred years. In the old days, a century or so ago, the beacon had been only a tar bucket hung at the top of a pole. It was meant to warn the new settlers of impending danger and, though seldom actually used then, it was enough to give the hill its name. Rounding the bend at the base of the hill, Hickey could see the Hancock house ahead. It was a downright shame, he thought, that a man had to leave a house like this. Didn't seem like a cause on earth could get him to move out of such a house. So much horse shit.

It wasn't the largest house Hickey had ever seen but it struck him as the finest. The two-and-a-half story mansion had a steep gambrel roof with three dormer windows in the front and, Hickey knew from the rough pencil sketch Adam had given him, three in the back. It was the detail which set the house apart. In the bright moonlight Hickey could see the roof rail around the top. It looked to be made of iron wrought in an intricate pattern. Stone quoins set off the corners and windows. Four chimneys broke the roofline. The house was set high on a hill and back from the road with a paved walkway leading to stone entrance steps. As he got closer, Hickey could see gardens at the sides of the house with flowerbeds mixed with the vegetable plots. Fruit trees, box trees and several tall mulberries lined the sides of the gardens. To the back, he could see the stables and coach house. Beyond them, pastures for the cows and horses.

Hickey was only a few yards from the gate to the walkway when he froze. He had been so interested in the house he had forgotten that he had no clue as to how he was going to get into the fine looking building which Adam had told him is now the residence for several British officers. He had been marching right up the path like he was going to knock on the door. "Oh, yes, excuse me colonel. I seem to have left a leather pouch here. Do you think you could be so kind as to allow me to fetch it for Mr. Hancock? No, not to worry. It only contains vital information about the treacherous rebel scum who are looking to draw and quarter yourself and the rest of the King's fine men. Won't be a minute, sir. Ta ta."

He had to regroup. He needed a few minutes to think. He quickly veered to the right off the road and into the knee-high grass. He made a wide arcing path through the grass, heading for the stable at the rear. Crouching at the southwestern corner of the newly-painted stable, he could see the full back of the mansion. The garret room on the left was where he was supposed to fine the grail that would earn him the gold. It was used by Hancock as a guest bedroom. However, in the last few months, Hancock had taken to using certain covert nooks and crannies as Sons of Liberty filing space. The secure third-floor location was great for an inhabitant's hiding place but without a doubt the worst possible target for an intruder. The drunkard ruse would not work to gain entrance. Trying to slip quietly into the front or back door of a mansion filled with British officers was, well, not even up for consideration. One would have to go up two flights of stairs, enter a room that might be occupied by a snoring redcoat, grab the pouch and then try and retrace all of those terrifying steps back down two flights and out the door. Not an option. Not unless there was absolutely nothing else to do.

Hickey studied the house. There was another possibility. The stone quoins set in the building's corners created a continuous, though minuscule set of thin stone ledges all the way to the roof. If he could make it to the gambrel roof, he could check the room from the window. He might be able to get in and out without being discovered. It was certainly not impossible. The roofline was, perhaps, twenty feet from the foundation. The trickiest part of the climb would be getting from the vertical corner onto the roof. But, if he got a good grip on the eave he might be able to swing up onto the roof. It was worth a try.

Hickey moved stealthily, keeping low, using the fruit trees as a shield. He made it to the corner of the house and began. His compact, muscular frame and thick steely fingers were made for the task. The quoins were cut from a kind of blue stone that he had seen used a lot back in Connecticut. The builder had graciously left a generous lip of an inch and a half around each block. The blocks were evenly spaced up the corner. In only a few minutes he was above the second story floor and within a few feet of grasping the roof. He wedged his left foot as deeply as possible into the narrow ledge and reached up for the outer edge of the eave. As he did, a door slammed. Hickey froze, his face pressed against the stone, one hand still stretched straight above his head and touching the wooden shingles. His heart hammered against the corner of the house so loudly he was certain it would wake up the sleeping officers. He heard footsteps coming out of the back door somewhere down below his hunched right shoulder. The footsteps passed directly underneath and stopped. Just when it seemed impossible for his heart to beat any louder, it received the next adrenaline flow and began to slam madly into his ribs. He waited for the musket ball to rip through his back and wondered if he would remember the fall twenty feet to the ground. But, there was no shot.

There was a slight rustling of cloth and then a low rushing sound, like water from a pump. The solider, half asleep and oblivious to the Irish scat bug clinging to the wall above, was relieving himself. For what seemed an hour but was more likely three or four minutes, there was silence. The urinating complete, the soldier lingered for the cool air of the hilltop. With each second, Hickey's grip loosened. He knew he would plunge to the ground killing either himself or the poor unfortunate soldier who would cushion the fall. A minute later, the footsteps slogged back into the house and the door closed.

Hickey's left arm was engulfed in pain, the blood running down into his torso. The fingers of his right hand, which had been squeezing the stone ledge of the quoin, were frozen in the grip. He brought his left arm down, shook the blood back into it and held onto the quoin on that side of the corner. He loosened the fingers on his right hand and readied himself for the delicate move onto the roof. Reaching up onto the roof again with his left hand, his fingers locked on a drainage lip that kept rain from running straight down the front of the mansion. He gripped it with all of his strength and walked his feet up to the next quoin so that now his rump was thrust out away from the corner, twenty feet in the air. Still gripping with his left hand, he brought his right up quickly to the roof edge. Now, he was almost standing on the inch-and-a-half wide lip. He pushed himself up with his arms and thrust his chest onto the roof. He quickly swung his left leg up onto the drainage lip. He was on the roof. He had made a loud thump in the final push. He pressed himself to the shingles and waited. There was no response. The night was still. Only the crickets talked.

His fingers and toes touching the shingles, he ape-walked up the gambrel roof to the dormer window of his target room. He leaned against the dormer, resting for a few minutes stretching his fingers and legs.

Gaining new strength in his body and in his purpose,

Hickey leaned slowly around the dormer and peered in. The sparsely furnished room, awash in the soft moonglow, was unoccupied! There was a bed, a small table, a fan-backed wooden chair and a fireplace. The wooden floorboards were bare. He pressed his palms against the wooden stiles and lifted. The window opened easily and he climbed in. Hiding places were at a premium. There were no closets in such rooms as this, a result of the very policy of taxation that was cited as the main cause of the current rebellion. Every room with a door was taxed, regardless of size. A closet was a room. Nor would papers, even in a leather pouch, have survived long attached inside the chimney. Hancock had hidden the pouch in the only place available. Hickey went carefully to the bed and lifted up the bed cover. Dropping to his knees, he looked under the mattress. The mattress rested on a grid of rope threaded through the bed frame. The tightly woven rope acted as a spring; the tighter the ropes the more resiliently comfortable the rest. 'Sleep tight' was the usual admonition. The leather pouch was wedged into the ropes. He pulled at it but it did not come free. He lay on his back and slid easily under the bed. The bed was high off the floor to catch the rising heat of the fireplace. He grasped the pouch with both hands and pulled. As it came free, the door to the room swung open in a flurry of activity.

Hickey, flat on his back, drew his knees up instinctively trying to get his feet as far away from the end of the bed as possible. He braced for the commands: 'Come out' or 'Drag him out from under there and let's have a look at this skulking rebel.' Neither came. The voices he heard, in fact, were jovial. One was female. There was a swoosh of cloth and a few quick steps and then the world caved in above him. They had leaped onto the bed with such force that the ropes stretched to his face before springing back and settling a few inches above him.

"I can't see a thing," said the female voice.

"No need, my dear woman, after all I am a doctor," the

man slurred, a nonsensical, alcohol-induced comment which set them both into a fit of laughter.

"Oooh, doctor, is there really a need for the use of such a thick, mean instrument?"

"The only thing that will cure your ailment, I assure you."

The woman was a howler, whooping and swooning with each thrust. Hickey liked howlers and, despite the taut ropes bouncing inches above his face and the fact that he was now trapped under the bed of what was obviously a British officer, felt himself getting slightly aroused at the fierce love-making just a few inches above his face.

It was over in minutes. The woman purred and shifted in bed and the man began to snore almost instantly. Hickey lay still for nearly half an hour. He had no choice but to try and make it out the window. When, at last he could stand the wait no longer, he slid slowly and deliberately out from under the bed on the side by the window. He reached down into his boot and pulled out a long knife, just in case. He clenched it between his teeth to free his hands. Clearing the bed, he rolled onto his knees and up into a crouching position. He kept his eyes on the love-spent couple as he backed toward the window. He had the pouch jammed into the front of his shirt. He took another step backward but his foot met resistance. It caught on the leg of the table and knocked it a few inches noisily along the bare wood floor. The woman sat straight up and, seeing Hickey's outline in deep shadow against the window, formed her mouth into the makings of a scream.

Instinctively, Hickey dove onto the bed, clearing the man and landed with his full weight on the woman, his hand over her mouth. She was stunned for a second and then continued trying to scream through Hickey's fingers. Hickey twisted her on top of him, swung his legs off the bed and stood up with the woman in front of him. He took the knife from his teeth with his free hand and held it to her neck.

"I'm a lover not a killer," he said. "You would like me to stay that way wouldn't you," he said, softly and steadily into her ear. She nodded. She had stopped trying to scream.

The man had still not fully grasped what was happening. The depth of his rum-induced stupor kept him from even the feeblest protest.

"Whas madder," he mumbled, his right eye still closed and his left open only to a slit.

Hickey slid around the foot of the bed, the woman still held at knifepoint in front of him. He moved her into the moonlight streaming through the window. The man seemed to come awake instantly. As a doctor, he no doubt, could expound on a man's heart under extreme emotional pressure. These juices pumped into the doctor's heart neutralizing the alcohol almost immediately. He got to his feet and stepped toward Hickey.

"Do not hurt her, sir, I implore you. Whatever it is you desire I shall see that you have it," he said in a prim and precise tone. Hickey thought the voice was vaguely familiar.

"I ain't hurtin' no one unless I have to," said Hickey. "You do what I say and there'll be no hurtin' of any kind. Understand?"

"Agreed," said the man.

There had been no response from anyone else in the house. Hickey figured that this was not the first lovemaking bout logged by this couple. The woman was, after all, a howler. The scream was probably worth little more than a knowing grin in the night by the others in their beds.

"I'm going to tell you what you gotta do if you don't want this pretty young woman to bleed all over herself and me. Understood?"

"Certainly," said the man, more alert all the time and now angry in his helplessness.

"I want you to take off that shirt and rip off the sleeves, then I want ..."

Hickey was interrupted. "I must protest. This cost me

dearly. It is the latest from France."

"The shirt worth more than her neck?" said Hickey making a show of tightening the grip on the woman's mouth and
drawing the blade up closer into the skin of her neck.

"No. No. Here. It is off. It is off already." He yanked
the shirt from his arms and ripped off the sleeves.

"Now, tear the front in half." The man did so, wincing at
the destruction of his prized import. Hickey then told him to
give the torn piece and one sleeve to the woman. "Not too
close," warned Hickey. "Hold them out."

The woman took the pieces of cloth.

"Now, come slowly toward me. Very slowly." Hickey
said as he backed himself and the woman until his back was
flat against the wall to the right of the window. The man
moved toward them. In this way the full brightness of the
moon shone directly on the man's face. Hickey was stunned.

It was clear now why the voice sounded so familiar. The
face was, indeed, quite familiar. Just two years ago, he had
gone along with a crowd from the docks to Old South to
participate in the third commemoration of the massacre. It
wasn't that he was so fired up about all of this liberty business but it was always a rousing occasion, lots of whooping
and hollering. And afterward, there was always plenty of
free drinks and partying into the dawn. Boston's finest orators worked the crowd. And, two years ago, this man had
given one of the best performances yet. He recounted how
he had been in on the very creation of the notion of liberty.
He was a close friend of Adams and Hancock. Since that
commemoration, his reputation had grown even stouter. He
had tended the wounds of the men at Lexington. He was
a respected member of the Massachusetts Provincial Congress. What was he doing here in British-occupied Boston,
in the usurped home of John Hancock now overrun with the
King's soldiers? What was he doing on the third floor of
that house in a sparse room with a woman young enough to
be his daughter? Yes, there was no doubt. The dark, pouty

lips and smooth, almost womanish cheeks were those of the man who only a few days ago had returned from Philadelphia where he had delivered a plea to the Continental Congress. Strange things, indeed, but not his main concern at the moment.

"Step closer," said Hickey. "Open your mouth."

When he did so, Hickey told the woman to stuff the torn shirt front into his mouth and to tie the one sleeve around his head, over his mouth. She did so, moving deliberately, her hands trembling.

"Now," said Hickey, "move to the bed and put your arms behind your back and through the bed railings." The man did this, too, without a word.

Hickey explained to the woman that they were going to move toward the man and she was to tie his hands with the other sleeve. She nodded that she understood and did what she was told to do. Hickey tugged on the knot to make certain it was secure.

Hickey made the woman lie on her stomach on the bed. He straddled her a knee on each side of her waist, warning her that any sound at all would bring disaster. He quickly stuffed the other part of the shirt front into her mouth and tied the other half of the shirt front around her head. He then used the back of the shirt to tie her hands to the headboard of the bed.

He backed slowly toward the window and slid open the sash. As he turned to go through the window, the hostage got a clear view of his assailant's face for the first time. From what Hickey could tell, there was not a hint of recognition. No reason why there should be. Hickey had been just another face from the docks.

Moving quickly down the roof to the corner, he braced for the trickiest part of the descent. He would have to dangle his legs out over the edge of the roof and feel for the quoin ledges with his boots. It was easier than he thought and in seconds he had a solid toehold. Holding on to the eave of the roof, he dug in with his toes and moved down from the roof onto the corner stones. The descent was much quicker than the climb. He jumped the last six feet or so, stumbled slightly, righted himself and ran to the front of the mansion. He was not going to fool around with the wide berth business this time. He'd go straight for the road, down Beacon to Tremont, from Tremont to Queen and then King Street. Right to the wharves where he could disappear for a day or two.

He sped to the corner of the building, his stride widening. As he rounded the front of the house, heading for the gate, someone shouted. "Halt!"

The unexpected voice, with its authoritative command, nearly sent him tumbling head over arse into the entrance path. Gaining his balance, he turned toward the front porch. He could see the britches of the soldier standing there but he was deep in shadow from the waist up.

"I was, er, drinking a little sir and, I, er, fell asleep in your barn. And, why, when I realized where I was I, wanted to, uh, get away from here. Yes sir, get away as quick as I could," said Hickey unconsciously grasping the pouch under his shirt.

"And, what is it that is hidden beneath your shirt, then," asked the man, seemingly forcing his voice deeper and sterner.

"Just my meager belongings sir, meager indeed."

"Those meager belonging wouldn't include some ill-gotten silver from a smuggling incident earlier this evening would it?" Hickey was stunned and stood agape. Before he could answer, the man said: "Or does it contain the key to my Peggy's bedroom door?" He stepped into the moonlight. It was Bill Oliver. Sgt. Willy.

"Bill, you rotten, red-backed bastard. I could kiss you or kill you. Or both."

"What ARE you doing here, Tom? On second thought, don't tell me. I don't want to know anything when it concerns you. Better be getting on down the road before the officers begin to stir."

"Thanks, Will. The next load is on me. The boatful. I swear." Hickey turned and ran down the center of Beacon Street.

Chapter Five

Carpenter's Hall, Philadelphia
11 p.m., Tuesday, June 20, 1775

The ritual had been over for several minutes now and the altar was being cleared of the blue cloth with the Star of Alexandria, square and compass and the like. The Freemasons randomly began to untie their aprons and place them on the wooden table for proper storage until next session. Washington, a Mason for twenty years, was never more pleased with the ancient order. These were men of substance, of commitment. When they swore themselves to the 10 principles, there was something at stake. Dr. Franklin, for example, had been the Grand Master of the first lodge in Pennsylvania the year before Washington was born. Nearly twenty years ago, Franklin had been inducted into the Royal Society, an organization in England at the very soul of Freemasonry. Even Hancock, as full of himself as he was, had not wavered in his commitment to his beliefs. He was, thought Washington, perhaps the richest man in the colonies. Local papers had lately pinned that tag on Washington himself but he knew Hancock possessed a fortune more readily turned to hard assets. While he never confirmed nor denied his own wealth, he figured — and he was always quite good with figures — that his holdings, though extensive, could not so easily be valued as Hancock's ships, wharves and other commercial

interests. Others present, such as Joseph Hewes, William
Hooper and Richard Stockton, the Paynes, the Whipples,
were all men of substance. It was, indeed, a group worthy
of membership and of his commitment. Gentlemen. Men of
means. Men of character. Men not shrinking from the challenge. Leaders.

Adding to the mood of the evening was the site of the
meeting. Carpenters' Hall was Washington's favorite building in this city quickly becoming noted for its fine architec-
ture. The exquisite, symmetrical structure built by the Carpenters' Company had been used last year by the Continental
Congress for its first session. Now, with the congress having moved into the Pennsylvania State House a block to the
west, Carpenters Hall was once again free for use by groups
such as the Masons. Tonight's session had been called to
order in the chamber to the left of the center hall, the same
chamber in which the nearly three score delegates had been
crammed last year. With only half that many at tonight's
lodge meeting, the chamber proved much more accommo-
dating. Carpenters' Hall wasn't a large building, barely fifty
feet on each side in a truncated cross shape, but its symmetry
and quality of construction were unmatched in Washington's
eyes. Set back from the street more than 250 feet, with well-
maintained lawn and gardens, it was dignified, ordered, re-
served, and yet, somehow, commanding. It was, so to speak,
a George Washington amidst the architectural glad-handers
and backslappers. There was something else. It had to do
with power. When he and the 55 other delegates had first
sat in these Windsor chairs last year, Washington knew he
was a part of something powerful. Rare and powerful. This
was where he belonged. He was not a lawyer as was nearly
half the assemblage. He was not a grand orator as almost
all of the others fancied themselves to be. But there was one
thing he did know. Washington understood power. Military
power. Political power. He understood it and, even more
importantly, he did not shrink from using it. It was, in fact,

his calling. He had known that from the earliest excursions west. Here, in this fine building eight months later, he had that same almost mystical feeling. These were men with power at their disposal. Power not for some enslaving cabal or for personal fortune but the power to take control of their own destiny. The vision and fortitude to take charge and to change the future. He wouldn't want to be anywhere else.

Glasses of madeira were being passed around now as the men settled into easy conversation. This was Washington's favorite part of the evening. Not the most verbose of the assemblage, he was, on the other hand, a good listener, a rare quality in this group. That made him a favorite among the competing egos of the several accomplished orators in the room. The seat by Washington's side was second in popularity only to that empty seat, rare as it was, that might be found next to Ben Franklin who at 68 was the oldest, most traveled and, certainly, the most glib of all. Though seen by many younger delegates as beyond reason or even a dottering old fool, Franklin was always charming in such social scenes as this.

"George!" said Ben Franklin, putting a hand affectionately on Washington's shoulder while settling with some effort his large girth into a wooden chair next to him. Washington did not like people touching him. Since his childhood days on Pope's Creek, he had cultivated a gentleman's distance, he had not liked the intimacy of being touched by acquaintances.

It made one more accessible than one wanted to be and certainly much more common than was desired. Many of the New England delegates were constantly slapping each other on the back or holding each other by the arm. Washington cringed at the thought. A person must be comfortable with himself. That was all one needed. That is not to say that friendship and comradeship were not good things. They were, most certainly. But, a man had to establish his own principles and, once established, there was no need for constant outside reinforcement. This was especially true for a military man. He was a student of the military. While he never cared much for most of the formal elements of school, — never bothered, for example, to learn French or Latin — he had read every military treatise and biography he could lay hands on since he was a boy.

But, Franklin's touch was something different. It spoke through its affectionate pat on his shoulders of a man with the same inner confidence. It was not so much a means of draining from him that which was his own as it was more of a signal; a message of kindred spirits.

"Congratulations, General Washington! Our distinguished congress of rebellious rabble couldn't have picked a better man for the job. And, despite your modest behavior, I daresay you relish the task," said Franklin, smiling and winking as he plopped the last few inches onto the groaning chair. Franklin's success came from industriousness. It came from inventiveness. It came from political savvy. All of these things. He worked at these qualities and perfected them. The real secret, however, was God-given. It could not be learned nor taught. After nearly seven decades on the planet, the sparkle of humor in his eye and the vigor in his attitude spoke of that most precious quality. After all these years, he had a genuine affection for the human species. Humans of all sizes and shapes; men of all talents and faults. Nearly a half century earlier he had sat down and drawn up a list of principles by which he would live. One of these was that we would never speak ill of another man regardless of how utterly unredeemable that individual might appear. He vowed to always find the good. It must be there, after all, somewhere in all of us, he had reckoned. He had come to practice that principle. Practice it and believe it.

"It is a formidable undertaking, Mr. Franklin. I have written to my dear Martha and I'll tell you what I told her. I can mark my decline and fall from this point on," said Washington with an exaggerated sigh that was meant to display his burden but only served to shore up Franklin's contention that Washington did, indeed, covet the leadership of an army. It was, after all, what he wanted to do since the days when, as a young boy, he would walk along the path which outlined the family property on Pope's Creek and dream of sailing off in a ship to do battle in some exotic foreign land for the honor of the king. Slight change of plans now, however. He was finally going to lead an army. The problem was he was going to lead an army of militia and volunteers against the king's army, against, perhaps, the greatest military force on earth. That deserved a hefty sigh. But, Franklin was right. He couldn't wait to get started.

The plan had worked. Wearing his Virginia militia uniform to sessions of congress had proven quite effective. The debate over selection of a general to go to Cambridge and take command of what was being called the Continental Army had not been without dissention. This congress had settled down into three distinct camps: There were unhesitating, immutable patriots; there were middle-of-the-roaders who still hoped for reconciliation with honor with King George; and then there were the delegates from the South who seemed to have their own separate agenda. The southern delegation wanted George Washington and no other. He was one of them. They understood and trusted him. New Englanders, among the most rabid of patriots, felt that, since the army at Cambridge was there basically to make certain the British were contained there, a New Englander would be best for the job. In fact, the militia and volunteers might actually resent a Southerner taking command.

There was one other factor. John Hancock. He wanted the job. He really wanted it. It was all that was left to satisfy his ego. General Hancock. It had a definite ring to it. Then, on Wednesday last, when John Adams rose to force a showdown on the issue, it had seemed clear that he was going to nominate Hancock. After all, they had been involved together in this business since the start. Meetings in the Green

Dragon Tavern. The heated discussions into the early morning hours at the Long Room Club. The rabble-rousing events staged under the Liberty Tree. As Adams spoke, Washington watched Hancock's face glow. He sat in the president's chair and beamed as the Adams introduction commended the qualities of the man he was proposing to lead the army. Although, Adams, said, he realized it might not be the proper time to actually call for a nomination, realizing that he had not secured the needed votes, he said he could not wait any longer in letting his desire be known.

"I propose," said Adams, staring straight into Hancock's eyes, "a man who I see as supremely suited to the task. A gentleman from Virginia, who ..." Hancock could not hear any of the words that came after. He was visibly stunned. His face reddened. He was embarrassed. He was disappointed. And then he was angry.

Washington, at the mention of 'Virginia,' rose from his chair and left the chamber through the door to the right of the center fireplace. It seemed the modest thing to do; to leave should the debate center on him. Besides, at that point, he knew he was in. There was no other Virginian who wanted the post and he had seen John Adams talking with his cousin, Sam, before the session. John Adams was much too astute to have made such a proposal without believing he could carry the vote. As it turned out, Sam Adams seconded the vote. He learned later that night that there had, indeed, been some debate but Adams had quickly circulated throughout the room signing up votes. The debate continued on Thursday and it was not until this morning that a commission had been drawn up officially naming Washington.

"Yes, indeed it is a formidable task, George," said Franklin, moving his head closer and peering over the top of his spectacles, eyes twinkling. "But, you haven't faced true terror until you've played the twigger, servicing two woman simultaneously in two adjoining suites while negotiating business with their husbands in the drawing room below. That, my dear Virginian farmer, is truly a formidable task. Heh, heh."

Washington, not prone to outright laughter, bared his latest set of ill-fitting, lead-molded false teeth and fairly chuckled.

"That could be a treacherous battlefield even for a general," said Washington, still grinning. "Have you led a wild, mindless soldier into such combat? "

"One never should discuss the battlefield whether made of dirt and clay or satin and down. It might be considered immodest," laughed Franklin.

They sat smiling and sipping wine quietly for several minutes. Washington broke the silence, noticing Hancock holding court at the far side of the room.

"I hope Mr. Hancock is not too disappointed that I and not he will be heading for Cambridge on Wednesday. I believe it is safe to say he was disappointed in the vote," said Washington.

"I consider myself a fair judge of men, George. Mr. Hancock may harbor some resentment against his old friend Sam Adams for not putting up a stronger opposition, or for that matter any opposition at all, but he will be over this quickly. His is one of those marvelous minds that has probably already decided that the job was actually beneath him and that he was not nominated because he is far too valuable right here as our congressional president. No, I don't think you have to worry about John Hancock. Whatever you may feel about his show of extravagance and his wonder of himself, I believe he is committed to his last dollar to resolving our disagreements with the mother country one way or the other. Beyond that, and I am still not certain it is our correct path, he seems to be leaning toward a total separation," said Franklin, disconcerting in his quick transformation from wag to political analyst.

"I have my own thoughts on that topic Dr. Franklin," said Washington, swirling the madeira in his glass, "but I do not think it my place as a general working now for the congress to make those ideas known."

"I told them you were the man for the job," said Franklin. "You just proved it. I have every confidence in you. Now, has Hancock mentioned to you the real reason I wanted to talk with you?" asked Franklin.

"He said you had received some 'information' that was all he said."

"Intelligence is more to the point," said Franklin, attempting to hop his substantial rump off the seat to push the wooden chair closer to Washington. "Some of us have begun to discuss the need for a special committee, a secret committee known only to a select few. As I said, I have spent many years abroad and amongst friends, I hasten to add, and there is a great deal of pain in all of this for me. Nevertheless, I am a Pennsylvanian first. And, if this is to be, then we must be prepared. My proposal is that this committee begin to secure 'friends' here and abroad to keep us apprised of the developments as they affect our cause. I have proposed to this select group of our brothers that we send an emissary to Paris to begin to lay the foundations of this intelligence network. As you know, I have many friends in Paris and can provide a lengthy list of trusted contacts."

"As a modest student of military matters, I believe such information has always been of great value," said Washington understanding that the references to 'friends' and 'brothers' meant that Franklin planned to operate this network of spies through the channels of Freemasonry. His European contacts within the brotherhood were extensive. The French, especially, could be valuable. The very French, thought Washington, who not so many years ago seemed like the devil himself.

"Hancock has always maintained a, shall we say, working relationship with the seamier elements of Boston. It is a holdover from his days working in his uncle's shop on the docks as a boy. Here are a few people to contact when you reach Cambridge. They may be of some use," Franklin slipped a folded piece of paper into Washington's large right hand, closed his fingers over Washington's and squeezed. "One other thing. Through some of my colleagues in the scientific community, I have learned of an invention that may be of some value to us. There is a notation on this list for you to visit 'The Turtle.' I won't tell you any more than that. I'll leave it as a surprise, and surprised I think you will be. I have seen it myself. Very interesting, indeed."

"I will be certain to make these contacts," said Washington.

"One final thing, George. Dr. Church. You know, Benjamin Church, who was here early last week? He was the fellow who brought the request to us for support for the army at Cambridge." Washington nodded. "He can prove very valuable to you as you begin to establish your command. He knows Boston inside and out. He, too, has been involved right from the start. He is a brother to call on him and seek his counsel."

"I will," said Washington, "and I thank you for your confidence."

"No need to thank me, George. We should be thanking you. You are aware, I am sure, that there are still some who are not as certain as I am that you are the man for this command. They may even fail to muster up any support should you find the going difficult. I hope that we will be able to support you so that you do not have to fight a battle both within and without our ranks. But, enough of this for now. Let's go fill our glasses again. I can see that a taste for madeira is something we share."

Washington nodded and followed Franklin to the table.

They had just filled their glasses when the gentle murmur of post-meeting patter was disturbed by the bang of the door. It flew open and slammed back against the wall. A young man, his shirttail hanging out and perspiration streaming down his cheeks, offered a quick apology for the noise and, before his apology could be acknowledged, stepped into the center of the room and made an announcement. He seemed on the verge of tears.

"Bloody battle. Near Boston!" he sobbed, breathlessly and seemingly in disbelief, "A bloody battle. On the hills above Charlestown. Breed's and Bunker's. Hundreds killed. Hundreds. The word just came. Just now. The militia boys had to pull out but not before they killed hundreds of the King's men. Happened Saturday. Early. "

There was silence and the young man, his mouth open, was frozen. If not for the dire message, it would have been almost comical. He waited to be released from his pose by some movement, some action on the part of the Masonic gathering to whom he had delivered this message. Finally, after what seemed an interminable vacuum, Hancock stepped forward and loudly began to demand specifics from the young man.

"How many of our men killed? What of General Ward? Where did you hear this? Who brought the message?" asked Hancock in rapid order.

The young man indicated that a rider had brought the message to City Tavern. He had been told to come to Carpenters' Hall and provide the news. He was sorry, again, for the intrusion but they had said not to worry about manners. His charge was simply to get the message to 'your honors.'

"They told me of no certain deaths but one. A Dr. Joseph Warren has been killed, sir. That is all I know," The young man slumped visibly having unloaded his burden.

There was an audible gasp at the announcement of Dr. Warren's death. Dr. Joseph Warren, president of the Massachusetts Provincial Congress and recently named major general, had been one of the earliest disciples of Sam Adams. Adams had convinced several young Harvard graduates that it was their duty to become leaders in the fight for colonial rights. Dr. Warren had been one of the most dedicated. When, in 1770, it had come time in Boston for the fifth commemoration of the Boston Massacre, Dr. Warren had begged Sam Adams to let him be the key speaker, despite death threats by the British against whoever spoke. Warren had donned a Roman toga for his speech, not only defying the threats but thumbing his nose at them. Now he was dead. Several of the meeting-goers had already taken their hats and were rushing out the front door for the City Tavern where they hoped to find greater details of the battle.

"Looks like you have your conflict, General Washington," said Franklin. "May the Supreme Power give rest to Dr. Warren. He was truly a patriot."

"I did not have the pleasure of meeting Dr. Warren but I am aware of his dedication to this cause. I, too, pray the Almighty guides him," said Washington with his cultivated look of solemnity, staring directly into Franklin's eyes but not seeing him. He was anxious to get to Cambridge. "I also pray he guides me as we set out toward a just end to all of this."

Franklin, with great effort, lifted himself from the chair and, finishing the last swallow of wine, began to gather his hat and stick to leave. Washington remained seated as the hall cleared. Dr. Franklin, nearing the end of his seventh decade and a quarter century Washington's senior, seemed to take all of this with stoic resignation. Washington sat for several minutes, his thoughts straying to images of playing soldier on the spit of land jutting out into Pope's Creek; and to his mother telling him she would not allow him to go off on some childish adventure with the King's navy; to the sounds of men screaming in agony as he ordered his men to fire on the French delegation he had come upon dressing for breakfast in the woods on the western frontier. He had later written to his brother that he had found the engagement exhilarating but, even then, he had exercised great restraint in describing his feelings. Truth be known, he had never felt more alive, more in tune with his destiny than at that moment. He blinked away these memories and stood, at last, to leave.

As he passed through the meeting room door into the center hallway, he realized that John Hancock was in the main foyer. At first, Washington thought Hancock was in conversation with other stragglers as they slowly left the hall. But, as he entered the foyer, he saw that Hancock was alone.

"George," said Hancock, "I waited to have a word with you."

The somber tone of his voice set off alarms in Washington's head. Was he going to confront him about the vote by congress? Did he plan to warn him that being named general and actually being allowed to be in command were two different things? That he planned to do whatever it took, considering his considerable economic clout, to see that Washington was unsuccessful?

"Mr. Hancock," said Washington, attempting to sound cordial and respectful.

"George," said Hancock, putting his hand on Washington's shoulder and drawing his ear closer. Washington wanted to pull away from such proximity but, something urgent in Hancock's manner made this instance acceptable. He did not withdraw nor complain.

"It looks quite clear now that we are in this to the end, whatever that end might be. A stirring in my gut tells me that many more bloody battles are in our future. Perhaps, you and I will follow Dr. Warren. At the same time, my heart tells me that this is the right thing — the only thing — we can do. I believe this. I've staked my reputation and, yes, my life on it. Not to mention a great deal of money. We are different men, George, from different backgrounds, but we are very much alike in many ways. I sense that you, as myself, are keenly aware of power and not afraid to accept it and use it. I also believe that, perhaps for different reasons, you, too, are in this until the end. I want you to know that I am behind you completely. I will support you in every way I can. Now, I ..."

"Thank you, John," said Washington, interrupting out of

initial relief and also with genuine appreciation.

"With what lies ahead of you, George, we should be thanking you," said Hancock. "Now, I have one other thing I want to share with you. I'm sure they'll be waiting for us at the tavern, wondering how we went astray. Perhaps, they'll think we stayed behind to duel over the generalship." Hancock laughed with unfettered delight, something Washington found disconcerting and that he personally rarely could do outside his family or immediate circle of close friends. "Seriously though, George, when you reach Cambridge, ask for Adam Hopkins. He has been in my employ for many years and, in recent years, has handled many of the more confidential elements of my business during the King's occupation. Find Adam and tell him to give you the pouch."

Washington knitted his brow.

"Just ask him for the pouch. He'll know what you mean. I have been gathering useful information for more than a year, detailed information that may be of some value to you. It is all in that pouch. It may prove to be of some value to you. Good luck, General Washington." With that, Hancock thrust out his hand.

They shook hands firmly. Washington was genuinely grateful. He thanked Hancock and together they left Carpenter's Hall for the City Tavern where conversation about the situation in Boston would continue over spirits until the early hours.

Chapter Six

New York City
2 p.m., Saturday, July 15, 1775

"The paper is the thing," purred Henry Dawkins through the bars of his cell to the red-faced man with the oily balloon nose in the cell across the passageway from his.

"With the right paper and a rolling press — has to be a rolling press because that is how the provincials are printed - with those two items a man can make a fortune in a hurry. Especially in these times."

The oily-skinned prisoner had been brought in two days ago for public drunkenness, his fourth such arrest this year. This time, they had not really told him his sentence. He understood it to be, simply put, that he stayed here until he changed his ways. He was now quite sober and Dawkins found him to be a great audience for his tales and an attentive listener to his schemes. He had his face pressed against the bars so that his peculiarly voluminous nose was protruding and his face made even redder by the pressure of the bars. He was in a large common cell room. Though he was alone at present, prisoners came and went. Sometimes there would be 10 yahoos and doodle dashers, coxcombs and wiseacres; the wretched of the city who drank too much, stole too much and who beat up on friend and acquaintance indiscriminately at the slightest provocation or for deep, abiding reasons that would be known only to the head basher for eternity or for no reason at all.

Dawkins, on the other hand, had been moved from his original cesspool into an individual cell along the north wall of the building. It was much cooler out of the direct afternoon rays of the sun and yet bright enough to allow him to draw, which, after all, was the reason for his new found jailhouse prosperity. He had enough food. Though certainly not a feast by anyone's standards, it was fairly fresh and varied. He had even been allowed a bath a few weeks back. A treat worth a week's food. He had been staying ahead of the lice in the daily skirmishes and a bath helped a great deal on that battleground. He had served about a third of his sentence and it was time to begin thinking about making a living after he got out.

He had learned through his now highly efficient grapevine that the Continental Congress had authorized $3,000,000 in paper money with each of the 12 colonies to have its own distinctive bills. That would only be the start. Not satisfied with this arrangement, the Provincial Congress of New York had decided to issue paper bills of its own. There was great opportunity in all of this.

"Know guys who can git it," said the nose with a mouth buried in it.

"What?" said Dawkins, surprised the man spoke.

"Said two guys I know can git it."

"Get what?"

"Printing press. 'Nother guy, paper."

"Really!" said Dawkins. "And where would these gentlemen be headquartered."

"Somewhere."

"I am certain of that," replied Dawkins.

"Somewhere away from here," said the nose.

"Where? Who? How do you know these men can obtain paper? The right paper?" Dawkins was interested and yet annoyed at his inability to communicate with the talking nose.

"Guy gets all that stuff. Seen him. All the time. Anything you want."

"Where would I find these upstanding gentlemen?"

"What'll ya give me?"

"The first sheet of provincial dollars off the press."

"Youngs."

"Pardon?"

"Youngs. Brothers, they are. Youngs. Isaac and Israel."

"The Youngs brothers, eh. Where would I find these Youngs brothers?"

"Huntington. On the Long Island. You still gonna give me a sheet?"

"I am a man of my word. You come back and see me before I am released and we will make firm arrangements for the transfer of the fresh goods," said Dawkins, who fully intended to keep his side of the bargain. If the tip proved valuable, it would be the least he could do.

Other short-term prisoners had, after seeing the remarkable detail of Dawkins' renderings, when the subject was broached, indicated that they could find someone to supply his needs. But, they were never specific. They'd ask around or check with their friends in that line of work and the like. The man with the huge and very ugly red nose was different somehow. He named names. He had felt the information valuable enough to ask for something in return. Dawkins would check it out.

"Now, excuse me, won't you. I have to get back to work. I'm going to need a little purse if I'm to enter into business with your friends."

"Sure," said the nose. He said nothing else but turned his back on Dawkins and walked to the bench on the far wall and sat, staring at his fingers.

The sketch business had made his stay at least bearable. The promiscuous renderings of the first week or so had given way to more conventional sketches and portraits of the jailers and, lately, their wives and girlfriends. Only the rich could afford to have their portraits painted but, here, in Dawkins cell was the next best thing. He would render their likeness and the likenesses of their friends and families. These were, of course, not elaborate colored oils. They were simple pen and ink drawings but Dawkins' talent was appreciated even among these wretches.

He took delight in these creations. He was pleased when he would finally turn the paper and show the man the exact image of his wife. He would watch as their eyes widened and they smiled. Sometimes, like what happened three days earlier, on Saturday, a tough old lockup would actually begin to cry when Dawkins rendered a vision of a child long dead or a near-perfect likeness of a late mother or father from description. It was a remarkable talent. But, such talent is not always rewarded in proportion to the needs and desires of the possessor. Dawkins painted and etched and drew and sketched for the gentry of Philadelphia. He went into their homes filled with their fine crystal and imported carpets. He was praised and paid a reasonable sum. Then, when he was done, he would be asked to leave. His creations were placed on prominent display but their creator was not worthy to stick around long enough to see for himself a visitor's reaction. Thanks for your prodigious talent. Here's the door. He wanted a house like that. And clothes. Other things. With the right enterprise, he could have them.

"Isaac and Israel Youngs ... stay healthy," he said to himself. Henry Dawkins seeks your acquaintance. Four months and a handful of days from now.

Chapter Seven

Scarlett's Wharf, Boston
11:30 p.m., Saturday, July 22, 1775

The Red Snapper sagged between a storehouse and a dreary inn frequented mostly by faceless sailors ashore in Boston for a few days before going back to sea. The Snapper, you might say, was in the third tier of Boston taverns. Among the top of the line were the Bunch of Grapes, the Coffee House, and Cromwell's Head. You'd be unlikely to be ducking a sailor's fist or flying chair in these establishments. In the Coffee House, for example, both as the British Coffee House and, later, the American Coffee House, you would more likely be concerned about disrupting a meeting of the Merchant's Club. Membership in the club included crown officials, military officers, lawyers and other gentlemen of high rank. The Bunch of Grapes was the site of the first Grand Lodge of Masons in America, organized there in July 30, 1733. The second tier of watering holes was the haunt of the skilled laborers, the mechanics and small business owners. The Salutation and the Green Dragon were among the more well known. The late Dr. Joseph Warren had been a frequenter of both the Salutation and the Green Dragon. Samuel Adams spent a great deal of his days in the Green Dragon, taking his meals and politicking.

Then there were the Red Snappers of the city. These were

the haunts of the drones, the dock laborers, the bull workers, the con men, the uneducated and the unredeemable. A manifest form of democracy existed here as well. You abided the beliefs and idiosyncrasies of others and they did likewise. Unless, of course, there was a truly egregious disagreement in which case democracy reached its purest form. The differing parties beat each other to a pulp until one remained standing, or at the very least, kneeling. This man, indeed, would be adjudged right and correct in the matter and life would go on in the Red Snapper as before.

Thomas Hickey liked the Red Snapper. Especially on nights like this. It was quiet and enjoyable. Such nights, once rare, were becoming routine now. General Gage, the British officer in charge, had decided to allow civilians to leave Boston if they so desired. The growing hodgepodge rebel army was attempting to encircle Boston and keep the King's troops isolated on the peninsula. Hickey estimated more than two thirds of the population had packed their belongings and moved into the countryside. Several thousand Tories remained.

He, Jack and Ezra had the table by the open front window. There were two gents playing cards across the room by the fireplace which, of course, had been snuffed out in April and wouldn't see action again for several months. Many of the finer taverns had signs forbidding card playing, dice or quoits. No signs here. One older fellow was sound asleep, his chair tipped back against the side wall and his chin buried in his large chest. The other three tables were empty. Mandy, the bar maid, was alone tonight. Before the recent military events, Mandy would be servicing the tables and Bill Cooper would be mixing up drinks and cooking up something edible. Sailors from the merchant ships would be singing and swinging by now.

Hickey took another sip of the Whistle Belly Vengeance and breathed in deeply the fishy saltwater coolness of the wharf. It was like a healing vapor. The Whistle Belly Vengeance was popular along the docks lately. Cider, rum and ale were the usual express routes to alcohol heaven. But, when you had more time and were with friends, you might have a Rumfustian, Whipt Sillabub or a Whistle Belly Vengeance. No one made a better Whistle Belly than Mandy. She made it with the usual hot whiskey, beer and molasses but she added fresh brown bread crumbs! Cheap enough, too. Three pence a quart. Hickey was on his third.

"Place is like a graveyard," said Jack Cuffs, a wiry, unimposing black man with a ready smile and close cropped hair. He worked for the cooperage near North Street but the military situation had just about brought business to a halt.

Jack Cuffs and Hickey had been friends since first meeting as enlistees in the war with France. He had gone off to fight at age 14, having convinced a British sergeant that he was 18. The British didn't ask a lot of questions. Didn't much care whether Jack was a free man or a runaway. They figured either way he'd have something to fight about and they needed bodies. Unlike Hickey, Jack had seen some heavy action. He was content now to work at the cooperage. At age 30, he had just about seen enough of most things in life, especially war.

"It's that doodle dasher Washington," sighed Ezra Gruch, dipping his finger in the top of his grog and then sucking it. Ezra was a caulker who worked free-lance along the docks. Balding and in his 50s, Ezra was six feet tall and weighed about 270 pounds, mostly fat. He appeared to have a foot in his grave already but, despite this lack of physical prowess, he was a poor judge of those rare occasions when his mouth was the equal of what little muscle he possessed. He was forever spouting off and challenging men, most of whom could have quickly slipped his other foot into the grave. He and Hickey had become fast friends when Hickey intervened in a nasty fight in which Ezra made some rather unkindly remarks about a sailor's mother. Hickey enjoyed Ezra's irreverence toward everything.

"What's His Grand Excellency The General of the Farm Hands got to do with this place being dead?" asked Hickey, puffing on a white clay pipe he had taken from the public pipe rack. The stem had been well chewed by previous smokers. Germ theories would not come along for another 100 years.

"Got everythin' to do with it," said Ezra emphatically. "I hear he's already got those poor bastards shining boots, washing clothes, saying 'yes sir' and 'no sir' and digging new fuckin' shitholes every day and on and on. I'd be walkin' away real quick if that were me."

"Those 'poor bastards' fought real good on Breed's," said Jack. "But, let's give the devil his due, Ezra, them men are mostly farmers and workers like you and me. They don't know nothin' about fighting a real war. Tom and I know about that. Me more'n Tom maybe," he said, winking at Hickey. "The King's men just keep marching and marching straight ahead. They wouldn't break ranks if you had a knife to their mamma's heart. General's gotta do something."

"Anyway," said Hickey, " what's that gotta do with the Red Snapper Graveyard?"

"I'll tell ya, Tom. I was in here last night and a coupla lobsterbacks came in and were talkin'. I had my eyes closed like Tommy over there and heard everything. The King's officers are worried. They didn't expect such a fight. Now, with the new Whig general and all his orders, they're really frettin'. These two said that had to sneak away just to get a drink. Officers got them cleaning and training and on sentry. That's why there's nobody here."

"I was over in Cambridge when Washington rode in," said Hickey. "He was supposed to show up to a big to do on a Sunday but it rained like in the Bible all day. Showed up on the Monday instead. A few bigwigs out to meet 'im."

"How you get to go over there and back alla time, Tom?" said Jack.

"You know me a long time now, right. You know I go

where I want to."

"Thinkin' of joinin' up?" asked Ezra, grinning.

"I'll be joining my foot and your arse if you keep that up," said Hickey, flashing his patented smile. "No. The way I see it this whole thing is about some soft, rich Englishmen fighting some soft, rich Colonials over who gets to run the shop. As long as I can make a pound or two, I'm happy."

"Well, ain't no way you or I could join up even if we wanted to," said Jack. "Some other general, Gates or something like that, put out orders just the other day to only sign up American-born men. No Negroes. No slaves. No vagabonds. And no deserters. That leaves you and me out, Tom. Fact is, unless Ezra here takes on some work real soon that vagabond name will fit him, too."

Ezra just shrugged and smiled.

"Why, I'm surprised at you, Jack, you know they'd want me. I ain't dark. Look it." He plopped his forearm next to Jack's and pinched up a clump of his own and Jack's skin. See?"

"Know that, Thomas. But let's see you pinch up a patch of that deserter skin."

"Oh, that hurts me now, Jacko. What did I do to deserve this?"

"Not a thing. I'm feeling poorly already. Ready for 'nother?" Jack called over Mandy and ordered another round of drinks.

"Good idea," grinned Hickey. "You can insult me all day at that rate. Deserting was the best thing I've done so far in this fair life of mind. I want no part of that military shit. Just one rich Mason taking over from another that's what this is all about."

"Your trade's dried up, too, hasn't it Tom?" asked Ezra with a look of real concern.

"Well, you heard about the colonials blowing up the guard station on the Neck. Lobsters have really tightened the noose now. I can barely get myself in and out of Boston.

Not to mention my wares." He did not mention to his drinking pals that his last mission had netted him what they both together might work a year to earn. It was safely stowed where only he could find it.

It had been more than a month since that special job. That night, he had moved into a room in the inn next to the Snapper and spent the next week just hanging around having a few drinks with the boys. Hosting a wench or two from the regular trade. An opportunity to deliver the pouch came along that second week. A ship Ezra was working on needed to make a day run up to Salem. Hickey went along, doing some deck work. Once in port in Salem, he left the ship and made his way back just north of Cambridge where he and Adam Hopkins met. He delivered the pouch and was paid. All during that time, he did not once open the pouch nor was he in the slightest way interested in what it contained. He spent the next two weeks in a small country inn. It was the most peaceful time in his life. He lay at night in the high, soft down bed and thought that this would be the way it would be all the time once he built that place out west.

He hadn't told anyone about that special mission. He was in no hurry right now for any more of the same. That night had exercised his heart quite enough for a while. In fact, he had also not told his friends that he was thinking of packing up and leaving for the western frontier a lot sooner than he had originally planned. With the Whigs and English looking more and more serious every day, it seemed like the perfect time to make the plan a reality. Head for the Ohio River. Settle on some land. No authority. No military. No politics.

Mandy came up behind Hickey, pressed her large breasts against Hickey's back and, with her lips next to his ear, said: "Can I get you something special, Tommy?"

"You're special enough, dear Mandy," crooned Hickey, kissing her softly on the neck. "But, maybe, just one more Whistle Belly."

"I've a whistlin' in my belly callin' just for you, Thomas Hickey," laughed Mandy, straightening up and clearing the empty glasses.

"Wouldn't you be wanting a real man, Mandy? Someone who won't come up short on ya," asked Ezra, his face reddening with alcohol and excitement.

"Well," said Hickey, teeth flashing that irresistible smile, "as Mandy here knows, I may not touch bottom but I wear the hell out of the sides."

"You are the devil himself, Thomas Hickey," said Mandy in mock disgust, swatting at his head with a towel.

Ezra chuckled, his face getting redder. Jack was laughing loudly at the exchange but his eyes followed Mandy's bottom as she walked to the bar. "Mandy's looking pretty good tonight, Tom," said Jack.

"I was thinking the same thing," said Hickey.

"Think you will?" asked Ezra

"She's by herself tonight," said Hickey.

"I can cover," said Ezra. "I can whip up a mean Sillabub. Go ahead. The woman is in distress. Can't you see that."

"I don't know, I ...," Hickey was interrupted by loud voices. Three men noisily pushed their way through the door.

The three were already seated at the table in the center of the room before Hickey had swung around to look. Two of the men, those facing him, were British army officers, a major and a captain. The other man, his back to Hickey, appeared to be well dressed. He sat erect, his head moving square to his shoulders as if balancing something on his head. Probably a god damned crown, thought Hickey. The sleeping gent, delicately balanced against the wall, came awake in a start, shook his head violently for a second and then, put his head on his folded arms on the table and went back to sleep. The card players looked up only briefly.

"Damned traitorous rebels," said the major, slightly slurred and loud enough to be heard by Hickey and friends. "We're stuck here in this rat hole of a city. Any civilized man would be returning from the theater on a night like tonight. Then, to say a man is not allowed a drink. That will never do. Never. Therefore, captain, I order you to drink hardy. It is just what the doctor ordered. Isn't it? They all laughed." The major was fortyish with thick, leathery lines common to career military men. He had thinning reddish brown hair and cold hazel eyes.

Mandy brought the new round of drinks for Hickey, Ezra and Jack. She then welcomed the newcomers and asked them what they would like.

"I'd like a breast. Chicken breast that is," snickered the blond captain, his thin lips pursed, making a weak little giggling sound.

"I'd like the thigh," said the major. "Both thighs. Don't bother with the plate. Just put them right here." With that, he slapped his hands tightly against his cheeks and pressed. The three men laughed loudly. Mandy, having heard such nonsense from the best of them, smiled good naturedly and explained that the cook was off tonight but that she'd be glad to get them a drink. They ordered rum. She went to get it.

The major had become aware of the trio by the window. He spoke loudly to his two companions while staring straight at Hickey, Ezra and Jack.

"I think it appropriate that we hail our grand sovereign and drink to his health," said the major, standing unsteadily, the chair falling over behind him.

The challenge to acknowledge the daft King Charlie was wearing thin, thought Hickey. Mandy brought the drinks and before she could set them on the table, the major grabbed one and hoisted it. The brew sloshed in the mug and splashed on the floor.

"To the health and long life of our good King George III." He took a long draught. The captain did the same. The other man, Hickey noticed, raised his mug but not as enthusiastically as the officers.

Hickey refused to meet his gaze. He stared at Jack saying: "Oh, shit. Just what we need to spoil a good night."

"I'm in no mood for this, Tom."

"Just be steady, Jack," said Hickey, "They'll be over it quickly. Looks like a few soldiers tired of the new regimen. No problem."

"I'll shove that sword up his arse if he forces that King George rot down my throat," said Ezra, puffing up his chest.

"Oh, sweet Jesus," said Hickey, "Just what I need, Ezra, you gettin' all brave again. I'm always the one wakes up with the swollen jaw."

The three of them chuckled quietly as footsteps approached the table.

"Pardon me, gentlemen. Is there something that strikes you as amusing in a salutation to our king?"

"Nope," said Jack. Ezra and Hickey simply raised their eyes to look at the major.

"Perhaps, you didn't hear me. I presented a toast to King George but I didn't see you loyal British subjects lift your glasses."

"Didn't hear you," said Ezra, "In fact, didn't pay much attention to you at all."

"Uh, what my friend here means, sir, is that we were deep in good conversation and didn't notice you and your men. Didn't hear a toast," said Hickey, quietly and with deference.

"So, I am to assume then," slurred the major, his eyes like a bird's, shallow and empty, "that you are loyal subjects and would have joined had you been aware?" Before they could respond, he continued: "And what of you?" he said to Jack, "Are you a free man? Papers?"

Jack got slowly to his feet. The major took a small step backward and braced. Jack smiled.

"I am a free man ... by birth," said Jack slowly and deliberately, "I served the king for two years in the war with France. I was only fifteen when I saw my first soldier die.

You, sir, I would imagine were still learning to clean your brass properly at the time. My friend here served for four years. And Ezra here is a fine craftsman who does much of his work for those sea captains loyal to King George. Now, I am sure that my friends and I would be glad to drink to King George and to the health of you and your men."

Jack picked up his mug. Hickey and Ezra did likewise. They held them up for a second and then took a sip.

"Good! Good!" said the major, laughing now. "Very good." He walked back to his table.

"I hope the king's cock falls off," said Hickey quietly, smiling broadly and holding his glass up again to the major who was out of earshot. The major and captain smiled back at him, holding up their drinks. Ezra and Jack laughed and winked at the officers. The third man at the table did not turn around. He hadn't turned around since sitting down.

"Now, what was I saying boys," said Hickey, toying with the idea of telling his friends he was thinking of going west but not ready to let anyone in on that plan yet. "Oh, my livelihood. That's right. Business is slow. That's for sure. I think I'll try and drum up some work in Cambridge or maybe back in Connecticut. Too hot around here for me to handle." His friends were, of course, unaware of his lucrative sideline in special projects.

Jack tried to talk Hickey into staying in the city. He said he could try to get him a job at the cooperage. After all, said Jack, he was thinking of getting married and needed to have his friends on hand for support. The marriage announcement came as a surprise and Ezra and Hickey told him that called for another drink.

Hickey turned to order the next round. Searching for a second for Mandy, he saw that she was serving a second round to the army officers. As she set the tankard of rum in front of the major, he plunged his hand into the deep cleavage between her breasts and freed her right breast from the bodice, placing a hard, wet kiss on the nipple.

"I said I wanted a breast," laughed the major, spinning Mandy around onto his lap, "but I've changed my mind. I do believe I'll have a thigh." He roughly brought his hand up under her skirt, groping for her crotch.

Mandy, who had been groped and fondled and squeezed by the best of them, drummed up her best look of disgust and freed herself, tucking her breast back into place. She turned to walk away. Hickey had seen this act before. Mandy could take care of herself. He started to turn back to their conversation when he heard a loud crack. He jerked his head back toward the major. He had grabbed Mandy, yanked her back to him and slapped her hard across the face. He slapped her again.

"No, filthy, wharfside wench turns her back on an officer of the king." He had her by the hair, dragging her back to his lap. Mandy reached out to scratch his face. He drew back out of range, holding her head like a doll and slapped her harder, opening a cut at the corner of her lip. A thin trickle of blood flowed onto her bodice.

Hickey, followed by Jack and with Ezra at the rear, sprung to the table. In a fraction of a second, Jack had a sharp, mechanic's knife to the throat of the young blond captain. Ezra had pulled the back of the chair occupied by the other gent. He toppled over backwards and Ezra pounced his considerable weight square on the man's chest.

Hickey caught the major's arm, and bent it behind him with a vengeance. The officer howled in pain, letting go of Mandy's hair. He tried to reach around and swat at Hickey and the source of the pain but couldn't reach far enough. The blond captain made a motion forward but Jack pressed the knife closer to his neck. He froze.

Keeping the major's arm tightly wrenched behind him, Hickey brought up his left arm and locked the officer's neck into an unforgiving vise of bicep and deltoid.

"Apologize to the lady."

"You, sir, don't know what you have done," spat the officer.

"I said, apologize to the lady." Hickey tightened the hold. The major began to gasp for air brushing weakly with his free left hand.

"Nev...uh," groaned the officer.

"Never is a long time," said Hickey, "and you don't have a real long time. Because if you don't apologize to the lady in the next couple seconds, you're gonna be nearin' the end of all the time you got."

The major thrashed wildly at this. Not being able to free himself, he lifted his right boot and brought the heel crushing down onto Hickey's right instep. The pain soared up through his leg and burst through his lips in a windy 'oomph.' But he didn't loosen his grip. In fact, the pain increased his resolve. He snapped up quickly on the man's right arm and heard a sickly snap. The major howled in pain. Mandy, who had recovered enough now to allow anger to return, kicked out and up hard with her shoe catching the major squarely in the testicles. He slumped with a weak sigh, his brain unable to sort out the pain of his arm and his crotch.

With the senior officer out of action, his arm bent in an unnatural angle at his side, Hickey turned his attention to the other two men. Mandy had returned with a pistol she kept behind the bar. She handed it to Hickey. He told Jack to release the captain.

"I'm sure, sir, a young gentleman like yourself is smart enough to realize when retreat with honor in his best interest. The major here got a little carried away with the rum and all. It looks like his arm is broken. Take him and go and we'll call it even. Agreed?"

The captain did not acknowledge the offer. He struggled halfheartedly against Jack's hold, looking first at the major and then toward the man on whom Ezra was still perched. Hickey had forgotten about the third man.

"Let him up, Ezra."

"You sure?"

"Yeah."

The man, freed from the embarrassing sitting hold, scrambled over on to his knees and got up quickly, brushing his clothes and sweeping back his powdered hair.

"Look, this has gotten out of hand. My friends, here, have been under a lot of strain and ...." All of this time, he had been obsessed with brushing his well-tailored coat and brushing dust from his trousers. Hickey knew that voice. He couldn't place it but an instant rush of apprehension made him strain to remember. Something about that voice. Now, the man finally looked up and met Hickey's eyes. The man gasped. Hickey gaped. He immediately recognized the thick pouty lips and the smooth feminine cheeks. Now it was clear to him why the earlier comment by the major had been so humorous. 'Just what the doctor ordered,' he had said. The third member of the royal party was none other than 'the good doctor' Hickey had tied up in the Hancock house. What was even more peculiar was that Hickey had since seen him enthusiastically welcoming Washington to Cambridge! This was twice now that Hickey had seen this pillar of Whig politics, this staunch Son of Liberty, in the friendly company of the enemy.

"You! You're the...," said the doctor, then, seemingly running through all of his options, he finished, "You'll have to forgive us gentlemen. We were only out to have a few friendly drinks. As I say, the pressures on these men are great these days. The major appears to have a broken arm. Allow me to tend to it. I do not deny that you have been justified in all of your actions. Allow me to aid the major and we will take our leave."

Hickey, still holding the pistol aimed at the captain and then the doctor, took a few steps backward and allowed the doctor to examine the major. "It does not appear as if any bones are broken but the shoulder has been dislodged from the socket." As he said this, he grabbed the shoulder and upper arm and yanked, quickly, professionally. There was a sharp click. "That may have done it. Come Captain McDermott. Give me a hand with him."

The doctor slid the major's hand inside his waistcoat to keep the shoulder in place. He and the captain helped the semiconscious major to his feet and the two of them dragged the officer to the door. Just before leaving, the doctor turned back to Hickey and said: "I'm certain nothing will be said of this. I hope we can count on the same discretion by you gentlemen." Hickey found a meaning in this hidden from Jack and Ezra.

***

Mandy's hair, freed from its tight bun, flowed off the pillow. Sweat beaded on her forehead and neck. Hickey lay propped up on his elbows next to her, running his fingertip in small circles around the nipple of her left breast.

"You're a strange one, Thomas Hickey."

"Strange? Didn't I put it where it goes?"

"Yes, you did it put it there quite well," she laughed. "I mean you're as hard as the worst of them but, there's something. Different. Soft."

"Soft! Did it twice. What do you want from me, woman? Blood?" Hickey mocked, putting his forearm in his even white teeth and biting in mock despair until Mandy came to the rescue, saving him from taking a chunk out of his own arm.

"I mean to say 'thanks,' Tom. You make me feel like one of them ladies up on the Hill. You can have me any time. You know that. But, each time you, ... you almost make it seem like you care. I want to thank you for doing that."

"I do care, my love. You're as special as any of them trussed up, powdered rich ladies. No one has the right to touch you, 'less you want to be touched. No one has the right to hit you. I don't care if it's the king himself. That's just how I feel about it."

"Like I said, Tom, you are the strange one."

"Strange?! I'll show you strange. Think this is strange," he rolled on top of her, stiff and fresh.

"Damn, don't you ever give up? My insides feel like jelly. You were right about wearin' the hell out of the sides."

"With a beauty like you, Mandy, I could go on for weeks." He rolled her on top of him, his fingers moving slowly, gently down the ample softness of her thighs.

"Not only did you wear out the sides, but, you touched bottom." She moaned, rolled onto her back and lifted her legs, spreading her knees wider for him.

Chapter Eight

Washington's Headquarters, Cambridge, Mass.
10 a.m., Wednesday, July 26, 1775

"It is not the farmers who come for a day and then disappear. This report shows one out of ten men absent for reasons other than illness! It is not the sorry state of their equipment that worries me. Nor is it the fact that most enlistments will be up by the end of the year. It is not the total lack of discipline that sticks in my craw," said Washington to the three generals. "What worries me, gentlemen, is information. The lack of it. Our adversary has us outflanked on every quadrant of the information battlefield. In a word, sirs, spies. They are among us. And what do we have? The pitiful dregs of the barrel. This has got to change. And quickly."

The three generals were indignant. They all tried to respond at once, filling the small meeting room in Washington's Cambridge headquarters with noisy rebuttals. Washington held up his hands, palms outward, and nodded to General Ward.

"Spies? Who? Where are they?" said Major General Artemas Ward. "If you have knowledge of who these traitors are, tell me. I will deal with them personally." Ward, a man who at 47 was only four years older than Washington but who seemed weak and elderly compared to the virile commander in chief, was visibly upset by Washington's challenge. His large body, bordering on obesity, began to shake. He had been severely criticized for, what some called, his lack of leadership on Breed's Hill. Ward had been in command and, had he shown himself as a true leader, thought Washington, Ward and not himself, might be commander in chief. Ward would bear watching. But, now, having been around Ward for three weeks, Washington did not consider him a real threat to his authority. One thing was certain, Washington did not doubt for an instant Ward's dedication to the cause.

"General Ward, I am not accusing any of you of harboring traitors. I am not suggesting that you are so green as to not recognize the possibility that there are these traitors amongst you. I do not know their names. I do not expect you to know their names. I am simply stating the facts as I see them. There was a major breech of secrecy concerning the battle last month. Our opponent knew far too much and too soon by all accounting."

"But, General Washington, we, too, have our sources. I myself have several young men regularly visiting Boston. They have given us much valuable information," said Major General Charles Lee. General Lee was a bird of a different plumage. A former British officer, he had regaled both Samuel and John Adams with his tales of past military expeditions. He had little care nor much concern for civilians; a soldier's soldier. He was 44 but seemed decades younger than Ward. Washington had determined that Charles Lee's knowledge of military tactics and warfare was far superior to his own. Lee could, indeed, be a threat to his leadership.

"Dammit, sir," spat Washington. For many years now, he had seemed to conquer what was once a legendary temper. The stresses of the past few weeks had already begun to chip away large chunks of veneer. "Must I repeat myself. I am not making accusations. I am not faulting your competency nor your information sources. We are in this together. We are fellow officers and, by God, we will treat one another accordingly. I will say this once more: We must build a network of spies at all levels. I have decided to authorize each of you a $500 purse solely for this purpose. These resources are scarce so you see the importance I place on this." There was a slight pause. Washington breathed deeply. "This is vital to our cause," in control once more.

"I'll rout out any spying bastards in my division, General Washington. Of that you can be certain," growled Major General Israel Putnam, an odd duck with enormous energy. His men loved him. He was without pretense, making it a point to talk to the rawest recruit the same way he had just responded to the commanding general.

"I'm certain you will, Gen. Putnam." Washington smiled. He regarded Israel Putnam as a good man, if not somewhat of a buffoon at times. An officer could not and should not get too close to his men. It was bad for discipline.

The generals, having been offered room to breathe, nodded and agreed to search for every available tributary of information on the King's troops.

"Fine," said Washington. "Now, let's move on to reports of supplies. Uniforms, I understand are especially in short supply. General Lee, how about your men? Do you think...."

Washington was interrupted by a young enlisted aide who, leaving the door open behind him, rushed to Washington's desk and handed him a message. Washington read the cover note and dismissed the aide.

"It's nothing, gentlemen, just another pesky detail. There seems to be a thousand of them each day. Well, then. Fine. We'll meet again on Monday." Washington simply returned to reading the reports on his desk. The generals knew they had been dismissed. The other two young men in the room remained. Joseph Reed served as Washington's personal secretary. He had recorded the minutes of the session and was now waiting to hear the general instruct him to remove the indelicate language from the notes. Washington went beyond that expectation instructing Reed not to record the meeting at all. Reed left.

Washington had also asked Thomas Mifflin, his 31-year-old aid-de-camp, to join the session. Mifflin wrote all of Washington's speeches. There already had been eleven in the first three weeks at Cambridge. Most of these were to local groups with social standing. Washington was indeed a hit already. His regal bearing had inspired Abigail Adams to borrow lines from Dryden in a letter to her husband, John: "He's a temple sacred by birth." She described Washington as having modesty etched into every line of his face and possessing "dignity with ease."

Much of this social success Washington attributed to young Mifflin's way with words. He had a knack for providing the right turn of phrase to suit a particular audience. Washington was still ill at ease when making a speech. But Mifflin seemed to have just the right touch for making his reserve appear to be genuine modesty. That's why Washington had asked him to sit in on this session with the generals. He wanted Mifflin to put his talents to work on words that would impress upon officers and men alike the need for security of strategic information. Also, it might help to open their eyes and ears to useful information from the enemy. Washington told Mifflin the type of speech material he'd like and nodded toward the door with a half smile. Mifflin left.

Washington sat silently staring out the window. Nearly an hour passed as he contemplated this latest problem. Perhaps, it would have been best to have said 'no' to the Congress and gone back to Virginia. This mess seemed more hopeless by the day. As strong of an impression as he might have made on his three generals, Washington was far more concerned with the spy situation than he had revealed. From his early assessment of the situation, there were, at this point, no well-defined sides. The "minutemen," as they were called, fraternized with the enemy regularly. They had no concept of "us against them." They regularly talked about the numbers of men on both sides. And how their new training regimen was coming from the Virginian sent to lead them. Or that when many of the enlistments were up at the end of the year and that might make an ideal time for the King's troops to overrun Cambridge. They were like feuding family. And why not? Every single man, woman and child in the colonies was connected umbilically to the Mother Country. Everyone had relatives in England or Ireland or France. Just a few months ago, they were neighbors. There was, of course, the possibility that this could actually help their cause. Such openness appeared to exist on both sides of the Charles. If he acted quickly, he might be able to put key people in place to shift the information balance. Lord knows this rabble is simply not ready to fight and win against perhaps the best fighting force the world has seen. We will need luck. Luck in great quantities. We can make our own luck if we know what the enemy is thinking.

But the realities of hour-to-hour existence of the army allowed little time for strategy or intelligence. Washington stared again at the report he had just been handed. Just yesterday, he had been told that there were four hundred and thirty barrels of gunpowder in the reserves. Now, this message says there are only thirtyeight. Thirty- eight barrels of powder! For 16,770 men. Ridiculous. And how could anyone be that far off in his assessment. A barrel or two? Sure. Four hundred barrels? With 1,598 men on sick lists and the other 1,400 away for god knows what, that left 13,700 men with 38 barrels of powder. A little less than nine rounds per man. Nine rounds each to keep the British locked in Boston! The British standard was 60 rounds per man.

If it weren't so pitiful, it would be laughable. This was not at all what he imagined command of an army would be. No uniforms. Little supplies. No discipline. And no one to trust. He couldn't even tell the three major generals of his staff that they were down to 38 barrels of powder because he didn't know if even they could be trusted. The enemy might know just how desperate was their situation.

Washington took a deep breath, stood up and straightened out his uniform. "You've had your moment of self-pity," he told himself. "Now, get on with it." Congress would have to provide more powder. Meanwhile, he would send men out into the countryside to get what they could. As for the spy situation, he would take care of that himself. He would find individuals he could trust. He would pay them himself and only he would know who they were and what they were doing. Armed with this information not only would he be better equipped to deal with the British but he would be better equipped to maintain discipline and control within his own ranks. He would also begin to send inaccurate information to Boston in an attempt to mislead the enemy.

He opened the lower right drawer of his desk and took out a leather pouch filled with papers that had been given to him by a Hancock associate. Hancock may, in fact, be a peacock but the information in this pouch was like found treasure. Hancock had compiled a list of more than a hundred supporters of liberty who were willing to help. Many of these men were well off or had a unique skill to contribute. A few of the names burst off the page in surprise as they were generally known as staunch supporters of the King. Hancock had included details as to the best way to contact these people and their specialties. He also had annotated the lists with footnotes as to favors owed him by these prominent Bostonians. Hancock had also secretly deposited sums of hard coinage, silver mostly, with many of these friends throughout the region, preparing for the inevitable day when he might have to flee. This could be put to good use now, such as in the purchase of gunpowder. Washington made notes on the margins of several sheets.

He would start with Benjamin Church. Washington had attended the brief ceremony yesterday at which Dr. Church was named the first "Surgeon General of the Continental Army." It was an interesting title. Dr. Church was to be the chief adviser on medical issues. Hancock and both Adams recommended Church as a key source of information. Dr. Benjamin Church had been there right from the start; a member of the top secret Committee of Safety; a popular delegate to the Provincial Congress; and he had even tended to the wounded at Lexington. It would be a good place to start. Washington was already formulating a method of operation. He would never confide fully in anyone on this list nor would he accept what was given to him as gospel. He would need at least two independent sources confirming the same information before he put it to use. Dr. Church, he had heard, moved in and out of Boston with ease. He might be a source of valuable intelligence. Then again, well, one never knew. There was talk.

***

Washington had lunch with three displaced Boston merchants and their wives. It was a pleasant affair. He wore his dress uniform and couldn't help noticing the admiring looks of the ladies at the table. In such small social groups, when he could relax, he found himself telling stories about his boyhood on Pope's Creek in Virginia's tidewater. Today he was particularly amusing, poking fun at himself and his early attempts at swimming. He had an innate ability to deal with pressures and problems by filing them away in neat packages while he took time out to recharge. He had arisen at 4:30 a.m., but with a little food and pleasant conversation, he was refreshed. The luncheon offered a respite from the morning's bad news and a pause before the distasteful but necessary disciplinary proceedings scheduled for the afternoon. He delighted in openly flirting with the merchant's wives, all three of whom seemed more than eager to join in. Often at such mindless affairs, he found himself fantasizing about these middle-aged women. The more pompous the woman, the more he fantasized about propping her over the side of his bed, hiking her skirts and sending home his message. It was good sport, this daydreaming, and certainly a well-earned respite from the pressures of his responsibility. It never entered his mind that the afternoon's disciplinary action resulted from another man's release of similar pressure.

***

"To command, Thomas," Washington said to his aide-de-camp as they walked from their horses to the field where the disciplinary action would take place, "one must first learn to obey. If I had a choice for these men to love me or respect me, I'd choose the latter. That reminds me, make a note to add to the Order of the Day that all officers should read Humphrey Bland's 'Treatise on Military Discipline.' I have a copy and I'm sure we can get another one or two to circulate." Mifflin made a note.

The sun was huge, magnified by the haze which hung over Cambridge. The temperature had been in the 90s all week and the humidity was nearly unbearable. Washington insisted, nevertheless, on wearing his full uniform with the dark blue woolen coat faced with buff. As they walked, small clouds of dry, powdery tan dirt followed them to their place in front of the third regiment of the second brigade under General Ward.

Supplies. Spies. Uniforms. Enlistments. Discipline. Putting the problems of what the British called this "rabble in arms" into any order would be next to impossible. High on Washington's list, however, was discipline. Without discipline, he knew his army would have no chance at all. Standing before the nearly 400 men, waiting for the line officers to call the motley group to attention, Washington thought of his dealings with the slaves at Mt. Vernon. In a lifetime of administering to these childlike beings, he had developed a set of rules and penalties. It was not their fault if doing right did not come naturally. Patience and tolerance were required. They needed guidance and discipline. The harsh reality of the lesson to be learned was that only stiff penalties seemed to bring the desired result. Of course, this was not only a problem with the Negroes. He had had just as many problems with others sold into his service for debt payment and the like. Just this past April — and didn't it seem like several years ago? — he had placed an ad in the Virginia Gazette offering a reward for two Scottish serving men who had run off from Mt. Vernon long before their indebted time was up. Washington had fed the men and provided shelter. He had provided them with firm discipline, showing them how to take pride in honest work for honest reward. How did they repay this civility? By running. Had they no sense of honor? No sense of dignity in wanting to fulfill their obligations? In many ways, the same was true with soldiers in his early war escapades. Soldiers, perhaps, even needed more discipline than slaves. After all, soldiers were expected to be responsible for their actions. He had moved swiftly during the past three weeks. There were eight courts-martial held after Breed's Hill. Dozens of officers were relieved of their appointments. Public lashings occurred nearly every day.

The first week of his command, Washington had written home that he found most of these New Englanders "exceedingly dirty and nasty people." To be fair about it, the "nasty people" thought little more of the "prissy Virginian stuffed coat" sent to tell them how to do their job. Soldiers packed their sacks and went home by the hundreds. Washington immediately got their attention. He asked Congress for authority to hang deserters. He had asked for the same authority from the Virginian House of Burgesses twenty years earlier. Congress said "no" but approved of many of Washington's stronger disciplinary actions.

As with his slaves, Washington realized that an important step in installing and maintaining discipline came in keeping the soldiers busy. He had them sweep company streets every day. There were daily inspections of camps and, especially, of the kitchens. Trash was collected and set afire daily. New latrines were dug and old ones filled in each week. Any sentry found asleep at his post was severely punished. Whereas the soldiers were used to just going and coming as they pleased, Washington installed strict rules for furloughs. They were rarely granted.

"General, the troops await your command," bellowed a young major snapping Washington out of his thoughts of the farm and its slaves.

"Thank you, major, put the men at ease." The major gave the order. Many of the men were already slouched at ease when the order was delivered.

"Men," said Washington, in a loud, strong voice, using words prepared for him by Mifflin, "It is not my intention to prohibit you from participation in all forms of diversion though in these difficult times such entertainments must be low on our list or priorities. When not about your duties, there are many such activities befitting a proper soldier in this army. All of you who have enlisted in this cause, have my commitment to you that you will be provided with proper equipment and training as our resources allow. I expect your commitment to this army as well. You will conduct yourselves in a proper manner at all times. There is no place in this army for bawdy or lewd behavior. Nor will drunkenness be tolerated. I have ordered all cider confiscated. I consider the offense that we are here to redress to be of particular distaste. Public fornication is a serious offense. I have already issued orders for the removal from our camps of all lewd women. This soldier, Daniel Green, was witnessed flaunting his disregard for my orders. He participated in an act of total disregard for modesty and decency with a woman in full view of the ladies of fashion in the surrounding neighborhood."

There was an audible snickering throughout the ranks. Most of the men knew that Private Daniel Green, having heard from his girlfriend that she no longer wanted anything to do with him because he had enlisted, had gotten drunk and paid a local prostitute to perform oral sex on him in broad daylight on a well-traveled foot bridge.

Washington ignored the impudent response and continued in the same even tone.

"I have stated in my daily orders to you that I have requested from the Congress the authority to deliver a maximum of 500 lashes with the whip. This request has been denied. Therefore, thirty nine of the maximum of forty lashes allowed will be delivered to this soldier for you to witness and take heed."

Washington stepped back as two uniformed soldiers led the offender to a post. The soldier, stripped to the waist, was trembling but silent. His hands were fastened to the post and a sergeant came forward holding the cat-o'-nine-tails, a whip made of leather thongs with lead pellets strung on them. The sergeant smoothed the leather thongs with his left hand so they hung straight then, in an instant, he brought the whip up and quickly down on the man's back with a relish and ferocity that made even the most jaded soldier wince. Wide welts immediately arose from the man's back and then, while the whip was being drawn back for another stroke, blood finally burst from the peaks of the welts. The man screamed.

Washington stood stoically, staring straight into the faces of the soldiers assembled as each blow was delivered. He had witnessed hundreds of whippings both on the farm and in his earlier military life. After a dozen or so strokes, the man had slumped, hanging from his hands. He no longer screamed. There was only a slight tensing of his body as the twenty-third and thirty-first and, finally, thirty- ninth strokes were delivered.

Private Green was cut down from the post. Two soldiers were summoned from the ranks to carry him away to the camp's medical tent. The major called the assemblage to order and reported to the commanding general. Washington acknowledged his salute, turned and walked away. Mifflin followed.

As they rode back to headquarters, Washington was aware of Mifflin's silence. "It is not a pleasant experience, Thomas. I assure you, however, that, with the exception of a few scars, that man will fully recover. It is very effective and makes it unnecessary to administer more drastic forms of punishment."

Mifflin smiled wanly and nodded. They rode in silence.

Chapter Nine

Sturbridge, 60 miles southwest of
Cambridge, Mass.
2 p.m., Saturday, September 16, 1775

Thomas Hickey glanced at the mantel clock over the fireplace of the small inn. It was already 2 o'clock. He had been waiting since noon. His patience was wearing thin. In the past two hours, only three people had entered the inn, two locals traveling in an open wagon and, an hour or so later, a lone rider. All three had a bowl of stew and a quart of flip and left.

Hickey, after leaving the Red Snapper in July, had settled into a room north of Cambridge. He had left the comfortable but well-worn inn he now called home just after sunrise, riding steadily west on the Main Road. It was a clear morning with the sun already burning off the dew as he rode by Old Mark. He had been this way a hundred times but the sight of Old Mark never failed to make him shiver, whether on a morning like this or in the dog days of summer. As the old folks told it, Old Mark was a slave who had decided that freedom was his destiny. He ran for it. When the master caught him, he bound Old Mark's hands and feet in chains and hung him from a tree. That was twenty years ago. For a year or so, chunks of Old Mark fell like autumn leaves. They left his bones hanging there as a reminder to runaways. A good lesson to anyone, thought Hickey. Anyone who thinks that freedom is something you get to by running away, is in for a long trip. A journey that just might end with your shiny bones whistling in the wind like porch chimes. A lesson some folks today might want to relearn.

Hickey shifted in his chair to look again at the clock. He was certain this was the place. Adam Hopkins said he was to be at the "Blue Fox" along the West Road by noon. Hopkins had said Hickey would be surprised by what he was proposing for his next "assignment." The pay, Hopkins said, might be even better than the pouch caper. Any job that paid in silver or gold could capture his attention. He already had just about enough booty to take him west. The rest would be gravy for the biscuits. But, he had been waiting two hours and he was bored and tired of waiting.

He got up from his chair and went out to check on his horse. The gray stallion was contentedly eating from a bucket. Hickey had removed the riding saddle and leaned it against the side of the building. He took off the underlay blanket, shook it out, folded it in half carefully and tossed it back onto the horse. He was about to mount the saddle when he heard the beat of several horses. He leaned back against the building and lit up the clay pipe from the inn's public rack. Arms folded, he pretended not to notice the new visitors.

The three riders were mounted on strong, young horses. They were dressed in bland browns and grays but there was something in their manner that told Hickey these were not locals, nor itinerant workers. One man in particular was very tall with a large, muscular frame. He sat erect in the saddle and, as he alit, he maintained the same stiff, upright bearing. He wore a large, floppy hat, which shadowed his face. The others wore loose jackets but Hickey could see the butt end of a pistol on each. The three whispered amongst themselves for a few seconds and then entered the inn. Hickey stared straight ahead. His alarms sounded. Had he been found out? Was this a set up? Had the British found out about the Hopkins-Hancock connection? After all, John Hancock was still on the King's list of prime enemies.

Hickey decided to get away as fast as possible. He grabbed for his saddle the minute the inn door slammed shut. He had slung it over his horse and was tightening the straps when he heard the door open and close behind him. He did not turn around, continuing to work on the saddle. Footsteps grew louder behind him. He braced.

"Here to see the turtle?" asked the voice.

Hickey was stunned. He had braced for a challenge and was ready to whirl around, kick out at the man's groin and be down the road before the others could make chase. He did not expect this question. He was silent.

"I said are you here to see the turtle?"

"Yes, but can turtles float?" answered Hickey, coming awake, repeating the answer Hopkins had provided to him. It had sounded ridiculous when Hopkins told him and it sounded fairly ridiculous at the moment. He turned around slowly. One of the shorter men with a pistol smiled at him.

"Mr. Hickey, I'm Sgt. James Curtis of the Continental Army. Thank you for meeting us. Please, if you will, come inside and talk with us."

The Continental Army! Hickey felt like bolting anyway. What the hell was Hopkins getting him into now? But, this young sergeant seemed amiable enough. It wouldn't hurt to hear them out. See what it was that could be worth a payment in silver. He decided to listen to the proposition.

"Be glad to," said Hickey, walking alongside the young man who was only an inch or so taller.

The sergeant held the door open and Hickey entered the cool darkness of the inn, his eyes adjusting to the dim light. The other two men were sitting at the furthest table from the door. Hickey could only see their backs. The sergeant motioned for Hickey to sit in one of the two remaining chairs at the table as he pulled out and sat in the other. The taller man was staring down at the table. He was still wearing the hat. The other man, a man in his thirties with dark hair and a deep scar on his left cheek, spoke: "Mr. Hickey. It is a pleasure to meet you. I'm sure Sgt. Curtis here has told you we have heard good things about your special talents from Mr. Hopkins. I'm Capt. Rawson."

Lowering his voice to barely a whisper, he said: "Allow me to introduce you to General George Washington, commander of the Continental Army at Cambridge." The words hit Hickey like a sharp smack in the face. General George Washington! Hickey stared at the man with the hat. Washington lifted his eyes to meet Hickey's but he did not remove the hat nor adjust the high collar, which further shielded his face. Hickey was impressed by the man's eyes. The blue-gray orbs met his gaze and didn't falter. Hard as flint, they were staring into his soul. Hickey returned the stare and, it seemed to him, there was a brief flash of acceptance, a recognition of a soul quite comfortable in returning the inquisitive stare. Washington extended his hand. Hickey grasped it firmly. Hickey was impressed by the size and firmness of the hand of this rich man from Virginia. For Washington's part, his first thought was that this short, stocky man had a hand nearly as large as his own.

"I thank you for coming, Mr. Hickey," said Washington in a calm, deliberate voice with the distinctive southern accent Hickey had heard on many of his sailing escapades. "I realize we are late. I take it you were entertaining the notion of leaving as we rode up. And, I certainly would not have placed any blame on you for that. As you can imagine, we have to be very cautious in our travels outside of Cambridge these days. We were required to take a detour or two which caused our delay. Nevertheless, I personally am grateful to you for accepting our invitation to this meeting."

"I enjoy a good challenge," said Hickey, purposely avoiding the use of any military or courtesy titles.

"General Washington!" said Sgt. Curtis, with emphasis like a teacher waiting for a pupil to repeat the lesson, indicating Hickey should use the general's proper title.

"It's been many years since I was in the military, sergeant," said Hickey. "In the King's army, at that. Been just a regular citizen for quite some time. Just trying to get along. Men are men to me. And that includes the general from Virginia here."

"Please, sir, a little respect or will I be forced to teach you respect?" He pushed his chair back and prepared to begin the lesson.

Hickey did not move, nor blink, nor change expressions. "I would sit back down if I were you, sergeant, or I might be forced to teach you how a pistol just about the size of yours is crammed up a young man's arsehole."

The young sergeant leapt to his feet and began to reach over the table.

"Sit down sergeant," said Washington, calmly, though the smile changed to the thin, dark lines nature has etched in marble. "Mr. Hickey is not an enlistee. We must treat him as we would any of our civilian neighbors." The young man reluctantly sat back in his chair. He sat stiffly, glaring at Hickey while Washington continued.

"I, too, once served the king, Mr. Hickey," said Washington, diffusing the moment. Washington was at once disturbed and impressed by Hickey's boldness. This was just the quality needed in a man who might accomplish the sort of tasks Washington had in mind. It was also these qualities that might turn a man's head from loyalty and duty. "What I propose is strictly a business arrangement between gentlemen."

"Never thought of myself as much of a gentleman," said Hickey, surprising himself with his incivility. Washington had that same patient-father attitude he had seen in so many military officers before. 'Oh, the boy has erred again. The burden is on me to show the lad the evil of his ways. This hurts me more than it hurts you.' And yet, there was something much deeper in this man; a steeliness which, Hickey thought, could stand up in any tavern brawl.

The young man with the dark hair winced and straightened himself in his chair as if just waiting for the order to crush the pesky bug.

"Merely polite conversation, Mr. Hickey. In fact, being a gentleman is not the most important quality in accomplishing the sort of employment I have in mind." Hickey had gotten his attention. From the farm to Philadelphia and, now, at the front line, Washington had become accustomed to deference by men of Hickey's social stature. Although he had seen this brassiness in many of the New Englanders who purported to be soldiers, it didn't take long for true discipline to get most of them in line. The lash of the cat o' nine tails was very persuasive. Discipline was difficult in any army. But, in the end, most wild horses are broken. The key word here was "most." There was that one rogue in a hundred that would never accept a man riding on his back. This man was somehow different, thought Washington. He would never accept another man riding on his back. There was good and evil in such animals. The question remained: what would it take to highlight the good and to suppress the evil. What would be the price?

"What kind of employment would ya be havin' in mind, Mr. Washington?" said Hickey, flashing his best and brightest smile.

"I would prefer to show you, sir," said Washington.

"Show me what?"

"The kind of work I have in mind." Washington stood. The two young men also got quickly to their feet. Hickey remained in his chair.

"Come, Mr. Hickey, let me show you something very interesting," said Washington, slightly miffed and yet not the least bit surprised that Hickey had not leapt to his feet in deference.

"Nothing else to do. Afternoon is shot," said Hickey, shrugging his shoulders and, with a great show of effort, laboriously climbed out of his comfortable chair.

Capt. Rawson and Sgt. Curtis took the lead. They opened the inn door and stepped out onto the narrow porch, looking both ways along the road. Hickey and Washington stood silently side-by-side inside the door. Satisfied it was safe, Sgt. Curtis opened the door for Washington.

"Thanks, gents," said Hickey stepping through the door in front of Washington.

The two men scowled and looked to Washington for redress. He smiled patiently, shook his head and walked toward his horse.

"Captain Rawson," said Washington, now in the voice of commander in chief, "you and Sgt. Curtis lead the way. I will ride with Mr. Hickey." The men mounted their horses and geed them toward a narrow dirt road which lead away southwest behind the inn. They had to wait at the entrance to the road while Hickey saddled up. Washington, too, waited in silence.

The four rode along the tree-lined dirt road for a mile still silent, with one or the other or both of the young soldiers glancing back every few minutes. The bright afternoon sun filtered through the dense trees causing patches of brilliant greens and yellows. Bluejays and robins stopped to investigate the travelers. Hawks and crows scoured the clearings for prey. A slight breeze kept the dust behind them.

"A beautiful day, is it not, Mr. Hickey?" said Washington, "Reminds me of my childhood days on Pope's Creek in Virginia. Summer still clinging to the earth. Fall creeping in at night."

"A nice one," answered Hickey.

They rode another half mile in silence.

"Retrieving that pouch from Mr. Hancock's house took a great deal of courage. I want to thank you personally for your effort. The information in that pouch has proven of great value to me."

"Didn't have a single clue what was in it. Never looked.

I'll do just about anything for the right price," said Hickey trying to disguise his surprise that the pouch had made its way to George Washington, general of the army at Cambridge. Then, feeling his response too flippant, he added: "Times that night though I thought I'd soil my trousers." He smiled his widest and whitest smile and Washington had no choice but to smile back, a barely perceptible twinge of envy over this man's perfect rows of white teeth.

"Mr. Hancock told me in Philadelphia that his house was occupied by a dozen or more British officers. How you managed to get into the house, retrieve the pouch and escape alive is a source of amazement to me. I am not certain, Mr. Hickey, if I have another man who might accomplish that same result. Enough of past exploits. I have been in Cambridge now for ten weeks. It has been difficult. We have many great challenges. Most of those men are farmers or laborers. They signed on because they believe in this cause. But, now many enlistments will be up in the next few months. We need uniforms, supplies, powder. There is a great need for training. Certainly it can be said that many of these men are excellent marksman. They lack, however, even the most basic concept of tactical maneuvers. These men have left their homes and families. They are as fiercely independent as you, yet they put up with it all."

Washington felt the best tack was to appeal to Hickey's passion, to talk to him as one man to another on equal terms.

"Certainly there is grousing. And, surely, many will leave as their enlistments end. But, just the simple fact that they are doing what they are doing shows the righteousness of our cause. They do it because they believe in their hearts that the King has betrayed them. He has ordered troops to fire on them, to forcefully chastise them for daring to question his tariffs and assessments. We will not abide it. There are those, Mr. Hickey, in the Congress who are already demanding full and complete independence from England. I myself do not know what form the just conclusion of this will take but, I can assure you, I left a comfortable home, and with great doubts and misgivings, I hasten to add, to do my duty. What is your duty, Mr. Hickey?"

"My duty, general," said Hickey, using Washington's military title for the first time, "is to me and only to me."

"Have you no duty to what is right, sir? The King's Parliament continues to burden us with tax on top of tax. Such a tyrannical system cannot be abided by just men. All men of conscience must rebel against such complete and total acts of tyranny."

"I don't own any land. I don't own a ship. Don't own a dock. Don't sell tobacco or import rum. Taxes haven't hurt me much," said Hickey.

"But, you pay in other ways. Higher prices for your smoke and drink. Royal agents telling you what you can buy and what you can't. And, what comes of these burdensome duties? You are deprived of any say in Parliament. Do you think the conduct of the people of Boston warrants their murder? Does the venting of frustration earn the killing of innocent farmers? Does the King have the right to lock up a city in a tight military fist because its people have complaints?" Washington's voice rose and the two soldiers turned back to look. He held up his left hand and nodded that everything was all right.

"Those are damned nice ideas to tell the ladies of fashion," said Hickey, "but to my way of thinking this whole rebellion business is about rich men like yourself wanting more. The way I see it the rich and powerful Masons of Parliament and the rich and powerful Masons of the colonies are just feuding over who gets what. Men like me, General Washington, do the fighting. And the dying. What do we get for our efforts? If we don't pay taxes to the King, we'll be paying them to John Adams, or Mr. Hancock or, perhaps, to you. You are a follower of the Masonic rites, aren't you?"

"For Providence' sake, Hickey, what does a social and

fraternal organization like the Masonic Order have to do with any of this? We are discussing the fundamental rights of every man, rich and poor. Where I come from in the south, Mr. Hickey, there are many landowners. Some beat and torture their slaves. Others, like myself, encourage them to have families and to be industrious. There will always be leaders. The Great Creator makes leaders and followers. This struggle is about what we expect of our leaders. I did not have to leave my comfortable bed at Mt. Vernon to come here where we may be overrun any day by, perhaps, the best army in the world. There is a reason."

"I suspect, General Washington," said Hickey, "you, in fact, wouldn't wanna be no other place. I think the title of general suits you just fine. I do believe right from my heart that you are doing your duty like you see it. Most of us, though, don't have so much control over what we can and cannot do."

"Why then, Hickey, did you risk your life to retrieve that pouch?" asked Washington.

"Gold."

"You can't breathe gold, Mr. Hickey. And you cannot spend it if you are a prisoner. Will gold provide a future free of tyranny for your children and grandchildren?" Washington was tiring of this shallow discussion of doctrine. The man would not be reasoned with nor persuaded by the usual appeals meted out to the general populace.

"It can buy me my future."

"What is your future?"

"The west," said Hickey with discernible reverence.

"West?"

"I plan to go out to the Ohio, maybe further. As far from here as I can get. I'm going to build me a house and do as I please. That, general, is freedom."

A price for each man, thought Washington. He now had the key. He would save it for the proper time.

"How did Adam Hopkins know you could be trusted

with that pouch?"

"I been working for Mr. Hancock, through Adam, for years. You know, general, I'm sure, that much of Mr. Hancock's fortune was made by his uncle in the smuggling trade, and that the good patriot, Mr. Hancock, is himself a smuggler. I have done hundreds of jobs in this tricky trade. Not once have I failed to deliver every ounce of goods I was paid to deliver. I may not believe — or even understand — your cause, but I am not a liar and I am not a thief. I earn my pay. I take nothing more than is due me."

Washington, had, of course, heard such stories about the Hancocks and was more and more certain Hickey was right for the job. Now was the time to proffer the offer.

"I will offer you a deal, Mr. Hickey. I will no longer question your view of the Sons of Liberty. I propose a strict business relationship. I offer to purchase your services. I pay very well. But, I must know that you will be, at least, a loyal employee."

"Never turn down the chance for honest employment," Hickey smiled and the tension visibly drained from both he and Washington.

"I mentioned to you all of the problems I face in turning the men at Cambridge into an army. There is one major deficiency I did not mention. Information. I view information about the enemy as among the most important commodities I can possess as a general. The enemy is better trained, better equipped and better disciplined. But, most importantly, the enemy seems to know all that we do while we know next to nothing about them. If we are to have a chance in this struggle, this must change. Immediately. This is where I see you being of great value to the cause of patriotism ... or to your own pocketbook, however you wish to view it."

"A spy?"

"Something like that."

"Maybe the general should just open his eyes a little wider and save himself a gold piece or two. It doesn't take a spy to see that there are whoremongers right there in Cambridge with you," said Hickey.

"Explain yourself."

"What I mean, general, is that the weasels are not sneaking around stealing your secrets. The weasels are burrowing into your own ranks. They're hearing the twaddle from your own mouths and taking it right across the river to the King's men."

"Spies on my staff?" said Washington stiffening his back in incredulously.

"Yes sir, Mr. General from Virginia. I've seen it with my own eyes at least twice. That's a fact. And such a fact as everyone knows that I won't charge you a halfpenny for the information."

"Who?" Washington's voice was loud and demanding. The two staff aides turned quickly around to see what had provoked such a response.

"It's certain that there's more than one but the biggest snake, as I see it, is Dr. Church. The reptile crawling about in the general's tent is none other than Dr. Benjamin Church, best friend of the congress and patriots everywhere."

Washington laughed, laughter born of surprise. The idea was absurd, wasn't it? Perhaps, he had read this Hickey fellow wrong. Maybe he was not as savvy as he seemed. Or at least not as trench-hardened as Hancock had made him out to be. Perhaps this was some kind of Hancock joke. A tweak of the nose as a sort of revenge for denying him the glory of wearing a general's uniform. The man was obviously repeating some drivel from a Tory tavern. It was inconceivable to most Bostonians who knew Church. Washington, himself, of course, had no long memory of experiences with Dr. Church from which to draw. But Church was a protege of Sam Adams. The doctor had been right there with Adams and Hancock and all the others as they met over the print shop. The Long Room Club laid the foundation for this struggle. Dr. Benjamin Church was chief physician of the army at Cambridge. He had the full faith and confidence of the Congress. It was Dr. Church who had been in on the Committee of Safety meetings two or three years ago, meeting at the Green Dragon Tavern with the likes of Hancock, Revere, Paine, the Warrens and the Adamses. Hancock had told him they had sworn on a Bible each meeting. It was Dr. Benjamin Church who had welcomed him to Cambridge and introduced him within the local society. Perhaps, he would have to rethink the kinds of tasks to be assigned to Hickey, although he might prove useful in sending messages back to the enemy.

"I can see you don't believe me," said Hickey.

"I didn't say I did or did not believe you, Mr. Hickey, but it is rather farfetched," replied Washington, unsure now of the nature of Hickey's tale. Could it be a bit of intentional misinformation? Had the King's men already gotten to him? Had Hickey reported about this meeting and been primed with a story or two to cause a rift in the ranks? It was best to be careful.

"I know Church is one of you. I know you think I'm a fool. But, I ask you, general, what have I to gain or lose? I am telling you the simple truth as I see it. I have been in a favorite haunt of the lobsterbacks and seen the good Dr. Church drinking pints with the King's officers. I might have thought that he was gathering information for you but, by the looks of your face, I can see you find it incredible that Church has even been talking with the British. Surely, you have heard the stories of how he wanders back and forth between Cambridge and Boston at will. He was in Boston right after the battle on the hill."

"I am certain there is good reason and explanation for his visits there," said Washington.

"Maybe so. Maybe not. But why would he be filling the doodle sack of a young woman right upstairs in Mr. Hancock's house — a house filled with British officers?" Washington said nothing, a little flushed by the man's audacity to use such language with him. Such choice of language was acceptable amongst gentlemen of equal status. That was understood. But, one should not use such bawdy language with a virtual stranger and, in particular, one of Washington's caliber. And yet, Washington's face also begged an answer to this latest barrage.

"That's right, Mr. Washington. That night when I sneaked into the Hancock house to get that purse, I saw the doctor with my own eyes. Sleeping with a young woman and, you might say, sleeping with your enemy I had to tie him up to get outta there and all the while he's tryin' to call for the lobsters to save him. Now, I ask you, is that a loyal patriot?"

What if it was true thought Washington. There must be some explanation. But what if it was true. Church did know all about the plans for fortifying the hills. He knew about troop movements. And times. The enemy knew all of this shortly after the plans were made. It was possible. But Dr. Church was a mason. What of the vow of trust? And yet these are extraordinary times and, should one think he's chosen the losing side, well .... On the other hand, what if this Hickey was telling the facts as he knew them. Even if he hadn't gotten the answers perfect, his willingness to report the facts was a good sign. Perhaps this Thomas Hickey should be given a chance to prove himself. Only he would know one way or the other. Nothing to lose really. He could always be shadowed by another specially selected aide.

"That is just the kind of information I am after," said Washington recovering his composure and returning to the general-like bearing with which he was very comfortable. "I'd like you to consider working for me."

"What does it pay?

"Why don't we wait until after I show you what we have invited you out here to see. Then we can discuss what needs to be done and how much I am willing to pay to get it done."

"Fair enough."

Hickey and Washington rode on in silence behind the two army officers for several more miles, both attempting in their divergent manners to sum up the other. By Hickey's estimation, they had traveled several miles since leaving the inn. Washington, Hickey thought, was indeed what he would have expected. He arrogantly believed he had been chosen by God to be a leader. Didn't they all. But, there was also what seemed to be a deep well of sincerity in this large, rich man. It was true what he said. He didn't have to do this. Power was certainly a motivator as was, to be sure, a real dislike for taxes. Yet Hickey felt that Washington was truly on a crusade.

Washington, on the other hand, could see those qualities Hancock and Hopkins had described. Toughness. Not afraid to speak up, to tell you what he felt. Washington wasn't used to that. It made him uneasy and, at the same time, he liked it. It was refreshing. Wouldn't it be nice to just pack up and go west. Didn't every man harbor such a notion at one time or another? His own wanderlust had been stifled by his mother at a young age and yet it had only made his desire to see action even stronger. This man could do whatever job was given him providing the price was right. There was still the gnawing question of loyalty. Could he really be trusted? If he gave Hickey $50, could the King's men wrest away his loyalty for $100? Hancock had said Hickey could be trusted. Was it just a way for Hancock to spy on him? After all, he couldn't have the title of commander in chief so why not keep track of the man who does. It certainly would not be beyond the realm of possibility that the Congress or, to be more specific, certain elements within the Congress would want to keep track of their new southern-gentleman-commander in-chief.

Washington had already made several important decisions about his intelligence operations. He would select agents personally. Indeed, many would be known only to him. If need be, he could use one to hold rein on the other. He would pay them himself. No one else would know who they were or what they were doing. Even trustworthy aides, such as Capt. Rawson and Sgt. Curtis, would not know the specifics of what he had planned for a man like Hickey. They would not know one another nor what were the others' missions. It was the only way he could be certain he was plugging the leaks.

"Just another mile or so, general," Sgt. Curtis yelled back.

Up ahead, the road dropped down into a hollow and, rounded to the right in a broad descending arc. Hickey saw they were heading toward the shore of a large, clear pond. The road leveled out again and they road close to the water. Hickey could see a large hay wagon halfway around the pond. Two men were standing by the wagon. Sgt. Curtis waved and the men waved back.

"I think you will find this very interesting, Mr. Hickey," said Washington. Hickey nodded that was a possibility.

As they came alongside the wagon, Capt. Rawson said: "David, Ezra. Good to see you both again. You already know Sgt. Curtis. It is a privilege to introduce General George Washington, commander of the Continental Army. General meet Sgt. Ezra Bushnell and his brother, David."

Washington alit and shook hands with each man. Hickey stayed in the saddle.

"Continental Army, eh," said David in a flat, nasally voice, "has a nice ring to it doesn't it. My little brother Ezra here, or should I say, Sgt. Ezra, is pleased and proud, General, to be a part of it. I can tell you that."

Hickey found it amusing that David Bushnell described his brother as "little." The military Bushnell was taller, thicker and obviously healthier than his older brother. Even his voice was deeper and stronger than the somewhat delicate man with squinty eyes. But Hickey was not paying much attention to the introductions and formalities. He was staring at a peculiar length of pipe sticking out of the hay piled in the wagon.

"Mr. Hickey, if you would," Capt. Rawson gestured for him to dismount and be introduced. He did so. "Mr. Hickey, this is David Bushnell and his brother, Sgt. Ezra Bushnell." They shook hands. David Bushnell's hand was soft and moist. The sergeant's was firm.

"I want to thank you, General Washington for sparing my brother these past few weeks. He has been a great help in the project," said David Bushnell. Franklin had told Washington about Bushnell's experiments and Washington had granted several extended leave periods to Sgt. Bushnell to help his brother with these tests.

"If this should work," said Washington, "it will have been duty well done."

"Well, shall we get to it then?" asked Capt. Rawson, climbing onto the hay wagon and grabbing armfuls of hay, tossing it into a pile to one side of the wagon. Sgts. Curtis and Bushnell joined him. David Bushnell stood watching with Washington and Hickey.

Washington and Bushnell exchanged pleasantries while Hickey's eyes were riveted to the wagon. As the hay was stripped away, a massive, black wooden oval emerged. It was as if some giant bird had nested in the wagon and laid an egg. An egg made of wood with metal pipes poking out the top. Thick bands of metal girded the egg to keep the monster's mucousy yolk from busting through its wooden shell. And there were windows! Small thick windows so the monster's fetus could look out and see what kind of a world into which it was being hatched.

David Bushnell saw Hickey's widened eyes and smiled. "Wait until you see it in action, Mr. Hickey. You will be even more amazed."

"What is it?" asked Hickey.

"It is my Water Machine, sir."

"Water Machine?"

"A sinkable boat! A boat that travels underneath the water instead of across the top. She's almost ready for action. A few minor problems to conquer and she'll be ready."

"Damnest thing I ever saw," said Hickey. "That is God's truth." He continued staring at the ovate contraption that was about a foot and a half taller than Sgt. Bushnell.

The three men finished kicking the remaining hay from the sides of the wooden base on which the Water Machine had rested for the wagon ride. The base had several wooden wheels. They used a metal bar to pry away a wooden stopper in the front and prepared a ramp on which to slide the egg down to the shore and into the pond.

"I've christened her "The Turtle," said David Bushnell, "because she acts a lot like a turtle. Just like that interesting little creature, my turtle can dive under water and attack its enemies by surprise. Besides, when it's sitting in the water, it looks a lot like a big turtle." He giggled, an effeminate little laugh that was filled with obvious pride and delight in his creation.

The wheels of the wooden base squealed and the ramp creaked as the ponderous wood and metal egg was rolled down the ramp. Ezra Bushnell laid boards from the bottom of the ramp to the water so that the wheels would not sink into the soft soil.

"I developed the concept back in May," said David Bushnell with precise diction as he affectionately watched his Water Machine make its way to a point where a low steep bank faced the pond. He, Washington and Hickey were following the Turtle. "I left Westbrook, Connecticut, and went to Boston to see how I could help the cause. I actually thought about joining the army. My studies at Yale were in mechanics and natural philosophy, which, I felt, might be useful to a general like yourself, Mr. Washington. Then, one afternoon, I climbed to the crest of a hill overlooking Boston and sat staring at the city. It was locked up by the British. A tight fist with a glove of men-o-war in the harbor. Then it struck me with utter clarity: without those ships the British army would be surrounded by the Sons of Liberty. It would be a total reversal. The British army would be forced to flee. The ships were the key. How could we get rid of those ships? I remembered an experiment I conducted as a freshman at Yale. I, in fact, had to perform the experiment because my professors refused to believe my claim — that gunpowder can be exploded underwater. Well, of course it can! I showed them it could. What if, I thought, we could somehow go out into the harbor unseen, place gunpowder charges on all of those ships and watch them go to the bottom. How do I get there unseen? A sub-surface vessel would do it. A boat traveling under the water. I learned that the Dutch engineer Cornelius van Drebbel had experimented with a sinkable boat more than 150 years ago. I sat staring at the harbor and thinking about my water machine and, the more I thought, the more I believed it would be quite easy to build. We've been working day and night ever since."

"Will it work?" asked Washington.

"It does work, general. It does. We have tried it twice. There are still some snags. We had one minor leak where the brass hatch cover is connected to the iron top ring. The other problem was corrected thanks to you. As you might have noticed my little brother is a much finer physical specimen than myself. He says I got the brains and he got the muscles. I tried piloting the Turtle first time out and I almost collapsed of exhaustion. It takes a great deal of energy to propel the craft through the water. That's when I requested that Ezra be allowed to come home on leave to Westbrook and help me. He can peddle that thing for miles."

The Turtle had reached the edge of the bank where a makeshift dock had been extended out over the water and Sgt. Bushnell was waiting for the signal to launch.

"Hold up there, Ezra," said David Bushnell, "perhaps the general and, maybe, Mr. Hickey, would like to see how she's put together before we put her in."

Ezra fetched a ladder from the wagon and stood it against

the wooden egg. He climbed up and unscrewed the hatch, which hinged back exposing the interior of the vessel. Washington at well over six feet only had to step up two rungs to peer inside. The hull was made of six-inch thick timbers with thick iron bands holding them in place. The outside was thoroughly coated with tar to make it watertight. Inside the Turtle was a thick transverse beam, which apparently served as a seat. The hatch screwed down leaving a sort of collar around the top. It was in this collar that a half dozen small, circular windows were set.

"Impressive work," said Washington, stepping off the ladder. "Mr. Franklin spoke very highly of your facility in the field of mechanics, Mr. Bushnell."

"Coming from such a genius, that is a great compliment indeed," said Bushnell red in the face. "How about you, Mr. Hickey?"

Without a word, Hickey was up the ladder, having to take an extra rung or two to get a full interior view. This was truly amazing! A boat that could move under the water. Think of the possibilities. Especially, in that age-old profession of smuggling. Hickey figured he could easily fit on the seat. He was confident he could make this little Turtle swim.

"Never seen anything near to it in my whole life. Ever," said Hickey. "How does the operator see? How does it move? How fast? How does a man breathe under the water? Can I ....?"

"Hold on, Mr. Hickey," said David Bushnell. "One question at a time. Here, before we put her in, let me give you a brief description. The hull is of virgin oak timbers with iron hoops. It is covered in tar as you can see. The transverse beam serves as a seat but also serves to keep the sides apart as the significant pressures under water try to crush our little Turtle. The hatch is of brass with a screw lock that is watertight. The small windows wind up just about eye height for Ezra as he sits on the beam. It allows the one-man crew to see when the vessel is just below the surface. I have used fox fire, which you may know is a naturally phosphorescent weed to illuminate the depth gauge and compass once the craft is deeply submerged. There is 700 pounds of lead ballast here in the base. About a third of that can be dropped away quickly if there is an emergency and the operator must surface. Normally, of course, we fill these bilge tanks to sink her and then use the pump inside to pump them dry when we want to come up. The screw propeller there is what makes her move. You can crank it forward or backward. Believe me, it is not easy. That's where Ezra comes in."

"Does work up a bit of a sweat," said Ezra, smiling broadly. "But, I'm gettin' the hang of 'er. I figure I can get her up to about where I can go about three miles in one hour. Must admit, though, first time out, I couldn't even climb out of the hatch right away. Just 'bout passed out."

"I added a vertical propeller there in the front on top because we had trouble with it trying to flop to the side. That seems to keep it stable. The rudder there helps steer her. As for breathing, Mr. Hickey, there's enough air for about a half hour. That's fully submerged. If you bring her up so that the hatch cracks the surface, you can breathe through these tubes as well."

Washington was amused by Hickey's childlike reaction to this creation. The man was certainly a complicated mix. Tough as horseshoes and yet like a small child with a new toy when it came to gadgets such as this. Washington was still not convinced the device would work, or that there was any real use for it even if it did work. He wanted Hickey to see it and, after all, it was part of his first assignment. But, the real assignment wouldn't be revealed for a few more months.

"This is, indeed, a work of genius, Mr. Bushnell," said Washington to a beaming David Bushnell. It was important not to discourage such innovation even though he himself was not fully convinced of its value.

"Thank you, sir."

"Genius it is," echoed Hickey, receiving a smiling nod of thanks from Bushnell.

"All right then, let's put her in."

Ezra and the two other military men rolled the Turtle down the planks and out onto the dock. For an instant, Hickey thought the groaning mass of lashed logs would collapse under the weight of the black egg. A hoist had been constructed and the men attached the three lines to rings around the belly of the Turtle. Pulling together on the hoist ropes, the boom creaked as the full weight of the big black, wooden Turtle lifted off its cart. Ezra put his back into the boom to swing it off the dock. It barely budged. Hickey quickly went out to help and, together, they managed to swing the monster egg over the side and lower it into the water. The water now supporting the Turtle, Ezra was able to shinny down the boom rope and slide into his seat in the Turtles innards. He screwed down the hatch and opened up the ports to take on water in the bilges. There was a perceptible collective gasp as the Turtle sank with only the hatch collar above the surface. They could see Ezra smiling and waving through the dollar-sized windows. The Turtle — and it did, indeed, look like a giant turtle cruising under the surface — moved around the pond and back to dockside.

"See here now, what I have built is what I call a torpedo that we can attach on the front of the Turtle. It has a heavy screw in the front so the operator would come up on an enemy ship and screw the bomb right into the hull of the ship. The charge would be timed so that the vessel can get away. Then. One hundred fifty pounds of powder goes off, blasting a gaping hole in the ship. Down she goes."

"If this should work as you say, Mr. Bushnell, it might make a significant difference in the way we confront the King's men in Boston," said Washington, reaching in to his pocket and handing a pouch to Bushnell. "Some additional funds to keep your work progressing. Thank you for the demonstration. I will be in touch with you about the most advantageous time to put your Turtle to work."

Hickey helped Ezra Bushnell, Rawson and Curtis hoist the Turtle from the water and roll it back into the wagon. He wanted to get another close-up look at this incredible device. The thought of royal ships just dropping to the bottom was etched in his mind. These colonials were serious. Not only were they serious, they just might have a chance to pull it off.

Washington and Bushnell conversed about the possibilities in using the Turtle before the end of the year while the men threw the hay back onto the wagon covering the monster's egg.

"General Washington," said Capt. Rawson, brushing his clothing, "it is getting late sir. It will be dark before we reach camp."

Washington nodded and shook hands with the Bushnells. "Thank you for your work," he said sincerely but returning to that fatherly tone of the army officer, "this task of ours will not be easy. However, we are right and, therefore, we have no choice but to continue. It is through the efforts of men like you that we will win this struggle. I thank you on behalf of the Congress, the army and all men of liberty."

Cpt. Rawson and Sgt. Curtis again led the way back up the road toward the inn with Washington and Hickey following.

"What do you think?" asked Washington.

"One of the damnest things I have ever seen in my life," replied Hickey.

"This is the passion that our cause evokes, Mr. Hickey. Men of genius struggle to create ways to help turn the tide. Farmers leave their fields to defend the city. It takes all types of men. Are you ready to sign on?"

"You still haven't told me what this job pays."

"I will personally pay you five dollars a month stipend plus additional payment for, shall we say, special assignments."

"What do I have to do?"

"You've seen Mr. Bushnell's Turtle. It has certain limitations and some development ahead of it but if the British were to learn of this device and if, let's say, its description was such that they believed it would work today, well, perhaps, we would benefit."

"That's it? You want me to tell the British about your top secret water machine? And, for that, I get five dollars a month."

"That will be the beginning. If I feel you are to be trusted, the tasks may grow more difficult and the compensation will grow with it. And if the task grows to a level of importance requiring a special payment, Mr. Hickey, I am prepared to offer you the land you so desire."

"What land?"

"I hold claim to thousands of acres in the west. I acquired this land on several missions during the French affair. If we are successful in this effort, I will be looking to develop that land. I would be willing to give you 100 acres of land of your own to do with as you wish. Again, that is providing the task is of sufficient merit to the cause of liberty to warrant such reward. It is beautiful country, the Ohio valley, Mr. Hickey. I can understand your dream. A hundred acres is a great deal of land for one man, Mr. Hickey. I'd venture you would meet your terms of freedom on that much land."

Washington had played his hole card. This was a prize he was certain Hickey would not - could not - resist.

"I'll go into Boston on Monday," said Hickey.

Chapter Ten

Sam West moved his finger slowly along the rows of symbols, drawing each new one on its own line on the chart he was compiling. It was his guess, his hope, actually, that there would be 26, maybe, 27, different symbols. If there were more, his task would be much more difficult. No matter. This was an enjoyable break from doing God's work. Reverend Samuel West, as he was known to the troops at Cambridge, had been assigned this extra task by General Washington. He leapt at the chance for a brief respite from ministering to the fledgling army which seemed to always have one foot in heaven and the other in Hades.

Rev. West had toyed with secret codes and messages as a boy. As a young man, he enjoyed creating codes for correspondence. It was a way to earn a shilling or two. There was always an eager merchant who needed to keep his business private. Enciphered letters were actually quite common. Heaven knows a wax seal arrives broken more often than not these days. He was certain, however, that this was no common merchant's message. If it warranted the attention of the general himself, there was something of great interest hidden amongst these symbols.

But even simple codes could be a challenge. This message had nearly 4,000 characters. Each had to be charted before the search for common symbols could begin. It was handwritten, too, which caused legibility problems and there were no breaks between words. No capitalization. No punctuation, just row after row of symbols. This could prove to be a real challenge.

***

At that very moment, in a small dining room of a whitewashed Cambridge home, Elbridge Gerry and Colonel Elisha Porter of the Massachusetts militia were finishing up their own count of the symbols. In a move that would become standard practice for the duration of the conflict, Washington had assigned the code-breaking task to two independent teams, each unaware of the other. The events of recent weeks, culminating in the discovery of this message, had hardened his resolve. He had to be very careful. Spies were everywhere. He could trust only himself.

Both Gerry and Col. Porter had some field experience with codes. They, too, were familiar with the basics of code-breaking. The first task was to catalog the symbols, add them up and then begin to substitute letters that most frequently appear in the English language. E, T, and O are the most often used letters. Sure enough, when they had completed their tally, three symbols made up almost a third of the nearly 4,000 symbols. And, at nearly the same time as Chaplain West, they discovered that the least-used letters — J, K, Q, X and Z — had not even been changed to symbols.

Gerry, who would go on to be the fifth vice president of this new nation, began immediately to substitute the letter E for the most-used symbol. Next, he placed Ts where the second most frequently used symbols had been written. Then he added Os. These, as the decipherers would discover, fit perfectly into the text. Cryptographers of the day knew that the next most frequently used letters were A, N, I, R, S, H,

D and L. These did not fit so easily. A few were out of sequence. It only took one to make the task more tedious.

***

Chaplain West had also substituted Es, Ts, and Os. He was now searching for patterns. The unbroken stream of symbols made the work tedious. He, too, turned to adding the next group of most-often used letters. Again, he searched for patterns. It was early evening when it happened. The puzzle door was breeched and a thin shaft of light shown through. There were four instances where the strings of substitute letters read "_hiladel_hia." It was like staring at one of those enigmatic drawings where a witch and a pretty woman are enmeshed in the same pen strokes. It's all in how you look at it. Stare at it long enough and the picture jumps right out. He penned in the letter P and Philadelphia could hide no longer. The second instance had an N and S at the end. Philadelphians. Separating the third instance from symbols at each end, revealed the next word as "_onne_ti__t." Obviously, Connecticut. He now went back and added all of the Ps, Cs and Us.

***

Gerry and Porter were moving at the same pace. Large chunks of the text were being filled in. It was a simple character substitution code and it was in English. The complete deciphering came quickly. What they read was obviously the work of a traitorous spy. The message was addressed: "To Major Cane in Boston, on His Magisty's Sarvice." Though spelling was not the forte of the author, secret intelligence was. The message described Bunker Hill and detailed troop movements and powder stores. It added: "This advice is the result of warm affection to my King & to the realm. Remember, I never deceived you."

Chaplain West, Gerry and Porter had quickly come to the same conclusion. Whoever wrote this is an enemy of the patriots' cause. Chaplain West and Col. Porter rushed off to deliver the deciphered message to General Washington.

***

"Ante up!" bellowed Washington, his blue-gray eyes sparkling with humor. "Ante up and you won't have so much of my damned money sitting there staring back at me."

"You have plenty," said Sam Hewes in an age-worn, high-pitched squeak, which Washington found amusing. "But me, I'm just a poor printer trying to amuse the great general who has come to this town to lead a great army," added Hewes with sweeping gestures of mock subservience.

"As fine a pile of horse plop as I've ever heard," replied Washington, waving his cards more animatedly now, gesturing for Hewes to put six pennies into the center of the table.

The other men at the table were chuckling uncontrollably at the banter. They had not seen the gentleman from Virginia in such a relaxed mood, although that was simply because they had never before been invited to the card game. Washington loved the repartee. He enjoyed telling and hearing an off-color story. He reveled in the stories men tell about the women they knew, especially the exaggerated tales of sexual prowess. He could swear with the best of them, mostly a result of his earlier military career, and, at his size, could drink with just about any of them. He knew it was important to maintain discipline. Fraternization was unacceptable. But a friendly card game with a few civilians or a chosen officer or two was one of the highlights of his week. Perhaps, second only to dancing with the ladies in Cambridge at one of the many parties given in his honor.

Vassal House, Washington's Cambridge quarters, was a comfortable wood-sided house but quickly becoming too small for the staff. The dining room, however, was just right for a spirited card game. There was plenty of wine and food and a buxomly, dark-haired woman to serve it. Two of the other men at the table were mid-level officers chosen to participate in the card game as a sort of reward for their fine work in the recruiting of the local citizenry. The fifth man was Ezekial Potter, a civilian from New York who had come to report on the status of Albany and northern New York. There soon would be great activity there.

Hewes tossed his coins into the center of the table with great agony and the bet came to Potter.

"I'll match that six pennies and raise the bet another six," said Potter smiling. Ezekial Potter, Washington had discovered, was as uncomplicated a man as he had ever met. He had been at Lexington and, ever since, had volunteered to do whatever task he could to help the cause. He was very comfortable to be around. There was no pretense. He was honest and warm. Washington had asked him to stay on for a day or two while he prepared an important message to be taken back to New York. Besides, he enjoyed his company. The information he wanted to send to the Albany County Committee of Correspondence had to do with the encoded material given to Rev. West and the Gerry-Col. Porter team.

On Saturday last, General Nathaniel Greene had requested an immediate audience with Washington. With him was Godfrey Wenwood, a baker from Rhode Island. The baker told an interesting tale. A few weeks earlier, a former lover of his had asked a favor. She asked that Wenwood deliver a letter to Sir James Wallace, commander of the HMS Rose, docked in Newport harbor. Wenwood, while doing considerable business with the British troops in Rhode Island, was a patriot to the core. His was one of the names listed in Hancock's notes. It struck him as odd that his former girlfriend would make such a request. He showed the letter to a friend who broke the wax seal and tried to read it. It was in code. Wenwood put the letter aside trying to decide what to do with it. A week or so later, the woman asked if the letter had been delivered. The baker said it had but, now nervous about the contents, decided to contact Henry Ward, the Rhode Island patriot serving as secretary of that state's general committee. Ward told Wenwood to forward the letter to Gen. Greene, a Rhode Islander now serving under Washington at Cambridge. Wenwood decided to carry the letter to Cambridge himself.

Washington immediately ordered the young woman arrested. Later that evening, she was brought to Vassal House and interrogated. Washington was an old hand at such tactics having learned the ins and outs of intimidation and exacting confessions while serving as a Virginia magistrate.

"For a long time, she was proof against every threat and persuasion to discover the author of that letter," Washington had told his aides the next morning.

The woman did not crack. Washington tried every trick. Finally, in exasperation, he told his staff to take her to Cambridge jail and lock her up until she was ready to talk. That made her shudder in fear. Somewhere in the shallow depths of the unfortunate woman's mind there was a dark terror of being locked up. She sang loudly. Her new lover had given her the letter to deliver. The name she confessed to Washington sent a shiver up his spine.

He sent troops to bring the man into custody. The man continued to profess his innocence. "I do not deny authorship of the letter but, believe me, there is nothing treacherous or treasonous to be found in it," he maintained.

"Then provide the key to its deciphering," replied Washington.

"I cannot," said the respected gentleman, adding some feeble excuse as to its personal nature.

It was at that point that Washington had an aide make two pen and ink copies of the encoded letter and charged Chaplain West and the other duo with attempting to decipher it. He had hoped to receive word of their work before this.

"I'll raise a shilling," said one of the officers, his voice cracking with nervousness but his cards seemingly too powerful to resist not raising.

"Not you, too, young man?" groaned Washington. "You want to make me a poor man, too. Don't we pay you enough?"

"Yes, sir, my pay is quite ..."

"Yes, yes. Here it is then. Another shilling."

Washington goaded Hewes into calling as well. The bet came to Potter.

"With all due respect, I find I can't decide with a dry tongue," smiled Potter, licking his lips.

"Elizabeth!" Washington called for the sensuous young woman who immediately showed with a carafe of madeira and filled all of the glasses, starting with Washington's. As she bent over to fill his glass, he shifted his eyes to her breasts, turned his eyes back to Potter and then back to the breasts. His eyebrows rose slightly. Potter smiled.

"I see you find my friend, Elizabeth, quite to your liking, General," said Hewes who often brought such talent to the game.

"She is a beauty and, indeed, a proficient server," said Washington.

"She may be persuaded to serve you even better," said Hewes. "Isn't that right, 'Lizbeth?"

The young woman blushed but smiled and stood her ground, thrusting her ample breasts out for the general to inspect.

"We'll see if there is a need for added service later on this evening," said Washington waving the girl back to the kitchen.

"For a crude fellow, you have refined taste in women," said Washington to Hewes.

"If I may, general, for a refined man you have crude tastes in women," replied Hewes. They both laughed heartily with Washington nearly losing his ivory and metal false teeth.

"Now, Zeke, are you betting?" asked Washington.

Potter tossed in his money and others called. The young officer with the hefty raise took the hand, sheepishly showing his cards but raking in the coins with relish.

"Son of a bitching whoremonger," growled Washington, an outburst that startled the others, especially the young officer, who dropped several of the coins on the floor. He hesitated in picking them up until he realized the commander-in-chief was not angry at all. On the contrary, he was thoroughly enjoying being one of the boys. Potter wondered where in Virginia plantation society Washington had learned to cuss so well.

"Deal them," said Washington to Sam Hewes, slamming the deck of cards down in front of the old merchant. "And they better be good ones or I just might send the army of the Congress down to inspect that Tory-loving press of yours."

Hewes smiled broadly, shuffled the cards and dealt a new hand, a hand that met with groans from Washington. Potter bet and the young officer again raised.

Washington was about to protest when a uniformed sergeant hurried into the room and, without apologies, whispered something in the general's ear.

"Gentlemen," said Washington, now once again General Washington, "I am afraid that the realities of the day cause me to end this great amusement. I have truly enjoyed your company. Perhaps, we may finish at some other time. For now, I ask that you excuse me while I tend to some distasteful business."

The two army officers nodded curtly and left quickly. Sam Hewes thanked Washington for his hospitality and said no more, asking no questions. Discretion was among his strong points. Potter, too, got up to leave.

"Mr. Potter, can I ask you to please wait in the drawing room? I may have that message for you so that you can be on your way."

Potter said he would stay while Washington, not waiting for his reply, left through the pocket doors leading to his office. Washington told the sergeant to bring in Chaplain West who had arrived first, followed closely behind by Col. Porter. Neither still was aware the other was working on the same problem.

"What have you found?" asked Washington

"It was really quite easy, general," said the chaplain handing over the deciphered message.

Washington thanked the chaplain for his great service and asked him to say a prayer for him. Chaplain West agreed and left. Col. Porter was ushered in. His report was more formal.

"General Washington, Col. Porter reporting as per your order. Here are the results of our assignment, sir."

Washington read the report. It was the same as what Chaplain West had given him. Washington stood and shook hands with the colonel thanking him, too, for his diligence and indicating he would receive a commendation letter. The colonel was most pleased by this and left smiling.

Washington sat in silence reading the deciphered letter, no longer able to hide behind fabricated symbols. Doors closed in other parts of Vassal House as Washington sat alone in the quiet of his study shaking his head. He was furious and at the same time saddened by this revelation. He read the letter again and then scrawled out a quick message on stationery. He sealed it with wax and called for the sergeant to give the message to Mr. Potter. He sat staring at the letter for nearly a half hour.

The letter was, indeed, written by the man in custody. That man was none other than Dr. Benjamin Church. Hickey had been correct in his judgment.

Dr. Benjamin Church was a spy.

The man who had been trusted by Sam Adams from the very beginning, thought Washington. He had been a participant in dozens of confidential meetings at the birth of the Sons of Liberty. I had been introduced to him in Philadelphia where he was privy to the highest levels of the Congress. I invited this man into my home. He ate my food, drank my wine. He toasted liberty. All the while, scurrying back to tell the King's cronies. Hickey had said Church had not even tried to hide his comings and goings in Boston. And what of the story of him sleeping with this woman right in Hancock's house filled with snoring British officers?

Washington read part of the decoded letter again: "I counted 280 pieces of cannon from 24- to 3-pounders at King's Bridge which the committee had secured for the use of the colonies. The Jerseys are not a whit behind Connecticut in zeal. The Philadelphians exceed them both. I saw 2200 men in review there by General Lee, consisting of Quakers & other inhabitants in uniform, with 1000 riflemen & 40 horse who together made a most warlike appearance. I mingled freely & frequently with the members of the Continental Congress..."

How many other Church's were there? Who could be trusted? When a man who was just named chief of medical care for a fledgling army can write to the enemy: "This advice is the result of warm affection to my King & to the realm. Remember, I never deceived you. Every article here sent you is sacredly true." What next? How many others would succumb to fear? Who would look at the mighty British military and see they were massing for total revenge against the upstarts and, out of sheer terror, go crawling back begging forgiveness to save their hide?

Who can be trusted? The only conclusion: no one. He drew several charts. He would show them to no one. The first chart listed the centers of conflict that required his attention such as the British troops in Boston, Boston harbor, Cambridge, roads to the west, New York City, Congress, recruitment, Canada, politics, intelligence, etc. Under each, he listed two to four names. He would personally contact each one individually. Relying on their patriotism if possible, paying them when necessary, he would ask these people to gather intelligence on each of the topics listed. He would pay them himself. Only he would know who they were. No one on the list would be aware of any other. On another sheet, he listed some key points to remember in these dealings. Limit personal contact. Use drop points. Use a separate code for each contact. Always assign the same task to more than one person. Allow the generals to organize their own networks but do not tell them of his.

On additional sheets he set up schedules for contacting these resources and listed some facts they might target on their first assignments. In these few minutes, he organized the first spy service of a new nation. He vowed never again to be caught by surprise, having to swallow the bitter pill of betrayal. There was too much at stake, both for the colonies and for himself. Liberty couldn't be trusted to chance.

He took another sheet of paper and wrote: "Purposely bad information has a good purpose." Below this he listed samples of the kinds of misinformation that could serve the cause should the British believe it to be true. From this point on, he would know what the enemy was thinking, doing, planning. They would not. This would be the great equalizer.

On a final sheet of paper he wrote the heading "expenses." Some would serve without pay, of course. Others, who might be forced to leave their regular employment, might need to be supported. Then there were still others who would provide a service at a price. Of course, there would be a price for all of this information, sometimes a steep price, both in monetary terms and in the loss of innocence. He scribbled some figures. Forty agents. Ten dollars per month. $400. Special purchases — $100 per month. This would include a new ink being developed by Culpeper which went invisible when dry. That could prove very useful. One could concoct a completely innocent letter to a friend with greetings and salutations. But, in between the lines could be written the true message. The materials, Culpeper said, might be costly. It would be worth the price. He would provide financing himself and keep a record of these "special expenses."

He sat staring at the papers for some time then neatly folded them and walked upstairs to his bedroom. On the dresser was the pocket shaving kit he had used for many years whenever traveling. The leather folding pouch contained two razors, shaving brush, comb, mirror and a vial of rose attar water. He slid the papers in behind the mirror and folded the kit.

Within that worn leather toiletry kit, on the third sheet of paper about midway down was a notation: "Thomas Hickey — New York City."

Part II

Chapter Eleven

New York City, 7:45 a.m., Friday, January 26, 1776

Thomas Hickey questioned his sanity. The coldest day of the winter and he was on horseback with everything he owned packed in two large sacks slung over his horse. His innards had shrunk to a rock-hard ball of ice; the ball rattled around, banging into his ribs. His teeth clattered and his frozen brain kept serving up the same image of Old Mark, bleached bones jingling in the winter wind.

What about you, Hickey? He quizzed himself as the image of Old Mark, running for his life, ebbed and flowed. This Ohio business? That ain't running. That's planning for the future. I'm earning my way. How had he gotten into this? What in hell's name was he doing? There was this gnawing pain in his head. What had begun as a clear plan to gain true freedom was starting to look more and more like anything but. A few gold pieces and some silver had turned a rather simple dream into a prolonged sleepless night. He was working for George Washington. Washington was his boss. Plain and simple. He gave the orders. Hickey obeyed. To be sure, it wasn't a military arrangement but it was just as effective. Money was the uniform of the day. And Hickey was donning the full dress uniform regularly. Washington's game was politics. He had everything to gain. For men like himself, it was more of the master/servant routine. And yet, Washington was so goddamned certain of the need for this fight. So certain of the rightness of it. And he paid well. In the three months since the Church discovery, Washington had gradually stepped up his assignments for Hickey. He required more specific information, more detail. Each time Hickey delivered. And there was always a bonus. But there was something else. He found himself, in moments of weakness, actually thinking about such things as freedom, liberty, and oppression. Call it what it is: politics. He had seen numerous men who seemed normal and reasonable suddenly turn into snarling, wild-eyed animals at the mention of liberty. Then there were those who couldn't draw a cup of water without detailed instructions who suddenly expounded on the philosophy of liberty or the need for representation in return for payment of taxes. It was, though a mystery to him, a powerful idea. He shuddered, wrapping the wool blanket tighter around his neck and shoulders.

Old Mark appeared again. Gray bones. Freedom's signpost. The sheriff was replaced by Washington. Washington was slipping the noose around Old Mark's sweaty, black neck. The terrified man's yellow eyes were wide and he screamed at Washington to let him be. He wouldn't ever run again. Ever, sir. Ever, ever. The dark face got lighter. The neck where the heavy chain tightened wasn't thin and dark. Now it was thick and tanned. The face was .... his. Hickey shivered again, forcing reality back into the frigid vacuum between his ears. He thought about the recent night when Washington had given him this latest assignment. There was a party to celebrate a new year. Hickey had not been invited but was called to the party by Washington. Boston was no longer a threat, he said. It was a matter of time before the real threat, the real battle. In New York. He confided in Hickey that he was about to send Gen. Lee to New York to begin to prepare its defense against the British attack which would surely come as spring approached. He wanted Hickey to go there in advance and report back on the mood of the city. Who was in control? What did the citizens in the shops think about the conflict? Was it really a Tory stronghold? Hickey was to listen for the bit of gossip, the whispered tale that could be of value. In this manner, said Washington, I will be able to support Gen. Lee as best as is possible from this distance. He gave Hickey a list of names of people who could carry weekly messages, encoded, of course, back to Boston. He confided that he had other men already in place in New Jersey, on the Long Island near New York, in Albany and elsewhere. Men even posing as Tory sympathizers and supporters. All sworn to provide needed intelligence. Washington said Hickey would be perfect. His still-thick Irish accent might be handy at times, especially if the need arose to pose as a King's man.

What Washington did not confide in Hickey was that Gen. Lee was not always pleased with his commander-in-chief's leadership. Lee was forever complaining about Washington's lack of willingness to attack Boston. Lee was forever complaining about everything. He was also constantly reminding the world that it was Lee and only Lee who could save them from their demise and, oh, what a burden but he supposed he would have to do it. He accused Washington, not to his face, of course, of wallowing in the trappings of being a general but not having the stomach for it. And make no mistake about it, Lee had his supporters in the Congress, including Sam and John Adams. The Church affair had shaken him. He could trust no one but himself. He would gather information from all sources and sift through it for what was needed to do the job. If that meant, in effect, spying on his own staff — his own generals — then it had to be. Lee had become irritating, for sure, but he might even be a threat. He was forever writing to Congress about Washington's inactivity. He wanted to hunt down loyalists and teach them the error of their ways. One night, he told a junior officer that the members of the congress were too scared to take on the King. They wouldn't take a fighting stance, he said, if they found their wives in bed with General Howe himself. That was going just a bit too far for Washington's taste. Besides, Lee, who fancied himself a much greater military strategist and leader than Washington, had been stirring up the troops. Washington had formally written to "suggest" that congress authorize Lee's going into New York to establish a military presence. Sending Lee into what was, at best, a lukewarm advocate of liberty, would keep him busy and, perhaps, even be his reckoning. With Hickey and, perhaps, another operative or two watching, he could keep an eye on the general.

"No," Hickey had told the general. "I don't know anything about New York. I've never been there. Don't wanna go there. Sneaking around Boston is one thing. Packing up and going off to New York is another." He reminded Washington that he was not a soldier. Fact of the matter was he wasn't even a patriot.

In the end, Washington had been very convincing. It was clear why he was an effective military officer. He was a natural leader and Hickey fancied himself somewhat of an expert on men who considered themselves leaders. Washington could look at a man and impose his will. Hickey reckoned that, for Washington, it wasn't a case of one man forcing his will on another man. Washington had the certainty of a patrician land holder; he knew it to be fact, pure and simple. He was chosen to lead. In that case, why wouldn't they do what he required? And when pure imposition didn't work, Washington was practical enough to know when to use other tools. When Hickey had steadfastly refused Washington's New York assignment, the general upped the stakes. "Go to New York City for me, and I will double the land you are to receive. Two hundred acres." Two hundred acres of land along the Ohio. Hickey asked to think about it but it was a weak formality. Washington knew the answer.

Hickey's horse kept a steady but shaky pace, its hooves

slipping in the dents of frozen hoof prints and wagon wheel ruts of the road. His work for Hancock had afforded him the luxury of a horse. Most folks had never even been on a horse, "shank's mare" being the standard means of transportation. And most folks had never traveled more than 20 or 30 miles from the place where they entered this world. He was a long way from home and heading toward a strange city. The temperature had inched above freezing yesterday under a bright noon sun, just warm enough to soften the surface of the road. Now it was a solid track of frozen ruts and ridges. This had already been one of the coldest and snowiest winters in memory and it had barely begun. The wide road, known simply as The Lane, carried Hickey past broad, snow-laden meadows and farms. Small signs proclaimed the estates of "J. Duane, Esq.," "T. Tiebout," and "G. Stuyvesant." The ride must be a treat in the spring or summer, thought Hickey, as he plodded on southward toward New York. The wind blew the wool wrap over his face but it was no protection as the icy blast stabbed through the cloth, sticking it to his raw face. Snow drifted three-feet deep across the roads with deep ruts where hooves and wagon wheels had plowed on through. The large estates were broken here and there by small groups of fine, though less luxurious, homes set on small lots close along The Lane. A slight ague was coming on. His knees and elbows ached. His head felt large, puffed up with fluids. He gripped the blanket tighter around his thick red nose, from which fluids dripped steadily into the blanket. For the past three hours, traffic had picked up considerably.

Two or three times an hour, a cart or wagon would pass. Some of the wagons were large, piled high with fine furniture. The owners would follow closely behind in a sleek, enclosed carriage. The men with their cocked beaver hats and warm camlet coats in browns, reds and blues sat stiffly alongside women with heavy woolen wraps clutched tightly at the neck. The drivers wore cocked hats and did not acknowledge him. These were most likely Tories, perhaps, a royal agent feeling the heat of the wild gangs posing as Sons of Liberty. Or maybe, they were third generation merchants who, having made a tidy sum off the crown's trade, needed to rethink their position. Other smaller wagons and two-wheeled carts carried plain, painted furniture with simple edges. Men with deep-cracked, leathery faces held the reins. Women with waxy white puffy cheeks, cheeks that not even the bitter wind of January could put a blush on, sat next to them. Sometimes children clung to the slats of the wagon bed, bouncing with each rut. They were all quiet. Often the wagons would carry only women and children as those too poor to own a wagon full of possessions had to rely on charity to carry their wives and children to live off the dregs of a benefactor while men and older boys remained in New York to dig fortifications and earn a mouthful of food. They would look at Hickey but they would not speak. There were individual riders, too. Some of these men would nod as they passed. That was all. These were the unfortunates disrupted in every struggle. For these hapless souls, it was more likely that a gentleman in one of the carriages had provided work. The gentleman had turned out to be on the wrong side of the argument and now, they were labeled by association.

New York was being abandoned. It was quickly becoming a city of black and white. Those who had not been swept up in the head-thumping activities of the rabble-rousing Isaac Sears, were labeled traitors. Sears' so-called patriots had taken to tarring and feathering anyone who wouldn't swear to the new cause. They had actually snatched Anglican clergyman Samuel Seabury from his home and kept him prisoner for days. Recently, James Rivington, publisher of the pro-British New York Gazetteer, had been the target. The mob destroyed his presses and dumped his type cases into the river. And, while the Provincial Congress was growing very weary of Sears' strong-arm tactics, he and his roving band of head-knockers were still enjoying the odd tarring and feathering in the name of liberty. On the other hand, if one felt no particular loyalty to the King's agents, there was little solace to be found in the reports that Gen. Howe would soon come to save the city for the King. The fact that the royal governor, the Honorable William Tryon, had been forced to move into the harbor aboard the H.M.S. Duchess of Gordon, was reason enough for other New Yorkers to move as well. Most people were somewhere in the middle. And they were scared. The Continental Congress was sending troops to fortify the city. The British wouldn't stand for that for very long. It was only a matter of days or weeks before the battle would come to their city. So, it was time to move in with cousin Samuel or Uncle Josiah. Or, if one's pocketbook was deep and full, it was best to move out onto the Long Island, where a summer home could be opened for winter use. Temporarily, of course. Just until it was safe to return. If one didn't even own a purse, then it was off to New Jersey in a public wagon to find a scrap until this ended.

Hickey was getting closer to the city proper. There were cross streets now, laid out in even blocks. Bullock Street, Grand Street, Eagle Street. They were lined with three- and four-story commercial buildings. At first glance, after the bleak winter landscape of the past two days, it seemed like it was business as usual. Shops were open. Hickey could see people moving about within the buildings. Smoke poured from the chimneys. The aroma of burning wood was a treat. But the closer in he got, the more Hickey realized there was something wrong. New York was wearing a mask. One out of every two people was a soldier. Instead of bags of feed and sundries, wagons were moving dirt for the berms and fortifications of the waterfront. People stared at him and then whispered to one another. Despite this tension and his empty gut and the miseries of his aching joints, Hickey was excited. New York was just slightly smaller than Boston in population but, he had heard, New Yorkers were much more appreciative of the pleasures of the body than the sin-wracked Bostonians. True, a papist could face harassment in most any colony. But, so far, he felt he could survive here for a while.

The streets were much denser now and the buildings more elaborate. Hickey became aware of the stench. He had been pawing at his runny nose, thinking it was the ague that provided the discomfort. He now realized it was the odor, a sickeningly sweet vapor that attacked his nose and his stomach. He thought he would vomit but held back the initial gasp and was able to block out the brunt of the smell by pulling a scarf tighter around his nose and mouth. He rode on, his horse cold and sagging. Neither of them would be good much longer. Where Division Street met The Lane, there was a large common area. Hickey geed his horse to the right side of the common, slowing as a man with a red scarf wrapped around his face walked by cutting from west to east across the common.

"Pardon, sir," said Hickey, his voice thin and shaky, "Know where a man could lodge and put up a horse?"

The man stopped, looked at him and pulled the scarf from his face. His eyes were gray and lifeless.

"Go straight up here to James Street. Go left. That'll take you toward the Ship Yards. Not too far. Uh, Bunkers. Rutgers. Then Cherry Street. Right along there you should find something. Colder than hell, ain't it?" He wanted to sound friendly, even made an attempt at a smile, but it never quite formed. He stared at Hickey for a second, shrugged and looked at the ground.

"It is that," said Hickey to the top of the man's head. He thanked him for the directions, then added: "What's that smell?"

"Garbage," said the man dully, "The fucking soldiers just toss it out the windows. Weren't so cold it'd be worse."

Hickey followed the directions. James Street was packed tightly with buildings. There was barely a walkway between them. There were wood-frame warehouses and solid, decorative brick mercantile offices. There was a bank with limestone lintels and trim. Hickey noticed each block had a tavern. He had been in motion so long that it took him almost the full block from Rutgers to Cherry to stop once he had the notion in his mind. He pulled up at a tavern with an inviting Blue Whale sign hung from an iron angle hanging over the door. There was a stanchion for horses and a trough for the animals. Hickey swung his right leg back behind him and stepped heavily down to the road. The move jarred his bones and made his head hurt. The water trough was frozen over. He took the pistol from out of his pack. Washington's men had insisted he carry it. He did not feel comfortable around guns. Maybe that was also part of his problems with the military business. He grabbed the hefty weapon by the barrel and crashed the butt into the ice. A jagged hole appeared and Hickey led the horse to it. The horse bent down to drink then jerked his head away violently, nearly ripping off Hickey's hand.

"Hell's wrong with you?" he asked the horse. The horse sidled to the right, bracing his muzzle away from the trough. "You ain't thirsty, fine. I am."

Hickey swung open the door to the tavern. The small, dark tavern room was warm. The fireplace popped and crackled. Hickey thought he had never smelled anything as wonderful as the burning wood mixed with aroma of food cooking in a small kitchen to the right of the bar. It was truly a miracle how an ounce of warmth could destroy a pound of cold in just a few seconds. A clock behind the bar indicated it was just after 11 a.m. There was no one in the room but the barkeeper who was cleaning some tankards and stacking bowls, making ready for patrons. He heard the door close and turned around.

"Come. Come in. Warm yourself," said the barkeeper, smiling perhaps a little too broadly.

Hickey nodded, taken by surprise by the loud, friendly greeting. He kept the blanket wrapped around him and sat in one chair of a small table that had two others neatly pushed underneath.

"I'm John," said the barkeeper wiping his hands nervously on an apron as he walked toward Hickey. "They call me Salty but that's a long story. Comin' or going'?"

"Coming," said Hickey, managing a small smile.

"Most going the other way.

"Noticed. Why?"

"Hard times these. People not knowing what to expect. Most just feel it's best to leave until things sort themselves out. Always do somehow. Don't they?"

"Guess so," said Hickey, warming up, loosening the blanket, letting it fall down around his shoulders.

"Come far?"

"Boston. Three days."

"Fast in this weather. Horse need tending?"

"Yeah. Strange. Wouldn't drink. Nearly took my hand off getting away from the trough."

The barkeeper laughed, an exaggerated laugh, his belly bounding and his hand slapping a thigh.

"Happens all the time. Public water is so filled with God knows what no creature wants to take it. Comes up outta the pumps like that. Seems like horses growing up on it don't mind so much. Every time a stranger comes to town, it's the same thing. Horses won't go near it. Smarter'n we give credit for. You oughta smell it in summer. Stink! Most don't drink it at all. Carts go round with water from the springs up north. We get it here. Try it?"

"Like something a little stronger."

"Sure can do that, too."

"Know how to make a Whistle Belly?"

"Good choice. Nice and hot."

The barkeeper walked back toward the bar but first glanced out the window at Hickey's horse.

"You oughta see to your horse before long. Looks beat," he said as he began making up the drink.

"Any ideas?"

"Got some rooms upstairs and a place at the back for horses. The owner, Mr. Ratzer, used to like to approve boarders himself but the way the city's clearing out he'll take most anyone who can pay. In fact, Mr. Ratzer is out on the island now. Leaves it to me to run the place. Otherwise, the soldiers just move in. Sometimes they pay; sometimes they don't bother. I'm sure it would be all right."

"How much?"

"Four pence a night for the room. Two pence for horse-keeping."

Hickey reached under his clothes for his pouch. He drew out six shillings. "I'll pay for a week," he said, sliding four shillings toward the barkeep and leaving the two for drinks and food. Hickey took a deep draught of the Whistle Belly and then, tightening the blanket back up around his ears, went out and led his horse around the back through a narrow walkway. The wooden barn was attached to the main structure and seemed to take in some heat by the connection. The horse seemed to shudder in gratitude as Hickey closed the door behind them. He took the two sacks of his belongings down, filled a small round bucket with water from a keg and the horse lapped at it with a vengeance. He spread some hay and went back to the bar, carrying the sacks.

Hickey took two bowls of hot beef stew and two more drinks. He sat in the corner of the room quietly eating and drinking, watching the midday crowd come and go. The patronage was made up of some army officers and a few who looked like merchants. Dock workers. Carmen and stablehands. A mixed group intent on enjoying the noon minutes before heading back to the reality of 18th century New York City. There were great conversations. Hickey was impressed by the breadth of knowledge of even the stable workers. "Common Sense" was the topic of choice. Hickey hadn't read this little pamphlet by a man named Thomas Paine. Seemed like just so much more drivel about this liberty business. More politicking. But, after overhearing the lunch crown, it might be worth a look. Anything that could rile up a mixed group like this might be worth looking at. Since its arrival in the city earlier in the month, it had been selling as quickly as the presses could produce it. At one point during lunch, Hickey had been stopped with spoon nearly into mouth.

One young man, not more than 17 or 18, had stood up and read a passage. Hickey was amazed the boy could read so well. "The period of debate is closed. Arms must decide the contest; the appeal was the choice of the king, and the continent hath accepted the challenge. The sun never shone on a cause of greater worth."

A fairly well-dressed man, a merchant, perhaps, added that his favorite passage was the part where Paine says "I challenge the warmest advocates for reconciliation to show a single advantage that this continent can reap by being connected with Great Britain. I repeat the challenge; not a single advantage is derived. Our corn will fetch its price in any market in Europe, and our imported goods must be paid for wherever we must go to buy them."

There was a great deal of discussion but little arguing. It seemed that there was general agreement on the message but debate on the meaning or the choice of words. Hickey made a mental note to get a copy of the pamphlet.

It was nearly two-thirty now. Having paid for the food and drinks in hard coin, with a coin for the barkeep, Salty was very friendly and a little more relaxed. They were alone again and the barkeeper brought another drink over to Hickey and sat down.

"Here's the key. Room's up the back stairs. Third door on the right. This one's on me," he said, sliding the fresh, hot drink over to Hickey.

"Thanks. Think maybe I'll go up and ...." Hickey was interrupted.

The door slammed open and three men, stomping the

cold off their boots, came noisily in, swearing and laughing.

The barkeeper looked at the men, sighed and stood up. "Good afternoon, gentlemen," he said, a twinge of anxiety in his voice.

"Heard you had a stranger here, Salty. That him."

"Look, fellows. Let him be. Man's tired. Just passing through."

"Love to," said the man in the deep blue longcoat. "But, we have a responsibility."

Salty, Hickey thought, looked at first as if he was going to protest but thought better and walked back behind the bar busying himself, his head down but glancing up now and again.

The three men walked toward Hickey.

"Doing the King's business, mister?" said the man in the blue coat who stood close to Hickey's chair on the right. The voice was deep but uneven, like yelling down a well.

"Doin' my own business," replied Hickey.

"Times like these no man should put his own business above the call," droned the man in the middle who was shorter than the man in blue but heavier. He opened his coat to reveal a pistol.

"Call to what?" asked Hickey, unsure of what these men were up to. Uncertain whether the topic was the call to the King's defense or the fight for this notion of liberty.

"He's a lobster. Tell I can. Smell 'em. Peel back that cape and he's a red one, sure tell. Red as red," cackled the voice from the skinny white face of the man on the left.

These were not loyalists. That still didn't say much about what they were.

"That's one thing I'm not, that's for sure," said Hickey, taking the middle path. "I'm just a man's lookin' for work. Figured New York might be the place."

"Listen to that voice. Straight over on the King's boat. Ireland, I'd say. Told ya. They're fillin' this city, they are. Filled with Tories it is. A cesspool of arse-kissing King lovers," came the cackled reply. "We takes our orders from the great Washington himself."

"Don't know nothin' about that. Only need to earn enough to keep me warm and my belly full. And, I'm not feeling so well at the moment so if you'll let me be I'd appreciate it"

"Let him be? Let him be!?" said the man in the long blue coat in a mocking deep voice, unexpectedly pushing right up against the table lowering his face across the table from Hickey.

The short one pulled the pistol and pointed it at Hickey's head. "As duly authorized agents of General George Washington and the army of the Congress and believing yerself to be an agent of King Charles and an enemy of the Committees of Safety, I hereby order you to hand over your purse and any other valuables you may have."

These thieves had never gotten within a hundred miles of Washington. If they had, they might have stolen the false teeth out of his mouth. Nor, probably, had they ever seen any member of any Committee of Safety in the flesh. The irony was not lost on Hickey. A smuggler and a spy who did work for Washington being held up by a band of highwaymen who claimed to be Washington's agents.

Shorty cocked the pistol hammer and suddenly Hickey was struck by an overwhelming sense that this man was simply going to shoot him and take what they had asked for. Who would care? What law was there left here in New York City to enforce? Who could spare the time to enforce it?

"Don't shoot," begged Hickey hysterically, while lowering his own pistol beneath his cloak. He had drawn the pistol the minute the men had entered the tavern. He brought the pistol out under the table and aimed it at the groin of the short man with the pistol.

"We got ourselves a blubbering baby lobster," cackled the chicken-like man on the left.

"Please. Please," begged Hickey, "Here's the only thing

of value I got."

He fired the pistol. He was close enough to hear the ball crack into the man's thigh. The man gave out a yelp and tumbled backwards, dropping the gun.

Hickey was coldly efficient now. With first-shot advantage, he had planned his next move. No time to reload. He dropped it and, despite the ache in his head, acted quickly. He flipped up the table grabbing the skinny birdman and slammed his face down as he brought up his knee. There was a sickening click as the birdman's beak snapped. He hadn't planned any further than this. He was surprised it had even gotten this far. He dropped to the floor groping for the short man's gun.

"Don't bother," said the voice from deep within the well. "Just step back against the wall slowly." The man in the blue coat had drawn a pistol and was aiming it at Hickey.

Hickey stood up and backed slowly to the wall. The man in blue came closer. He stood three feet from Hickey, raised the pistol level with Hickey's face and slowly pulled back the hammer. Hickey's mind raced. Terror had replaced the fever. He could clearly see the man in blue beginning to tighten his finger on the trigger. He was smiling, his dark eyes deeper than his voice. Hickey also could see that, to his right, on the floor the man he had shot was coming awake from the shock. He had picked up his pistol and was fumbling with it, trying to aim it at him. He was furious. It was a matter of who would shoot him first. The fat man shook his head, groaned from the shattered leg and cocked the hammer.

The cocking hammer drew the man in blue's eyes for an instant. Hickey reached out with his thick hands and snapped the man's wrist upward while yanking him to the right. There were two gunshots. The ball from the blue man's gun plowed into the soft wood of the wall but not before scraping over the surface of Hickey's left cheek. The shot from the fat man lodged in the skull of the man in blue.

Hickey swiped at his cheek with the back of his right

hand. Blood dripped onto his chest but the wound was not deep. He picked up his pistol and wrenched the empty weapon out of the fat man's hands.

"Get someone to take care of this," Hickey said to Salty who had already put on his coat and was heading for the door.

The skinny, birdman was still out. Hickey slipped a long, sharp knife from its case, tied to his right calf. He was alone with the fat man. Hickey knelt and pressed the blade to the man's throat.

"Why me?"

"Why not? Good as any," spat the fat man, minding the blade cutting into the tender flesh of his neck while trying to reach down and comfort his shattered thigh bone. "Just another easy purse is all."

"I could kill you right now. Say you came at me again. Should kill you."

The fat man suffered in silence, tightening his jaw in defiance.

"I ain't no King's man just as sure as you ain't working for Washington. If a man had an itching to find out a little more about either side in this city, where would he go?"

"Wuh?"

"Where do men still loyal to the King gather?"

"Don't know. I swear. Ain't no King lover."

Hickey pressed the knife blade tighter against the fat man's neck. The razor-like edge drew blood.

"Er, uh," screamed the man, trying to think, "Corbie's! Corbie's Tavern! Spring and Wooster." The blade cut slightly deeper. "And ... the Sergeant's Arms. Those two. Only two I know. Honest."

Hickey released the blade.

"Now, what about a man who wanted to join up with the Sons of Liberty here in New York?"

"Fraunces," said the fat man without hesitating.

Thomas Hickey had begun to earn his pay.

Chapter Twelve

Lockup, New York City
4:30 p.m., Saturday, January 27, 1776

"Almost sorry to leave," thought Henry Dawkins as he folded his clothes and stuffed them in the sack. "Almost."

"Quite cozy, actually," he smiled, carefully rolling up his pens and pencils and placing them in the sack with all of his worldly possessions. "But, opportunity awaits."

Dawkins had served his full seven-month sentence and today was liberation day. The portrait business had allowed him to do his time with hardly a hardship. From the coolness of the north cell, his friend the gap-toothed guard had moved him into this cell as the weather turned cool, then frigid. This particular cell just happened to be located on the other side of the stone wall from the guardroom. And, as the fates would have it, there was a roaring fireplace serving the guards and in the grandest stroke of luck, that fireplace was cut into the other side of this wall. With his back cozied up to the wall, it had been downright warm for the last six weeks. He put his two books of illustrations into the sack and tied the string. He sat on the cot waiting for the guard.

Once again, he went over the plan. He would get started immediately. By spring, he would have enough cash to buy a house and send for Priscilla and the kids. He might even open a small gallery. From then on, he would dump the toads and sluggards and be legitimate. Make up for lost time.

The shuffling gate of the red-headed guard brought Dawkins to his feet, sack in hand waiting for the key to be turned in the lock.

"Gunna miss ya, Henry," said the guard.

"And I you, I'm certain," said Dawkins, insincerity oozing from his oily smile. "Here. A little going away present for the girl. She's a real beauty. You should be very proud."

Dawkins handed the dim-eyed guard a sketch of the painfully plain, puffy-cheeked, brown-haired girl the guard had once introduced as his betrothed.

The guard grinned, the gap between the upper front teeth widening. "Thank you, Henry. She is a beauty, ain't she?"

"For sure. For sure," agreed Dawkins. "Now, can we get on with the formalities?" he gestured toward the lock.

"Oh? Oh yeah. Sorry. Here you go. Good luck to ye." The guard swung open the cell door and Henry Dawkins, once again having paid his debt to society, was a free man.

Four days later, following the directions of the inmate with the swollen nose, Dawkins was in Huntington on the Long Island knocking at the door of Israel and Isaac Youngs.

The harsh winter wind slapped his face and he turned his back to it while, again, reaching out to knock on the door. His hand went several inches further than before but met no resistance. Dawkins turned back to face a thin, innocuous man in his thirties with prematurely white hair, thinning in the front, puffed out at the sides. He wore spectacles and smiled like a Sunday school teacher.

"Yes? May I help you?" The voice was soft, almost womanish.

"Indeed! Indeed!" said Dawkins, stepping right past the man into the warmth of the comfortable clapboard home.

"Do come in," said the Isaac Youngs, not in the least taken aback by this stranger who had invited himself into his home.

In fact, it was Dawkins who was uncomfortable, like the fly invited with open arms into the web.

"I am Isaac Youngs," he said, extending a thin, moist hand.

"Dawkins. Henry Dawkins."

"What can I do for you?" said Youngs.

"A mutual acquaintance said that you and your brother are investors always with a keen eye toward a healthy profit. And I have an enterprise which could make us a tidy sum in a very short time."

"Well, we do pride ourselves in our ability to succeed in commerce," said Isaac Youngs. "Let me get my brother. That way you'll only have to present your proposition once." He led Dawkins into a small, warm sitting room and left to fetch his brother. Dawkins examined the furnishings. Several small porcelain statues were displayed on a shelf. A silver dish on an end table had been etched with a sailing ship. Mediocre work, thought Dawkins. Large framed paintings on the wall were nondescript except for the frames, which were of good quality.

He was examining the signature on one painting when the Youngs brothers returned.

"Mr. Dawkins, this is my brother Israel."

"A distinct pleasure," said Dawkins, warmly grasping Israel's hand with both of his own. Dawkins barely contained a chuckle. The Youngs brothers might have been twins. Both appeared almost fragile and yet both had the grin of a snake.

"Well, I am not going to deceive you. I have only this week been released from jail. These are terrible times, you know. A horrendous miscarriage of justice. Charges concocted to keep me from earning an honest living without choosing between my King and my country. You know the difficulty in that. Out here on the Long Island, there are many who remain loyal to King Charles. Why you yourselves may even ...." He paused waiting for a reaction to his admission to being a convict and, a fence sitter in terms of the struggle. The brothers Youngs were noncommittal but smiling.

"Any way, my reputation may precede me. I am, in all modesty, an engraver of some renown. Many of my works have appeared in major publications. Benjamin Franklin himself has purchased several of my works." This part was true. But the Youngs did not alter their expressions.

"I propose a small printing enterprise," said Dawkins, uneasy now at the almost insane grinning by these men who sat patiently listening to a stranger tell a tale in their home. "An enterprise, I envision in which we would produce labels for the hat industry ... among other printed products. These labels would be of my own custom design and surely would find a market. We might save the expense of shop rental by installing this press, say, in the attic of your home here."

The Youngs brothers were almost laughing now. Nodding with great zest and, yes, giggling.

"We understand, Mr. Dawkins," said Israel. "We understand fully. How much will you need?"

Caught off guard, Dawkins had no ready answer for such a straightforward question. "No silver, sir. A press would be all. A rolling press."

"Of, course, a rolling press," chuckled Isaac. "A rolling press is the only kind. The only kind."

"But, you will also be needing paper, won't you?" added Israel. "Any special paper?" He beamed.

"Why, now that you mention it, there is one type of paper which makes the very best hat labels. I believe it must be purchased in ...."

"Philadelphia," filled in Israel.

"Er, that's right, Philadelphia," said Dawkins cautiously.

"We know just the agent to purchase our paper," said Isaac.

"Yes, the perfect man," agreed Israel.

"Actually," said Dawkins, "I also know of a man who can provide this kind of paper."

"Isaac Ketcham!" The three of them said the name in unison.

It was Dawkins' turn to grin now. The Youngs brothers were seasoned professionals at this kind of enterprise.

"We have a spare room in the attic right alongside a nice open space that will be perfect for the press. Let us show it to you," said Isaac Youngs.

Chapter Thirteen

Fraunces Tavern, New York City
5 p.m., Monday, March 18, 1776

The food was untouched. The drink going cold. Thomas Hickey could not take his eyes off her. He studied the way she cocked her head to the right when she took a customer's order. He followed her with his eyes; table to kitchen, table to bar, table to table. He strained to hear her voice across the room. It was like music. No, more like a hymn. A mother's lullaby. His mother's. Just for him. Listen to him. Invoking his mother's lilting lullabies. What rot. Had to be his dick talking. But more than that. Her skin, he thought, glowed, reflecting the lantern light. Nutmeg. Cinnamon. Other spices. A brownish red. Perfect. Not a blemish. She was young but obviously a woman. She wore white. White skirt. White bodice. White ruffles around her breasts that made them appear even darker. Full breasts but not too large. Not over-stuffed melons like some nowadays but select pears, round at the base, pointed outward. Her neck was long. There was a small crease in her chin. Her legs were like those of a young mare, always set at the right balance. Her eyes were dark, nearly black, against a white that was whiter than her bodice.

He had tried to look into her eyes when she took his order but he had to look away in order to remember the words:

food, drink. She was the most beautiful creature he had ever seen. What she did to him was something that had never been done to him before. She made him weak. She made his usually certain hands fat and clumsy. She made his ready confidence drain away. His easy smile was nowhere to be found. Hickey had come here every day for the past week, ever since seeing her for the first time last Tuesday. Each time, he would order food and a drink. Nibble at the food. Have a swallow or two of the drink. Sit for an hour or so. Leave.

He would go straight up to the Holy Ground, New York's raucous den of thievery, murder, and prostitution, which, ironically, surrounded St. Paul's Church and infested property owned by Trinity Church. Salty had told him that, at last count, there were 267 taverns in New York City. New York was quickly becoming a garrison town and soldiers liked their drink and they liked women. Merchants were upping their prices almost daily to take advantage of the new military inhabitants. The whores of the Holy Ground were also doing quite well selling the blessings they had to bestow on the military. There were also daily reports of whores slicing off soldiers' testicles and slitting each other's throats to get to the fattest purse. But Hickey felt comfortable. He knew how to talk to these women. They were like Mandy at the Red Snapper in Boston. They had opened their legs as young girls and didn't need long, clever stories to do so every night. Just a shilling or two. He knew the smells. The sounds. The talk of the men was his kind of talk. The trouble was familiar trouble, easily handled. So, for a week now, he would watch the Fraunces girl and then go to the Holy Ground and get rid of the tightness she caused in his belly.

He knew her name now. Phoebe. Phoebe Fraunces. Daughter of the owner, Samuel Fraunces. Black Sam is what his oldest friends called him, although now he was becoming much too prosperous and respectable for such a tag. The tale was that Samuel had come to New York from the French

West Indies and, at that time, was known as Samuel Francis. After the last war with the French and Indians, he decided to make it more French, changing the family name to Fraunces to capitalize on his talent for preparing French cuisine. He had operated a tavern or inn in the city for twenty years and now owned not only this building and an interest in a couple others but had operated perhaps the most popular place in the city, Vauxhall Gardens. Hickey hadn't been there but he had heard that old Sam was selling the place or had sold it. It was supposed to be a grand place with elaborate wax figures and beautiful gardens. Great food. Sam was much more interested in what was taking place in Philadelphia. He wanted to be on the right side when all of this played out. So, he was selling his New York properties and getting closer to the men of the congress.

From what he had overheard, Phoebe was 19. Fraunces watched her very closely, not letting any patron get too close nor too friendly. Word was any one who was a mere patron was not right for his daughter. There were older brothers who saw to this while Sam was away.

"You're not eating."

Hickey's mind raced through the list of words. Pick a few. Put them together. Say them.

"Me? No ain't..."

Wrong ones. Stupid choice.

"Perhaps, I can warm that up for you," Phoebe said, bending over, her breasts just inches from Hickey's face, starting to pick up the plate.

"Not really...going away now..." He stood up and tried to make his legs work. They were loose, soggy and barely carried him to the door. He looked back through the window to watch Phoebe shrug her shoulders and carry the dishes to the kitchen.

He began to walk the mile or so to the Holy Ground. By the time he reached Wall Street, his legs had returned to him. By Crown Street, he was cursing himself for being such an

arse. By the time he caught sight of St. Paul's, he was ready
to regain his manhood. She was just a young girl. Wouldn't
know what to do anyway. A man like me needs a woman. A
real woman. A woman with certain talents.

He bypassed the Gilded Rose. He wasn't in the mood
for talking and doing a dance around the issue. Even though,
at the Rose, one ran less risk of getting an important part of
one's anatomy lopped off. He wanted to get right down to
business. The Jolly Bear was tonight's place of worship in
the Holy Ground. Good drinks and rooms right up the stairs.
Some good looking women, too. One who called herself
Betsy was as good as he ever had. Didn't mind a few little
extras if the money was right. The first night in the Bear,
Hickey had talked with the barkeeper and, after a generous
bribe, was told which women were known to be clean and
which would make a man's doodle turn black and run with
puss.

Hickey could hear the noise from the Jolly Bear. It was
half a block away but he could already hear the singing and
the laughter. He felt much better.

Pushing open the door, thoughts of Phoebe Fraunces
faded. It was hard to talk, let alone think. A small group of
soldiers, well into the rum, were betting on who could hold
his breath the longest with nose and mouth buried deeply
between the giant breasts of a woman with gray hair. They
were laughing so hard, they could barely stand up, leaning
shoulder to shoulder like butting rams. By the fireplace, four
men, each with a woman on his lap were singing and pouring
cider or kill-devil or something into the gaping mouths of
the women. The women had their skirts hiked up over their
knees and two of the men had their hands high up on their
white thighs.   There were couples lining the stairs. Pairs
kissed and groped standing up against the walls. Hickey's
ready smile returned. He ordered a drink and, before it was
served, a hand covered his eyes and another his crotch.

"Gueth who," slurred the woman he knew by the name

of Betsy.

"Why just the most beautiful women in New York," he said, "No, in all the colonies. A woman to make any man sell his soul. And that I would do for you my Betsy. That I would." He turned, grabbed her by the waist and pulled the inviting body toward him. He kissed her long and wet. Her breath smelled of alcohol and even a pipe but that made it all the more welcome. He ordered another drink and walked up the stairs with Betsy clinging to his waist. She would be extra good tonight, he thought.

A few hours later, as Hickey came down the stairs, the Jolly Bear was quiet. The soldiers had left and so had the women who entertained them. Some alone, some together. A couple of older gents were deep in drunken sleep at the tables. It was nearly two in the morning. The Jolly Bear never actually closed. It ebbed and flowed. People came and went. The staff cleaned up around them, maybe even stopped serving for a while, but never threw anyone out into the street. Hickey was wide awake. He had only had a single drink. Betsy had tried her best but her best wasn't good enough any more. This was another new experience for Thomas Hickey. They were coming fast and furiously now. He could perform drunk, not having slept for two days with a wharf rat for a bed partner. Not tonight. Betsy's breath was repulsive and the pasty, sickly pallor of her skin made him want to wretch. She didn't mind. He had paid her the same as ever. She took the opportunity to plummet into a deep, snorting sleep while Hickey lay with the tightness still twisting his gut.

The tall man with dark, deep-set eyes behind the bar was cleaning up. He noticed Hickey and, without annoyance, made up another drink. Hickey paid him and took the drink to a table by the fireplace. He inched the chair back against the wall and sipped on the drink. Phoebe Fraunces was not so easily glossed over anymore. He would have to find a cure for this ailment. Perhaps, tomorrow or, rather, today, at supper. A most peculiar thing.

Hickey hadn't paid much attention to the three men sitting at a nearby table except to notice that they did not appear to have been partying. They seemed quite sober. One by one the words piled up until he found himself trying to listen to what they were saying. It was difficult because they were leaning forward over the table, cupping their drinks in front of them. They were talking naturally, not whispering but Hickey still had to strain to hear.

"Stores of powder and shot. North of the city. We have to find where they store it," said the man with the black hair and clear, strong voice.

"Yes. We must see to it quickly. It can only be a matter of days now," added a well-dressed man, perhaps 40, who had refused a drink but puffed on a carved wooden pipe. "Sir Henry Clinton has come through the narrows and the word is that Washington is sending that court jester Lee down here with thousands. Tryon will never allow that. We must act now."

The third man had listened to the others, nodding, considering. He spoke and they listened. "We have time. Sir Henry, I am told — and by a very reliable messenger — is only here on a social visit. He plans to sail to the south within the week. As for Lee, that is true. The rebellious rabble is marching this way. There is work to be done but we will get it done. My man tells me that an agent acting in secret on behalf of the crown has delivered a half million in sterling to Tryon to be used for, as he put it, 'spying and corresponding and for corruption.' We will have the resources and we will complete our task. But there is time."

"How can you be so sure? Sunday past the church bells nearly rang themselves down from the belfries of every church in the city. It was a warning. People are afraid. Someone will get itchy and fire and we'll be off. Just like at Lexington. We must act now," said the younger man.

"I have told you what they expect from us," said the man

who had brought the news of the large war chest for spies and subterfuge. "The Sons of Liberty won't act until Lee or Washington himself arrives. They are too busy digging ditches and fouling up our city to pay much attention to the real strategic points along the river and at the north and east. We will work our plan. There is no great urgency. We'll meet at Corbie's on Monday as planned. I expect to have some news that should help our financial pinch. I believe there is some fresh, new money on the way."

The other two men nodded halfheartedly but agreeably. They stood, drew on their cloaks, and left.

Hickey left for the long walk to his room, drafting his message to Washington as he plodded through the snow. Hickey was not certain of the importance of what he had heard. After all, grousing and swearing oaths against one side or the other had become the general sport of New York. The reports from the Long Island were frequent and boastful. Virtually every pub he entered had its resident Tory rooster squawking about how the Sons of Liberty would be getting what's due them. They all pretty much sang the same tune; out on the Long Island, there were nearly a thousand loyalists ready to take up the King's arms and block the retreat of the rebels once the royal navy was in place around Manhattan. Others spoke openly of as many troops being stationed north near Goshen. These loyal enlistees would block the way to the north and cut off this festering bit of Whig folly. Enough of this. Leave it to New York to return some sanity to the King's colonies. Most patrons either ignored the babbling or cheered the diatribe in jest, drinking the good health of the mad King. No harm done. Hickey had reported to Washington on these ravings but also indicating that it was probably true to some extent although he not yet managed to get close enough to any real subversive activity.

He had been here two months now without much consequence. He was beginning to think seriously about just packing up and riding west. He didn't have enough money but what the hell. He'd be away from this mess. Or he could double up. The Tories were always looking for runners or a scrap of information here and there. Nothing big. No harm. Collect a bit from both sides and then get the hell out while they slit each other's throats. Washington had promised him 200 acres of land. His own land. But who really knew whether the arrogant southern sail full of wind would make good on the deal. What if he did? It was a lot of land. And then there was this girl Phoebe.

Hickey decided, once again, to stay for a while longer. After all, Washington was paying regularly. A report like this would probably earn a small bonus. Besides, he had to straighten out this thing with this Fraunces girl.

***

Two hundred miles to the northeast, while Thomas Hickey trudged through the gray snow of New York City, George Washington, surrounded by aides and a mounted guard, entered Boston Common for the first time since the British evacuation.

"It appears to be undamaged and the path safe, General," said the sergeant who had been sent ahead of Washington and the small cadre of military officers riding with him.

"Thank you, sergeant," said Washington, stiffly, dismissing the enlisted man. Turning to an aide, he said: "I still want to examine the house myself."

"Of course, general, I thought it prudent, however, to be certain there were no traps set or obstacles in the route," said a major riding with the Washington party. What he really wanted to say was 'Why are you so damned concerned about this one house when all of Boston is ready to welcome you as an emperor?'

Boston Common, thought Washington, was like the Indian encampments he had come upon in the Pennsylvania woods. There was no life, no movement, but it was almost as if whoever had been living there had left in such a rush as to leave something of their very soul behind. One could feel it. There were campfire pits with wood still stacked nearby. Bits of cloth and wood scattered about. But it was more than that. There was a reluctance; a feeling as though those who had been here had been ordered to leave but weren't anxious to go. Proud men who had no desire to be seen as cowards, thought to have run away, tails between their legs.

The thought did not linger. Washington was more interested in the realities of the moment, in Hancock House. He told the staff that the first thing he wanted to do upon entering Boston was to examine the Hancock House. It was, he told them, a promise he had made to John Hancock when they met in Philadelphia. This was true as far as it went but Washington simply wanted to see how this house, built by the richest man in Massachusetts, stacked up against the manors of Virginia. As the group rode past the cemetery where Thomas Hickey had briefly rested before making his way into the house, Washington had to admit that the view from his high point on the Commons was very attractive indeed. The general alit at the front of the house but, before going in, walked around the grounds. He took note of where the gardens would be blooming in the spring and of the out buildings. Though smaller in scale than Mt. Vernon, it was of finer quality. The detail of workmanship was impressive. Washington took note of the stone ledges formed by the corner stones. That would be where Hickey had climbed to the roof. He entered and toured the house. The British officers had remained gentlemen. Nothing appeared damaged. In fact, it looked as if the house had been cleaned before the royal tenants moved out. None of the expensive furnishings had been taken. Hancock may be crude and brash of manner but he has good taste, thought Washington.

Assured the Hancock mansion was untouched and his curiosity about Hancock's lifestyle sated, Washington toured the British fortifications. "This town of Boston was almost impregnable," he said to an aide. He thought to himself, however, that the one major battle he had wanted to initiate would have taken the city and perhaps have ended this conflict right then and there. He had reluctantly abandoned the idea on the advice of his council of generals. Congress had taken him at his word when he humbly had sought their prayers and assistance in carrying out this duty. When his stated modesty hinted that perhaps a council of generals could help fill in whatever blanks may exist in his military training, they had not slapped him on the back, encouraged him, told him he was the best military mind ever and not to worry. They took him at his word. A council of generals was a good idea they said. Asking us for help in the really tough decisions was also a good idea, they said. This was not what he had in mind and it would, he felt, come back to haunt him before this business was through.

Admiral Lord Howe had left Boston the previous morning. Several small boys from Boston picked their way through the crows feet, the devilishly pointed traps set out by the British on the Boston Neck to slow any final advance by the enemy before they could board the ships in the harbor. The boys ran into Roxbury shouting the British had left. Brigadier General John Sullivan was not convinced. Looking from a telescope he could see sentries still standing guard at Bunker Hill. He was cautious. He didn't want to tell General Washington until they were certain. It remained for Thomas Mifflin, quartermaster general of the new army, to prove a nagging suspicion he had having stared through the telescope himself. He sent several soldiers to Bunker Hill to make an assault. What they found was a scarecrow force. Stuffed uniform shirts and pants standing guard. The goal, again, to slow any final push by the rebellious colonials.

Shortly thereafter, Washington was notified that the British had left Boston. He allowed a half smile and asked for the details. Once convinced that Boston was ready for occupation, he mounted his horse and road to talk with Artemas

Ward, the senior general from Massachusetts.

Ward, nearing fifty, had been suffering with a defective gall bladder and was recovering from a most painful episode. He was surprised, and not pleasantly, by Washington's visit to his quarters so early on a Sunday morning. Ward was a loyal general to the commander-in-chief but still begrudged Washington's selection. The Congress felt he should have taken a more energetic role at Breed's Hill. It was all the reason they needed to back the selection of the Virginian over the man who had been chosen to raise 13,000 troops and head the Provincial army.

"Gen. Ward," said Washington with warmth and a genuine smile, "I have confirmed that Boston has been abandoned by the King's men. I would like you to be the first officer of the army to enter the city. Would you prepare to do that?"

"Why, er, yes, of course, general," stammered Ward, surprised by the honor Washington was bestowing upon him. "But, I feel, sir, the honor belongs to the commander-in-chief."

"No, General Ward," replied Washington, "This is your land, your Massachusetts, your Boston. You and your men shall be first to reenter your homes. I would suggest one thing. We have reports of rampant smallpox. I believe you have suffered through this deadly ailment, have you not?"

"Yes sir."

"Then select 500 of our men who also have already faced this disease. Take them with you. You may select whom you want. My only suggestion to you is that you select your fellow soldiers from Massachusetts and that they have the immunity to the pox."

Ward beamed and saluted. Washington returned the salute and rode back to his quarters. He had learned the ways of the politician well during the past nine months. By allowing a Massachusetts general to be first into Boston, he gained the respect and support of the Massachusetts Congressional delegates and the residents of Boston. He had nothing to gain by being first. Congress would still give him a gold medal and Harvard bestow upon him an honorary doctorate. Moving quickly to fortify Dorcester Heights had been Washington's best tactical move so far. While the British leadership had been planning to leave, it forced their hand.

Most of Boston had not fared as well as the Hancock House. Even the grand Old South meeting hall had been turned into a stable. Wood for cookstoves was plucked from the nearest source, whether church pew or classic facade. Patriots returning to their property were irate. Washington, eager to capitalize on the liberation of Boston, said: "One or two of these deplorable Tory sympathizers have done what the great majority of them should have done long ago, commit suicide."

But, assuaging the insulted Boston property owners was not his primary concern at the moment. Washington knew the British had moved out of Boston for reasons other than sheer terror at his fortifications. They would return. New York would be the target. Reports from New York were sketchy. Hickey had begun to provide information on what seemed to be a strong Tory presence as well as a growing discontent with the Patriot troops. Two other regular sources, including one Washington had decided to use to corroborate Hickey's reports and vice versa, unbeknownst to either man, had also begun to hear talk of Tory speeches and city officials communicating with Governor Tryon aboard the Duchess of Gordon offshore.

It was time to move the troops to New York.

Chapter Fourteen

Broad and King Sts., New York City
2:30 p.m., Thursday, April 4, 1776

Tension smothered the bursting of spring. Tulips peeked out of green bulbs warily pushing out into the dense air of a city irrevocably marching toward confrontation. Continental troops poured down the Post Road, plopping down under the elm trees of Bowery Lane to rest before finding a place to sleep. Such places were scarce. Many soldiers had taken to sleeping in carts or under porches. Small tent cities were forming throughout the northern boundary of the city. Grog shops and brothels became home to others. And still, day after day, the clomp of boots on cobblestones could be heard. Those merchants who remained tripled their prices while riding the sharpened rail of Tory versus Whig.

Amid this city-turned-garrison, Thomas Hickey and Phoebe Fraunces walked side by side, enjoying the new sun, higher in the sky each day as spring was forced on a city undecided or uncaring about the change of seasons. They now spent every free moment together. It had taken him almost two weeks to get up the courage to ask her to go for a walk with him. She had readily accepted and within the first few steps he found it as easy to talk with her as with his own sisters back home. He had never been in love before. This must be it, he thought. To say Black Sam Fraunces approved was to say His Honor George Washington loved Good King George III, mad as a hatter though he might be. Her father considered Hickey a poor, drifting, low-life deserter with nary a single redeeming feature. Black past. Gray present. No future. But that did not stop Phoebe from listening to her heart and wanting to be with this man, an inch shorter than she, and a tongue-tied stranger just a month before. She still did not have the courage to be seen with Hickey within range of the tavern. But that time would come and she would face down her father if need be. There were moments when Hickey frightened her. With her, he was gentle, almost docile. But, at times, she sensed a savage presence in him, a foreboding and yet compelling primitive core. She knew he had seen and done things she did not want to hear of, at least not just yet. And yet, she felt drawn to him, wanted to be with him. She was, at once, embarrassed and intoxicated by the way he looked at her, listened to her every word and delighted in her laughter.

Hickey was certain she had bewitched him. It was like one of the soldiers had told him: "Beware of those natives from the Indies. They can make a man crow like a rooster or bark like a dog." He told Hickey tales of incantations. Spells. Worship of plants. Black magic. It didn't matter. Hickey would hop on one leg, drop his pants and blow farts to the tune of Yankee Doodle, if that's what she wanted. On the other hand, if old Black Sam started slicing off chicken heads and burning candles while wailing at the moon and cursing the Hickey name, he might get concerned.

The spy business had picked up in the past few weeks. Perhaps it was Phoebe's influence on the outlook of his future or maybe it was simply that this city was racing toward the inevitable showdown. Whatever the reason, he had sent Washington some interesting material. He reported on the numbers and types of people fleeing the city and where they were going, mostly Long Island or New Jersey. He described in detail the roving bands of thugs operating in the name of liberty. Rogues, both Whigs and Tories, terrorized those who were trying to live their lives oblivious to politics. The loyalist thugs were known as "cowboys" while the roving thieves and head-bangers who felt closer to the Sons of Liberty were known as "skinners." He listed names of taverns suspected to be Tory strongholds. He detailed the work on fortifying the city, his reports often more honest than official reports sent back by Major General Charles Lee. He was even bold enough to mention in one report that it was his gut feeling that getting caught on this island would be a very bad tactical blunder by the army. There was no defense, he had written; no way out.

He prepared these reports carefully as instructed. He used the paper and the ink that was as white as the paper. Washington had told him that he personally had paid a lot of money for the development of this ink. It was invisible for all practical purposes. He wrote innocuous letters of greeting in visible black ink between the lines of invisible messages. He folded these reports and gave them to the coach driver who delivered them to the addressee in Hartford. From there, they were delivered to Washington. Return instructions would be placed in the false bottom of a snuff box. The box, seemingly dropped by someone fleeing the city, was left beside a tree stump just north of the city.

In return, Hickey had received word from Stephen Moylan, a Washington aide, that the British had begun to make preparations for evacuation of Boston. It was likely that troops would begin to pour into New York from Massachusetts. The news about Boston had been like whacking a beehive with a stick for the Tories in the town. Rowboat activity increased between the city and the Duchess of York in the harbor. Less than a week ago, City Mayor Whitehead Hicks passed the official seal of mayor to David Matthews who had been serving as water bailiff. Matthews, a real estate speculator with a keen eye for a fast dollar, had already come to Hickey's attention. The new mayor loved the title but wasn't about to let official duties get in the way of his enterprise. A man of medium height and build with a non-descript face under a patch of blonde hair, Matthews had a wicked, rascally laugh. Word was that Matthews could be led around by the nose provided that the hand pinching the nose also contained a gold piece or two. A woman at the Bear had told him that the new mayor was also receiving messages from Tryon. Hickey decided to wait until he had more information before labeling the new mayor as a British puppet in his reports to Washington.

"Have you found work yet, Thomas?" asked Phoebe.

"Not much work to be found," he answered, knowing the question was, in part, prompted by Black Sam's harping to her that Hickey was lazy and really good for nothing at all. He wanted to tell her he was earning a rather steady income but could not. Then, seeing a small squad of soldiers marching up Broad Street with shovels and picks, he got an idea.

"Been thinking of joining up with the Continentals. Pay ain't much but it's better'n nothin'." In the same flash of brilliance, he thought, he'd ask Washington to let him wear a uniform. It would provide an even better cover. The Sons of Liberty wouldn't give him a second look and the Tories might think they were turning one of Washington's men.

"A soldier," Phoebe echoed, letting the word come from her lips slowly, as if trying the concept on for size. "It might be dangerous. I wouldn't want anything to happen to you Thomas. Not when we're just becoming friends. My father says that the city will almost certainly come under attack."

"It's a helluva long way beyond friendship for me, Phoebe," said Hickey ignoring the war talk. "You know that. I'm madly in love with ya, girl. Can't think of anything else. You're the most beautiful woman I've ever laid eyes on. The most beautiful thing my eyes have ever seen. And what's inside is even more beautiful than what's out." The words came easily now. Natural and heartfelt.

"Thomas!" Phoebe blushed. "These words from lips that tied themselves into little knots just ordering a plate of peas not even a single month past."

Hickey watched the blush grow in her cheeks, a rose tint against cinnamon, barely discernible. He was overwhelmed. This girl was the most perfect creature he had ever seen. He wanted to grab her and hold on so she wouldn't disappear. He wanted to kiss her, feel her skin, caress her, consume her. He grabbed for her hand and brought it to his lips almost afraid that the touch of her skin would cause his brain to explode. He had been very careful. Hadn't so much as sought to kiss her. He could control his desire no longer. He brought her hand to his lips and lightly touched his lips to the first knuckle of the index finger, gently, and only briefly, taking the knuckle into his lips, like a suckling new babe. His heart exploded. It was the greatest draught at his greatest thirst. The most delectable meal when he was most hungry. Her skin was soft but textured like silk. And sweet. The sweetest dessert ever tasted by man. He closed his eyes wanting this moment to last but feeling certain she would pull back, chastising him for being too bold. She did not. She let her hand rest on his lips. Her hand had, at first, been taut but now relaxed and he felt her giving herself through this first touch.

He opened his eyes and looked at her. She looked gently back into his eyes and smiled like she had never smiled before.

"I thought you would never touch me, Thomas," Phoebe said softly, almost with relief. "I thought that, well, maybe, you did not want to."

"I've thought of nothing else since I first saw you. Nothing. Not a thought goes by that doesn't begin or end with you. Phoebe, I haven't been the best ... I mean, I've done many things that ..."

She stopped him, moving her finger tips to his lips.

"There is no need, Thomas." With that she stepped forward and, closing her eyes, pressed her lips softly but generously against his. Hickey thought he would swoon. The effect was overpowering. For an instant, he thought it best to run away but the intoxicating pleasure wouldn't allow it. The kiss deepened. He had been attracted by the girl Phoebe and was being held now by the woman. He pressed himself to her, holding her firmly. She did not shy away. She put her hands softly on the back of his head and pulled him even closer.

The world moved on as they remained locked in this embrace, drinking every drop of the clear spring stream, touching their tongues to every fresh snowflake of the first winter storm. Ages came and went. When they eventually forced themselves apart, each was somehow different. They continued walking, now hand in hand, oblivious to the beat of drums and the shouted orders of the troops. They walked east toward the river, talking and laughing as men hacked and wretched from the ravages of malaria, typhoid and smallpox which rampaged through the troops like an invisible enemy. Phoebe had only been as far as Murray's Wharf once before, with her father. She was fascinated by the dark men enslaved on the docks. Some of this blood was in her and yet they were so much different than people she knew. The East River docks were home to the largest population of Africans enslaved in the colonies. Nearly half of the population of the waterfront and warehouse area were Negroes, Africans, darkies. Men with skin as wet black as some of the fish brought to her father's restaurant early in the morning. Like well-oiled black leather. They had masses of wooly hair with bits of debris clinging to it. They chomped on clay pipes and seemed at ease with one another but tense when a white man and coffee-tinted woman holding hands walked nearby. Some laughed. Some just sat, feet dangling from the pier, staring east across the water oblivious to the growing tension in the city.

As they turned back west toward Queen Street, their conversation was interrupted by shouts and raucous laughter. They were coming up on a narrow side street that accessed several large warehouses. The voices came from that opening. Instinctively, they both hurried toward the intersection. About a dozen roughly dressed men were standing around a small horse-drawn cart. The men were shouting and laughing, clapping each other on the shoulders and then turning their attention back to the main attraction.

"Pour it on his head!" shouted one man with crooked yellow teeth.

"Hurry it up. Hurry it up. Coat'em good. How'dya expect the batter to stick to this fish without a good coatin'?" yelled another, a tall broad man with a rumbling voice who was tearing apart the seams of a pillow and pulling handfuls of feathers from the opening.

The object of these shouts was a naked, terrified middle-aged man, his head shaved and one end of a thick rope around his neck. The other end was held by a large thug with a flattened nose and ugly animal eyes. He was cackling convulsively, his shoulders heaving but his hand yanking tightly on the rope. In his other huge hand, he wielded a thick club, ready to smack the man's head should he decide to escape.

Hickey recognized the third man in the cart. He had sent Washington a report on this man. This was Isaac Sears. "King Sears" as he was often called among the dock workers. Sears' father had been a Yankee fish peddler. Sears grew up on the docks, among the ships and went to sea as a teenager. Later, he commanded a privateer and then, in middle age, had made a comfortable living as a merchant. He was called "King Sears" because he was king of the wharves. He could organize hundreds of bullymen in a heartbeat. Almost from the start, Sears had taken to the idea of liberty. He was quick to join the Sons of Liberty. He attracted the attention of the Delanceys. James Delancey, who controlled the New York Assembly and Council, openly sought Sears company. When Gen. Lee arrived, Sears was named his adjutant general. Now, all involved in this struggle for liberty in New York wanted to take a step back from their charge. Sears had taken to the job too greedily. He personally took on the challenge of cleaning out this "filthy Tory Nest" known as New York. And, while he had gained legitimacy in the political cause, he remained a head-banging, waterfront thug at heart.

His latest victim was a tavern owner charged with selling food and drink to be taken out into the harbor for the HMS Duchess of Gordon, serving as floating home now for William Tryon, Royal Governor of New York. Sears clamped one hand on the shoulder of the cowering merchant and pushed him to his knees. He lifted a large teakettle and slowly tilted it forward.

"In the name of liberty, I hereby sentence you to be marked as a King-loving Tory. Let this be a lesson to all of those who would steal our freedom from us and climb into bed with the King and his royal lackeys."

With that, thick, viscous tar poured from the kettle and onto the top of the shaved head of the merchant. The tar was hot enough to pour and to blister the skin but not hot enough to burn the flesh from a man's bones. That would defeat the purpose. After all, the idea was humiliation not execution. But it was still quite hot and made hissing noises as it splashed onto the man's head and shoulders. Instinctively, he put his hands up to cover his eyes. Sears took aim, pouring the tar over any white patch. The tar ran out with only the man's legs from the knees down uncovered. There was a slight hesitation before the other men started grabbing at handfuls of feathers from three pillows and pelting them hard against the tar-covered body. Half stuck in the black goo, half hung in the air, slowly floating to the cart.

The men took great delight in the look of terror on the merchant's face. Sears was especially proud of this latest creation. He stood at the front of the cart, hands clasped behind him, admiring his work.

Phoebe was appalled. She had never seen a tarring and feathering, although she had heard dozens of conversations about such cruelty in the tavern. She was surprised that the victim hadn't cried out in pain. He had simply just whimpered, humiliation being the prime source of his hurt.

Hickey had drawn Phoebe back from the cart and up against the brick facade of the warehouse. He had seen this particular form of punishment before and was aware that the men worked up to such a frenzy could get out of control.

When the pillow sacks had been emptied, the noise level dropped and there was a rumble of admiration for the feathered Tory statue they had created. Then they tired of this one, removed the rope and sent the merchant tumbling off the cart with a kick. He scurried up the road, the cooling tar making his muscles jerk as he fled like a giant spasmodic chick just hatched from a huge mythical black egg.

"Next," announced Sears, a judge calling for the next case.

"Nother good'n," said the man with the club. From the midst of the thugs came another man, his hands tied in front. The rope was roughly pushed over his head and the knot tightened as they yanked him onto the cart.

Hickey recognized this victim. It was Ketcham, the paper merchant who had been the center of attention at last evening's session of the back room group at the Sergeant's Arms.

Twice a week for two weeks now, he had made himself a fixture at the Sergeant's Arms Tavern. He was getting closer to much more substantial information. If what he suspected proved true, it would make Washington take notice and maybe even prompt a large bonus payment. There seemed to be a well-planned, elaborate scheme under way to counterfeit several of the currencies in circulation. This money would then be used to somehow sabotage the patriotic effort in New York. He drank rum and sat by himself at a table that butted up against the right rear and back walls of the tavern room proper. This wall, unlike the case with most other taverns he had visited, did not form the rear exterior wall. It held another room where larger parties of 15 to 20 could all sit around a large round table. The opening to this room was six or eight feet wide with no doors or curtains. From his vantage point, Hickey could hear the conversations in this rear room and he could see most of the table although he was careful not be caught looking. It was the same routine each day. Up late. Go to Fraunces for a meal. Try to sneak away for a walk with Phoebe. Take up this spot at the Sergeant's. Drink a few rums while looking bored and tired with life. Some easy detection work had resulted in a list of characters. He was beginning to know them quite well.

It was usually about six o'clock on Tuesdays and Thursdays when the participants in the rear room gatherings would arrive. They would order dinner and drinks and engage in general conversation about the day and the events of the continent. They toasted the king and peace. This was still not unusual in New York, though becoming less and less acceptable. The vast majority of the colonists still hoped that all of this would just go away and the king would relent and agree to some kind of self-rule. No one in his right mind really thought about total independence. Did they? Then, when the plates were taken away and another round of drinks ordered, they would get down to the business at hand. What had gotten Hickey's attention at first a week ago were the minor oaths and toasts that came after the formalities. A young man, perhaps in his 20s said: "At least the king will have New York." A thick, puffy, red-faced man with an ill-fitting white wig, whom the others referred to as Forbes, said: "The Sons of Liberty will find no liberty here." Agreement all around.

Much the same had occurred last evening, except for the addition of three new cast members. Two frail little men with white hair and squinting eyes with lids that blinked constantly over snakelike grins — they looked like brothers

— said almost as one: "May we live to see the king himself
come visit our New York." These two new additions to the
round table were accompanied by a third newcomer. Hickey
slumped and, balancing his head in his right hand, his elbow
jutting across the table made like he was about to doze off.
He was more awake than ever. The third new man Hickey
thought could be an actor. He made great sweeping gestures
with each word and spoke in grand, flowery language dripping with honey and sweetness. His smile was that of a stage
actor. Life was a role in which he was currently starring. As
it turned out, once the introductions were made, this man
was, indeed, involved in the creative arts but he was not an
actor. His artistic specialty was engraving. Henry Dawkins,
newly released from the city lockup, had been invited to
tonight's session along with the other two newcomers, the
Young brothers. This Dawkins character was especially interesting. He had eyes like a ferret, darting constantly from
side to side as he spoke. His voice was calm, seemingly
friendly but mostly condescending. He seemed to be a conspiracy of one, his personal gain was the principle goal here.
The Youngs, Isaac and Israel, had made the arrangements.
This group would introduce them to Isaac Ketcham. The
paper man.

"You did say, my good man, that Mr. Ketcham would
be joining us this evening. Did you not?" said Dawkins to
Forbes with a broad smile.

"He'll be here or I'll have him printing stationery for
George Washington," said Forbes. The others laughed loudly. Dawkins laughed, too, but was really in no mood for this
frivolity. Since his first visit to the Youngs, he had been putting the pieces in place. He was nearing the deal of his life;
the big one that would finally allow him to live the way he
had meant to live. Ketcham, he hoped, would provide the
final element.

They had finished dinner and the waiter was filling up
the wine glasses again. Dawkins was getting less and less

bubbly, Hickey noticed. He kept looking up at the mantle clock. Forbes had the others in convulsive laughter with tales of customers at his gun shop.

It was after eight when a short, compact man in a heavy dark brown coat hurried through the front door of Sergeant's and went directly to the rear meeting room. Hickey could hear the muffled apologies for lateness and distinctly heard the words "stopped by ruffians" and the payment of "$20 colonial." Someone at the table said something about the highwaymen would be lucky if the payment was worth a shilling. Everyone laughed.

This must be the Ketcham they were waiting for, Hickey thought, sliding his head further down along his elbow, his cheek pushing into the table like a sot about to doze.

He was in luck. Ketcham had a clear, resonant voice and was obviously proud of his product. Hickey could hear most of what Ketcham said word-for-word. The comments and discussions by the others were broken, some voices clearer than others. Ketcham was displaying some special paper for the group. As the samples passed around the table, Ketcham described the unique properties of the paper and proclaimed it perfect for the project being undertaken. Hickey heard no protests to the contrary from the others. In fact, the smooth actor-type who had seemed most eager for Ketcham's arrival, was nearly ecstatic. He was rushing about the table proudly showing off the sample he held, oblivious to the fact that each person at the table already had a sample.

"About the supply...," started the actor. But before he could finish, Ketcham spoke.

"Unlimited. I have two thousand broad sheets I can have within two days. Ten times that much in a week or two."

"Perfect! Perfect!" said the actor. "This will be the best I've ever done. The best."

"How much do you need?" asked Ketcham.

Hickey saw that the group deferred to a compact sandy-haired man who had sat quietly through the proceedings. He hadn't said much or, at least, much that was audible. But Hickey heard clearly his next words.

"The governor says we are to begin with 100,000 and, perhaps, go as high as half a million." Hickey learned later from the barmaid that this was none other than David Matthews, Tory mayor of the city.

"Hallo!" thought Hickey. "That's it." He had begun to surmise what this eager group was up to. The mention of 100,000 threw him, at first. Could have been leaflets or something like that but, there is only one commodity that involves paper and "half a million." Money. Paper currency. This cozy little club was about to get into printing Colonials in a big way. Counterfeiters. Tory counterfeiters. Dumping $100,000 to half a million Colonial dollars into New York City right now could have disastrous effects. Already, the legions of small counterfeiters, coupled with the overprinting by the colonial committees, had made the paper currency sink like Washington's "turtle" with a hole blown in its side.

This little group, it seemed, was involved in more than just rum-fortified braggadocio in the name of the King. Now, thanks to this idiot Sears, he had an opportunity to, perhaps, get closer to the situation.

"This'un here, my fellow lovers of liberty," proclaimed Sears with a broad, thick-toothed grin, "swore to the good health of that pitiful diseased sovereign Georgie Three and ..."

"So did a hundred others in that tavern," exclaimed Ketcham. He was small but he had courage, thought Hickey. You had to give him that.

The man with the yellow teeth cuffed Ketcham on the back of the head. Ketcham tried to duck but didn't quite evade the attack. He took the blow, shook his head and stood even taller.

"And a feisty king lover he is," said Sears. "It's time we ..."

Again, Ketcham interrupted, shouting to the crowd watching the spectacle. "The only reason I'm up here is because I couldn't come up with a bribe large enough to please this ugly bilker."

Sears' smile disappeared. He grabbed the kettle filled with molten tar with his right hand and Ketcham's hair with his left. Ripping Ketcham's head back, Sears tipped the kettle, aiming for his mouth but the kettle wouldn't come forward. It was caught, something was holding it back.

Thomas Hickey, much to Phoebe's surprise, had leaped onto the side of the cart and grabbed Sears' wrist. Sears was a bull of a man but Hickey's huge hand easily encircled the man's wrist. There was a second of helplessness when Sears looked at Hickey, attempted to move the kettle downward and, when it wouldn't budge, looked back at Hickey in disbelief.

"What the hell do you think you're up to?" shouted Sears, regaining his bully's stance. "Yer interferin' with a duly appointed committee of the colonial congress. This is treason. Unhand me or tar 'n' feathers will be mild to what'll happen to you. Get this man off me!" Sears screamed at his thugs. He tried to move the kettle again.

Hickey tightened his grip and gave a short tug upwards. Pain raced up Sears' arm toward his brain. His hand opened and the kettle bounced off the cart rail and landed on the road, tar bubbling out in a slick, dark puddle.

"Whoa, gentleman, before you do anything you'll regret. Let me tell my story."

"Let him tell nothin'," screamed Sears', saliva spraying from his lips. "I told you to get him off me." The man with the yellow teeth and the tall one who had been in charge of the feathers, took a step toward the cart.

"This is for your own safety," said Hickey. "I'm trying to stop you from making a big mistake. I do this in the name of liberty, believe me." Hickey had formulated a quick plan from the moment he recognized Ketcham. He was making the rest up as he went along. "Obviously you have been given bad information. This man is a merchant, a well-respected merchant from Philadelphia. I overheard him talking in Fraunces Tavern about having business with His Excellency George Washington himself. You all know General Washington is on his way here right now. My lady friend is Black Sam Fraunces' daughter. The Fraunces believe in liberty. All of you know what side they are on. I've overheard that this gentleman has business to do with the general from Virginia himself. Isn't that right, Miss Fraunces?," Hickey looked at Phoebe for approval.

"Why, I, uh, yes. Yes, I believe so," said Phoebe too surprised to think about an answer.

"So, you see, gents," said Hickey quickly not giving Sears' or his men time to think about what he had said. "I am certain that Sons of Liberty such as yourselves would not want to be tarrin' and featherin' a man who has business with the great Washington himself. Would you now? Follow me here, gents. If I am wrong, you can always come back and get me and the gentleman from Philadelphia and make a pair of black barnyard roosters out of us both. Ain't that right? There may be a shortage of a lot of things but ain't no shortage of tar and feathers is there?" Hickey flashed his most brilliant smile, carefully loosening his grip on Sears.

Sears pulled his hand away as quickly as he was released. Sears was a thug. He was a bully of the first order. He had some clout what with his connections to Delancey and Gen. Lee. But, in the end, he wasn't stupid. Gen. Lee was not around. The colonials found his services useful but they, too, were getting very nervous. He was going too far. When Washington arrived, the political balance would change. If this story was true, maybe this short but incredibly strong stranger with the giant balls had actually saved him from trouble. After all, all he had on the guy was that when Will Cobbes and his boys had stopped him on the North Road a week or two ago, the man had made some remark about damned, lawless hooligans "masquerading as Sons of Liberty." The heat was on throughout the city with Tryon out in the harbor and Washington on his way. It might be best to skip this bit of fun. And, maybe, there's an added benefit to all of this ... I'd like to have this "friend of the Fraunces" cracking heads for me.

"Never let a man in this city say that Isaac Sears is not a man of reason and a true believer in liberty," Sears said pulling out a sailor's knife and cutting the bindings on Ketcham.

Sears climbed out of the cart and, the excitement over, the crowd broke into a several smaller groups joking and laughing as they spread into the side streets, discussing the sound of the tar on flesh and the look on the man's face as the feathers snowed onto the sticky mess.

"You got one helluva strong arm on you son," said Sears to Hickey. "I can use a man with your talents, especially one who believes in the cause."

"I don't believe in much," replied Hickey. "I believe in myself." He paused as if thinking. "About it, really." Taking Phoebe by the hand, he began to walk back toward the Broad Way.

"I'll be talking with you," added Sears, talking to Hickey's back. Hickey did not answer.

"Thomas. I have not seen you like that. You could have been killed. I was ..."

Phoebe was interrupted by the earnest voice of a man hurrying to catch up with them.

"Sir. Sir. Let me thank you for saving me much pain and even greater humiliation," said Ketcham.

Hickey turned and smiled. "My pleasure."

"How did you... I mean, I am a merchant and I, well, I do come from Philadelphia. How did you ... why did ...?"

"Just happened to be in a tavern a couple days ago when you arrived. Overheard someone say they were waiting for this merchant from Philadelphia. And, in you walked."

"What about General Washington? I wouldn't recognize him if he popped up right in front of us right now. I've got no business with the general nor Mr. Fraunces."

"You know that. Now I know that. But that arsehole Sears don't know that. Men like him flit from scent to scent changing their ideals and notions on the spot. I don't think you have to worry about him. In fact, he tried to offer me a job and he don't know me either."

"A job knocking heads for the colonial committee?"

"I told him I don't really believe in one side or the other. Believe in me and...," Hickey looked at Phoebe, "this most beautiful living creature on God's earth. Those things is all. That's what I believe."

"Perhaps I might buy you a drink some time," said Ketcham, his voicing returning to its normal resonance.

"I'd like that," said Hickey, "Never pass up a free one. I'll be at Corbie's tonight at 8. If I see you then, I'll gladly drink your health."

"I'll see you there," said Ketcham, buttoning his shirt and slowing his pace. He took one last glance at Hickey and Phoebe and turned into Wall Street.

"That was a courageous thing you did, Thomas," said Phoebe. "I was frozen. I don't know whether from terror or fascination. You've got a mighty strong arm there, Mr. Hickey," said Phoebe, hooking her left arm in the crook of his right. "I must say you make my life much more interesting to say the very least. But what of this visit to Corbie's Tavern tonight? I know I have no hold on you, Thomas. But must you go to these taverns every night?"

Hickey had not given a second thought to the fact that he said he would meet Ketcham at Corbie's. Corbie's, according to his last bit of espionage, might be the center of Tory activity in the city. It had never crossed his mind to lie to Phoebe. He told her the truth when she asked what he would be doing on a particular night. He did not tell her why he was frequenting these taverns but not volunteering all the facts was not lying.

Phoebe read his face and, seeing him search for an answer, said: "Thomas, your business is your own. It is just that, well, I worry you'll meet some one more to your liking at one of these places. Someone more, uh, accomplished in what a man needs and wants. And, I ...."

Hickey stopped, turned himself in front of her and kissed her. "I go to the tavern at night for a few rums to help me sleep. Otherwise, I lay awake thinking about being with you."

"Perhaps, some time, I will be able to ...," her voice fluttered and she drew in a gulp of needed air, "... help you sleep better." They kissed again.

Chapter Fifteen

Abraham Mortier Estate, Richmond
Hill, just north of New York City
11:30 a.m., Friday, April 26, 1776

It was one thing, thought George Washington, to rally a sorry-looking army of farmers against the British encampments at Boston. At least the farmers had a vague idea that they were fighting for a cause. New York City was another tale altogether. Loyalism was rampant. The New York Committee of Safety and the Provincial Congress of New York loathed the idea of total independence, although they continued to support the fortification of the city against the British. The city itself was virtually indefensible forming a one-mile square at the southern tip of Manhattan Island. An island, for God's sake. It was like changing places with the King's men in Boston. This morning's report said he had only 8,300 men fit for duty. Fitness was a relative term. Perhaps, half that number actually could be counted on in battle. And who would the opponent be in the defense of this island? The greatest navy the world has ever known.

This was the first opportunity since arriving in New York to sit at his desk and catch up on correspondence. He had been in New York for ten days. It seemed like months. For better or worse, he had inherited a plan for the fortification of the city from General Lee. Batteries were already under construction. It was too late to start from scratch. The work

continued with Washington concentrating on bringing some
military discipline to the restless soldiers crowded into the
city. More than two dozen courts martial had been held in
these ten days. Offenses ranged from desertion, drunkenness and disorderly conduct to succumbing to the temptations of the whores of the Holy Ground and trafficking with
the enemy. This latter offense was the most troubling to
Washington. There was a regular commerce between soldiers and Tories. Several reports had soldiers even loading
small boats with goods bound for Gov. Tryon aboard the
HMS Duchess of Gordon in the harbor.

Congress had not yet been able to pressure the New
York Committee of Safety to recruit troops. Washington
had already issued an appeal to the committee as well as the
committees of New Jersey and Connecticut to send 2,000 to
2,500 militia men to help defend the city. There was no response. It might be true that The British had gone to Canada
to regroup but, as far as he was concerned, the assault on
him personally had already begun. Congress was busy puffing and snorting and sparking egos. They voted him a gold
medal which he basically had to design himself. But they
never stopped for an instant the fretting and second-guess-
ing. The safety committees were just biding time trying to
gauge what side to support. Several of the congressionally-
appointed generals had made it clear that Washington had
not improved much in military skill since the French and
Indian conflict. And now he was blessed with an army of
puerile hooligans with their brains in their crotches. But that
is precisely why God chose him for this task. The country
needed his granite-hard resolve and leadership.

It was a lot like the inscription on the honorary Doctor of
Laws degree given him by Harvard earlier in the month. He
knew it was not born of intellectual inquiry but, nevertheless, considering his early aversion to school, he delighted
in the honor — only the second time Harvard had granted
such an honor in 140 years. The inscription read: "There

is the greatest propriety in conferring such an honor on ...
the accomplished general who ... without hesitation left all
pleasures of his delightful seat in Virginia, and the affairs
of his own estate ... without accepting any reward that he
might deliver New England from the unjust and cruel arms
of Britain."

He would not be deterred. It was a lot like operating
Mount Vernon. Get a little lazy and all goes to seed. These
men, like his slaves back home, needed discipline. They
crave it. They want it but don't know it. And when they get
it, they produce. Great things result. Look at Mount Vernon
on a glorious Virginia morning in May. All of this glory
comes from hard work, discipline and leadership by the few
who know how to lead. No, he wouldn't be deterred. The
single most important element was loyalty. He must have
their loyalty. Now, it seemed, there were major doubts about
the loyalty of New Yorkers. He would have to get to the root
of this. They had already gone too far to turn back now.

Mustering all of his tact and political skill, Washington
had begun to politely but firmly force the Provincial Congress to do his bidding. All communication and fraternization with the men-of-war in the harbor was banned. Severe
punishment was to be dealt to those who violated this most
basic concept of military discipline. He has also persuaded
the congress to name a local commander to head the city's
militia. It was simply amazing to Washington that the command of the militia had up to this point rested in the congress
as a body. Every order had to be voted on. They were reluc-
tant to lose the slightest hint of control. But they had come
around. Brigadier General John Morin Scott was named
commander. He was a solid, likable man and an outspoken
patriot. He would answer only to Washington.

None of the other New York State militia generals answered to Washington. The new commander-in-chief was
especially miffed by the status of Brigadier General Nathaniel Woodhull. The Provincial Congress had given him total

control of the militia on Long Island. He could order them into direct conflict with the British, without "delaying" for directions from the Provincial Congress. This was, in fact, a license for Woodhull to fight his own war without consulting the Provincial Congress, the Continental Congress or the commander-in-chief. It didn't hurt, of course, that Woodhull just happened to be the president of the Provincial Congress as well.

As annoying as these problems were, Washington relished the challenge. It had been a year already since Lexington and Concord and the freedom movement hadn't been snuffed out yet. Besides New York held some fond memories for him. He had visited the city at age 22, enjoying the miniatures of the Microcosm in the Royal Exchange at Broadway and Pearl Streets, and the amusements of the gardens along the Hudson. He remembered feeling a certain worldliness, New York, even then at half the size it was now, seemed more cosmopolitan than most of the southern cities with which he was familiar. He had carried with him his well-worn copy of "The Gentle Art of Polite Behavior" and had fallen hard for Miss Mary Phillipse, sister-in-law of Beverly Robinson, son of the speaker of the Virginia Assembly with whom he was travelling. Mary had rejected him falling instead for a British captain.

He was responding to a letter from John Adams informing him he had been awarded a gold medal by Congress for his efforts at Boston.

"That it will ever be my highest ambition to approve myself a faithful servant of the public," he wrote. Always aware in his writings that destiny would have others read his letters besides the addressee, he had begun this letter several times. Too humble. Too weak. Too ingratiating. He had to strike the right balance of strength and humility. There were factions in the Congress still not pleased with his stewardship of the army. He added, "...and that to be in any degree instrumental in procuring for my American brethren a restitution of their rights and privileges will constitute my chief happiness." This, he felt, was just right. He had originally written "a restitution of their freedom" but felt that would be misconstrued as a call for total independence. He would end with giving credit to his men. "They were indeed at first a band of rabble...." No. Not rabble. Too demeaning to the congressional representatives who had delivered the recruits to him. "They were indeed at first a band of undisciplined husbandmen but it is (under God) to their bravery and attention to their duty that I am indebted for the success which procured for me the only reward I wish to receive, the affection and esteem of my countrymen."

He paused and looked out the window of the second floor study of this elegant Mortier residence high on a knoll of the Lispenard Farm. Abraham Mortier, a major in the King's service, had built Richmond Hill on a hill facing Hudson's River. The view was unobstructed. Washington could see the shore through groves of trees whose leaves were just now beginning to burst from the bare limbs of the stands of aspens and maples. The view to the right or north stretched all the way to the tiny hamlet of Greenwich Village. To the south was the city. From the balcony over the tall columns at the front of the house, you could see all the way to the Common, inside the city wall with only trees and gentle hills in between. Washington knew he would enjoy this place from the moment his carriage entered through the large ornamental gate and passed by a beautiful little tree-lined water collect known as Burr's Pond.

There was a knock at the door.

"Yes."

"Your madeira, your excellency," said the lovely young teenaged girl shyly.

"Yes, yes, bring it right in, my dear. Set it right there. Thank you, Miss Fraunces, eh, Phoebe isn't it?"

"Yes, sir. You're welcome."

"I cannot thank your father or, of course, you enough for

volunteering your services to help with the domestic require-
ments. My Martha will be along shortly but I would be lost
in the household duties without your assistance." He smiled
a thin grin to hide the large, fake teeth and his eyes would
not give up the sight of her smooth brown skin. It almost
glowed. Her breasts, straining against the bodice were not
lost on him either. What a wonderful addition to the elegant
furnishings. Washington felt a brief tightness in his stomach,
a small barely perceptible ache. Fraunces had volunteered
to cater the meals at the headquarters and, when asked for
domestic help, had readily insisted his own daughter was the
only one to be trusted with such a responsibility.

Phoebe didn't mind at all. It was a welcome change
from the tavern. She loved the gardens encircling the mansion. She took long walks about the farmlands. The work
was quite easy. Washington was not very demanding of her,
although she could not help notice the way he stared at her
when he thought she wasn't looking. She had heard many a
conversation in the tavern about the general's appetites. But,
so far, he hadn't made any unseemly requests. It was quite
nice. Of course, the fact she was near to Thomas and away
from her family was far from last on her list of why she liked
this new position. Washington had given Thomas a position
on his personal guard staff. Thomas looked so handsome in
his uniform with the special sash of the Life Guard. When
he wasn't on duty, they would walk and talk for hours. There
was, however, one disappointment. Despite the position of
responsibility on the general's guard staff, her father had not
softened his view of Thomas Hickey. Hickey he told her
doesn't give a thistle about patriotism.

"He muscled his way into that job just to impress you. In
fact, I believe he used you to get that post. His excellency,
George Washington, deserves better from us in this city."
Black Sam had said, "I don't trust that Hickey. Never have
and never will."

"You don't even know him, father. Thomas is gentle and

kind. He makes me feel alive in a city that is dying before our eyes. Just look around."

"I won't have you brokenhearted, Phoebe. Thomas Hickey is not the kind to settle down to gainful enterprise. He will have nothing of children and a wife. One day, he will be gone. I must insist you stay away from him."

He would come around. It would take time but eventually her father would see the gentleness and goodness that she saw.

"Phoebe?" Washington saw the sweet young girl lost in thought.

"Er, yessir. Will there be anything else?" Phoebe asked.

"No, not now. Perhaps, later." Phoebe left, closing the door quietly behind her.

Washington drifted from his work. How did an unrefined oaf like Hickey manage to attract such a prize? He wondered if Hickey had managed to bed her yet. If Martha didn't arrive soon, he was certain the idea would grow stronger in his own mind. But, Phoebe Fraunces was one luxury he could not afford. It would be political suicide. No, satisfying his needs required much more subtlety. Of course, he had some skill at that as well. Besides, Black Sam Fraunces had taken care of that, too, just fine. In fact, the ache in his groin would be gone within a few hours. It was, after all, the one small vice he required. A negligible price for the responsibilities he had assumed. Men who assumed the burden of power were to be forgiven for their needs.

Washington continued staring out the window, deep in thought. Hickey was an interesting case. Washington had recruited him for his toughness and his seeming indifference to the moral struggle in which they were involved. Their argument at the test of the Turtle was, at least for his part, a sham. Washington cared not a whit whether Hickey was a patriot. In fact, it was his indifference to politics that had attracted him. Hickey was only one of dozens. He hadn't expected a great deal. The conversation at the Turtle test site left little to the imagination. Hickey was no genius. He might provide a nugget or two to earn his keep but that was all. A nugget here and there from a score of informers and Washington might develop a solid intelligence base.

Hickey had surprised him. From the start, there were regular reports, sometimes two and three a week. It was good, usable information. Nothing of major consequence but very workable intelligence. He had provided names of ardent Tories. He had listed locations of meeting places for Loyalist groups. He had reported on the mood of the troops and the bribes being collected for protection in the name of the commanding general himself. Then there was the latest report of a counterfeiting ring. Not really unusual throughout the northern colonies these days. But, nevertheless, an interesting cast of characters. And, if it turned out to be the basis for something larger, he would take action. Yet, Washington had to agree with Sam Fraunces that a soldier who deserted one army could desert another. Washington, not revealing Hickey as one of a corps of personal spies, had a long talk with Sam Fraunces at a Masonic meeting the fourth night after he had arrived. They agreed that Hickey was out to take care of only one patriotic cause -- his own.

At first, Washington dismissed the idea that Hickey be named to the Life Guard. Spies were invisible. Intelligence agents did not parade around in the uniform of the general's personal guard. That defeated the purpose. But Hickey had been persuasive. He made a good argument for the notion that the best place to hide is in full view. "No one thinks to look there," he said, smiling that entrancing smile. "If I wear my Guard uniform into a Tory tavern and get a little drunk and curse the good general and his heavy-handed discipline, I just may get more information than if I scurry through the gutters trying to scrounge up tidbits here and there," he said. Washington had seen the value in that but it was Hickey's insistence that he needed the legitimacy of the uniform to be able to court Phoebe. He had actually used the word "court."

Washington found that very funny. Hickey had cuckolded.
He had poked and prodded every orifice of every shape and
size woman made. He had charmed and smiled and plied
with rum women of all ages. He had worn his doodle to
a thread in the doing but courting was not something one
associated with a man like Hickey. In the end, Hickey was
so sincere, so earnest about Phoebe, that Washington had
consented figuring the end of a single source such as Hickey
would not mean much. In fact, he might make a good body-
guard. He was tough and looking to impress the Fraunces
girl. If someone decided to do away with the commander-
in-chief, Hickey with his bull-like shoulders and bear paw
hands just might spoil their plans. Washington agreed.

The commander-in-chief turned back to his desk. He
checked his list of correspondence. Next on this: Write
mother. He had not written to Mary Washington since leaving Philadelphia. Why bother? It would be more of the
same. He would write friendly greetings and talk of his
work. She would reply that she had been abandoned by
her son and was destitute, having no money with which to
live a civilized life. She was forever overspending. She
would spend far beyond the income of her estates and then
complain to her son that he neglected her needs. Everything
from money for butter to bolts of silk was on her list of commodities she felt he should secure for her. He scratched the
note from the pad and went on to the next item.

He was working on a plan to organize the New York
troops into four brigades. Though thin, the brigades would
provide defense where needed. One brigade along the Hudson, another to the north, a third on the Long Island and the
fourth in the city itself. He could probably defend the west
end of Long Island with four or five thousand men. Cross-
fire could keep the East River fairly secure. The various
batteries along both rivers could hold off the British men-
of-war for a while. The fortifications and batteries around
the city proper would hold if they could prevent the ships

from direct attack. He made notes assigning Heath to the Hudson brigade and Spencer to the Rutgers Farm and Jones Hill brigade area. Greene was placed in charge of the Long Island troops and Stirling was to center his brigade along the Bowery Road. There was another knock at the door.

"Come in," he said, anticipating another look at Phoebe.

It was not Phoebe. It was a man dressed as a farmhand, in patched breeches and vest, rough boots and a beaten brown cap. He said nothing. He walked to the desk, pulled a slip of paper from his pocket and slid it toward the general.

Washington, too, said nothing. He unfolded the paper and read.

"There is a deadly plot afoot. Your man Hickey has been seen with those who are known to be involved. Regular traffic between Corbie's Tavern and the Royal Governor Tryon speaks to this plotting. I will have details for you within a few days."

Washington waved the farmhand to the door. He left.

A plot. Hickey, too, had mentioned several Tory plots overheard in the taverns. But, he had not reported anything of substance. It was certain that Hickey would be mentioned in these reports. He frequented those taverns where the plots were hatching in order to secure information. He had gained their confidence. His plan to have spies answerable only to him was working. At this point, such plots seemed little more than rum talk. He could have one agent check another. He could get two or three views of the same situation and draw his own conclusions. Still, Hickey would have to be watched. He might be persuaded for the right price to send the same information to the Duchess of Gordon.

Deep in thought, Washington turned in his chair to again look out over the blossoming countryside toward the river. There was movement along the path to the left which led down to the orchards. It was Phoebe. She was holding hands with a man wearing a uniform with a Guard sash.

Hickey. Was he using her, too. Or had this ruffian really fallen in love? To be 30 or so and exploring the virgin territory of a Phoebe, could make a man do strange things. Nevertheless, Hickey would bear watching. They all would. There was treachery afoot these days. He would have to be very careful.

A few hours later, he was being jostled along the Broad Way toward the southern tip of the city. Guards rode ahead and behind. One couldn't be too careful.

"See what happened to young Private Meeks?" said Tom Barnes. "Got his jewels sliced off. The bitchfoxy hag cut'em clean off. Left his cock. Barely."

Hickey winced at the thought, reining his horse to avoid a hole in the road. He glanced back over his right shoulder to see if everything was all right with Washington. He, Barnes, Green, Martin and Lieutenant Gilbert Lockner, who was riding in the carriage with the general, had drawn duty this evening. Their job as members of the general's personal guard staff, was to escort Washington's carriage to the Masonic meeting at Fraunces Tavern. The meeting and social gathering afterward would take about four hours. Lockner, who was a Mason, would stay with Washington. The others could do as they pleased as long as they were back at Fraunces by 10 o'clock. It was an unusually warm spring evening. A perfect night, in fact, for a walk with Phoebe but he had some other business to which he had to attend.

"Don't go up to the Holy Ground much anymore," said Hickey. "Everybody's too crazy now. You can't even have a drink without someone breaking a chair over your head or some whore sticking a knife in your neck. Besides, I got other things to worry about."

"Like how to get the virgin daughter of Black Sam in bed," chuckled Barnes.

"Yeah," said Hickey bristling at his fellow Lifeguard bringing Phoebe's name into a conversation in the same breath as the strumpets of the Holy Ground. But he recog-

nized the good natured joshing for what it was and, taking
Barnes by surprise, said: "She's the most beautiful woman I
have ever seen. I'm going to marry her."

"Marry!? Settle down? Tom Hickey? Never thought I'd
hear that. Besides you don't want no used goods in your
wedding bed. Word is that old General Crotchthrob here is
putting the boots to her already."

Hickey whirled in his saddle, leaned toward Barnes and
grabbed a massive handful of his guard sash, nearly yanking
him with a single hand out of his saddle. Surprise and fear
swept over Barnes' leathery, gap-toothed face.

"No one gets near Phoebe! No one. I don't care if he's a
general or the goddamned king. Get it? Fucking Washington
puts one Virginia gentleman's hand on my Phoebe, I'll kill
him. Understand?" Hickey's voice was taut and quivering
with emotion.

Barnes, now slightly recovered, tried unsuccessfully to
dislodge Hickey's handhold. "Tom. Tom. Look, it was just
a joke. We all know the general's got a steady stream of
female visitors applying to take care of his needs while Mrs.
Washington is on her way to the city."

Hickey continued to yank on the sash. A shout came
from the carriage. "General wants to know what's going on
up there."

Hickey released his grip, slightly at first, then completely. "Nothing," he yelled back to Lockner, "just a lark."

"The general says to look sharp. People are looking to us
as good examples."

"Right," said Hickey.

Hickey and Barnes road on looking straight ahead but
still talking. Hickey had regained his composure.

"Didn't know you were so touchy, Thomas," said
Barnes.

"Look, didn't mean nothing Barnes. But I see the way
he looks at her and I want to strangle him. I don't like her
working up there. Don't like it at all. Surrounded by all

those fine things and him practically falling over her with his Virginia gentleman's charm."

"I wouldn't worry none, Thomas," said Barnes, "I see the way that young lady looks at you. Nothing to worry about."

Hickey nodded but was not convinced. He would have to talk with Phoebe again about working for Washington. They road on without talking. The driver of the coach made a mental note to tell the general about Hickey's vow to kill him. Might be nothing but it might also mean a small bonus.

Fraunces Tavern was in a fine brick building along the southern wharves near where soldiers had constructed a new battery. Washington had been to Fraunces twice in the two weeks since arriving in New York but this was the first Masonic meeting. Lieutenant Lockner, whose father was a banker on Long Island, had been a Mason for only a few years but it was proving to be an asset in his young army career. Washington seemed to enjoy his company and preferred the young officer for such off-duty hour activities.

Barnes planned to set himself in the rear room of a tavern not far from Fraunces along the docks. There he could find a hot dice game to occupy the next few hours and, perhaps, make a few dollars.

Hickey was still doing double duty. He would like nothing better than a few hours with Phoebe on such a warm evening. During the past week, their relationship had become slightly more passionate though they were still far from fully consummating their love. Hickey discreetly adjusted his pants as his groin swelled at the mere thought of Tuesday night. He and Phoebe had walked toward the river from Washington's quarters. Stopping along the path out of sight of the mansion, Hickey had embraced Phoebe and they kissed long and deep. As he held her face in his hands, staring into her eyes, she had reached down to his hips and had pulled him close to her, his hardness pressing into her belly even through the several layers of her clothing. In a burst of sheer delight, she took his hand and dragged him playfully into the tall trees just now budding after the harsh winter. Surveying the perfect spot, she lay on her back and pulled him down on her. He propped himself on his elbows, a little surprised at her exuberance and concerned he might crush her. She wrapped her arms around his neck and pulled him down and they rolled one over the other, kissing. Drinking in large draughts the love that was welling between them. Every move was new to Hickey. Not that he hadn't done all of this before. But never with someone he cared about as much. He didn't want to make a mistake, to make her think he only wanted her body. Sensing this, Phoebe became the aggressor. She pushed him off, sat up and lowered the shoulders of her bodice, pulling the cloth down to her waist. Hickey gasped. Phoebe smiled and, rolling him on his back, sat on his hips, lowering her breasts to his lips. Hickey's groin exploded and moistened his pants like a virgin. This hadn't happened to him in 20 years. They kissed and lay in each other's arms for an hour. Hickey could not even imagine what it would be like to fully make love to Phoebe.

***

Now, instead of heading for Phoebe's arms, he was heading to Corbie's Tavern, a Tory stronghold not far from Washington's headquarters. This spy thing was wearing thin. Not only was he required to perform the duties of the Lifeguard, so as not to draw suspicion, but he had to spend his "off duty" time combing the city for information useful to Washington. But, it would all be worth it. One thing Washington did was to pay promptly. He had a substantial amount saved already, including a couple of bonus payments for especially valuable reports. If the city survived the coming battle, regardless of who was the victor, he would be in good shape. He had made certain of that. He and Phoebe could move west, have a family. Their own home. It was worth it.

After escorting Washington into the building, Hickey got back on his horse and headed north. A half hour later, he pulled up outside the small tavern that was openly known as a hotbed for Tory sympathizing. This was not unusual in a city in which the mayor was still a supporter of the royal governor and the Provincial Congress was not yet fully convinced of the need for independence or anything even closely representing such freedom, despite their pronouncements to the contrary.

Hickey tied his horse and pushed open the heavy, leaded glass door and stepped into the warmth of the main sitting room. Night temperatures were still in the 40s and a fire had been lit in the cut stone fireplace. Hickey looked around for a recognizable face. The thin man with the long nose and sharp point of gray hair in the center of an expanse of reddened scalp sat at a table in the darkened rear corner of the room. Henry Dawkins appeared to be explaining some great joke to the two reptilian-looking men at the table. The two white-haired men, looking like twins, seemed to be thoroughly enjoying the conversation. Their eyes darted at unpredictable angles as they spoke and their long tentacle-like fingers walked in the air. The Youngs brothers, Israel and Isaac, had joined Henry Dawkins to show Hickey their grand creation.

He had been introduced to the three men by Isaac Ketcham that night in the tavern after having saved Ketcham's soft body from the ravages of boiling hot tar. He was surprised to find he wasn't the only member of Washington's Life Guard invited. Sitting at the table already was Private Michael Lynch. Lynch was more upset than Hickey. He seemed to search for an escape route until Hickey smiled, put his hand on the young man's shoulder and sat next to him. He was amazed at how quickly they had taken him into their confidence and told him their plans. Even now as he walked to the back of the room in this den of King lovers wearing the sash of Washington's Lifeguard, the men jumped from their seats and embraced him. Ketcham had told the members of the cabal that Hickey had saved him from the blistering tar of Sears' tribunal. He had been invited to several meetings since then, accepted as one of them. Even when Hickey turned up in the Life Guard uniform, they were more interested in hearing about Washington than distancing themselves from him. He explained he needed the job, talked about Phoebe and said he might even help the conspirators from his new position. They had nodded impatiently and moved on with business.

"Something wonderful it is we have to reveal to you this fine evening," hissed Henry Dawkins.

"Yes, yes, fine it is. Fine," said one of the brothers. Even after four meetings, Hickey could not distinguish between Israel and Isaac.

"Perfection. The best ever. Simply and utterly the best," squealed the other brother.

"Give me time to get a drink first," said Hickey settling into the chair.

"It's coming already," said Dawkins. "Here look at this work of art!" Dawkins handed Hickey a small piece of paper.

Hickey studied both sides of the paper. It was a New Jersey Three Pound Note. A strange looking leaf formed the center of the note with small dingbat bugs and flowers and the like around the border. "Printed by Isaac Collins," was printed under the leaf and it carried the date, "Burlington, 1776." Isaac Youngs joked that Dawkins had toyed with the idea of printing Isaac Youngs rather than Isaac Collins on the false bills. In an ironic twist, the Dawkins masterpiece copied the slogan on one end of the bill, "'Tis Death to Counterfeit." Hickey turned the note over, studied the printing, ruffled the paper through his fingers. It looked just like the real thing. In fact, it looked even better than the real thing.

"A work of art," said Hickey feigning enthusiasm.

Dawkins reached into the wide, deep, patched pocket of his coat and pulled out a cube of these notes tied with string. "Here's two hundred," he said. "That's 600 pounds! Pass them around. Have a good time. Just give us a little something as you put them into circulation."

"That's too much," protested Hickey.

"Nonsense," said the Youngs in unison.

"We're all putting them out. There's plenty more where that came from. Forbes wants 100,000 pounds!"

Forbes, Hickey knew, was one of the men in the conversations at the Sergeant at Arms. Was he passing counterfeit notes part of some larger scheme? Washington might pay well for the answers to questions like that.

"What's the matter, Thomas?" asked Dawkins, "A problem?"

"No," said Hickey, not at all. "How much have you printed?"

"Well, we haven't finished the Forbes order yet but we're close. We also have 100,000 Continental Dollars ready to go."

"At the rate prices are going up," said one of the Youngs, "we'll have to print faster and faster. West Indian rum is more than twice what it was last year. Sugar has doubled since January — two shillings six a pound! Unbelievable. And salt, forget it. If you can find some to buy, it costs 8 shillings 6 pence, three times what it cost just a few months ago. It's this war. It is much too costly. But, of course, we have no worries about prices now. Do we?"

Hickey was quite certain that neither Dawkins nor the Youngs brothers were involved with anything beyond counterfeiting. For them, this was the grandest scheme of all. They were proud, and rightfully so, of their masterpieces. From what he could tell, when the Youngs or Dawkins were invited to a meeting at the Sergeant at arms, the topic was limited to counterfeiting. There was no discussion of doing the King's bidding or any such business. In his meetings with the trio, they had not themselves ever mentioned being part of a larger scheme. Pure and simple greed was their motivator. Were the backroom conspirators simply making use of Dawkins' talents to finance their goals? If Hickey could determine that, it might make his final pay day. One way or the other. Hickey slipped the pack of three pound notes into his pocket and sipped his drink. He had another hour before heading back to Fraunces.

***

As Hickey was pocketing the bogus money, the Masonic ritual in the Long Room upstairs at Fraunces was coming to a close. Washington was impressed by Sam Fraunces deep, resonant voice, which seemed to vibrate the windows as he spoke. Fraunces brought the session to a close and then walked directly to Washington.

"I am worried, general, that my Phoebe is getting in too deeply with this Hickey fellow," said Fraunces in the same clear voice but much now much lower and more conversational. "I don't trust him. I have men tell me all the time that they see him in Sergeant's and Corbie's and all over the whorehouses. I personally don't care if he rots from the syphilis but if he ever ... if my Phoebe ... I'd kill him, general. No doubt, no hesitation."

"Sgt. Hickey does his job for me quite well. That's all I can tell you. Other than that I know very little about him," said Washington not revealing the duality of Hickey's employment.

"Can't you order him to stay away from her?"

"You and I both know I can't do that. It would do no good, Sam. We cannot watch them every minute. Let me thank you again for sending Phoebe to help with the house. She is a joy to be around. Very efficient. All I can do is keep them both as busy as possible. I will tell him about your feelings. I will try to make certain he knows how you feel and that I value your services and would not want a solider of mine upsetting the citizenry," said Washington, knowing he could solve all of Sam Fraunces concerns if he could tell him that his daughter's suitor is a spy for the patriotic cause. That was out of the question.

"All I know is if he soils my Phoebe, I will kill him."

"I promise you I'll support whatever you feel you have to do but give it some room. Give it a chance."

"I will try, sir. There is so much treachery in this city now, so much anxiety. I just know Hickey is in the thick of it. You know what they say about my people from the West Indies. They have a sense about these things. I sense Thomas Hickey is not what he seems. In fact, I would be careful if I were you, General Washington."

Fraunces went to attend to the cleaning up of the room and to direct the serving of the wine and refreshments.

Washington exchanged pleasantries with the other masons and was offered the first glass of madeira which he accepted and from which he took a hefty first sip. His eye caught a man who he had noticed during the ceremony. A stranger. A trim, athletic looking man in his early thirties, the stranger had looked directly at Washington several times during the ceremony. Again, the man stared at him and this time walked toward him.

"General Washington, it is an honor. James Gibson, sir. Of Connecticut."

"Mr. Gibson," said Washington coolly but politely. "What brings you to New York?"

"I have a message for you," said Gibson, lowering his voice and turning his back to the room. "A message from Dr. Benjamin Church."

Washington was surprised. Church had been convicted of treason. Washington and his staff had made the judgment. Washington wanted to hang Church but the Articles of War, in particular Article 28, provided only that a person caught communicating with the enemy should suffer such punishment as a court martial saw fit. Unfortunately, Article 51 limited this punishment to 39 lashes or a fine of two months' pay and/or cashiering from the service. That was a year ago, since then Washington had petitioned the Congress for the death penalty for such an offense and they agreed. But it could not be applied retroactively. So, Dr. Benjamin Church, former chief physician of the new Continental Army, former confidant of patriots at the highest levels, languished in a jail in Connecticut. He still maintained his innocence although the deciphered message clearly implicated him as a traitor.

"I am afraid I have nothing else to add on that matter," said Washington curtly.

"I understand, sir," said Gibson. "As you know, Dr. Church maintains he was simply protecting his position among the British which, in his eyes, enabled him to provide very valuable information to you and your cause."

"We examined all of the available evidence at the tribunal, Mr. Gibson. As I said, I have nothing else to add."

"Dr. Church understands that position. He simply asked me to deliver information to you that may prove valuable. He does this only as a gesture of good faith and in the hopes that you can help with his release in the future."

"I would not rely too heavily on that event taking place, Mr. Gibson."

Unperturbed, Gibson continued: "General, you have on your personal staff a member of your own guard named Thomas Hickey. Sergeant Hickey, I believe. Word had reached Dr. Church of this and he felt you should be warned that Mr. Hickey may be a Tory sympathizer. Dr. Church, who as you know, was able to move in and out of Boston freely during the occupation, personally saw Mr. Hickey roaming freely through the upstairs sleeping quarters of a home used as quarters by British officers. On several other occasions, Dr. Church saw Mr. Hickey moving among and in the company of British soldiers. He was quite friendly with them, sharing drinks and toasts. Please be careful, Gen-

eral Washington. Dr. Church provides this information to
help your cause and to protect you from the possibility of a
breach of information."

"I will take this matter under advisement," said Washington not committing to helping Church in any way. Hancock
had told Washington that Hickey went into Boston frequently
for him. But, he never mentioned that Hickey had dealings
directly with British officers or drank with the troops. Had
Hickey ingratiated himself with Hancock? In fact, asked to
be put in the confidence of the new commander-in-chief for
other reasons? Thomas Hickey was becoming more of a nui-
sance than anything else. Sam Fraunces knew the power in
this city very well. He couldn't afford to offend him. Now,
Hickey was getting in deep with his daughter. He was too
visible. Two reports tonight alone had Hickey in with the enemy. But that was why he was being paid. Was he being paid
from both sides? It was time to set Hickey straight. Maybe
he should just sign off on the land now and send him on
his way. But, from a practical standpoint, Hickey was very
close to revealing the details of this counterfeiting ring.

He also had hinted at a much more serious plot. His pragmatic side took over. If he could be seen as foiling a major
Tory plot, it might be just the political ammunition he needed
to gain support from the Continental Congress, New York's
Provincial Congress, the congress in New Jersey, and even
the great mass of fence-sitters here in the city. He would let
Hickey run a little further but the time was fast approaching
when he may have to set him straight or set him adrift. He
had actually earned his pay and what was a few hundred
acres of raw land? He owned tens of thousands of acres. Let
Hickey contend with the savages. Hickey could crack the
nut and then, after the war, he could enjoy the sweetmeat.

Chapter Sixteen

Washington's Private Office
8 p.m., Saturday, May 4, 1776

Hickey jimmied the makeshift wire key in the keyhole of the upper right drawer of Washington's desk.

"Turn, you son of a bitch, turn,"

It didn't. He angrily yanked out the slightly rusted piece of fence wire he had formed into a skeleton key, bent the tip a little more and thrust it back into the keyhole. He made a tighter loop at the other end for a handle, adjusted his grip and turned. There was resistance at first, then, it turned with a click loud enough to make him instinctively turn his head to the door to see if anyone heard.

It had been a brilliant spring day and the remnants of the bright sun still sent enough light through the window by the desk for him to see. If he didn't find what he was looking for soon, he might have to risk lighting the desk lamp. That might be dangerous. Other guards were posted throughout the grounds. They might spot the light in the general's office and wonder why someone was burning a lamp while the commander-in-chief was at Fraunces for a birthday dinner for a fellow mason.

Hickey was off duty but, as a sergeant in the Life Guard, could generally come and go as he pleased throughout the Mortier estate, especially in uniform. He had entered through the main foyer, telling the private on duty that he had to fetch some paperwork for the general. He set himself up at a small desk in the drawing room and, when the private went out to relieve himself, Hickey went up the main staircase and into Washington's office. The private had never thought to question where Hickey was or how he had left without being seen. Pitiful, really, he thought, how the hell he thinks he's going to win a war against the King's finest with an army made up of dumb farmhands and lecherous sots.

The drawer was half-filled with sheaves of papers, neatly packaged in folded outer wraps or tied with thin white ribbon. There was a small wooden tray set within the drawer that held pens and nibs, a small knife and some trinkets. Hickey took the entire stack of paper out of the drawer to set it on the desk. As he did, a smaller clump of papers fell from the middle and crashed into the floor. The sound was deafening to his nerve-tensed ears. He froze. Waited.

There were no footsteps rushing up the stairs. The only sound was laughter from guards down below in the back garden. They were oblivious. He sat in the general's cool, high-backed leather chair and picked up the first sheaf of paper. The top sheet was marked "Expenses for the week ending May 4." There were notations such as "five shillings, horsekeeping" and "10 shillings, wine for meeting." This log went on for three full pages of detailing every cent Washington was spending. Proud and honored to serve without pay .... my arse. He'll probably bill the congress for every cent, thought Hickey. That is, if he or any of them lived to submit a bill. Hickey was not interested in the expense accounts, except for one peculiar entry at the end. A heavy line was drawn across the bottom of the accounts and below the line was written "special services" this was followed by a dozen sets of initials each with an amount next to it. One set of initials was "T. H." and the amount next to it was "2 dols. Sp." Two dollars Spanish. Exactly what he had been paid by Washington this week. Did all of these initials represent people spying for Washington? Special services. That's what he's calling it. Washington had a dozen, perhaps more, just like him. Some were paid more, some less. The largest amount next to a set of initials was three pounds, 15 dollars. Must have been a report of special importance. Were they, too, in the Life Guard? He quickly ran down the list trying to put names to initials. There were no quick matches. "J. J." Was that James Johnson, the fifer? Or was William Green the "W. G.?" Didn't really matter. He was looking for something much more important.

Several of the packets were reports from officers in charge of fortifications. There were detailed status reports on the work and the amount of shot and powder available to defend each. This was the kind of information for which the King's governor might pay nicely. But, where was the paper he wanted? He quickly shuffled through the remaining packets. Nothing. He set them on the desk, lifted the wooden tray to see if a slip of paper might be hidden underneath. Nothing there, either. It was getting dark. He could barely make out the writing. He put all of the papers back in the top drawer and opened the middle drawer. He couldn't see into the drawer at all nor could he risk dropping something again. He would have to light the lamp. He took the oil lamp off the front of the desk and placed it on the floor near the chair. This might mask some of the light from the soldiers at the back of the house. Now, to light it. It was too warm to hope that there was a nice hot coal in the ember box by the fireplace. Chipping flint was noisy but he'd have to risk it. He opened the tinder box on the desk and was delighted to see Washington had a new fire pistol, a device that looked like the flintlock of a pistol but without any barrel or handle. He cocked the pistol and held a tinderstick in his left hand. One click and the tinder glowed. In a few seconds he had the lamp lit with the wick turned down low.

The lamp gave off a soft, gold glow that flowed in a pool of light for several feet around the lamp, trailing off into darkness in the far corners of the room. Grabbing the next pouch of papers from the middle drawer, something crashed to the floor and bounced to the base of the lantern. Hickey drew back unable to identify the object, white and pink and hard. When he realized it wasn't alive or moving, he moved closer. It was a set of the general's false teeth. He picked the teeth up with his thumb and forefinger and dropped them back into the drawer. Sitting on the edge of the chair, bent at the waist, he displayed the papers on the floor, examining one at a time and placing them back into the cloth pouch. Nothing. He wrapped the pouch in the ribbon, tied it and set it back in the drawer. He took another packet of papers from the desk

The sound of the door was deafening. It crashed back against the wall in a thunderous blow. The rush of air seemed to suck the papers from his hand and they crashed to the floor. In a knee-jerk reaction, he slammed the drawer shut as he braced himself back in the chair gaping at the door.

"Thomas?!"

Hickey couldn't comprehend. He was expecting the tight, harsh voice of the general or, at the very least, the inquisitive shout of a guard. The voice was soft, female. His brain wouldn't work.

"Thomas, what are you doing?" said Phoebe Fraunces, her open hands splayed in front of her, frozen. Her voice was at once bewildered, shocked, accusing, and questioning.

"I was just try...I, I mean..." His voice quavered.

"You told me you would be in the city...just what are you doing?" Phoebe had regained her senses enough to step into the room and close the door behind her. But she remained with her back pressed firmly against the door not moving toward him. "You told me you were not on duty but had things to do. Is this what you had to do?"

"I was looking for something...something about me that I heard...."

"The general is in the city at a Masonic meeting," she

interrupted, "and I find you sneaking around in his office, lamp on the floor, guilt all over your face." She was near tears, her mind racing through all of the things her father had said about Hickey. 'He's a taker, not a giver. He's looking after himself. When he gets what he wants, he's gone down the road. You'll be left standing girl. Trust me. He's slicker than whale oil. He could charm the teeth right out of General Washington's mouth. I don't want you falling under his spell. I don't want you hurt.'

Hickey had never seen Phoebe like this. He didn't know whether she was going to cry or leap at him in a catlike rage, tearing at his eyes.

"You haven't answered me, Thomas. What are you doing in here?"

"I'm protecting myself. Protecting us."

"Us? Protecting us from what?" her voice still shrill and accusatory.

"I have reason, uh, someone I know told me that Washington has been given information about me. Stories that say I'm a traitor. Or worse. I was just trying to find something, find out who. So I could fight back," his voiced cracked and quivered. Phoebe could not tell whether this was from honest emotion or from being caught in the act. He stepped towards her but her voice sent him back.

"Don't. Don't come near me, Thomas, or I'll scream and you'll have twenty guards in here and you can explain to them." Phoebe's heart was pounding and her head throbbed. Was it all true? Was this man she so readily took to just a good actor? Could it be that this man with bear-like paws who had held her hand so gently was a spy? She had overheard her father and brothers talk of leaks. The royal governor out there on the ship knew everything that went on. Was this man with the broad smile that melted her insides a Tory spy sending the general's secrets directly to the ship?

"Phoebe," said Hickey, collecting his emotions, gaining control again, "I know how this must seem. I know your father thinks I'm a no good bounder who's out to have his way with you. But," Hickey spoke slowly as if in pain, "have I ever been improper with you?"

Phoebe started to answer but said nothing.

"I have never been this happy in my short, rotten life. My innards turn to corn mush every time I see you. I feel like I drunk a gallon of callibogus when I touch your skin. Last week, in the field, I, well, it was like, I don't know, like holding the rarest bird in the world, studying its beauty not wanting to hurt it. Hoping it would never fly away."

"Stop it," Phoebe began to cry. "Just stop. I'm so confused, Thomas. It's all just so much words. My father. My brothers. They all say the only thing you care about is yourself. They say you're into everything from counterfeiting to spying. I hear all the time how you're in every tavern in the city. Then I find you here with some lame excuse about looking for some paper that has something bad about you. Maybe this paper contains the real truth you don't want me or anyone else to see. Maybe you'll take this paper and whatever else you can find of value in here and be gone into the wind. Not a single glance back to the foolish little girl who threw herself at you. Laughing. I feel as if you are laughing at me, Thomas."

"I will never laugh at you, Phoebe," said Hickey quietly, softly, stepping toward her. She backed away, turning her head so as not to see that smile.

"Phoebe. Listen to me ...," he stepped closer.

She did not shy away. He stood in front of her and took each of her hands in his. She turned her head and looked into his eyes. Her face softened.

"I love you, Phoebe. I want to spend every hour of my life with you. There is only one way I can prove it. There is no other way. It doesn't matter what happens to me. You come with me now and, together we'll go down to the captain of the guard and I will turn myself in. I will tell him exactly what I told you that I was looking for papers about

me. I will tell him I was wrong to come into this office and
let him do what he thinks is right. That's the only way you
will believe me. It doesn't matter what happens to me without you. Let's go do it now," Hickey tried to pull her away
from the door to open it.

"No. I....," she was whispering now, her voice soft,
breathless. Her hands and arms went loose and she pushed
Hickey away from the door. "I believe you, Thomas. I do.
It's just that you gave me such a start, and all the talk and I
... we ... I'm so torn. I've never felt this way. I don't know
what to think, who to believe." She knew one thing for certain, believe him or not, she wanted this man. She wanted
him with such a burning desire that it scared her. She gently
pulled her hands out of his and slid them up to his neck, pulling his face close to her. She was the aggressor now; he was
the unsure one. She kissed him, opening her mouth, holding
the moist embrace for what seemed like hours.

When she finally drew her mouth away, she said: "I love
you, Thomas. I want to be yours. I don't care what you have
done or are doing. I don't want to know."

He picked her up effortlessly and carried her to the leather settee to the left of the desk along the wall. Careful as to
not kick over the lamp, he lowered her gently, supporting
her head as if cradling an infant. She shifted closer to the
back of the settee, the cool leather exciting her skin. She
undid the hairpin and released the long dark hair, which re-
flected the lamp light like satin. She lay with her hands back
over the arm of the settee, above her head. Hickey quickly
pulled open the buttons of his shirt and tossed it aside. He
knelt and, as if picking delicate new spring flowers, undid
the buttons of her bodice and freed the corset. Phoebe's
breath came in small gasps as if she were crying but there
were no tears now. Her eyes fluttering to near closed, she
arched her back as he removed the restraints of the cloth
and tossed it into a clump with his shirt. Still kneeling, he
bent over her his left arm sliding underneath her waist and

his right behind her neck. He drew her cool, softness into his sweaty chest and they kissed, long and deep. He kissed her eyelids and her ears. He ran his tongue along the length of her neck. His lips followed the whitish hollow between her breasts and then found a nipple. He took it gently between his lips and plucked at it with his teeth. Phoebe shuddered, a ripple from her neck to her toes and she moaned low and pleadingly. The strain in his groin was almost painful. He stood and undid the buttons of his trousers and let them fall to the floor, slipping off his shoes in one movement. A breathy gasp came from Phoebe's lips and she reached out and grabbed his hardened manhood, a bit awkward in the newness and yet utterly seductive in its honest need. Hickey thought for certain he would explode but he called upon every ounce of strength and experience not wanting to disappoint. She stood up, freed herself from the rest of her clothing and pressed herself tightly to him. She wanted more of this man. She wanted every part of him. She reveled in this first experience of womanhood, thrilling to each new touch, each new sensation. It seemed that there was too much of him. The hardness, it seemed as they stood pressed against one another, covered her entire front. Would she be able to do this? Would she satisfy him like so many women had done before? The answer came readily. She knew she would. It was so natural. The two of them. It was a perfect fit. None of these thoughts mattered. What mattered was the emptiness. The hollowness was aching, almost painful. She needed this hardness within her, not pressing against her. Instinctively she knew the only remedy for this most pleasant and strangely new ailment.

They slowly turned and rocked, knowing together that the settee was too small for them to lie on and the floor too hard.

"Here," said Hickey softly in her ear as he sat back on the settee. He gently, silently, guided her, showing her how to put one leg on either side of his. She straddled him readily and slowly lowered herself down on to him. He used his hand to guide the way but there was little resistance. Phoebe gave a short, crisp shriek, like a cat startled from sleep. Innate movement took over. She raised and lowered herself with abandon, her brown eyes misty, a thin sweet smile on her lips. Thomas Hickey realized then that all of the women from age 16 to that moment had only been the prelude to this. It had never been like this before. It had been good, even great but never like this. This was sex and love. And the combination was indescribable. They moved in waves, slow then faster, then slow again, for some time.

Phoebe shuddered gently again and moved her hips more quickly. Hickey grabbed the small of her back and made several long deep thrusts and they clutched one another as they fell. Waves passed through them, oceans of strange mixtures poured from their souls, blending and soothing.

Hickey held Phoebe's face between his hands and smiled. She smiled back. They said nothing. He kissed her gently, barely touching her lips.

" I love you, Ph...."

The door of the office banged open.

"What is the meaning of this?" said Washington, holding a fresh candle and, straining through his surprise, to see who had intruded into his private office.

Phoebe grabbed her frock and held it in front of her. Hickey doubled his hands over his crotch, now a manageable size to be hidden by his cupped hands.

"Miss Fraunces! Sergeant Hickey! This is goddamned appalling!" said the general, furious, the veneer of his civility stripped away. "What the hell are you doing in my office, stripped naked like a strumpet. When I tell your father of this...."

"It's all my doing...," said Hickey.

"Be still, Sergeant Hickey. I'll deal with you later. You, young lady, go into the bedroom there and get yourself dressed."

Phoebe gathered her things and, still clutching them in front of her, ran past Washington into the hallway and then into the next doorway on the left, one of four upstairs bedrooms. Washington, despite his anger and shock, still took notice of the round buttocks and hefty curve of her bouncing breasts as she ran into the hall. He slammed the door and walked to the desk. He picked up the lamp, slammed it on to the desk and cranked up the wick. The light burned bright enough to fill the room. Hickey stood hands cupped in front of him.

"Explain yourself, Mr. Hickey," demanded Washington.

The shock had quickly faded for Hickey, too. He was torn now between outrage that Washington had interrupted their lovemaking and concern that he not say anything that might get himself or Phoebe into real trouble. The general had treated them as his children or, worse yet, as common slaves to order as he saw fit. He decided that it was best to tell the truth.

"I love her, General Washington, sir." Hickey felt that was too much. He hadn't ever used the title 'General Washington' when they were alone. He only used it when out with the other Guards. And, he never said 'sir.' Together they sounded almost as if he was mocking Washington.

"You love her. You love her! So you drag her into my private office and deflower her on my sofa without regards to her future or yours? You are aware, Hickey, that Samuel Fraunces thinks you are worse than the lowest sot of the Holy Ground. I do believe he or his sons would slit your throat in a minute. This coupled with the fact that I have received certain reports about you that, well, make me wonder just who you are working for....I have a mind to just call in the guard and court martial you tonight. You could do little more harm sitting in the city jail."

"Court martial! Reports! What reports?" Hickey was beyond embarrassed, beyond concern now. He was angry. "You think I'm just one of your damned troops. Think again.

You know what I have provided for you. What are these reports? Who are they from? What do they say about me?"

"Sergeant Hickey, must I remind you that, despite any other arrangements, you have officially signed the papers to serve in the Life Guard. You are, indeed, a solider in my command and I will dispense discipline as freely with you as I will be any other troop in my command. As for reports, I will comment no further than to say that a great deal of very private information has been making its way to the King's ship in the harbor. Important strategic information to which few are privy. I want to know how this is happening. I demand to know how this is happening. I suggest you put your talents to work. Or, I am afraid I will be forced to make some changes."

"What are you saying?"

"I am saying, Mr. Hickey, that you had better find the source of this traitorous activity or I will be forced to terminate our special arrangement and, with uncertainty about your public future as a member of my Life Guard, I may have to suggest to Mr. Samuel Fraunces that he take steps to prevent his daughter from going down an unpleasant path."

Hickey understood now that Washington, despite being startled, could care less about him and Phoebe or their lovemaking on his precious settee. He might be a bit upset by it taking place in his own office but that was simply an affront to his arrogant power. What mattered to the general's pragmatic mind was that he get something in return for this insult.

"I'll see what I can find," said Hickey tightly.

"You'll do better than that," said Washington. "You find the source before I leave for Philadelphia. That is approximately two weeks. I will report to the Congress on the source of these leaks. Understood?"

"Perfectly," said Hickey, sliding into his pants and buttoning up his shirt.

Hickey turned his back on Washington and walked toward the door.

"Two weeks, Mr. Hickey. Is that clear?"

Hickey nodded and left.

Washington was now fully recovered from the shock of finding the couple. As Hickey had surmised, Washington was much more upset by the fact they were in his office. He was the damned commander-in-chief. This was his office. Sergeants and their lovers don't just march into a general's office and copulate on the sofa. It meant something was weak: His leadership? His authority? But, if he could get Hickey to unearth the mole whom was burrowing into his ranks and coming up with extremely sensitive details of his plans, it would be worth the use of his office as a love nest. Washington recalled to his thoughts the sweat-coated brown buttocks and the round whitish breasts that bounced by him and ran into the bedroom.

He was feeling a touch of envy as he turned to leave.

Then he saw it. What was this?

He grabbed the twisted wire and pulled it from the key-hole. He pulled open the drawer. Unlocked! Someone had used this makeshift key to open his drawers and rifle through his papers. There were papers on the floor under the desk. Hickey? Then it was true what Church had said. Or was it Phoebe? She was so enthralled with Hickey she'd do whatever he demanded. Even spy on those fighting for her freedom. Or, perhaps, it was neither of them. Maybe it was true that they just stumbled into this room in the heat of passion, victims to circumstances, unknowing about the key or the break in. One of the other guards. A gardener or a cook, perhaps.

He would see what Hickey found out. He would give him his two weeks. Then he would take decisive action. He would get to the bottom of this and he would do it quickly. Hickey would be cut loose; his usefulness was at an end.

Chapter Seventeen

Corbie's Tavern, Spring and Wooster Sts.
8:30 p.m., Monday, May 20, 1776

Corbie is Scottish for raven. It was most appropriate then that the ominous black scavenger should hover on the sign outside this tavern on this particular May evening only a short distance southeast from Washington's Headquarters at Richmond Hill. The proprietor, one William Corby, an Americanized version of the old Scottish bird, was on hand along with a formation of other loyalist vultures. This motley congregation had been meeting for months but it was the first session for one fledgling, albeit a crusty crow like Thomas Hickey.

Since Washington's ultimatum, Hickey had pressured all of his contacts. Washington would be going to Philadelphia tomorrow to meet with the Congress. It had been necessary to physically impress his urgency on a few tight-lipped pub-goers. He had been especially tough with Private Lynch, whom he had discovered at the counterfeiting sessions. It seemed that one young Michael Lynch was heavily in debt to a free black man named, Bubaki Lews. Mr. Lews ran a high stakes dice game and, after the baby-faced young private had lost his entire month's pay, had advanced the hapless gambler nearly 20 pounds. Lynch had proceeded to quickly lose it all back to Lews who gave him three days to come up with the money. When the money was not in hand on the third day, Lews sent out the word to slice the young private's throat. Lynch, hearing about the counterfeiting scheme from another Life Guard, whom — unsure of Hickey's loyalties — he refused to name, had decided paying Lews with counterfeit scrip might be a quick way out. It worked. The new fake bills were so good Lews never looked twice. He simply shook his head, half in disbelief that the private had gotten the cash so quickly and half in dismay that he would miss the opportunity to slice up the young private's pretty white face.

Threatening to expose his gambling to the officer corps, Hickey had coerced Lynch into telling all he knew about rumors of Tory plots. Once he started singing, Lynch found the tune to his liking and gave Hickey several leads, which seemed to be the real thing. Yesterday, Hickey had paid a visit to Gilbert Forbes, a gunsmith who operated a shop in the Broadway.

Forbes, a heavy set, red-faced man with two tufts of bright orange hair jutting out from over his ears, was aghast at suggestions of plots against liberty, cursing the king.

"Why you most certainly offend me, sir, and all righteous citizens of this city who stand in favor of liberty," crowed Forbes. "Most offended, indeed. His excellency, General Washington is like a god right here on this earth."

Hickey offered to buy a large quantity of guns to be used for a "special purpose" and produced a wad of the counterfeit bills given to him by Dawkins. Forbes' brightened at the prospect of such a large sale but just as quickly as it came the smile disappeared. He examined the notes and, his demeanor dissolving into back street thug, demanded to know where Hickey had gotten the paper. Hickey, who had been told that Forbes might be aware of the counterfeiting scheme, feigned innocence.

"What?" said Hickey, "you don't want my business?"

"Most certainly, I do. Certainly, indeed. But, I do not

like the money I am paid with to be worth less than this oily rag," he said, waving a yellowing piece of cloth in Hickey's face.

"What are you saying, Mr. Forbes?"

"I am saying your money is only as good as the printing talents of one Isaac Dawkins."

Hickey smiled knowingly.

"His Excellency High Horse Virginia Tight Arse works us long hours and for the dregs. You can't blame a man for trying to have a little extra. Besides, the Whigs are facing a hopeless cause and I want to cover my flanks. I want to be sure I'm on the right side when the time comes."

He said he knew of a private who was "doing the right thing" and that he himself had once served the king as a soldier and could feel quite comfortable doing the same once again. He said he might be of particular use to Forbes and friends having access to the southern general himself. He let loose the Hickey smile and within minutes Forbes was telling him about the secret society he belonged to and offering to introduce Hickey to the group.

Hickey didn't hold out much hope for uncovering a widespread, organized conspiracy, such stories were just tavern talk with lots of grousing and grand solutions but little substance. But, he just might discovery enough to get Washington off his back. Tories throughout the city's pubs openly bragged about their part in the plot that would send old Washington packing while they waited on the dock to greet the Howe brothers in doing the King's work. But this was the first lead of any consequence. Forbes not only talked about such plans he was actually a part of a group of sympathizers, so he said, who were making plans to carry out such actions. It really didn't matter, Hickey thought, whether they do or don't carry out their plan. I won't be around long enough to find out.

Later in the evening, Hickey met Forbes in the Corbie's bar and followed him through a back room and up a flight of stairs to a large, open room with chairs around an undraped, scarred oak table. Hickey was surprised by the number of people standing about chatting, drinks in hand. It seemed more like a party than a meeting of conspirators. Hickey and Forbes made a total of sixteen, all men. He recognized three of them. They, too, were members of the Life Guard. He also recognized the faces of four or five others he had seen in his tavern travels. The light banter and laughter died as the others realized there was a stranger in the room. They took their seats. Forbes introduced Hickey.

"Gentlemen, it gives me great pleasure to introduce to you Thomas Hickey, recommended to our cause by Henry Dawkins and the Youngs, God save them as they writhe in the clutches of their rebel jailers."

Hickey looked at Forbes. Jail? This was news. He hadn't talked with the counterfeiters for nearly a week, since he set out after information that would satisfy Washington. He could see that this was not the time to question Forbes about their fate.

"Mr. Hickey," Forbes continued, "has been deeply involved in the distribution of this new currency. He is the fourth member of the rebel general's elite private guard to seek to join the King's cause — the cause of righteousness, of duty, of loyalty, and, yes, of sanity itself.

"Mr. Hickey, or should I say Sergeant Hickey, is the highest ranking guard to make a commitment to the cause of justice. Gentlemen, a toast. To the glorious constitution of Great Britain, we remain and will always be loyal subjects of our gracious sovereign, King George the Third." Forbes held his mug high and the others did likewise then all took a hefty draught of their chosen poison.

Hickey did likewise with natural enthusiasm as wary eyes peered over tipped mugs to see if the newcomer would, indeed, join in. Forbes introduced each person. The members of the Life Guard he knew. There was William Greene, a dour young man who was one of the guard drummers.

Private John Barnes smiled at Hickey when introduced but James Johnson, a guard fifer, simply nodded not making eye contact.   There were four businessmen, including two publicans, James Houlding, operator of a beer house in Tryon Row, and George Lowry, a short, fat man with a bright blue coat, who owned a tavern opposite Oswego Market. It seemed that the taverns and beerhouses of the city had been the spawning ground for much of this loyalism.   The tall, thin man with the sunken cheeks and look of a grave digger was introduced as William Forbes of Goshen.   No occupation was stated but Gilbert Forbes made it clear they were not related. The wheezing old man at Hickey's right was introduced as former sergeant of the King's Royal Artillery William Graham.   He smiled through puffy old eyelids and sagging, pink baby-smooth skin, the result of 50 years of being scraped layer by layer with a razor. Next to the old wheezer was a man who, before Forbes could make the formal introductions, stood up and leaned toward Hickey, introducing himself.

"Clayford. John Clayford," he said in a firm, clear voice. The handshake was firm and strong.

"Uh, yes, John Clayford," stumbled Forbes, not expecting Clayford to introduce himself. "Mr. Clayford is in charge of, shall we say, special arrangements for our committee."

Clayford grinned, a thin, frigid smile, his eyes focused directly on Hickey's eyes. Hickey met his gaze directly. Neither blinked.   This is the strong arm of the group, thought Hickey, from experience.

William Corby, the owner of the tavern and host for the evening, was a nervous but earnest participant, looking uncomfortable throughout the meeting but among the most vocal supporters of the King. Almost, too, enthusiastic, thought Hickey.

Gilbert Forbes had waited until last to introduce the two men seated at the far head of the table. They were clearly a cut above all of the others at the table. They wore starched linen shirts and dickeys and well-tailored coats of subdued colors, one dark brown the other deep blue. These two were not nervous. They were in full control. They patiently waited for the introductions. When all of this frivolity was over, they would deem to address the others. The man in the brown jacket was William Leary, a prominent city businessman. He allowed a barely perceptible royal nod when introduced, a thin condescending grin frozen on his face. The other man, medium height with sandy blond hair falling over the collar of his obviously expensive blue jacket was none other than the Mayor of New York David Matthews. If this went as Hickey thought it might, he would be golden. If he could report to Washington that Mayor Matthews was involved in some way, he would have earned his keep and maybe Washington would give him the deed to the western land and send him on his way.

The introductions over, Forbes looked to Mayor Matthews.

"Thank you, my fellow loyal subject, Mr. Gilbert Forbes. The Honorable William Tryon, Royal Governor of New York, sends you pleasant and honorable greetings from aboard his ship, the H.M.S. Duchess of Gordon. He is in constant correspondence with the Royal Court and with the King's subjects here in the city. He has given his seal to our latest plan and wants each one of you to know that you will be rewarded when this city is freed from the wicked artifices of an ambitious minor faction of rabble rousers. He heartily and sincerely pledges himself to this covenant and to our honorable and sacred endeavor to restore legal, constitutional government to these colonies."

The men around the table broke into applause and raised their glasses and mugs.

"Now, to business. Report of the North Country. Mr. Forbes."

William Forbes, the man who had been identified as being from Goshen stood and, reading from notes, outlined what he had accomplished in the lands north of the city since the group's last session.

For the first time, Hickey realized this was the real thing. These weren't half drunk idlers boasting to fellow drinkers as he had expected. These were men with money, position, and power. They had a plan. And the plan was a stunner. No matter that none of this might ever come to fruition. The simple fact that these men were here in this room was enough to cover the Washington debt. Then, he'd be out of this uniform and out of the rich Virginian's fist.

"We have, thanks to the funds given to us by Governor Tryon through Mayor Matthews, enlisted nearly seven hundred loyal citizens. Each who enlisted in the King's service will be given 200 acres of land, western land, with 100 acres more for a wife and 50 additional for each child. Others not enticed by the land were given one to five guineas and will receive regular payments thereafter. These men are willing to risk their lives for the king. We have them organized into eight groups, each with a clear task. Twice now, we have had mock runs and they have proven to be very dedicated and efficient. We have detailed maps of all cannon emplacements along the North River. When the signal is given, they will spike these cannon making them so much scrap. Ammo stores will be ignited. The major roads through Newburgh, Middletown and Goshen will be blocked."

"How about the King's Bridge?" asked Leary.

"I have formulated a plan," answered Forbes, "But General Washington has taken an interest in the strategic value of the bridge and has added some fortifications. I believe, however, that with the help of our soldiers here," he gestured toward the members of the Life Guard and to Hickey, "we will be able to infiltrate the bridge fortifications and cut it down."

Hickey's heart thundered in his chest. He wondered if Gilbert Forbes, who was sitting next to him, could hear it. It took all of his concentration to appear calm. His mind raced.

All of the talks with Washington, right from the first day at the Turtle test, had not prepared him for this. His was a strict business arrangement, money for information. He felt no loyalty. The more he saw of Washington, the more he realized he was just like the British officers he had known, clawing and scratching for glory over the bodies of expendable men like himself. All of the idle prattle at a hundred taverns did not come close to shattering his composure as was this cool, professional report on proposed acts of terror. This struggle had never really been his struggle. It was a means to an end. A way to earn hard cash. He said it all along: this was a struggle between the haves of England and the haves of the colonies. Now, in this first report, the struggle became a reality. This was no game. No cat and mouse charade. These men were deadly serious. Spiking cannon meant lodging metal into the bore. The men who fired them would be killed as the cannon shattered into thousands of powerful shards ripping through their flesh. There were bound to be men on duty at the ammo and armament storage areas. And at the bridge, too. These men felt so passionately about their loyalty to the King that they were willing to kill for Georgie III. Hickey could understand killing if someone was trying to kill him. He could even understand killing to protect the honor of someone he cared about, like Phoebe. But to kill a stranger for a king or a general from Virginia was not something he could, at this moment, understand. However, Washington would drool down the front of his spotless uniform for information like this. Once he had traded this information to Washington, he would take Phoebe out of this city and head west. It was too dangerous for her here.

One by one, the members of the "society" as they called themselves, stood to make their reports. Gilbert Forbes told of having four hundred rifles ready and thanked Mayor Matthews for the prompt payment. Sergeant Graham, the crusty, ancient artilleryman, had quite innocently strolled throughout much of the city. He had made extremely detailed maps

of each fortification, assessing their strengths and weak-
nesses. Furthermore, in order to present this intelligence,
he was conveyed quite easily from the city to Tryon's ship
and back without a question. Two of the businessmen, Jacob
Duryee and William Savage, were responsible for organiz-
ing the loyalists on the Long Island. They, too, had enlisted several hundred citizens willing to take up arms to stop
Washington's troops from retreating in that direction. The
arrogant southern general, they said, who had always been
a laughing stock among the great generals of England and
France, would be trapped on an island, surrounded by the
greatest navy the world has ever seen. There would be no
escape. Hickey wondered if Washington knew of his tenu-
ous position. He must. New York was a strategic gem. If
the King's men controlled New York, they could divide the
northern and southern colonies and end the rebellion before
it had ever really begun. Washington knew New York had
to be defended. But, Hickey was certain, he also knew it
couldn't be held for very long. How would all of this organized resistance sit with Washington? It would be interesting
to stay around and watch him respond. But, he and Phoebe
couldn't afford that luxury.

However, the lightning bolt of the evening was still to
come.

When John Clayford stood to make his report, the silence
in the room became palpable.

"Gentlemen," he said, slowly, firmly, his deep resonant
voice rock steady, "my little part in the King's garden party
is ready. With the valuable assistance of the loyal members
of General Washington's own Life Guard, we now have full
access to his schedule of activities and can grab him at any
of a dozen points. Generals Heath, Sullivan and Greene will
also be taken along with eight key colonels. Special transport has been prepared to immediately convey Washington
to the Duchess of Gordon. He will be taken to England to
stand trial for treason. As you know, that was not my original

recommendation. I have carried out plans for his transport based upon this society's decision. But, I believe we have agreed, that should he attempt to escape or should there be any danger of our losing him in transport, he will be executed --- on the spot. Do we agree?"

Everyone nodded. Most, thought Hickey reading their faces, were uneasy with such a proposition. Only Mayor Matthews spoke.

"General Washington," he said, now seeming a bit nervous, "is much more valuable to our cause alive than dead, Mr. Clayford. If the great leader of the rebellious farmers of New England, is brought to trial, it will take the heart and soul out of this nonsensical Whig folly. However, as a last resort -- and only if all else fails — we cannot and will not allow him to return to command. On that, we agree. This is where our newest member can help. Sergeant Hickey, we would like you to study our plan and be prepared — I repeat, as a last resort only — be prepared to eliminate General Washington."

He explained how Hickey and the other members of the Life Guard were the insurance for this essential part of the plan.

"General Washington is key. I know this is all new to you but we have not the luxury of time. If you would like another assignment, Sergeant Hickey, speak up now."

Hickey shook his head.

"We will attempt to bring him to trial and, if he attempts to escape, Mr. Clayford has permission to execute him. However, if the general manages to remain fortified in his quarters and out of reach, we will rely on you to carry out this part of the plan. We know that you are, shall we say, intimately involved with the general's housekeeper. It, therefore, shouldn't be difficult for you to put this element in place. A bit of nastiness in his meal. Quite easy and quite clean. Mr. Forbes can provide you with the necessary materials. Do you agree to this?"

"Of course," said Hickey firmly, "I'll do it without a second thought," said Hickey knowing he and Phoebe would be 1,000 miles away before that day ever came.

The others nodded their approval of the new man. The other soldiers of the guard tried, unsuccessfully, to hide their discomfort that Hickey had just agreed to assassinate the general.

'I'll do it without a thought,' Hickey repeated in his mind. But he had plenty of thoughts. They were ready and willing to kill Washington. Now, if need be, they wanted him to do the deed, to poison the holier-than-thou southern windbag. And, to use Phoebe, to do it. The plot had been deeper and more well-formed than he had ever imagined. He was not certain he would tell Washington all of this. He would tell him enough to get clear — but how much would that be?

Once again, for the second time in his life, he was in far deeper than he wanted to be. How had this happened? Just a few short months ago, he was his own man free to do as he pleased. A nice neat dream. A well-thought plan to make it come true. No Washington. No intrigue. No rich man's battles. No Phoebe. The words came slower the second time...no Phoebe. It was beyond imagination. All of the 'yes sir' and 'no sir' shit. The double life, always thinking two thoughts, showing two faces to the world -- it was all worth it. Because without the meeting with old tight arse Washington at the Turtle showing, he would never have met Phoebe. Or would he? Was it meant to be? No, he didn't believe in that kind of twaddle. Nevertheless, he was here and Phoebe was here. Here in this city retching its gut between crown and who knows what. Yes, he would do what he had to do. Whatever he had to do.

"These packets are filled with additional monies for all of you," said Matthews, handing out thick wads of paper currency. Hickey could not see whether this cash was real or fake. "Those who are in recruiting may need more, see me afterward and I'll arrange for drop offs for you. We don't want to be caught with large sums, that might be suspicious."

He continued passing out the packets as the conspirators loudly pushed back their chairs to refresh their drinks and await the special report of the evening.

Mayor Matthews took Hickey by the arm and led him to a corner of the room.

"Here's a special welcome package for you, Sgt. Hickey." He tried to look at the packet without being too conspicuous. It was as thick as his finger.

"Go ahead, look at it, sergeant. You'll find nothing in there but good crown silver. Sterling notes. You were expecting, perhaps, a Dawkins' original?" said the mayor, his voice rising and filled with sheer delight. Hickey smiled a caught-in-the-act smile and asked, "What about Dawkins? And the Youngs? Forbes said something about jail."

"Yes, that is correct. Unfortunately, Mr. Dawkins was arrested about a week ago. The Youngs brothers as well. Charged with counterfeiting. This is in the normal course of events a fairly simple offense. One pays a fine, perhaps spends a few weeks or months in jail and is sent out of town with the admonishment never to return. But, as you are well aware, Sgt. Hickey, these are not normal times. That disgraceful farce of a tribunal the Committee of Safety has talked with each of them. They are being held indefinitely. I hear Ketcham was already in jail when they were arrested. I wouldn't be surprised if Ketcham was responsible, although I am told that Dawkins got drunk and pretty much gave himself away. But, Ketcham....well, I never have trusted him. I can see him singing away the minute they took him in. Fortunately, I believe they knew nothing or little about our real purpose, at least Dawkins and the Youngs. Ketcham is a different story. He asked a lot of questions. Questions that had nothing to do with paper or printing or even counterfeiting. Given an ounce of opportunity, he will tell them anything they want to hear. So, he might be of concern."

"I was on the list for receiving some of that bad paper,"

said Hickey.

"I wouldn't worry too much, Sergeant Hickey. Who'd believe a member of the good general's Life Guard would be involved in such a horrible crime against the saviors of liberty?"

Mayor David Matthews laughed loudly at this attempt at humor and continued chuckling as he walked away to refill his drink.

Hickey stood watching the others. The members of the Life Guard were fully engaged in small talk with their fellow conspirators. Greene caught Hickey's eye and quickly averted his eyes seemingly to avoid Hickey. Then, as if having second thoughts, he broke away from his small group and walked straight to Hickey, holding out his hand. Hickey had a flash of familiarity. It was difficult to distinguish between this group and the masons who met at Fraunces or the counterfeiters. They all wanted to come up on the right side when all of this washed.

"Welcome to the party, Thomas," said Greene, forgoing the usual military courtesies. "I always thought you were one of the few with any brains. Never quite figured you for the Life Guard type."

"Thank you, William," said Hickey, as sincerely as possible. "A man has to do what he feels in his heart is right for him."

"Between you and me, Thomas," said Greene, leaning in real close, "I don't think much will come of any of this. Once the King's fleet arrives in the harbor, the Washington party will be over. These are smart men. They'll deal. I just wanted to make sure I was covered on all sides. Cover your flanks. Right, fellow soldier? You know me, I've always been one helluva card player. Got to know the odds. Play all angles. Now that I see you here, I know I made the right bet." He, too, walked away smiling and heading for Privates Barnes and Johnson, the fifer, probably, to report that Sgt. Hickey was fast in. It was true. Hickey was just making everyone smile this evening.

Hickey filled his mug with ale from a pitcher and took a long, pleasant draught. Being such a bearer of good cheer was thirsty business. On the downswing of the mug, he noticed Clayford coming his way. His stomach tightened.

"Well, Sergeant Hickey, you certainly have made a quick ascent in the ranks of the King's chosen few," said Clayford. "From newcomer to executioner of the great general himself all in a few minutes. Perhaps, success so easily come by is not so well appreciated. I'll be honest with you Hickey, I was not and am not in favor of you being here at all. I especially am not pleased with your being tapped for what I consider to be a critical element of our plans. The good mayor and the distinguished man of commerce, Mr. Leary, were quite anxious to enlist a sergeant in the private guard of the rebel general. A great asset, they feel. A coup. My feeling, and rather carefully thought through I must tell you, is that one does not get to be a sergeant a general's private guard force without having earned one's keep. To my thinking, the very status that makes you so attractive, is what makes you so unattractive. I consider you a risky venture. I have done my best to have my sources examine your past and your current status. Of course, I had so little time to do so. So far, you are what you say. Believe me, Hickey, I am dead serious about this mission. I consider it my duty to my King and my home to do this. I will let nothing get in my way. I will not hesitate to eliminate any thing or any person who gets in my way. Do you understand?" He was face to face with Hickey now staring into his eyes.

Hickey returned his stare.

"When you were checking on me," said Hickey smiling, "you didn't find out about the one-eyed woman with the parrot and the whip over in the Holy Ground, did you?"

There was an instant before Clayford realized he was being mocked. His instinct was to pounce but he quickly, though visibly and with great effort of restraint, settled himself and replied, "You are quite a humorous man, Sergeant Hickey. I hope you are able to maintain that wonderful quality."

He walked away with Hickey sizing up the thick, broad shoulders and tall, thick legs. He began to think twice about once again letting his mouth get in the way.

Hickey had been so engrossed in the power struggle with Clayford he hadn't noticed the arrival of yet another guest, the seventeenth member of the society and it's only female. And this new addition was very much female, indeed. She moved among the men with ease, saying a few words to each little group, which would, in turn, break into raucous laughter. Something bawdy, no doubt. She was tall, a good three inches taller than Hickey, most of her height in her long legs. She had a high, thin waist and large, round breasts, the full, broad tops of which were exposed as they were thrust out by a stiff corset. Her skirt now rode high on her thigh as she propped one foot on a chair and showed her legs to a couple of the men who had issued some sort of challenge to her. Hickey wasn't the only one to drink in that leg with its long tapering thigh and calve ending in a purple shoe. The issuers of the challenge seemed to agree she was right and she brushed her skirts down, straightened her shoulders and flung her hair back over her shoulder. The straightening of her shoulders made her breasts stand out further which, apparently, prompted another comment. The new conspirator cupped the sides of her breasts, pushed them together and said something that sent the men to fits of laughter.

This extra-loud burst prompted Mayor Matthews to recall the group to order. The woman sat next to Clayford, very close, her thigh pressed against his leg. She seemed at ease in this closeness.

"Gentlemen, and, of course, Miss Gibbons, let's finish our business here. It is getting late."

There were two brief committee reports. These dealt with evacuation routes for friends of the crown and alternate channels for communication should a member be waylaid or arrested. Then it was Mary's turn.

"We know you have pressing business, Miss Gibbons, so let us hear what you have and you can be gone."

Standing, one hand, Hickey noticed, slipping out of the fingers of Clayford's bear paw, Mary Gibbons said: "These should prove very interesting to you gents." She reached into the center of her breasts and pulled out several small bits of paper. "Copy them quickly, if you would. I sort of promised I'd get them back to their owner," she laughed heartily.

Forbes, Houlding and Lowry took the papers and, dipping pen in ink, scribbled furiously while Mary went on to explain that she might not have much information during the next few weeks. "I'll be taking a break boys but I'll be back at it soon enough. "

Mary Gibbons, who was obviously no stranger to a man's bed, then told a joke about a cuckolded parson. As she spoke, Hickey saw in her face the face of a hundred women he had been attracted to in taverns and whorehouses all over Massachusetts and New York. Just a few short weeks ago, he would have been on her like Corbie's crow on a dropped lunch. Now, she did nothing to him or for him. This thought was at once frightening and satisfying.

Hickey, sitting next to Houlding, tried to read the notes he was scribbling without appearing too interested.

"General Washington. We advise you to begin immediate organization of a War Committee. Such council should be chosen carefully from the resources of the city's leadership faithful to the cause of liberty...."

Houlding's hand covered the next few lines but Hickey watched as he finished up copying one note. "Our sincerest best wishes and God speed in your most formidable task, John Hancock, president, Continental Congress."

"Hancock!" thought Hickey. This was a personal message from his former employer, the richest man in the northern colonies to General Washington himself.

Were these notes the real thing? If so, how did Mary Gibbons, barely a step above Holy Ground strumpet, get them. A War Committee! This was the first mention he had heard of such an idea. Were the rich men in Philadelphia really thinking about going to war with the King of England? Despite all the intrigue, he, too, had been pretty much convinced that this was a power play. There would be some concessions and that would be that. This was all becoming much more than he bargained for. Perhaps, this group had the right idea. Because, if it, indeed, came to war, there would be no chance for the unfit farmers of liberty to win. They had gotten lucky at Boston. The island of New York was a different matter altogether. But maybe this was all a ruse, a way to make this group and others feel more confident in their plotting.

"While we're waiting for these messages to be copied," said Mayor Matthews, "here's one interesting little report I think we safely share with the entire group. The rebellious upstarts have developed an underwater boat! That's right, a boat that a man can propel under the water. They plan to attach explosive charges to the King's ships in the harbor. We understand they're having some problems actually operating these craft but nevertheless it is something we will convey to Governor Tryon. We may be able to prepare the hulls of ships against such attack."

This report provoked lively chatter among the conspirators but nothing to rival the chatter in Hickey's head. They knew about Washington's Turtle. This was, indeed, the real thing. Somehow this bitchfoxy Miss Gibbons had a direct pipeline to some serious information.

Within minutes, the papers were copied and returned snugly to the warm home between Mary Gibbons ample mounds.

"Thank you very much for your valued service," said Mayor Matthew, "we apprecia...."

He was cut off by someone who said loudly, "You haven't

seen any of her valued services yet." The mayor's face was bright red which, along with his light colored hair, made him look like an embarrassed school boy. "Gentlemen, please. Let's finish up here. Thank you, Miss Gibbons. If Private Greene and Mr. Houlding would remain, please. The rest of you we will see on Wednesday. Same time. Thank you."

"Well, boys," said Mary Gibbons as she rose and headed for the rear door, "off to pay the King's ransom." She was waylaid on her way to the door and paused to drink a final pint.

"Where does she get this information?" whispered Hickey to Houlding, trying to sound conversational, as they rose to have a final mug before leaving.

"Someone real close to the general as you might guess," said Houlding, not in the least surprised or suspicious of Hickey's interest. "She has provided some invaluable information. True numbers of available soldiers. Sick rosters. Enlistment figures. Problems in fortifications. All she tells us is that she gets it from a 'beautiful young thing close to the heart of the rebels'."

Houlding gathered his notes and walked to the bar.

Hickey positioned himself near the hallway to the back stairs, his back to the wall, feigning disinterest. Mary Gibbons expertly slipped through the crowd, avoiding all efforts to get her to have one final drink. She walked straight to the door and disappeared down the back stairs. Hickey hoisted his mug and, downing the remaining ale, looked around. He waited a few seconds and slid out into the hallway. The rough-hewn wooden stairs would echo footsteps so he waited until he heard the bottom door bang shut. He took the stairs two at a time and carefully opened the bottom door a crack to see Mary Gibbons half running up the Broad Way.

Chapter Eighteen

Spring Street, north of New York City
11:15 p.m., Monday, May 20, 1776

The days were much warmer but spring still had not given up its hold on the nights. Mary Gibbons wrapped her dark shawl tightly around her shoulders and over her head, clutching it at her neck forming a hood with just enough room to see where she was going. She moved quickly. Thick clouds dulled the moon and the air was heavy. Rain was on the way. She had spent far too much time at the meeting. She enjoyed the way they looked at her, the way they all wanted her, but she knew half of them wouldn't last a minute. Clayford knew how to take care of her. He had already proven this. And that new one, the soldier, Hickey, there was something about him. He had potential. He was short but thick and she certainly had a knack for telling the men from the boys. When all of this was over, she would make good use of all these King's men. She would fleece them one at a time. But now it was important to finish the business at hand.

Hickey slipped out the bottom rear door of Corbie's just as Mary Gibbons rounded the corner of the building into Spring Street. This area immediately north of the city proper was just starting to develop when Washington settled into the Mortier Estate. There was more and more traffic along Greenwich Street, which followed Hudson's River along the western shore of the island. Unlike the city below the palisades where streets had grown up along the old Dutch roads and buildings crowded side by side from Pearl Street to the Common, there was room here for gardens and trees. The Broadway Street, if it continued its relentless pace, would soon push north through here, moving along an ancient high ridge once walked by the Indians but, for now, small homes and businesses were widely spaced along streets like Spring and Wooster, still little more than country lanes.

He walked briskly, not wanting to run and alarm Mary Gibbons. Once away from Corbie's, he would move off to the side of the road and be able to move more quickly to keep her in sight. He never heard the door to Corbie's close for a third time in as many minutes nor the third set of footsteps move into Spring Street. Once away from Corbie's, it was difficult to see in the heavy gray night but Hickey managed to catch sight of Mary Gibbons as she turned south into Hudson Lane just before Greenwich Street. Once she had turned, Hickey broke into a full run. He would be lucky to pick up the trail now. She might be anywhere. Perhaps, a carriage was waiting around the turn. She may have seen him and was already doubling back across the fields behind him.

Rounding the corner into the dark street, Hickey, at first, saw no sign of Mary Gibbons. Then, staying under the cover of a tree, Hickey saw movement ahead. Mary Gibbons had apparently stopped to catch her breath she was only a few hundred feet ahead, moving now in and out of the deep shadows of the tall virgin trees. For the first time, she turned back to see if anyone was watching. Hickey thought she saw him but, by sheer luck, he had been within the deep shadows of another tree. She did not bolt. She hadn't seen him.

They moved briskly along, the prey and the tracker, in and out of shadows. Suddenly Hickey could see Mary Gibbons quite clearly. He realized that she had moved out into a lengthy open expanse of the dirt road. There was a single house on the right about a quarter mile ahead. The house was dark. Hickey would have to decide quickly. He could end the intrigue and hope to discover her secrets some other night. Or he could take his chances moving into the open road. Faint thunder rumbled and, although the clouds were crowding in over the island, he would still be seen by anyone for some distance either behind or ahead of him. He had just about decided to call off the game when Mary Gibbons provided an answer. She stopped, looked back down the road, and then quickly ran up the front steps and into the house on the right.

Crossing the road and stepping down an embankment into the grass, his head below the level of the road, Hickey ran to a point directly across the street from the house. He studied the structure while crouched in the high grass. It was a one-story wood-framed house with white clapboard siding. Large dormers protruded from the roof on either side of the peak to allow the inhabitants to make use of the attic space. The interior was dark. The nearest structure was barely visible perhaps a half mile down the road. Hickey could see a light flickering from a window. To the left of the house, as he looked across the street, was a neat side yard with fruit trees and a small garden. Closer to the house, a single, healthy tree, a sugar maple or, maybe, a pin oak grew to a height well above the roofline.

Wait. He could see the tree much more clearly now. Light eased out of the left side dormer and rested on the upper limbs and leaves of the tree, clearly a maple.

"Thank you, Miss Mary Gibbons, thank you very much," Hickey whispered.

Hickey sat on his haunches and went over his options. He could cozy right up here and wait until Mary came out or the "beautiful young thing close to the heart of the rebels" came out or someone came out. This might just be a decoy, a stop along the way to throw off any followers. He could then follow Mary or whomever to the real mother lode. Maybe they used a runner. In a few minutes, a scruffy errand boy would emerge from the front door, pull his cap down over his eyes and go off in to the night. He sat for several minutes his thoughts bouncing between what to do right now and how he would present this security leak to Washington if he did find out anything worthwhile. In the midst of these dueling thoughts came the gnawing pang of guilt over an idea that had first popped into his mind at the meeting. "A beautiful young thing," he thought, "close to the heart" of the liberty crowd. The only one he knew who fit that description was Phoebe. That, of course, did not mean it couldn't be someone he didn't know. Phoebe wouldn't be involved in such a thing. What a ridiculous idea. Could it be that Phoebe, too, was a spy? Maybe Washington hired her to spy on him. Or was old Black Sam worried about business once the Tories won? Had he put his daughter into the service of Washington to mine for gold? Old Sam might be playing both sides waiting for a clear winner.

But how would he tell Washington of any of this? If the leak was someone he knew or someone Hickey knew that Washington knew, it would be easy. He would run through a brief description of the evening's events, trailing Mary and the outcome. There's your problem. Pay me. Leave.

But what if Phoebe was somehow involved? Black Sam had showed his survival instincts once before. When it looked as if the French were winners, he changed his name to Fraunces. It wouldn't be much of a surprise to find he was doing what was necessary for his survival once again. Who better to gauge the hopeless nature of the cause than Fraunces? He could hear the swarthy Fraunces with that clipped not-quite-French accent saying: "So, my daughter, you say you love this Hickey even though I tell you he's no good. Once a traitor, always a traitor. You want to insure he lives? Just provide a few papers to Mary Gibbons and I'll see nothing happens to your Hickey." Right, Sam, thought Hickey, you'll take care of no one but yourself.

Hickey rattled his head. It was his feelings for Phoebe that were clouding his reasoning. He had seen her only once since being humiliated by Washington. She had found excuses not to report to Richmond Hill for several days and, then, when Hickey met her in the city, she said she couldn't stay long. She was nervous. She mumbled something about her father being more concerned about her safety now that the rioting had grown and the King's ships were expected to appear in the harbor at any moment. She looked as if she were about to cry. That night, Washington became more insistent on Hickey plugging the information leak. It was almost a threat. Hickey had to provide some valuable intelligence before the fat-arsed Virginian went off to Philadelphia or there might be "consequences." Hickey didn't have a clue what that meant. At just about any other time in his life, he would have described in great detail just where the old Yankee Doodle could plug his spy money. Right now, however, he was concerned about losing Phoebe and, somewhere in the back corners of his survival brain, he was concerned about what Washington meant by "consequences."

Hickey had no choice but to track down what Washington wanted. It was the only way he and Phoebe might be free of this entire business. Tomorrow he would report to Washington. Then he would explain everything to Phoebe and they could make plans to leave this place, a city growing more ugly every day. Rioting continued in the Holy Ground with scores of whores and soldiers being arrested in a lump and tossed, men and women together, into the prison at Bridewell to be sorted out a day or a week later. He had to get out of this. Take Phoebe and get away. It was never supposed to have gone this far.

He shook the thoughts from his head. Back to business. He had been crouched in the grass for ten minutes. A courier or go-between would have been anxious to return the material. Had he missed something? Had someone, Mary Gibbons herself, perhaps, walked out the back door almost

immediately? Was the light a decoy? Hickey got quickly
to his feet furious he hadn't even thought of a rear door. Or
maybe Mary Gibbons was operating a little dice game of her
own. Maybe this was bogus information. There might not
be any "beautiful young thing." She might have picked up
some cuttle at the taverns and then, scribbling a few official-
looking notes, buy the gratitude of some of the most powerful people in the city. It was time to find out.

As he crossed the street, he was exposed by a sudden
burst of lightning. He froze for an instant and then ran to
the base of the tree in the yard. Heavy rain slapped into the
leaves and made little pits in the dirt. There were shadows
moving on the curtains of the dormer window. If Mary or
someone else had left through a rear door, nothing could be
done now. But, if he climbed the tree, he might be able to
see in the window. He could at least identify someone who
lived in this house. Even that information might be valuable
to Washington.

Keeping the trunk between the window and himself,
Hickey studied the branches, looking for a quick path up.
The first branch was a couple feet out of his reach. He tried
walking his way up the tree, his palms and insteps clinging
to the slippery bark of the rain-soaked tree. He made it up
a few feet and then slipped, landing on his back with a slapping sound. He quickly got up and pressed himself against
the tree trunk in case someone had heard the fall. The rain
and thunder muffled the sound of his fall. He measured his
grip again and figured that, instead of trying to muscle his
way up, he could sort of run up the trunk and leap for the
branch. On his third try, he got his hands around the branch
and managed to swing his full weight onto the branch.

The branch he wriggled onto was about 18 inches in
diameter. It was sturdy and comforting and about 10 feet
below where he had to be in order to see into the dormer
window. He had to get higher. Standing on the limb and
holding on to a parallel limb over his head he sidled back

to the main trunk and surveyed the limbs above his current roost. It was the natural order of a tree's upward spire that the higher you went the narrower the limbs, Hickey jammed his right foot into the snug joint where a branch entered the trunk about three feet above his stance. Bear-hugging the trunk he stepped up, his left foot lightly resting on his right. Stepping to another branch on the same level but more around the trunk, to the south where it seemed the most branches extended toward the warmth of the sun, he managed to virtually walk up another four feet. His head was near the level of the window's sill, about 20 feet from the dormer. The window was open a crack and he could hear voices and see shadows. But, he still needed to be a few feet higher. These branches were only four or five inches thick. They supported his weight but not without bouncing under his steps and giving way as he stood. Carefully stepping up a notch, Hickey was aware of the severe pounding of his heart, a combination of tree scaling and anticipation. If he could balance his weight properly he could see into the window. He set himself and looked toward the window. Damn. He was high enough now to see into the window but he was looking at a rear wall and the occupants of the room were to the left of the window opening. There were clearly two people in the room. He could not see them exactly but there were two clear shadows on the wall. The shadows, cast by a lamp burning at mid-flame, were apart for a second and then blended together, both people standing. Hickey heard a soft, breathless gasp as the shadows melted into a single translucent gray form on the rear wall, like the hulking monster of a child's nightmare. If he was to see who was in the room he would have to move further out onto the narrow branch, already sagging under his squat but solid mass. He was standing straight up now his legs spread and his arms straight above his head holding a branch no more than a couple inches thick above his head. It was like one of the basic calisthenics positions the troops were now required to do each morning. Only Hickey was not about to do any jumping or clapping his hands over his head. His was on a delicate perch. Still, if he wanted to see the occupants of the room, he would have to get further out. Inching another few feet, the rain slicker now on the more slippery skin of the young tree growth, he felt his heart thudding now. He stopped to reassess and, as he did, the shadows broke apart, as if the monster was giving birth. A thinner portion of gray disappeared and then reappeared in front of the window, no longer gray but pink flesh with a swirl of white cloth. Hickey held tightly with his left hand and wiped the rain from his brow and eyes with his right. This was definitely a female. The white cloth ended at the waist, an undergarment had been peeled down revealing large, seemingly heavy breasts. Pink breasts. Breasts that bounced and jiggled side to side as the form swirled around. She was laughing and teasing, although Hickey couldn't hear what she was saying. He wiped his eyes again and, as the figure swirled a little slower this time, he saw the not-so-delicate earthy face of Mary Gibbons, if that, indeed, was her name. Hickey's mouth was dry, despite the rain, and his heart was beating out a steady quick-time march.

His arms began to ache from being held over head and gripping the branch so tightly. There was a vague sense of relief and excitement. Phoebe was not one of the room's inhabitants. He could see Mary and the other form was much larger than Phoebe. Then guilt wafted through him with the blowing rain. Of course it wasn't Phoebe. Why had he even thought such a thing? He quickly dismissed the painful idea, attributing it to his newness to the whole idea of love. It was like a madness. It was this love, too, that caused a bit of the guilt to remain as Hickey watched Mary Gibbon's hefty breasts and hips playfully cavort for her visitor. He wouldn't mind a turn at that, he thought.

Shaking the rain from his dripping hair, he alternately wiped his hands on his pants to get a firmer grip. The rain was coming in buckets now. He inched further out on to the branch, which sagged noticeably toward the ground some 20 feet below. He found himself letting his feet get ahead of his hands, realizing that was because the branch above his head was running out. It was much shorter than the one on which he stood. In fact, to get a glimpse of the other person in the room he would have to hold the end of the branch in his fingers like a rope and lean out. He was near the end of the finger hold and he could see, through watery eyes and rain-clouded windows, the rather hefty pink midsection of the figure watching Mary Gibbons do her dance of Salome.

If he could stretch just a little further out he might see a face. He carefully slid his feet another two feet out on the delicate perch that sagged and, Hickey thought, actually seemed to whimper. He adjusted his hands. He was now fully extended from the waist up, holding the end of the branch like a safety rope on a catwalk. He looked into the window. A nose. A bit of forehead bobbing in and out of view. Just a little more. A bit further.

As Hickey strained to see, lightning burst overhead, slamming into earth somewhere close by. The deafening roar of thunder, like the unearthly wail of the monster that had been projected on the wall, shook the tree.

In that instant, that fleeting window of opportunity in which the night and the window were lit as clearly as a cloudless summer day, the two figures moved together, framed in the center of the window.

What Hickey saw, the crystal clear images leapt from the window, screamed into his eyes and slammed into his chest as surely as if he had been struck by lightning. It propelled him back from his perch, as if his mind wanted to retreat at all costs. There was an interminable instant in which he was suspended, his back laid out almost parallel to the ground far below and the slick, sticky feel of the small branch and its leaves oozing through his grip. Then he was airborne. The descent was oddly slow, as so often happens in those instances when the body and mind check out of normal ev-

ery day time, and enter that cloud-filled world of fetal floating, of endless pasts and futures, a world of slow time, special time, like swimming in molasses, thick but as clear as a
mountain spring.

He hit the branch below on his left side and he bent like
a saddle. Pain shot through his chest and slammed into his
head. The branch had bruised his ribs but it slowed his descent. He tried grabbing for a branch as it passed by but,
in stretching his arms, he expanded his ribs. The pain was
instant and unbearable. He drew his arms in to his chest and
fell. There was nothing left to get in his way. He dropped the
last 10 feet face down, managing to turn to the side slightly
before slamming into the cold, wet ground.

In that last second, as he fell through the thick, rain-swol-
len night for what seemed like hours, Hickey saw the dormer
window and the two figures as clearly as he had in the instant
of the lightning flash. It was as if he was falling through
molasses and the scene in the windows was being played out
before him very slowly, deliberately.

He knew that high forehead with its hair pulled back in
a knot. He was quite familiar with the large prominent nose
above the tight lips, bulging a little from the hefty false teeth.
He recognized the large frame well over six feet, now quite
thick at the waist, although he had never seen it in the raw
before. In fact, it would have been the last guess on his list
if someone had said anyone in the city had seen this naked
form. Especially Mary Gibbons.

Then, as the molasses ran out, and just before a lightning burst of pain exploded behind his eyes, Thomas Hickey
formed one last thought.

It was George Washington. The Virginia gentleman. His
Excellency, the General of all the Troops of Liberty. It was
Washington himself who was the security breech. It was the
grand Virginia patrician who was taking relief in the loins of
one Mary Gibbons.

The "beautiful young thing" Mary Gibbons had been

talking about was none other than Mary Gibbons.

There in the window he stood, in all his glory. The "horse's mouth." The deep, dark source from whence came the bits and pieces of information flowing to the plotters. The antithesis of the sharp-toothed wharf rat slithering from redcoat ship to shore. The tall, somewhat paunchy, pasty complexioned sire of a new order. It was none other than the buck naked father of this seemingly hopeless cause.

Mary, it seemed, would entertain the good general with ample madeira and ample Mary. And, despite his excellence as a horseman, she would ride him into exhaustion. Perhaps, some nights, when the general refused to doze, she went to fetch more madeira or to a promised visit to a sick friend in the next house or whatever excuse would get her out of the nest and into the Corbie's den. While he dozed, she would rifle the pockets, blow out the lamp, take the papers to be copied and return them before arousing him for a nightcap. Of course, some nights, there would be no prize. But, as Hickey knew, Washington trusted no one but himself so, indeed, it would be quite logical for him to carry late-arriving bits of information on his person. Washington the spymaster was spying on himself.

Hickey went black. He never felt the large hands with the bear trap fingers digging into his arms and dragging him away from the tree.

Part III

Chapter Nineteen

On the road, north of City Wall
1:10 a.m., Tuesday, May 21, 1776

Hickey was rocking in Phoebe's arms. She was so warm, so gentle. She was singing to him. Then, for no reason, she began rocking him harder. Bouncing his head on the floor. And her voice ... it was getting deeper and not sweet at all. It was coarse and demanding. This wasn't Phoebe! It was an imposter, a man pretending to be Phoebe but in a wicked, crude skit. The man was yelling, taunting him.

Hickey's eyes slowly opened to the realization that he was not being rocked at all. He was being bounced along in the back of a wooden delivery wagon, a wet, mildew-slicked tarp tossed over him. The voice was that of the driver yelling at the horses. Two horses, Hickey guessed. He tried to sit up and push the tarp aside to see who was at the reins but was surprised by the resistance he met. He could move his body but his hands were restrained. He became aware of the rope around his wrists and then knew that the rope was fastened through a ring bolt in the bed of the wagon. His feet were also lashed together but they were not fastened to the wagon.

He tried calling out to the driver and, for an instant, thought the wagon slowed but there was no answer and the full pace resumed. He shifted onto his right side hoping to get a glimpse out from under the tarp but, as he turned to the right, his chest exploded in pain. He quickly fell back. The fall. He had fallen out of the tree. The Washington Tree. It did not hurt to breathe when he was on his back so, more than likely, the ribs were not broken, just bruised.

So, who had tied him up and was hauling him away? And where were they taking him? It could be a Washington Life Guard, someone assigned to watch the house while Washington was inside. That would mean someone who would know of the great general's need for an evening's poke. Who could he trust that much? Offhand, Hickey could think of no one in the Guard he would trust with that information. Maybe he had been discovered in a lump on the ground by another resident of the house. Or, perhaps, a neighbor had happened by and thought Hickey a robber and had tied him to be safe. In which case, they would be speeding to the city authorities. How long had he been out? The Mary Gibbons' nest was not more than a couple miles from the Common. It would only take twenty minutes or so and besides, even at night, once through the palisade wall, you could tell you were in the city. The wheels made a different sound on the packed city streets and, well, your nose could tell the difference between city and pasture. No, they were heading away from the city.

The wagon stopped. The horses shuffled and wheezed, catching their breath, and the driver jumped down and walked to the side of the wagon bed.

"Is the liberty boy awake yet," said the driver in a deep, deliberate voice. Hickey immediately recognized who it was. "Time to wake up and answer to the King."

John Clayford pulled the tarp away from the wagon bed and held a lantern close to Hickey's face. The sudden light made him blink and turn away.

"So, we are awake from our little nap. Good. 'Cause you and me have some serious discussion ahead."

"Cut these ropes, Clayford. What the hell are you doing?"

"For the near future, Hickey, I'll ask the questions and you provide the answers."

"Jesus Christ, Clayford, I got fuckin' broken ribs from fallin' out of a fuckin' tree. I've had a bad night. Don't make it any worse," Hickey was making a conscious effort to sound just plain angry. No fear. No guilt.

"I said: I talk. You answer," hissed Clayford, poking a thick black cudgel into Hickey's bruised ribs.

"Yeegodd!" yelped Hickey, the pain shooting from ribs to brain. "What the...."

"Now, listen Thomas Hickey, sergeant of a rebel general's private guard, I am going to explain how this will work. I am going to cut the loop so you can sit up. Keep in mind, your hands and feet are still bound, we are miles from the city and, I have several delightful tools that I will be more than willing to put to use. I have this beauty of a headknocker, this very sharp blade, and I have a loaded pistol right here," Clayford said patting the weapon tucked into his belt. Clayford reached over the wagon bed and slit the loop that attached his hand bindings to the ring bolt. Hickey was able to sit up and prop his back against the front wall of the wagon. The pain in his side eased a little.

Clayford, still standing alongside the wagon, set the lantern down in front of Hickey. He held the cudgel in his left hand. He drew the pistol, cocked the hammer and rested it on the wagon side panel, leveled at Hickey's face.

"Let's start with the basics. Who are you?" said Clayford calmly.

"What the fuck you talkin' about," said Hickey, genuinely angry now. "I'm Thomas Hickey. You know who I am. Who the fuck are you?"

"I ask the questions," said Clayford coolly, a thin, evil grin playing at his lips. He cracked the cudgel smartly across Hickey's right cheek, splitting the skin. The same spot that had been grazed by the Sears' cronies his first day in this fair city. Blood trickled into his mouth. "As you can see, the good Lord has given me equal use of both hands."

Hickey was furious. The whack on the cheek brought him to his senses. He could kick out at the pistol and be on Clayford in a heartbeat. He could get the hand bindings over Clayford's throat and throttle him in seconds.

"I don't think I would do that, Hickey," said Clayford, reading his thoughts and pulling the pistol back out of kicking range. "Now, let's start again. Who are you?"

"Thomas Hickey." He decided to buy time for a new plan while answering the questions. Besides, he was truly interested in knowing just what this was all about.

"Let me change that," said Clayford, "What are you?"

"What....?"

"Are you a sergeant in the Life Guard who has decided to return to the King's service? Or are you still a loyal Son of Liberty?"

"I don't give a warm turd about any of this liberty business. I don't want to hang when the King's ships arrive tomorrow or next week or next month. Simple as that."

"That simple, eh?" said Clayford, "Why is it then that you followed Mary Gibbons home? Why would you want to know the source of her information? Unless, of course, you wanted to warn the general."

"Are you quite done! That's what this is about? Christ, Clayford, I followed her home to poke her. You saw the way she bounces her delicious ample ass around, flirting with the old men. I got a healthy wooden soldier just watching. I figured I could help her sleep better by putting the boots to her for an hour or so."

"First of all," said Clayford, showing no emotion, "no one, as you say, puts the boots to Mary Gibbons 'cept who I say. Second, you're lying." He whacked Hickey in the same spot with the club. A purplish lump grew out of Hickey's cheek.

"Why didn't you catch up to her on the road? Walk with

her a ways, break her in to the idea? Why did you hide in the grass and watch her go into the house? No secret lover climbs a tree first."

"I lost her in the dark. I wasn't sure which house she went in."

"I was right behind you. You knew exactly where she was going. You didn't lose her. I never once lost you. Was right behind you from Corbie's. Now, I told you I needed the truth." Clayford struck another blow to the egg-sized lump on Hickey's cheekbone. A pulse of pain distracted Hickey for a second but the blows were easier to take now. Anger and numbness were seeing to that.

"Now, Thomas Hickey, I am going to ask you two questions. I want you to think carefully before you answer. First, what did you see spying on Miss Mary Gibbons? Second, who is the bad apple in our little orchard? Who tipped you to our plans and let you into our little circle?"

Hickey thought very carefully, all the time staring into Clayford's eyes, dark eyes made even deeper by the lantern glow. He also carefully planned his defense against Clayford's response to these so-carefully thought out answers.

"I saw her bare ass and it was your mother who told me where to look," said Hickey, readying his bound feet.

Clayford swung the cudgel and Hickey's heels met the attacker's forearm. The club popped out of his hand and banged off the wagon onto the ground. Surprised, Clayford leveled the pistol closer to Hickey.

"That was not a wise thing," he said, still quite calm but the stone coldness in his eyes was as raw as any animal Hickey had ever seen.

"You might as well shoot, Clayford, 'cause the next chance I get I'm gunna cram it up your arse and pull the trigger."

Clayford smiled. This Hickey was a lot like himself. He would have to work a little but, eventually, he'd get what he wanted.

"Get down out of the wagon."

Clayford backed away, keeping the pistol aimed at Hickey's face. Hickey rolled onto the bruised ribs, grunted and got on to his knees. Then, with a little hop, he was on his feet. He hopped to the end of the wagon, squatted down to sit on the end and then jumped off. His cheek was pulsing with each beat of his heart and his damaged ribs made him walk bent at the waist like an old man.

"It's time for a bath, Hickey, you smell like hay and horse manure."

Hickey didn't have the slightest clue what a bath had to do with their present situation. Then, as the moon moved out from under the dissipating storm clouds he could see a massive dark structure a few hundred feet up the hill from the road. Now he knew where he was.

They were not more than two miles from Mary Gibbons house and even closer to Washington's headquarters at Richmond Hill. They were on high ground along what some Tories called Great George Street, an extension of the Broad Way outside the city. This was the water engine, that amazing bit of technology started two years ago by a young visionary named Christopher Colles. Hickey had heard all about it in the tavern talk and in the papers. He was struck by the similarities between Colles and himself. Both were in their mid-30s. They were both Irish and they both had been in the colonies for five or six years. However, while Hickey was getting himself deeper and deeper into the unwanted and unsought intrigue of this rich man's struggle, Colles was busy creating a true marvel of mechanical ingenuity — a steam driven water pump. The City Council had given him a couple thousand pounds to start the project and Colles had purchased this land and built a huge reservoir. The wood structure was, Hickey remembered, something like 60 feet wide by 100 or 150 feet long and 10 feet high. The roofed structure could hold more than half a million gallons of fresh clean water from a huge well on the property. But the real stunner of the project was that it would operate with a steam-powered engine. Most people laughed when they first heard about it. "Next, they'll have steam-powered horses," said one tavern wag as he and Hickey discussed the project.

Colles was not to be denied even though the only other steam engine ever brought to the colonies was burned in a fire three years earlier. He decided to build his own. Just last month, people were out in the streets looking north as Colles unfurled a massive flag celebrating the successful test of the engine. You could see the flag all the way down in the Bowling Green. Colles had cast an 18-inch cylinder, fired the boiler and the steam power had pumped water 50-feet up the well at a rate of 200 gallons a minute.

The City Council was so excited that it approved another seven thousand pounds sterling for the construction of more than 10 miles of hollowed out pine logs to be used as pipes bringing fresh water to most city streets and alleyways.

Hickey recalled how his horse had shied at drinking the trough water when he first arrived in New York. Some wealthy residents had their own wells but most either spiked the brackish water with spirits or bought it from the tea-water men at three pence a hogshead. The watermen got it from Fresh Water Pond north of the city early in the day and then peddled it on the streets. But, now the work had come to a halt because of the impending conflict and the fact that most of the city's laborers had already fled. Those remaining were kept busy in the construction of the fortifications.

Hickey had not bothered to visit the water engine site but it was much larger than he imagined. It seemed to move off into the night for miles, like some dark, hulking ship abandoned by its crew. There were no windows and the wood was very dark from the tar pitch mixture used to waterproof and seal the joints.

"Impressive isn't it?" said Clayford. "I helped build the engine. Works as smoothly as a mantle clock. Walk up that path on the right. Quickly!"

Hickey shuffled along as quickly as the leg bindings would allow. There was a path leading up the hill to the south end of the structure. Once at the top of the hill, Hickey saw some steps built into the side of the building leading to a small enclosure seemingly stuck on the side of the large reservoir building. The floor of this small structure, supported by wooden trestles, was just about at the roofline of the larger building. The enclosure extended several feet onto the roof of the main structure.

"Up the stairs," ordered Clayford, first allowing Hickey to remove the leg bindings. Hickey hesitated and Clayford pressed the pistol firmly into the back of his neck. Clayford told Hickey to remove the beam across the door, open it and step inside. Hickey did and Clayford stepped in. Clayford ordered Hickey to put his hands on the low wooden railing of the small platform and not turn around. Hickey felt the pistol withdraw from his neck while Clayford hung the lantern on a bracket next to the door and then pulled the door shut.

They were on a small platform from which attendants could monitor water height and flow. When the reservoir was filled to capacity, probably only a foot or so from the main roof, the platform would be only inches above the water line. The lantern gave enough light so that Hickey could see there was water in the structure. The light faded quickly in the sealed building so Hickey couldn't see more than twenty feet ahead nor could he tell how much water had been left in the reservoir after the tests. He kept staring straight out into the darkness.

"Several test pumps have worked without a mishap," said Clayford. "Probably three or four feet of water in here right now. Fresh spring water. Nothing like it."

Without warning, Clayton, having tucked the pistol in his belt, lunged at Hickey slamming into his shoulders and, grabbing his belt, dumping Hickey out over the railing. Hickey grabbed at the air.

Hickey had no time to think about the fall, hitting water

almost instantly. He hit the hard surface of the water on his right side, slapping his bruised ribs. He went under, struggled to right himself and then realized he could stand. Hickey was not afraid of pistols and knives. He hadn't found a man yet who made him cower. The concept of authority never set well with him. He often thought that, perhaps, the good lord had not given him all of the necessary ingredients for normal fear. Fear was not a big part of his makeup, except, perhaps, that rather peculiar form of fear he experienced when he first met Phoebe. But, here was the one thing that caused uncontrollable fear -- drowning. He had never learned to swim. A man had no control over his limbs in the water. Everything was slow and dangerous underwater. Water was insidious. It creeped into places it wasn't supposed to be and stayed well beyond its welcome. Boats were all right. They were dry and there was always something to hang on to just in case. But, being in water or under water was a different story.

The water in the reservoir was deeper than Hickey had guessed. It had to be only a few inches under five feet because it was up to his neck. The floor of the reservoir was solid, stones or timbers. He couldn't tell. He hopped over to the wall. The walls were slick with pitch. There were no hand holds. No way to climb up. No way out. He was losing control, his mind raced down a narrow, watery shoot toward panic. Clayford spoke.

"Now, Sergeant Hickey. Let us go through these questions once again."

The reality of Clayford's voice nudged the panic aside and Hickey took a deep breath.

"Why don't you come down here and ask me?" Hickey said, carefully masking any fear.

"It is truly amazing that you have lived this long being so stupid, Hickey," said Clayford. "I told you several times that I am asking the questions. You are providing the answers."

"I don't think so," said Hickey strongly, while bobbing in the water directly under Clayford. "Now if you'll just go away and let me swim in peace...." Hickey bobbed backwards until his back was against the cool, wet, pitch-covered wall, his feet searching for the smallest node, the tiniest foothold to get him up further out of the water. The walls were smooth.

"I'm losing patience with you, Hickey. I'll ask you one last time. Why did you follow Mary? And who tipped you to our little party group?"

"I wanted to get my hands on those tits. And your horse's arse told me all I need to know about you," Hickey shouted his voice echoing off the water and walls.

"Fine, Sergeant Hickey. I'll let you stew for a while. Maybe you'll feel like talking later." Clayford slammed the door.

The panic slammed into his head. He wanted to shout to Clayford to come back. Please come back. He would tell him everything. I'm just a heavy-handed rogue smuggler in over my head. I don't give a horse plop about the Kings or the Washingtons of the world. I'm just out to carve a space for myself and maybe someone like Phoebe. Someplace far from people like you. Washington is giving me gold but not enough gold to drown here in this huge water-filled coffin. Come back. I'll tell you everything I know.

All that came from his mouth at the sound of the door was: "Hey!...."

Hickey gulped in air and tried to stave off the panic. The faint post-storm moonlight through the open door above had allowed him to at least see the surface of the water and the walls near on each side. Now, he could see nothing. He hopped on his toes to his right, found the corner and pushed his back hard into the angle. It made him feel slightly less vulnerable. Concentrate. How could he escape? He had no way of climbing the five or six feet up of the platform. He would have to move carefully around the walls searching for something, anything, that would help him. He took several more deep breaths and began his hopping exploration of the walls. He had only gone six or seven feet when he was startled by a deep clunking sound, like the muffled sound of a blacksmith's anvil when heard from the street. This sound continued but was joined by a soft whoosh like fast-moving mountain stream. Then, he felt it.

The water was moving. At first just slightly but, within a few minutes the surface of the water was lapping against his face. And it was getting deeper!

Clayford had started the water engine and was filling the reservoir.

Hickey lost control. He screamed something incoherent at Clayford and began clawing at the wall kicking his legs hopelessly at the shiny surface, trying to climb up. Panic quickly sapped his strength and he stopped, pushing his back deeper into the wall. His calves were aching from the strain of balancing on his toes and yet the water was already right up under his chin. It had gone up about three inches in just a few minutes. At this rate, it would be above his nose in just a few minutes more. He had to do something. Then, as often happened when he was faced with a crisis, whether the redcoat patrols on the Charles or an irate whore wench, his mind became very clear and calm. He quickly went over the details of the reservoir building as he remembered them. That's it, he thought. The water is stored here to be pumped into the city. The way out was the way the water got out. Several of the hollowed out logs that were to be used as pipes were already hooked to the outlet hatch. If he could pry open that hatch, he might be able to let the water out and buy sometime. But, the hatch, as he remembered, was at the other end of the building, 100, maybe 150 feet away. Hopping along the edge would take much longer than he had. He had to speed up the process somehow. He remembered seeing the soldiers swimming off the docks in Boston. They would roll over on their backs, cock their legs into a crouch and push off the dock and shoot out into the river. Of course, they would then swim back for another push. Something he always envied, especially on the rare occasion when he even consider the notion of a ship or boat he was on going down. All the while he was thinking, he was positioning himself tight against the wall under the platform. He wasted no time. He was mostly in control now. He took a deep breath, drew in a huge breath and rolled over on his back. With all the strength of his thick legs, he dug in and pushed against the wall. He shot across the reservoir, water rushing over his face. It was difficult to say how far he had covered. Even more of a problem was determining in which direction to continue. If he had sometime gotten turned around, he would waste his last few minutes hopping back to where he had started. He didn't hesitate. Straining to keep his mouth out of the water, he bobbed forward. He found that, with momentum, he could bob up out of the water to where the water was around his chest. Then he could lunge forward, gaining a few feet each time. The lunging, however, caused the swollen jaw to throb and the pain to shoot through his chest. It also quickly drew the strength from his legs and back. A few minutes at this pace and his legs would barely hold him up. He was considering a precious minute or two of rest when his hand touched a wall. Knowing the outlet hatch would be to his right, if this, indeed, was the far wall, he bounced along the wall. The steam engine continued to hum. The water was at his nose now. He had to time his breaths as the mini-tides of water moved into and away from his face.

Just a few feet down the wall he felt it. It was like discovering gold. Or making love to Phoebe. There was a change in the contour of the wall. A square corner of pitch-covered wood standing an inch or two out from the smooth wall. Hickey traced his hands round the full shape. It was a square hatch about three feet on each side. The hatch was, of course, set low in the wall so that the water would be drawn from the bottom of the reservoir tank. He could get a foot up on the top ridge. He couldn't manage to balance for very long but he knew now that he could buy time. He could, if needed, get up out of the water. Hickey began working on the hatch. The outlet mechanism was on the outside. An operator would more than likely shift a hefty lever and trip the hatch panel aside to start the water flow. Whether he could move the panel from inside was a different story. He smoothed his hands around the panel and found what seemed to be the ends of bolts, probably the bolts that held the lever mechanism. He pushed to the left and nothing happened. He pushed to the right and thought he felt movement. Bracing his back against the wall as best as possible, Hickey grabbed the frame of the hatch with his powerful fingers and put his right foot against the bolts. His legs were weak from all of the hopping on his toes but he was getting a second wind now. There was hope. He strained his legs and, just as he lost his grip, the panel slid ever so slightly. Able to hold himself comfortably above water, Hickey gave himself the luxury of a few minutes rest. On the second push, he dug his fingers into the wood and concentrated on pushing with the large muscles of his thighs. The panel slid nearly three inches. Hickey stood quietly and felt it. There was movement. Water was rushing past him. Water, held captive in this dark cavern just as he was, rushed through the opening and down the log pipes. With water streaming out, Hickey waited even longer to recharge. Then, instead of using his feet, he slid his fingers into the hatch opening and locked them around the thick hatch panel. Jamming a foot into the frame he strained with every ounce of strength left.

The combination of newly-found energy and the ever-increasing rush of water, snapped the hatch panel fully open. Thousands of gallons of water raced to freedom sweeping Hickey in its wake. He splayed out his arms and legs, catching the sides of the panel but the water pressure crushed him into the opening. He let go, took a final gasp of air and went head first into the pipe. He had no time to think or to panic. The surge of water forced his wide frame through the hollowed logs with ease. In seconds, he shot out the open end of the test piping. The pipe was only three feet off the ground on thick wooden trestles but the force of the water carried him straight out in the air for about eight feet. The water flow cushioned the fall and carried him on a small river down a gentle grass slope for nearly 50 yards.

Hickey rolled onto his back, staring at the gray moon, water racing over and around him trying to find a lower level. He laughed and howled like a mad man.

Hickey lay on the ground for nearly an hour resting his body as well as his emotions. His jaw was now numb, certainly better than the pain. His ribs were still wracked with pain. He considered all of his options. There was only one thing to do. He had to get to Washington before he left for Philadelphia. Confront him with what he had witnessed. End this spying business right now. Get out. And take Phoebe with him.

Clayford had not come running to the water drop. His captor, it seemed, had left the water engine site. He had either written Hickey off or was going to let him soak for several hours figuring a water-softened prisoner would be much more cooperative.

The details of the countryside were slowly being filled in by the late spring sun. It would be full daylight in less than an hour. He had to get to Washington. But he also had to avoid Clayford. He used a jagged rock to slice the wrist bindings.

Washington was due to leave for Congress in Philadelphia today, probably shortly after daybreak. It was possible that he might use the Greenwich Road but more than likely the carriage and escorts would come out Richmond Hill on the Mortier estate road and then go north on The Lane north to the King's Bridge. He was only a couple miles from where the estate road met The Lane. He could travel through the fields along the tree line and probably be there in less than an hour.

The walk was easy and refreshing. Hickey's clothes were drying and the bright, clear sun promised a spectacular late spring day. He reached the Delancy estate in quick order and moved rapidly through the just-budding grove trees of the Stuyvesants. When he reached the junction of the Mortier road and The Lane, the sun was just breaking fully above the horizon. There was no one else in the road. He had either missed Washington or was early. He picked a vantage point on the northeast corner, climbed into the lower branches of an evergreen tree and waited. From here he could see several hundred yards west into the Mortier road. That would give him time to scramble down, wait alongside the road and get to Washington in the coach as he went by. The night's rain had left the road messy so the entourage would not be moving very fast.

Less than half an hour later, Hickey heard the faint rumbling of a carriage and saw the general's coach and the mounted Life Guards in front and at the rear. Hickey jumped down from the tree but still kept the trees between him and the road. The entourage turned slowly into The Lane and was coming toward Hickey. Hickey stepped out and started walking to the road. He thought about what he would say. He would give Washington the benefit of the doubt. After all, Hickey, too, had spent many a night in a woman's bed. He would state the facts of the previous night, tell Washington he was through and insist on partial payment of what the general had promise him. He hoped it would go smoothly but he was prepared to insist and even to break Washington's secrets to the other Life Guards present if the discussion got out of hand. He was clearly in view of the guards now though still a couple hundred feet or so away.

As he took another step toward the approaching carriage, Hickey froze. Three horses were approaching from the south coming up the road behind the Washington contingent at a gallop. Hickey instinctively dropped back from the road and watched. The sergeant on duty of the Life Guard halted the carriage and rode to the back. The four Life Guards faced the approaching horses. The leader of the newcomer said something to the sergeant. He rode back to talk with the general. The newcomers waited. The general apparently approved of what was reported and the men got off their horses and walked to the carriage. Hickey squinted, opened his eyes wide, and squinted again. He couldn't believe what he was seeing but it was right there in front of him. The visitor was John Clayford.

Hickey shrunk back into the protection of the fir tree. Clayford was talking with Washington. Now he was signaling to the two men riding with him. Together they looked in the direction of the fir tree and prodded the horses into a run. They were heading for him.

Hickey's instincts took over. He wasn't in water now. He crouched low and moved back away from the fir, keeping its protecting limbs between him and the riders. He had bound his shirt tightly around his ribs and the pain had eased. He was able to cross the narrow Stuyvesant lane and squat, almost completely invisible, among the row hedges. He watched as the riders rode around the tree and then looked up and down the estate lane. They split up. Fatal mistake thought Hickey. One rider road into the Stuyvesant Lane toward the main house while the other swept slowly back and forth in the fields. Hickey waited behind the hedge. When the rider broke through the hedge, Hickey, surprise on his side, grabbed the man's arm and yanked him from the horse. A few short, powerful blows from Hickey's thick hands and the man lay unconscious. Hickey stuffed a kerchief into the rider's mouth and bound him. The man's horse had been shied away by Hickey's ambush. The other rider was not in sight. Hickey moved out toward the road again. The Washington entourage was already a half mile north. Clayford was riding slowly toward the Stuyvesant Road to meet his riders.

Hickey crouched once again and moved swiftly east toward the protection of the thick woods which stretched from the lane almost all the way to the East River. Who could he trust? Was Clayford another of Washington's agents? Did they think that it was Hickey whose coat was turning bright red? Was Clayford really one of the King's men who had somehow gotten the confidence of an unsuspecting Washington?

The first order of business was safety. Washington was not due back from Philadelphia until June 7. Getting to Washington was still Hickey's best hope. Maybe he should just leave. Head west right now. Washington could go play with his doodle for all he cared. He'd be labeled a deserter once again and face possible charges. Not a big problem. But what about Phoebe? It was unthinkable to leave without her. But Clayford and crew would be looking for him. Who knows what he told Washington. The entire city might be after him right now. His first objective was to make it to the Salt Meadows, a low-lying scrub area along the sound. He would be safe for the night. There, in the soft marsh hidden by acres of wild grass, he could work out a plan. He would rest and work on a plan.

Chapter Twenty
Philadelphia and New York
May 22 to June 5, 1776

Hickey came awake with the light of the late spring sun rising quickly over the East River. He had slept soundly, perhaps too soundly, on a rather comfortable bed of grass and reeds but felt damp as if someone had wet him down for the night like a saddle horse. He had slept for several hours yet was bone weary. The throbbing in his cheek had subsided and was only sore to the touch now. His ribs hurt and his right hip was tender, bruised by the squeeze through the water conduit. He had simply tried to talk with Washington. He hadn't been prepared for this. He had no blanket. No food. He began to walk north, keeping the sun at his right shoulder. His boots were stiff from being soaked and then drying. He stayed in the tall vegetation listening for the slightest sound or movement. Clayton's men might be out looking for him this morning. If he could move around to the northwest, past the small pond near where the Jews buried their dead, he would find some small farms.

After a half hour of slow going over lumpy terrain, his stomach empty, Hickey stepped out into a clearing. An expanse of crop fields stretched for several hundred feet to either side and half again as far up to a small white and red house. The house was too far away for him to see anyone or be seen. The field in front of him had just been plowed. Dark brown soil with clumps of gray stretched in neat furrows away to the north. To his right, however, a smaller field was green with small plants. Hickey walked toward the plants, his stomach now howling.

Farmers here in New York often made two potato plantings; one as early as weather would allow for harvesting in summer and the other, planted in June, would allow for harvesting in September. Hickey grabbed at a few of the small green plants and pulled. It was still about a month too early for the harvest but there were a few small nodes at the roots that were edible. Hickey pulled out his shirt and formed a small sack to hold the stunted potatoes. He quickly plucked the plants and popped off the small brown lumps from the roots into his shirt. When he had several pounds of the deformed little tubers, he ran back along the tree line buffering the fields from the river. Finding some dry kindling, he used a flint to start a small fire and tossed in the brown lumps, then he sat with his back against a thick tree and thought about what he had to do.

***

Washington found the Philadelphia of 1776 much different than the one he had left only a year before. The stiff formalities of the Congressional delegates of 1775 had been replaced by impassioned rhetoric and a heady sense of destiny. This despite the "most shocking and unaccountable misconduct" of the Canadian invasion as one delegate referred to the northern campaign.

"What do you think of the proposal of your fellow Virginians, General Washington?" asked John Hancock. The peacock from Massachusetts referred to instructions to the Virginia delegation that had come from Williamsburg a week ago. They were to propose that the Continental Congress pass a resolution declaring the 13 colonies free and independent states.

"I believe it to be a noble vote," said Washington, with caution, "but it is my opinion that our first order of business should be to draft a constitution. Such a document, Mr. Hancock, cannot be the work of a single day. There is much to be done. This is a document that may very well render millions happy or miserable depending on the outcome of all that we strive for."

"Well said! Well said, George, but why so formal?" Washington had taken, on this visit, to calling all of the delegates 'mister'.

"I am a general in the service of this Congress," replied Washington stiffly. Congress was not pleased with the debacle to the north. There was a great deal of infighting. Fingers were being pointed. John Adams had written a letter to James Warren in Massachusetts asking, "Where shall we lay the blame for this most ignominious defeat?" Ben Franklin had been asked to investigate and had reported flagrant mismanagement of military events.

Washington took these charges personally. Hancock himself had complained to him about a lack of discipline. As the commander in chief, Washington felt it was his responsibility though he had little input prior to the debacle that ensued in the north. He took such charges personally. While Hancock did not seem to make the connection between criticizing the military's discipline and Washington's responsibilities, he was taking no chances. He would remain professional. He would report his needs, offer his opinion when asked and, when he returned to New York, move quickly to make certain the New York campaign was not a repeat of the northern border fiasco.

"Two items before I forget, George," said Hancock, either not noticing or choosing to ignore Washington's pensiveness. "Don't forget the committee meeting tomorrow. This will be your best opportunity to get what you need from Congress. You know how I feel about the disaster in Canada.

Our troops were ruined before the fight began. There was no discipline, George. Troops need discipline, as I am certain you are most aware. I am afraid, George, afraid that we are not prepared for any new attack by the King's forces. New York, as you have so correctly pointed out to us all, is obviously the next test. We must be ready. The troops must be ready. I will support you in what you need.

"On a more personal note, I don't know whether Martha told you but I have commissioned Mr. Peale to produce portraits of you and your charming wife."

"Yes, she has insisted that I sit for an hour each day until we leave. I am grateful for the thought," said Washington, "but I have tried every tack to escape. But, I can find no outlet," said Washington, allowing a wan smile, and not commenting on the state of the troops.

"You're most welcome, General Washington," said Hancock, laughing loudly and slapping Washington's shoulder. "We must record these times for history, George. In whatever fashion, our world will be much different after this business." Washington nodded slightly, readily agreeing their world would never be the same but uncertain as to the outcome. Hancock was, indeed, a supporter despite the initial rivalry for the job, but he was also a politician. It was becoming clearer with each day that New York was key to his maintaining the role as commander in chief. Several delegates had confided in him that there were opponents to his command. Canada was an embarrassment and, although the ambiguity of command was not directly his fault, as commander in chief it became part of his record. He could not afford to suffer such a defeat in New York. He had a long list of items to bring before the committee tomorrow. If he got what he wanted, New York would be prepared.

***

Meanwhile, in the New York City jail, Henry Dawkins

was not in a position to change the world. Nor was he in a laughing mood. Once again, the unwise application of his god-given artistic talent had landed him behind bars. This time he would be drawing for three. The Youngs brothers had been arrested at the same time and they had been unceremoniously tossed into the same cell. All were charged with counterfeiting. The reptilian Youngs had spent the first day sitting on the edge of the cot, pressed together ankle to shoulder, rocking back and forth.

"I told you I would take care of it and I will," said Dawkins impatiently when the brothers whined that they had been taken in by Dawkins; had, in fact, been 'dragged into this mess' against their will.

The brothers had continued rocking and moaning until the first visit by the gap-toothed guard.

"Mr. Dawkins!" gushed the guard with unrestrained delight. "What brings you back here?"

"How's that pretty woman of yours?" purred Dawkins.

"Just fine. Still treasures the drawin's ya did."

"My pleasure, my pleasure, indeed. Now me and my friends here could really use something to eat...."

The guard hurried on down the dank, hollow hall to find food for Dawkins and the Youngs. As he did, he passed by another cell holding a solitary prisoner.

This prisoner was not as much as ease within the foul-smelling confines of the city lockup. It was his first such confinement. His mind worked overtime. What would happen if the liberty boys tried him as a traitor? What if the King's ships arrived and began destroying the city? He'd be left to die, the fetid blocks of the jail walls falling on his head. He had to get out. And soon. What did he have, what did he know, that would help in the bargaining? They had questioned him several times already. None of his answers were of any value, they said. Think harder. Why are you holding back? His worry was for naught. Within a few days, he would have the perfect tale to tell.

In yet another cell just a few feet away, Isaac Ketcham went over each day of the past few months. He, too, was charged with counterfeiting but for some reason he was being kept away from Dawkins and the Youngs. The military officer who read him the charges said he was also being charged with conspiracy. What conspiracy? He bought some paper, paper that was a lot like official scrip, but paper nonetheless. He knew that Dawkins and the boys may have been peddling the paper to the Tories but so what? Half the people in the city were Tories. What had Dawkins conveniently forgotten to tell him? Counterfeiters were as plentiful as whores in the Holy Ground. But conspiracy didn't sound good at all. Who knew what craziness the Whigs were after? And the Tory plots were rumored in every tavern. If he were somehow caught up in this conspiracy business, he might waste away in this cell for years. What would happen to his family?

He could not stay in this rotting cell. He had to get out. He tried to concentrate. How could he convince the authorities that he was just a paper merchant who had used bad judgment to make a quick profit? He wouldn't hesitate to turn over Dawkins or the Youngs. They were lowlifes anyway. What could he use to bargain? He went over his first meeting with Dawkins. The Youngs had slithered in and explained that the trio needed a "very special" paper order. He shuddered at the thought of almost being tarred and feathered by Sears and his thugs. And how Sgt. Hickey had, well, had saved the day, saved his skin. Or had he? And why? Why would a guy like Hickey risk his own hide to save a stranger? Unless it was planned that way. Hickey may have been looking for a quick way to fatten his purse. Hickey! That was it. He was certain the good general from Virginia would be interested in knowing that one of his private guards was involved in a counterfeit ring. He spent the rest of the evening going over his plan.

***

Hickey, his stomach filled with baked potatoes, had decided three things. First, he had to get to Phoebe and tell her everything: spying for Washington, Clayford, everything. Second, he had to find out just what Clayford was up to. Was he working for Washington? For the King? For himself? Third, he had to confront Washington as soon as he returned to the city.

He had decided that the first step in accomplishing these three things would be paying a visit to Mary Gibbons. Her house was not all that far away. He would get what he wanted from her, one way or another. Charm or force. He was certain she knew the Clayford story. Depending upon what he learned from her, he could find Clayford and get down to business. If he could clear up this business with Clayford directly, he would go to Phoebe, explain everything to her and together they would wait for Washington's return. Then they would leave and let the rich men fight their war.

If for some reason he couldn't get to Clayford, he would have to be more careful. There was no way of knowing what Clayford had told Washington. He might have reported seeing Hickey pledge his allegiance to the Daft King. If Clayford was in Washington's pocket and knew about Hickey's arrangement, then he might be telling Washington that he was selling out. Perhaps, every soldier in the city was looking for him. That would not stop him, however, from seeing Phoebe. He had a little over a week before Washington returned. It would be plenty of time to accomplish the first two parts of the plan of action.

He set off for Mary Gibbon's house. His route would take him to the north of the burial ground, north of the water engine, just to the south of the fresh pond and across Ranelagh Gardens into Hudson Street. This route would provide adequate cover and should take no more than an hour.

***

Isaac Ketcham put down the pen and reread the petition to the Provincial Congress. He had done a fine job. There was plenty of humility. He especially liked the part where he claimed to be "deeply etched with shame and confusion for my past misconduct and only now can I see that my wife and six poor children will starve unless I am set free by bail."

But it was the last paragraph that would get him freed. "Sir, I the subscriber have something to observe to the honorable house if I could be admitted to do so. It is nothing concerning my own affair. But entirely another subject."

Isaac Ketcham had no way of knowing that this bit of creativity would get him out of jail nor could he know that it would have much graver consequences for one Thomas Hickey.

**

"I hope you have what you need to do the job, General Washington," said Benjamin Harrison, one of Washington's best friends in Congress and one of the few whom, at six feet four inches, could look him directly in the eye. A fellow Virginian, Harrison, while as tall as Washington, was not as trim. Even though Washington had gained twenty pounds since his young scouting days, Harrison outweighed him by fifty pounds.

"I think it went quite well," replied Washington, adjusting his uniform after having sat for the last three hours in committee. He, Harrison and delegate Elbridge Gerry, another Washington supporter from Massachusetts, were headed for a late lunch at the City Tavern a few blocks away.

"The report on the Hessians tipped the scale," said Harrison. "How did you get that information?"

"I have made it a point to invest in information, Benjamin. I have scores of men out looking for such knowledge of the King's men. This particular fellow had been captured but escaped. As soon as he got the message to me, I rushed it to Congress. King George hiring 17,000 Hessian troops to fight against us makes for quick argument. Combined with the fifteen regiments on their way, we face 30,000 trained troops."

"I believe your advice to the Congress was straightforward," said Gerry. "If nothing else, the suggestion that our men at the north fight for every foot of ground will help morale. I am not certain of its chances for success but, perhaps, it will slow down the advance from the north."

"I am certain of that," added Harrison. "But more important was the approval for 20,000 militia and the 'flying camp' idea was brilliant, George."

Washington accepted the compliment readily although the idea was not exactly new. They would form a force of 10,000 additional troops ready to move at an instant's notice. In actuality, Washington was not certain such a force could be raised, or that it could be moved that quickly. But, again, it gave Congress the sense of taking matters into its own hands. It was good for morale and also boosted their confidence in their chosen commander in chief as a man of action.

"I would have much preferred that Congress paid for enlistments for regular troops for at least three years as I suggested," said Washington.

"Benjamin and I agree with you, George," added Gerry, "but, there are many in Congress still not convinced of the necessity for any kind of separation or independence. Also, resources are scarce. So, I guess the future rests on the militia and how well you can lead them, George."

Over lunch, the trio discussed the growing movement toward independence. John Adams had been for complete independence since the start. He was forever lobbying for a resolution to that effect. But it had never gotten very far. Many delegates, acting on their instructions from home, were taking the cautious route. Concessions and a degree of freedom, both politically and economically, were fine. But, a break from the King was just not reasonable, not achievable and certainly not necessary. This entire affair had gone way beyond what many in Congress had subscribed to from the start. The colonists had one of the highest standards of living in the known western world. Many farmers, professionals and businessmen were taking in tens of thousands of dollars each year. Fortunes were being made. All the King wanted was a small share to help pay the bills. Was that too much to ask? Somehow the notion of liberty had been intertwined with economics. There was simply no going back now. Fortunes and freedom had been wagered. George Washington stood to lose a great deal as did many others. Washington knew with certainty that independence was the only path remaining.

"Our Pennsylvania hosts are the staunchest opponents to independence," said Harrison, sloshing through double portions of meats and cheeses. But, I think we now are close to a vote."

Pennsylvania had never considered itself a royal colony in the first place. The highly sophisticated political engine in place was being run by John Dickinson. It had been put in place by William Penn and his offspring. John Adams and his cousin, Sam, had been quietly and steadily making progress in breaking up this Penn control over the Pennsylvania assembly. "Common Sense," Tom Paine's impassioned call to liberty had come at just the right time. But, it took a somewhat suspect attack on a British frigate patrolling the Delaware to bring the conflict close to home for Pennsylvanians.

"I think they were stunned on Wednesday when old John Adams read the resolution from Virginia calling for new local governments that are best for independency."

"I believe it must come and soon," Washington confided. "I only hope we are prepared."

"The Board of War and Ordnance should help, George.

That was an important item. I think you made a logical plea for its creation. And the staff changes were a good idea. Joseph Reed will make a fine adjutant general and we all agree that Moylan was needed in the Quartermaster role."

"Yes, I have gotten all I could have expected, with the exception of the regulars. But, is it enough? Even now I think I should be hurrying back to New York. There were rumors when I left that I was coming here to resign. Hopeless cause and all of that. God help us as I suspect we have a bloody summer ahead of us."

"Enough doom for the moment," said Harrison, "As I said to Elbridge earlier, I weigh twice as much as he does. So, if they hang us for being separatists, at least I will have a shorter agony. Dear old Elbridge here will swing for an hour. He's so skinny they may have to fill his pockets with rocks."

Washington laughed, the first laugh in weeks, and took a long, satisfying draught of madeira.

***

Hickey formed his hands into a cup and drank from a stream that passed near Hudson Street. As he dried his hands on his shirt, he could see Mary Gibbons' house a quarter mile or so away. Once again, he stepped off the road to walk in the high grass. He stood staring across the street at the house, suddenly overcome with anger and dread. He was angry that he had been forced into stalking around in the weeds and breaking into houses and strong-arming women. But the anger was tempered with a strong sense of dread. He did not want to go into this neatly painted house.

Certain there was no traffic, pedestrian or horsebound, he quickly crossed the road and was pressed, once again, against the tree from which he had made an abrupt exit. He decided the back door would be best and so he quickly ran to the rear, staying low. He tried the door. It was locked.

He looked for a rock and found a smooth gray one that fit nicely in the palm of his right hand. He wrapped the rock in his shirt and gave a short, sharp jab at the window. It shattered. He reached in. The key had been left, twisted a half turn in the lock for safety. He unlocked the door and stepped in, closing the door behind him. He listened. There was no sound. The silence was overwhelming. His ears rang with the blood pounding through them. Maybe the house was empty. Maybe Mary Gibbons was out searching for an additional bit of intrigue. Or, perhaps, she and Clayford were enjoying an early afternoon tussle. Maybe he could find some evidence in the bedroom where he had seen her and Washington. He moved through the kitchen alongside the base of the stairway, turned and went up. He figured the bedroom was on the left. The floorboards creaked and he froze, waiting to be discovered. Nothing. Something crowded in on the deafening silence. An odor. A sickeningly sweet smell battled the silence for his attention. He creeped along the hall. There was a door ajar to a room, which, he guessed, would be the bedroom he wanted. The odor grew stronger.

Hickey pressed his back against the wall, reached his hand over palm against the door and pushed.

The sickly smell rushed from the room and leapt down his throat. He clasped a hand over his mouth. His stomach flipped and he began to retch but fought hard, swallowing forcefully. He stepped in the room.

Mary Gibbons was home.

But Mary Gibbons would never entertain the general again. Not unless he was into stranger pleasures than Hickey could imagine.

The pleasant rosiness of her cheeks was a pale bluish purple. Her body was half on, half off the bed. There was a strip of white cloth pulled tightly around her neck. Her once sensuous hips and thighs were covered with material from her bladder and bowels.

Someone had made certain Mary Gibbons couldn't tell

anyone about her little secrets.

***

Washington's carriage was being readied as he kissed Martha on the forehead.

"You take care, my dear, I will see you shortly," Washington told his wife, gently patting her arm as she lay in the large feather bed.

"Yes dear. And George, do take care of yourself." To some, the marriage of George Washington to Martha Custis may have seemed more a convenience to both than a great lover affair. Martha needed a man to handle affairs and George needed the resources and prestige of the Custis fortune. But, over the years, a true affection had grown between them and they were quite comfortable and happy in each other's company.

Martha was suffering the effects of a smallpox inoculation. It was thought that she should stay behind in Philadelphia and rest and, perhaps, join her husband in New York later, providing it was still safe.

Washington had left Gen. Israel Putnam in charge of New York City with instructions to sound the alarm if the enemy fleet appeared in the harbor. There had been no such alarm arriving in Philadelphia but he felt he had accomplished all he could hope for with Congress at this time. Whether it was enough was yet to be seen.

After one final kiss for Martha, Washington and staff left Philadelphia early on June 5 for the ride back to New York.

***

Fraunces Tavern was buzzing with activity this evening in early June. The Masons were meeting in the large upstairs room and a separate small celebration was being held downstairs.

Thomas Hickey had been watching the building from the shadows across the street for more than hour. He had not seen Phoebe but she was more than likely inside serving one or both of the gatherings. He had seen, however, an interesting group of participants, including John Clayford. It made sense. Clayford was a Mason, along with Washington and Black Sam Fraunces and William Forbes, one of the conspirators from the meeting he attended. Even the wheezing old Royal Artilleryman Graham, from the same session, was a Mason. Proves the point, thought Hickey. There ain't no Tories and Whigs just Masons and the rest of us.

All of his suspicions had been confirmed. While making his way south on Broadway a few days ago, Hickey had come face to face with a private from the Life Guard who had come staggering out of a tavern right into Hickey's path. Through his drunken haze, the young man recognized Sgt. Hickey and his jaw sagged.

"Whaaryadoin' here, sergeant," mumbled the man through a tongue swollen with alcohol. "Their lookin' for ya. All of'em. Looking for you, sergeant."

Despite the drunkenness, Hickey was able to determine that the word was out that Hickey was involved in some kind of conspiracy and had something to do with counterfeiting, too. Word was he was to be taken on the spot.

"It's all a mistake," Hickey had assured the young soldier who was only too willing to ignore the entire chance encounter.

Hickey had decided to wait it out in the small inn north of the city where no one would know or care about a renegade soldier. He had continued to pay the rent for the room and to board his horse. It seemed half a lifetime ago that he first arrived at the inn and was nearly killed by the bandits posing as patriots. He had stopped on his way from Mary Gibbon's house to get his horse and ridden to within a mile of Fraunces'. With Washington due back in the city in a day or so, he had to make an effort to get to Phoebe. He had waited until dusk, rode to the Bowling Green, set his horse and walked to Fraunces. Now, with the Masonic ritual underway, he felt it safe to move closer to the building. Instead of walking across the street, he stayed close to the buildings strolling casually as if out for a breath of air. He wore a weathered tricorn that flopped down over his brow. As he neared Fraunces, his heart beat faster. He could now see through the first floor windows. There was a whirl of white and yellow as waiters served the downstairs group. Stopping by the large window to the right of the entrance, he took out a pipe and went through the elaborate ritual of lighting it all the while looking into the window.

There she was!

Phoebe, her delicate face dark against the white frill of her bodice. Smiling, nodding, taking requests, oblivious to the fact that he was watching. He could not wait any longer. He had to talk with her. Even if it meant risking confrontation with Clayford. His heart thumped hard against his ribs and he found himself breathing heavily. Dragging on the pipe, he took the first step slowly. Then the next. As he was about to step onto the entrance landing, two men came through the front door. Hickey recognized them immediately. They were Clayford's henchmen, the ones who had chased him into the thicket as Washington left the city. Hickey snapped his head down as if coughing from the pipe smoke. His spine went rigid as he waited for recognition. He would put up a good fight. But, neither man said a word nor even looked his way. They simply did not expect Hickey to be walking through the front door.

The steps to the right led up to the large meeting room where the Masons were in session. Straight ahead was the smaller room where a handful of loud sailors were having a drink. The small entranceway continued down a narrow corridor to the serving kitchen. A small room off of this hallway was used for coats in the winter and general storage in the summer months. Hickey slipped into the room and waited.

Footsteps grew louder as they approached the kitchen door and, once the door was opened, they became quite distinct. Hickey prepared himself but the footsteps belonged to a Negro man with white gloves carrying a heavy tray. The footsteps continued and then carried on up the stairs to the Masonic meeting.

Within minutes, lighter footsteps came through the door and, as they passed the opening to the storage room, Hickey saw her. Phoebe. Just a few feet away. His rehearsed speech disappeared. He could not move nor speak. He was stunned by her beauty. He didn't want to talk. He just wanted to hold her and kiss her. Just leave. The two of them. Forget Washington and this damned city. He could carve out his own landhold. She was almost to the end of the corridor when he stepped out behind her.

"Phoebe." He choked, not being able to manage any other words.

Phoebe halted as if struck on the head and about to slump to the floor. She turned. Hickey stepped toward her but she backed away. He had not seen this look before. There was fear mixed with sadness. Tears streamed down her cheeks. She seemed as if she wanted to speak but just made little gulping sounds.

Hickey moved closer.

"Don't! Thomas," she blurted. "I loved you Thomas. You said you loved me. I know I'm just a silly girl but I thought you really loved me. Now I don't know what to think. They say you are a spy. I saw you in the general's office...and, well... They say you killed that woman ... the one you were seen following from a party .... A party you went to after you left me. The entire city is looking for you. My father says ...."

Hickey began to protest. He moved toward her.

"Stop!" she said, loud and firm.

Hickey froze and slowly backed away, trying to calm her with his hands folded as if in prayer. His voice was quavery like a school boy and tears welled in his eyes. "Phoebe, I DO love you. I did not kill anyone. They did. I'm in the middle of something much bigger than I know about. Just come with me. We can leave the city. Just you and me. I loved you from the first time I laid my eyes on ...."

"Stop," she pleaded, sobs bubbling up from deep within. "Just stop. I can't .... I don't know what to ..." She backed away from him toward the entrance foyer.

Hickey came for her now but she turned and ran into the tavern area. As he followed, he saw the two Clayford henchmen hurrying back through the entrance, alerted by Phoebe's screams. They had not left but had merely stepped into the street for a pipe. They saw Hickey and came after him. Hickey slammed into the kitchen door, nearly knocking it from its hinges. He careened into a cook sending him sprawling into a tray of vegetables. The two men were through the door now. Hickey spotted the rear exit door, which led out on a small garden where patrons could order food and drinks in the summer months. He scrambled up onto a counter and leaped to the edge of the brick cook stove and came down hard by the door. He ripped at the knob, banging the door open and was out and down the few steps into the ale garden.

There was an eight-foot high wooden fence enclosing the garden. Six tables were placed against the fence at intervals around the enclosed area. Hickey, surveying on the fly, selected a table, which he figured was nearest the alleyway that might offer some escape. The table was occupied by a heavyset gent who was diving into some meat chops. Hickey ran toward the table hurled himself onto the surface and went for the top of the fence. His foot had landed squarely in the greasy, meat-filled plate. His ankle twisted and gave way. His fingers clawed at the top of the fence but couldn't hold the full weight of his body. He slammed down hard on his knees. He tried to get back up for another go at the fence but pain shot up from his ankle to his brain. His ribs seemed to give way and pain engulfed his brain. He slumped back to one knee.

Clayford's men were on him, each grabbing an arm and pulling it back behind him. Hickey struggled but the pain wouldn't allow his brain to concentrate on the battle. The larger, dark haired man put the blade of a broad knife to Hickey's throat and told him to end the struggle. He did.

Several other men, summoned by Black Sam, were now in the garden. Hickey was tied and carried away.

Chapter Twenty-One

Washington's Headquarters
7:30 p.m., Monday, June 10, 1776

Hickey ached with rage. Anger grew in him like a dry barn fire out of control. His head throbbed with it. His muscles were sore with the tension of it. For five days, he had sat in this small brick-walled out-kitchen. Guards were stationed in front of the locked door. He had not been beaten or abused. Simply ignored. That added to the rage. They brought him food but he could eat little, his body preferring to nibble away on itself one obsessive minute after another.

Again and again and yet again he went over all of it. Washington, Phoebe, Clayford, the conspirators. There were never any answers. Just more and more questions. More doubts. More anger. If he could get hold of Washington, he would take his arrogant neck in his powerful hands and squeeze until his face turned blue and his false teeth popped out.

Hickey had been taken from Fraunces last Wednesday. Five days ago. Washington had returned from Philadelphia on Friday. He knew that from the talk of the guards. It was now Monday and yet Washington had still not called for him, nor was there any indication that he would. Hickey had pounded on the wooden door, demanding answers. The guards either laughed at him or ignored him. Both, response and lack of response, angered him even more. He had developed real pain in his gut, his stomach like granite from tension. He would realize his fists were clenched, relax them and minutes later they were balled up anew.

At night, as he tried to allow for the release of sleep, he went over and over what he would say to Washington given the chance. He would tell him everything he knew, everything he had seen. He would threaten to expose the entire arrangement if the slate wasn't wiped clean.

He was allowed to shave and wash in a basin that was brought each morning and evening. But he had not been allowed out of the room that measured about 10 feet square. He was pacing now, trying to work off the pent up energy. He sat down on the edge of the wooden cot. The sun was low in the sky with bright orange rays coming through the window and emblazing the far wall. Another night. Another chance to think about what he should do; what he could do. He had just turned to the full length of the cot and rested his head against the wall when a guard came to the door.

"Hickey, here's a basin. Clean yerself up. The general wants to see you." As was the usual drill, Hickey stepped to the back of the small room with his face to the wall. The guard unlocked the door and set the basin on the floor while another blocked the door.

The minute the door closed Hickey ran to the basin, grabbed it and threw it at the door. Water splashed on the floor and walls and the basin clanged into a corner.

"Have the fucking general come down here and wash me," Hickey shouted. "If he kisses my arse, then I might wash it to get rid of his rotten stench."

The guards just laughed, one calling back over his shoulder: "Suit yourself. We'll be back to get you in half an hour."

The thought that they expected him to clean up in order to meet the general sent him further out over the edge. He paced quicker now, smashing his fist into the door each time he reached that end of the small room. After a dozen passes, he sat on the cot working the fingers of his left hand over the knuckles of his right which were cracked open and bleeding from the assault on the door. He put the large knuckle of the first finger in his mouth to lick away the blood just as the door of the kitchen opened. Three armed guards entered the room. The sergeant leading the trio told Hickey to face the wall with his hands extended behind him. Hickey hesitated and then, facing the bayonetted muskets, did so. His hands were bound and, with a soldier on his arm and the sergeant following, they led him out of the kitchen building across a brick-paved path and into the main house.

The familiar surroundings of the house seemed to temper his mood. He was no longer lost in his own rage but a part of the real world again. He was still angry but at least now he could think. Washington would know he was angry. He would know that the deal was off. Hickey was out. He would know what he thought about the arrogance of the rich. But now, passing through the dining room of the Mortier house, Hickey knew he had to be free. The unfettered rage of the past few days would have to be harnessed. He had to convey his outrage to the general but he also had to ensure that he gained his release. He had to talk with Phoebe once more. He knew he could convince her given just a few more minutes alone.

Hickey was led up the main stairs to a wooden bench in the hall outside of Washington's office, the same office in which he and Phoebe had shared their desire. The arrogant, fatherly face of Washington the patrician came clearly into focus as he remembered that night. Washington had scolded them like children. Hickey's heart beat faster, blood thumping in his temples again. He fought hard to quell the rise but it grew to a heavy pounding as the door to the office was opened and Hickey was pushed through the door.

"You arrogant whore's son! Who the fuck do you think you are? I'll snap your sluggard's neck you ...." Hickey had

charged straight through the door, breaking the armhold of
the two surprised guards. He rounded the desk, his hands
bound, and intent on ramming his head into Washington's
face. Just as he made the corner, another guard who had
been standing near the general was able to get a foot into
Hickey's shin. Hickey slammed to the floor, unable to use
his hands to break his fall. His knees crashed into the hard-
wood surface and the momentum carried his head down and
he smashed his forehead into the floor.

Pain raced from his head down his spine and back to
his brain. Yet, overshadowing the pain, was the fact that
his aborted charge had left him kneeling before Washington,
prostrated on knees and forehead, hands behind him, like a
royal subject.

One of the two escort guards raised his musket and was
about to crack the stock into Hickey's head but was stopped
by Washington.

"That won't be necessary, corporal," said Washington in
a quiet, even tone as if he were telling a house servant not
to fuss over a bit of spilt tea. "Set Sergeant Hickey in the
chair."

The guards lifted Hickey by his crooked elbows and
slammed him into an unpadded wooden chair directly in
front of Washington's desk.

"I can understand your anger, Sergeant Hickey," said
Washington in his formal, general-like voice. "I have been
quite busy since my return from Philadelphia. I should have
sent for you earlier. But, these are quite serious charges
which have been brought to my attention. Quite serious,
indeed, for one so trusted as to be part of my personal Life
Guard. Counterfeiting is not to be taken lightly in these dire
times."

"I ain't no part of your fucking guard, Washington! And
you know it. I'm a paid whoremonger spy. Every coin comes
out of your purse you fucking weasel."

Washington's surprise was genuine. His brow knitted

and he looked at the other four soldiers in the room as if to say 'Has he gone mad?'

"Whatever are you talking about, Sergeant Hickey?"

"You know godamned well what I'm talking about. You hired me to come to New York and to spy on your own troops and to tell you about any plots that might break up your little game. And I did my ...."

"Sergeant Hickey, I'm afraid you are delusional. I don't have the slightest hint as to what you are talking about. It's obvious that we cannot communicate. Guards, take him back to the kitchen and make arrangements for his transfer to city authorities."

The sergeant of the guards began barking orders and, this time, three soldiers surrounded Hickey to lead him away. Hickey knew if he went through the door he would never get back. Never see Phoebe.

"No! No! Wait. Maybe the wait in the heat has made me mad." Hickey said, his mind racing for a story good enough to buy him a few more minutes. "What I meant was that I feel being in your service on the Guard led me into things I didn't expect. Like counterfeiting. I got dragged in. I have things I know. Certain things which you must hear. Private things." His voice pleading now and submissive.

The guards, ignoring his pleas, were dragging Hickey through the doorway. Hickey had jammed a foot against each side of the jam and the guards were whacking his feet with their rifle stocks to free his grip. There was a lengthy silence. The guards had Hickey sideways now and just about through the door.

"Wait," said Washington. "Perhaps, Sergeant Hickey does have something of importance to say. We must use everything at our disposal in his struggle for liberty. Bring him back."

The sergeant of the guards looked at the general as if to say 'Are you certain?' Washington nodded and gestured to the chair. Hickey cooperated as the guards yanked him back through the door and slammed him into the chair.

"Alone," said Hickey firmly but more a question than a demand.

Washington studied Hickey's face and then told the guards to leave.

"But, general," said the sergeant, "I don't think it's such a good idea to leave this ..."

He was cut short by Washington.

"It's all right," said Washington.

"Yes sir," said the sergeant, "but we'll be right outside if you need us, sir."

"Fine," said Washington, sweeping the back of his hand toward the door, ushering out the soldiers. The door closed with the sergeant taking one last look to make certain the general was safe.

They sat staring at each other. Hickey spoke first.

"Why are you doing this to me?" asked Hickey.

"Doing what to you, Mr. Hickey?"

"Doing 'what?' You know what I'm talking about. Tracking me down. Locking me up. Telling Fraunces I'm a counterfeiter. That's 'what!'"

"Come now, Thomas," said Washington in a maddeningly calm tone. "That's what I pay you to do. I have paid you several thousand dollars over these last few months. This is a healthy sum for someone of your status and capabilities."

"My status!" said Hickey raising his voice. With that, the door opened and the sergeant looked in at Washington.

"Sergeant," said Washington, "please do not interrupt. If I need you I will call." The sergeant shook his head and closed the door leaving Hickey and Washington alone again.

"My status!" Hickey continued. "Remember, Washington, you came to me. I wanted nothing to do with your little war or your politics. You're all alike, whether patriot or Tory, Virginian or Londoner. You sit in your grand houses and go to your Mason's meetings while the rest of us sweat and die so that you can have even grander houses and more things. You came to me. And, now I want you to give me answers."

Washington ignored the insults. "This is not some little tavern card game or a brawl over a wench," Washington said with the smooth drawl of the Virginia gentleman. "This is very, very serious business we are about here, Mr. Hickey. The fate of nations is at stake. Tens of thousands of lives depend upon this army and my leadership. I paid you very well indeed. And, if that means that you have to face a bit of adversity well so be it. If that means that you are locked up for a few days, then I'd sooner see you in shackles than an entire nation. This is a grand experiment we are involved in. I will not have it defeated by a pathetic cabal of misfits, by counterfeiters and kidnappers, or Tory sympathizers. If that means using you in the battle, then, again, I say, so be it. I have paid you well beyond what you might ever have earned otherwise."

The small office boiled. The open window behind Washington did little to cool the June heat. Sweat streamed from Hickey's brow and burned his eyes. With his hands behind his back, all he could do was to wipe his eyes on the point of his shoulders. Washington didn't appear to be sweating at all.

"How can you sit there and talk about liberty and such while you got me tied and thrown in an outbuilding with guards keeping watch on me like I was a criminal? How can you go on about right and wrong while you tell lies to Fraunces and turn Phoebe against me. Yer worse than the king. You do the same miserable acts to regular folks but you call it liberty."

"You simply do not understand," Washington said, still with outrageous calm and patience. "I have been involved in matters of such import since I was a boy. I cannot expect you to understand. I do not judge you ill for your lack of understanding. I simply tell you that you do NOT understand. That is why I am in this position. That is why I left my family and my home to come here to this wretched city. Because I do know of these things. I make this sacrifice for you just as much as for every patriot from here to Virginia. Rather than dissolve in anger, Mr. Hickey, you should be thankful that men like me have accepted this challenge. You should be ready to help at any turn with any task."

"I told you at the start," said Hickey, shifting on the edge of the chair, his hands still tied behind him, "this was a simple business proposition for me. I would find out what I could and pass it to you ... for money. No speeches. No loyalties. You broke that agreement. Things have gone too far. You think I'm some kind of Son of Liberty or some such nonsense. Ours was a straight business deal. Now it's over. Just let me get out of here."

"Thomas," said Washington, smiling a grotesque toothy grin of painted, wooden teeth, "much has occurred since we first met at the exhibition of the Turtle. By the way, it is ready for action now. I expect we will put it to good use in the next month or so right out in the sound. We'll see if we can't sink one of the King's ships. But, as I was saying, a great deal has transpired this past year. It is, perhaps, the most momentous single year in history. I did not do this to you. History did this to you."

"Well, I want you to undo my little part of history. Set me free and Phoebe and I will be out of the city tomorrow. You owe me that much for all I have provided you."

"I owe you nothing, Hickey," said Washington, just a tinge of peeve entering his attitude for the first time. "In fact, there are dozens of others like you who have provided much more usable information and, I might add, much cheaper. Like it or not, you are a soldier, a sergeant in my personal guard. You are a sergeant who has been accused by a prominent and respected citizen of participating in a plan to distribute counterfeit money. Other of my troops know of this. I must deal with this in a manner in which I can preserve my leadership and credibility."

"That's horseshit, Washington, and you know it. I am the one who told you about the counterfeiting in the first place. This business of my being a sergeant shit. I'm not a soldier and you know it. I didn't take any oath to you or any other puffed up reptile from Virginia."

"Listen, Hickey," said Washington lowering his voice and looking straight into Hickey's eyes. "Listen, very carefully because I don't think that I am getting through to you. I have grave responsibilities that go far beyond what you can conceive. I do not hold you responsible for your lack of imagination in these matters. There are those, yes, even those in Congress, who would see me out of the way. They would like for New York to collapse as easily as the northern frontier. There are political and military plots and subplots the likes of which you could never conceive. The Congress has, I have learned today, just postponed a vote on independence for three additional weeks. Why? So, that the colonies can have more time to consider the consequences. There are plotters undermining our efforts throughout the colonies. I can ill afford to have New York waiver at the very birth of our struggle. I have managed so far to stay ahead of these designs against me and against this cause. I have done so by hiring people such as yourself to provide me with the needed information to combat these evil intentions. I have hired dozens of men who pass out misinformation to the Tories. All with a single purpose. To win. To triumph over the King and his agents. I do this because I believe it is the right thing to do. We will be much better off deciding our own destiny. Believe me when I say to you I have expended dozens like yourself and will do so without hesitation in the future to protect my command, this army and this idea. I don't know how to put this any more clearly, Mr. Hickey ... you, sir, are expendable."

"Expendable am I," said Hickey, suddenly shaken from his paralyzing anger and back to the tavern brawler, the survivor he had been all of his life, "Well, Your Excellency,

O Great General, that shows just what your cause is worth. Because if a single man or woman is expendable, then your cause is no better than any other before it. You and the rest of your kind who want to pay less taxes so you can grow richer. You want to take control of the political reins so you can lord it over the rest of us. We're the ones that do the real work. Our sweat fills your pouches with gold and silver. So, we're expendable, eh, well then we might as well work for the king."

"I say to you again, Hickey," said Washington with definite annoyance, "you simply do not understand. I do not hold you responsible for this ignorance but only plead with you to try to grasp the import of this cause. Soldiers die in battle. Soldiers die for a cause, a cause in which they believe strongly enough to give up their lives. When I say you are expendable, Hickey, I am saying that you and all of us are soldiers in the battle against tyranny. In that respect, we are all expandable. You are not the common citizen you talk about. You, sir, are a soldier; a well-paid soldier."

"But," said Hickey, "shouldn't we have a choice? If we are fighting for freedom from tyranny, as you say, and your cause is such a special one, shouldn't we have a choice? Shouldn't the very freedom you claim we desire mean that we can choose our course in life?"

"One day, perhaps. But we must sacrifice now for that day," said Washington. "We have no choice but to go ahead from here."

"Well, I'm taking my freedom early, General Washington. I'm taking mine right now. Untie me and I will show you what a great experiment liberty really is."

"I would like to do that but, if I let you go, then the conspirators will think I'm soft. The populous will grow even more afraid than they already are. There already is talk of great conspiracies with popular support. The people are afraid. My soldiers are beginning to feel the same way. I must find a way to quash this talk of conspiracy and show them they can rely on me to protect them when the King's forces arrive. I need you to carry out a swift, firm counterattack on the plotters."

"I'm not doing another thing for you, Washington."

"I believe you will, Hickey, or you will never see the light of day outside a jail cell again."

"Oh, I don't think I would threaten me if I were you," said Hickey, saving his ace card for just the right moment. "What do you think would happen if Mayor Matthews, or the Committee, or Congress knew that the commander in chief was doodling a local whore with ties to the very conspirators themselves?"

Washington's staid demeanor cracked.

"What are you talking about? Explain yourself. I demand it." His voice was loud and demanding. The door opened and the sergeant again stuck in his head.

"I told you to wait until called now close that damned door," yelled Washington. The sergeant quickly slammed the door, nearly catching his own nose in the jamb.

"And, furthermore," continued Hickey, now quite calm and in control, "what if these men of authority knew that the source of many of the greatest information leaks came right out of the pockets of the command-in-chief himself? How do you think that would do? Would they think less highly of their general then?"

"This is nonsense," said Washington, unconvincingly.

"No, not nonsense, you pompous ass. The truth. I saw it with these Irish eyes. I saw you doodling in the hefty sack of Mary Gibbons. That, mind you, is quite all right in my reckoning. I wanted to twig her myself. Although, I dare to guess that Mrs. Washington might care. But that's not the best part. While you rested your cock and slept off the madeira, good ole Mary Gibbons was carrying notes from your pockets to the conspirators. That, too, I know first hand. You asked me once how they knew about the numbers of troops, the count of powder barrels, fortifications plans, and the rest.

They knew it because you told them! You told them by carrying around details of such things. You're so fucking arrogant you think you are above being whored yourself. Yes, indeed, I think the Tory Mayor David Matthews might make very good use of such information."

"I wouldn't be so...," Washington started but was interrupted by Hickey.

"Wait! The best is yet to come. How would the Committee of Safety and the Assembly take to the idea that their gold medal award-winning general also had the strumpet murdered once she was found out? Now that would really be useful information don't you think?"

"I didn't know she was...I mean....," Washington surprised Hickey with a look of genuine shock.

"Don't tell me you didn't know old Mary with the great ass and tits is gone. Yep, dead and rottin'. My guess is it was Clayford. He was the one who discovered me at Gibbon's place. Then he tried to drown me. When I finally made my way back to the Gibbon's place she was already blue. Lord knows what color she is now. I was trying to reach you to tell you...that's right, I was still trying to do what I thought was the right thing seeing as how you paid me well and regularly. Then, with Clayford's men chasing me, I see him riding out of town with you. That's when I made the connection. So, now I don't know whether he's a real conspirator and he's spying on you. Or he's one of your men and he's plowing the same field I am. I don't know who's the good guy or the bad guy. All I know is I was almost killed. A woman was killed. And now you have me bound and ready to be thrown into jail. All the while Clayton is drinking it up at your Masonic meetings. You're right general, I may not understand. I may not understand being that devious. I may not understand how arrogant it is to do one thing and say another for some great cause. I may not understand the necessity to set friend against friend, your own kind against your own. One thing I do understand, however, and it is something you've taught me, you have to use whatever is at your disposal. You can count on me to let everyone know your little secrets."

Washington had regained his composure.

"Surely, as one man to another, Thomas, you can understand the need for, let's say, certain services. I had been long deprived. Mrs. Washington had been apart from me for some time. Mary Gibbons was introduced to me by Sam Fraunces. You yourself remarked about her ample assets. I was not aware of her spying but, I can assure you, I moved quickly to nullify the effect of any information that may have been provided by my trysts. As I have said to you before, there are scores of others like yourself, providing information to me and misinformation to the Tories. So, I don't believe my indiscretions have caused irreparable damage. But I assure you, Hickey, I did not know about the death of Mary Gibbons. Clayford has always concerned me. He is a zealot and I don't deny that I believe he is capable of what you have described. I also was not aware of your personal ordeal. That is the truth. I simply suggested to him once that you may be getting in too deep and that he might want to check on you. I have done that with many others who provide me information. I cannot take anything at its face. As I have said, there are powerful forces at work here. I cannot be too careful. I wish that you had come to me earlier with this news about Gibbons and Clayford's attempts on your life. I have had others check on Clayford but I see now he must be dealt with."

"That's not my concern now, Washington," Hickey said. "I'm out of the information business now. All I want is to walk away from you, this city, this liberty bullshit. I want a chance to convince Phoebe that she should go with me. That's all. I won't hold you to your promise of land, though I think I have earned it. I just want to be away from here."

"I'm afraid that is not so easily accomplished, Hickey," said Washington with a deep sigh, "I can't let you interfere with matters that are ...."

"I'm not asking, general," said Hickey, "I'm telling you that I will tell everything I know if it doesn't happen."

"Let me finish, please, Thomas," said Washington carefully and, seemingly sincerely. "I want you to be free. You have provided some useful information. You could, indeed, tell people what you know but, at this point, who would believe you? Mary Gibbons is gone. Clayford will swear you're a liar. We would simply charge you with the information leaks. You see, Thomas, while there is a great deal of responsibility that comes with being commander-in-chief, there is also a great deal of influence and credibility. No, I don't think what you have would be of much use to you. But, and I hope you will believe me when I tell you that I am committed with all of my being to this cause. I will see nothing stand in its way. Having said that, you may at some point become a part of something that would, indeed, jeopardize this great cause. So, I do, indeed, want to see you away and with Sam Fraunces's daughter if she so desires. But there are some loose ends that must be taken care of before I can let that happen."

"I'm sure the mayor would believe me," said Hickey in a less-than-convincing tone. He knew what Washington had said was true. He was an eyewitness but Gibbons was gone. They would dispose of the body. Washington could have Clayford kill him and then claim it was Hickey all along who had been selling out to the King's men.

"Here's how the situation stands," said Washington, ignoring Hickey's feeble counter attack. "Public opinion is that my tenure is an even bet to continue. Newspapers in Connecticut, New Jersey, Pennsylvania and elsewhere talk about the hopelessness of defending New York. They talk about greatly-exaggerated conspiracies which can overrun my command in a matter of hours once the King's ships arrive. There are whispered concerns even within the Congress and local committees. What we need is to show them that we are completely in command and that the fire of conspiracy has been dampened. Not all battles are fought with ball and powder. We have to fight the battle within the minds of New Yorkers and all patriots. Doubt is as dangerous as a hundred enemy ships."

"I told you that is not my concern. I want you to cut these ropes and release me. I need to..."

Again, Washington interrupted.

"Hickey I am being as honest with you as I can. I said you were expendable. I could shout right now and they would burst through that door and, if I so ordered, shoot you on the spot. I can do away with you at any time. I want you to clearly understand that. But, that would not send a clear signal to those who may be doubting this command. 'Why he can't even control his own guard.' That's what they would say. I propose a new arrangement between you and me. I want...."

"You ARE the most arrogant man I have ever met. You drag me out of my life, turn me into a spy, sour the only love I've ever really had, tried to kill me, locked me up like an animal, and now you want to make another 'arrangement'? I don't know what to say."

"Hear me out," said Washington, his mind now deftly maneuvering over all of the possibilities. "I cannot simply release you without explanation. The political situation is too fragile. Black Sam has a great deal of influence. He says you are deeply involved in a counterfeiting plot. I must appear to be fully in control and to have eliminated any conspiracy. That will give the people of New York great confidence. It will dishearten the conspirators. It will secure greater support from Congress and, thus, go a long way toward victory. As I said, I cannot simply set you free. However, if you agree to this final assignment, I will guarantee that you will go free. I will guarantee you 300 acres of land in the Ohio territory. I will even talk with Black Sam Fraunces and convince him of your service and patriotism. I will tell him you are more than fit to be a husband to his Phoebe. I, sir, will do all of this if you will take on a final assignment."

"Sam Fraunces would say I held hands with the devil himself," said Hickey. "You believe him? He just wants me out of the way."

"As I said, Fraunces has a great deal of influence. People believe what he tells them. I have to deal with you in a fashion that will appease him but also send a message to anyone else who may be concerned about conspirators. I can think of only one way to do that. That is for you to take on one more assignment."

"What assignment?" said Hickey impatiently.

"I will tell the guards that you are being charged with counterfeiting. Despite all of the talk, you know as well as I that counterfeiting is rampant. Most are given a slap and released and sent away. I will be seen as dealing firmly with guard members who break the law. Also, I have certain reports that certain inmates in the city jail are involved in another conspiracy. One group you have reported on in the past. Another that has come to my attention, plans to blow up all of the bridges surrounding the island. Several of these conspirators are in the city lockup on a variety of charges. While in jail, you can learn more about these plots. In fact, I can tell you right now that you will discover a major cabal. This conspiracy may involve Mr. Clayford and others. I will expose this conspiracy, dealing firmly with every individual. It will be cut off in the bloom. We will gain firm control over rumors and give the residents of this city great confidence and hope. You will be released due to the great service you rendered. Then, Mr. Hickey, I would be glad never to see you again."

"You want me to go to jail!" Hickey said incredulously

"It would be for just a few short weeks. I could bring all of the necessary plans together quickly. While in jail, in addition to finding out what you can, you can spread some false information. You can be an angry young soldier caught trying to make a few extra dollars through bad scrip.

I promise it will take less than a month."

"Can I see Phoebe first?" asked Hickey, seeing an opportunity to bargain.

"If you accept, I will have her visit you. You will have plenty of time to set the truth in her mind."

"I don't know," said Hickey hesitating. His mind raced through the possibilities, filtering through each outcome. Washington was in control. He could, indeed, do anything he wanted with him. Who would believe the word of a deserter, a moon-cursing smuggler, and counterfeiter against a Virginian gentleman chosen by Congress as commander in chief?"

"Why should I trust you now? Look what you've already done to me."

"We could argue this forever, Hickey. I tell you once again. I paid for your services. Handsomely. You entered the job of your own will. Fate has thrust you into a position with few alternatives. I cannot afford to simply let you go. Hear me clearly on that. I cannot let you go. You would either come to an untimely end with your name forever linked to the conspirators. Or, you can perform this last task and we can find a way out for you while helping our cause here in New York."

Hickey slumped visibly in the chair, his shoulders, pushed forward by the ropes with which is arms were tied behind his back. His chin sagged deep between the shoulders.

After several minutes of silence, Hickey's shoulders relaxed in resignation. From the day he was born, people like this had lorded over him. The farm. The King's army. Nothing would ever change. The one slim hope he had was to be released and get as far away from men like this as possible. Hickey looked at Washington. There was no more contempt. No more anger. Only resignation. This was the way it was in his world. He stared into Washington's eyes and slowly nodded.

Chapter Twenty-Two
New York City Jail
June 20-24, 1776

Thursday, June 20
Three guards came running to the northeast corner of the jail. The high-pitched wailing was like a cross between a newborn with the cholic and a cat in heat.

"Yeoooww! Let me go. Let me go. Hellpp!"

Israel Youngs' lizard eyes darted frantically back and forth, his arms flailed at his sides like a loon trying to take wing. His mirror-image brother, Isaac, was standing nearby making the same kind of flapping motion. Thomas Hickey, his arms thrust through the bars separating their cells, had both hands firmly around the scrawny neck of the duplicitous counterfeiter. If he had wanted to snap Youngs' thin neck, he could have done so quite easily. He was simply trying to scare the Youngs. It helped sell his rebellious act and also might get him some new information. Since arriving in jail on the weekend, he had put on quite a show. He was loud and obnoxious, uncooperative with the guards, rude and rough with the other prisoners and, most importantly, clearly proud of his part in the plotting against "the powdered doodle dandy from Virginia, General Fucking Go-to-Hell."

Yowwwooooh," screeched Israel, not realizing that Hickey was barely squeezing tight enough to keep him from pulling away. It was Youngs himself who was banging his head on the on the bars.

"That's right scream like a little girl, ya bastard son of a wharf whore. I've a good mind to snap this little twig of a neck in two just for fun," said Hickey, loud enough to be heard throughout the north end of the low brick jail building.

During this almost comical display, Henry Dawkins sat on his wooden cot, a broad smile on his face. He wanted to throttle the Youngs himself, blaming them for his latest arrest. At the same time, there was relief that it was Israel and not himself who was being throttled by the little Irishman with the devil's voice and the mean spirit. Dawkins had been making mental notes of everything Hickey bragged about over the past few days. It just might prove useful.

Israel Youngs had shifted his howl to more of a moaning by the time the guards arrived. "Whooahhooo. Whooaahhoo."

The three guards, one of whom was the red haired, gaptoothed young man who had befriended Dawkins in his previous stay, quickly opened the cell and rushed in. The other two were older and seemed to be gasping for every ounce of air they could find in the stifling, fetid heat of the jail.

"Let him go, Hickey," said the balding older guard whose whitish belly protruded from his shirt. They flung open the door and began prying Hickey's hands off of Israel Youngs. Hickey did not let go easily. He made them work for it. The red haired younger guard got an arm around Hickey's throat while the other two each took an arm and a hand. In a few second, Hickey let up, gave in and Israel Youngs popped out of the death grip. Israel backed to the opposite wall still gawking at Hickey as if the devil himself had nearly claimed him.

"One more time, Hickey, and we'll be chaining you to the basement wall with the rats to keep yer company," said the other older guard who had a snorting, nasally voice which made Hickey laugh out loud.

"Funny is it? You'll get a real laugh out of this....," said the guard flailing at Hickey's shoulders with a thick, heavy black cudgel.

Hickey blocked most of the blows and, feigning temporary compliance, retreated to the bench in the corner of the cell.

"We've had just about our fill of yer shit," said the guard. "Stay away from the other prisoners and keep yer maw shut. Understand?" There was no answer. "Understand?! I said," asked the guard heading for Hickey with the cudgel.

"Leave me the fuck alone," said Hickey, "before I shove that stick up your arse."

"You think so, well I....," the guard made a move toward Hickey but the other two restrained him and ushered him from the cell.

Within minutes, the jail had returned to what passes for normal in such places. There were a few muffled shouts from somewhere. A couple of other prisoners shared a laugh, probably over some lewd story. The Youngs and Dawkins hissed and whispered sentiments that couldn't be heard outside their cell but that had to do undoubtedly with Hickey, the animal in the next cell.

Throughout this commotion, Hickey's cellmate had remained stoical, sitting back on his cot, his back to the wall and watching the proceedings. He said nothing. Did nothing. Just stared.

"Fucking idiots," said Hickey, "I can't wait until the King's ships arrive and save me from these liberty lovers. I'll see to those fuckers first. Just as soon as the King's men set us all free. And, you know what? That's just what will happen. Should be here any day now. I'm glad I joined the winning side before it was too late." Hickey was really getting into this act. This was due, in part, to his wanting to do this final job and get it over with and, in part, because it felt good -- and perhaps a little bit too natural -- to be rooting for the King and against Washington and cronies.

Isaac Ketcham, the paper procurer who had been saved from the tar and feathers by Hickey, looked on with approval in his eyes mixed with a healthy dose of skepticism. Wasn't it ironic that the two who had crossed paths so fortuitously would now be sitting here awaiting judgment? Ketcham had been walking a fine line. On the one side, he wanted to point his finger at Hickey and tell the guards, the congress and the world that Hickey was a chief conspirator while he, himself, was just a victim of greed. On the other side of the line was the need to carry on this fiction of commiserating with this short, stocky man who had saved him from, if not death, a great deal of pain. Ketcham felt his future rested with the latter.

"You really believe the King's men will bother to free us?" asked Ketcham. "I'm thinking there will plenty more to occupy them. We'll probably just sit right here while the royal ships bombard the island and us as well." Hearing Hickey's rantings these past few days, Ketcham had slowly conned himself into believing that the act of kindness Hickey had shown him on the streets was a Trojan Horse. Hickey had used him to get closer to the center of the plot. Hickey, he figured, had become more and more a leader of the cabal while he remained just a paper merchant who needed some extra cash.

"Listen, Ketcham," said Hickey, sitting next to him, "I have it right from the top that they'll take care of those who took care of them. And, I don't think that day is too far off." Hickey had affected an air of greater importance than that afforded by the simple plot to saturate the city with counterfeit money. Since being tossed into the cell five days earlier, he had 'confided' in Ketcham. He had raved about much more elaborate plans for the attack of New York and concocted details of such plans with great relish. It was the bait for his fishing pole. He figured if he trolled long enough some one would bite. They might say, for example, 'Oh no, it's not the

North Bridge that will be blown its the bridge to the island
lane.' He needed details to appease Washington. Then he
would take his arse out of this forsaken city. He was actually
enjoying the role of a turned Life Guard in the general's service. He was hoping that in confiding such detail, he would
prompt Ketcham, Dawkins or one of the others into returning the confidence and providing information that would
take care of Washington. So far, however, Ketcham had not
said much. Hickey was beginning to believe that Ketcham
simply did not know anything more. He had probably just
provided the special paper for the counterfeiters in return for
a healthy share of the return.

Ketcham, on the other hand, was, like Dawkins, noting
every detail in Hickey's braggadocio. All of Hickey's con-
coctions had been noted as fact. Hundreds of cannon hidden
just north of the city. An arsenal of powder and shot stashed
in farmhouses. Thousands of folks enlisted in the King's
cause. Thoroughly rationalized now, the plan to implicate
Hickey would soon be carried out. Yesterday, Ketcham had
handed a petition to the guard to be delivered to the Provincial Congress. He did not reveal what he thought he had
learned from his cellmate but simply whetted the appetite
of the congress for anything having to do with the many rumored conspiracies festering throughout the city.

"I have something of import to obsearve (sic) to the honorable house," his petition had stated.

The two older guards who had subdued Hickey were
back less than an hour later. They ushered Ketcham from
the cell. He made a great act of asking where they were taking him and why, looking back at Hickey questioningly. The
guards said nothing.

When Ketcham had gone, one of the two prisoners in
the next cell, opposite the Youngs and Dawkins, called to
Hickey to come nearer to the wall of masonry and iron bars
which separated them.

"I'll bet that one is telling them all about you, Hickey,"

said James Mason in a low controlled voice which belied his seething gut. This prisoner, the one who had spent weeks alone, separated from the others, had quickly discerned that this loudmouthed squat soldier might provide a key for his exit as well.

Mason was not a mere counterfeiter. He had been compromised by the conspirators early in the game and had been receiving a steady stream of cash in return for his reports on Washington's troops. These reports had been delivered routinely to Gov. Tryon ensconced aboard the "Ducthess of Gordon" in the harbor.

Mason knew he was in deep trouble. He was routinely taken from his cell and interrogated about his part in the plot or plots which now seemed to be epidemic throughout this city on the brink. Last night's session had been especially intense.

At the start of these grueling interviews, he was actually telling the truth when he swore he knew nothin more than he had already told them. Now, however, he could give them Hickey. He had also provided a long list of other 'conspirators'. Some of these he knew to be involved, others he had overheard from Hickey or Ketcham or one of the other prisoners. He threw them in for good measure.

It was, the inquisitors had said, enough to exchange for leniency. Mason's list included William Greene, a drummer for the army; James Johnson, a fifer; and James Barnes, another soldier. He also tossed in his current cellmate, Private Michael Lynch, another of Washington's soldiers. Private Lynch had also been charged with passing counterfeit scrip. The Mason song named Gilbert Forbes as very heavily involved.

As he continued to sing, the list grew longer until it featured Tory Mayor David Matthews and a dozen other prominent city leaders, businessmen, and professionals.

About midway down the detailed list of supposed conspirators was the name, "Sgt. Thomas Hickey, Life Guard."

Friday, June 21

"I have been made to look like a fool for the very last time in this city," Washington told Peter Livingston, president of a special committee of the Provincial Congress. "I thought your men were observing Mr. Delancey. Now I understand he has simply walked out of his house. He strolls down to the river, gets in a rowboat and is now safely aboard Tryon's ship. This is outrageous."

Washington had prompted the congress to summon scores of loyalists for interrogation. All of his information pointed to one or several organized conspiracies to sabotage his efforts to defend the city when the King's forces arrived from the north. Washington had felt Oliver Delancey, one of the most powerful men in the city before the troubles with the crown, was the key to much of this. If he could show that he was, in effect, holding such key leaders under house arrest, he could nip this plotting business right in the bud. Now Delancey was a guest of the Tory governor aboard the warship out in the harbor.

"Gen. Washington," said Livingston, "with all due respect, sir. We had nothing with which to hold Mr. Delancey. The committee is extended to its limits. Each day we receive reports of scores of others who may be involved in such endeavors. I had assumed, sir, that those with whom you were especially concerned would be watched by the army. You have 10,000 men. We have only a handful at our disposal. I don't think you can lay the blame for Mr. Delancey's 'escape', as you put it, on the Provincial Congress for any of its committeemen."

"Yes, I have 10,000 troops, Mr. Livingston. About a third of them are ill with one malady or another, but I do have enough men to defend this island. But, in matters of political security, I would hope you and the congress would take the lead." Washington softened his tone not wanting to alienate the congress. Delancey had escaped his control. This was very embarrassing and exacerbated the talk of whether or not he was fit for the job. The news of Delancey's stroll to the river and subsequent lodging with the enemy would make its way into every tavern in the city. It was time for action.

"I am sorry, Mr. Livingston, if I appeared to blame you for this. The fault lies with me. I stand willing to support you with men whenever you give the word. I appreciate the cooperation of the congress and all of its committees. But, I am sure you can see the damage done by such a simple act as Delancey's little boat ride."

"Yes. Yes, indeed," said Livingston, a tall proper man who reminded Washington of the prissy Frenchmen of Philadelphia. "We will support whatever you have in mind. Along those lines, general, we have received two quite disturbing affidavits in the past two days. One comes from an Isaac Ketcham who is presently locked in the city jail. The other is from another prisoner, James Mason. Both, independently as far as we can tell, have petitioned us with information that one Sgt. Thomas Hickey, a member of your own Life Guard, and several other soldiers, are deeply involved in a plot to aid the King's efforts."

Washington's surprise appeared genuine. "Sgt. Hickey! What is this? I know he has been charged with passing some counterfeit scrip. A rather common offense these days, as you know, Peter. But I cannot believe he would be a traitor."

"We were skeptical of this man Ketcham's claims. The man is pretty much a common criminal. Never passes up an opportunity for an illicit dollar. However, when we received the petition from Mason not 24 hours later we became concerned. Mason has admitted to having been corrupted by the conspirators. He has come clean on his dealings with the King's men. He has told us about every dollar received and given us a lengthy list of those he knows to be involved. Sgt. Hickey is on this list. Mason says Hickey was involved in a plan that would have kidnapped you and other leaders. There was even, Mason said, talk of, well, doing away with you and the other generals."

"Do you have this list?" asked Washington.

"Yes," said Livingston, removing several sheets of paper from his breast pocket.

"I'll take care of this personally, Mr. Livingston," said Washington. "There will be no mistake this time."

12:10 a.m. Saturday, June 22

Henry Dawkins folded the blanket containing all of his possessions and stood by the door of the cell. The Youngs brothers snored and whistled in harmony on their cots. A few seconds later, the red haired, gap-toothed guard turned the key in the lock and Dawkins quickly exited.

They walked down the hall to the guard area, which was empty. Red was on duty alone tonight. The gold piece felt large and warm in the young guard's pocket. Two months pay it was. Mr. Dawkins had given it to him as he left the east door to the prison and disappeared into the darkness. Hey, prisoners escaped all the time. And Mr. Dawkins was too talented to be locked up with all of these common thieves and head-thumpers anyway. The gap in his teeth was dark and wide in the middle of the broad smile as the guard admired, once again, the Dawkins portrait of his wife.

12:30 a.m., Saturday, June 22

George Washington slipped out of bed and got dressed, trying not to disturb Martha. She stirred, rolled up onto an elbow and said sleepily, "Can't this wait until the morning, George?"

"No, dear. Don't worry yourself. Go back to sleep. I'll be back in an hour or two."

Washington closed the bedroom door and went down to his office. Several officers were waiting there for him.

"Is everything in place, gentlemen?" asked the commander-in-chief.

"We're ready," said the officers in unison.

"I want an immediate report."

"Yes, sir," they said again in unison and quickly and deliberately left the office.

Washington stood and looked down from the office window as more than a hundred mounted soldiers formed up as the officers barked orders. Within a few minutes, they were off at a gallop.

The raids had been planned and executed with precision. Washington had been serious when he told Peter Livingston he would not be embarrassed again. He had personally taken charge of planning the raids.

Less than an hour later, one detachment of the Continental Army formed a barricade around the Flatbush residence of the Mayor David Matthews. Washington was taking no chances this time. He had selected officers and men he felt he could trust. He had kept each raid separate and independent with the officer in charge alone knowing the target. Each residence would be surrounded. There would be no slipping out the back door this time. The principal in question was to be arrested on the personal warrant signed by Washington and the premises searched for any evidence.

"What is the meaning of this outrage?" demanded Mayor Matthews, flinging open the front door to end the persist pounding. He was startled to see a dozen mounted soldiers with torches set out encircling his home.

"David? What is it?" A woman's voice, edgy with concern, came from the top of the hall stairs.

"Get dressed, dear," said the mayor, now backing into the hallway, pressed by a major and two enlisted men.

"Mr. David Matthews. We have a warrant signed by the Commander-in-Chief of the Continental Army, His Excellency George Washington. Your house will be searched and you, sir, are under arrest."

"Preposterous," sputtered Matthews, a round faced, pink skinned man with unruly yellow hair. "Leave my home this instant! I am the duly appointed mayor of this city. I order you to leave my home this instant."

"I am afraid I cannot," said the army officer, continuing with due efficiency. "Mr. David Matthews you are charged with dangerous designs and treasonable conspiracies against the rights and liberties of the United Colonies of America."

Two soldiers gave Matthews time to dress and then escorted him to the city lockup. The others thoroughly searched the house, looking for incriminating evidence. They had been instructed to look for diaries, log books, receipts, cash or any evidence to connect Matthews with the loyalists. Mason had said Matthews had contributed a hundred pounds sterling to the cause. Washington had not acted solely on the word of Peter Livingston and the petitions from the jail. A top secret committee, headed by John Jay, had been working to trace a connection between Mayor Matthews and other prominent city officials and Royal Governor William Tryon.

Shortly after 2 a.m., Gilbert Forbes, the Broad Way gunsmith, was taken by another cadre. He was immediately taken before the sitting congress which had decided to deal immediately with those arrested, regardless of the hour. Forbes refused to say a word and was sent to the city jail. An hour later, a local minister was sent by the congress to visit Forbes. The minister told Forbes he was there to care for his immortal soul as he had been told by the congress that Forbes had only three days to live before being executed. Forbes sang like a canary. He said Mayor Matthews had given him 140 pounds sterling on direct orders of Gov. Tryon. Forbes implicated scores of others.

By sunrise, 34 prominent citizens were in custody and charged with treason. Several hundred soldiers were sent to Long Island to take more Tories. Several were locked up in the Jamaica jail on Long Island. Others were brought in to the city.

The list of those arrested read like a Loyalist honor roll. James Matthews, the mayor's brother, who resided in Cornwall, Orange County, was seized along with Counselor William Axtell, Dr. Samuel Martin, and John Willet of Jamaica. The first list of New York suspects (There were two lists for New York and separate others for King's, Richmond, Queens and Westchester Counties.) included William Newton, Linus King, John Baltres Dash, Theodore Hardenbrook, Samuel Burling, John Woods, Benjamin Williams, Christopher Benson, William Bayard, Frederick Rhinelander, James Coggshall, John Milliner, Benjamin James, Theopolist Bache, Peter Mclean, Samuel Galsworthy and Francis De La Roach. The Second List held 24 more names.

Congress sat almost continuously to hear the extent of the Loyalist plot. Most, especially the more prominent of the city's English sympathizers, were allowed to post bail and return to their homes under orders to stay put until they were told otherwise. These bonds ranged as high as 2,000 pounds sterling. In all, some 500 people were suspected of being involved, in one way or another, with some kind of plan to support the British in the battle for New York.

8:30 p.m., Saturday, June 22

George Washington sat alone in his office sipping a glass of madeira and looking over the lists of those who had been arrested. The number was impressive and the raids had been carried out with true military precision. He was pleased with that. On the other hand, the extent of the plotting was staggering. Everyone knew of course, that New York was pretty much evenly divided between Loyalists and the boys of liberty. But to have this many, including many of the most prominent citizens, be directly involved in plans to subvert his military efforts and abet the King's men was disconcerting to say the least.

Washington realized that, while he needed to gain control of the situation and send a message to all that he was in charge, it would not be a good idea to publicly announce the full extent of the various conspiratorial plots. That might have the opposite affect on those residents who might be wavering in their loyalties.

He kept returning to a single sheet of paper sent by the Provincial Congress and signed by Peter Livingston.

It read: "Keep in mind, General Washington, that while we may detain these men for awhile and, perhaps, in some well-defined instances see that they leave the city, we cannot put them on trial because there are no laws against treason within the purview of the Provincial Congress."

Washington knew Livingston was correct. The united colonies were still embryonic. While they were prepared to fight for their liberties, there were still many details that were normally spelled out in a nation's body of laws-- such as treason and sedition -- which had simply not been addressed.

Washington knew the raids could blow up in his face like a sparked powder keg. What would be worse than discovering an evil plot and rounding up hundreds of conspirators? Having to slap them on the wrists and let them go? Let them go back to their plotting and, perhaps, open antagonism. This was the last thing he needed at this juncture. Word was that the King's fleet would arrive any day now.

He had one card left to play. There was one person who could be tried. There was one person who could be held accountable. Made an example of.

3:30 p.m., Monday, June 24

Hickey froze as Phoebe approached the bars of his cell. He had just been raging and sputtering like a mad dog about "the liberty traitors" and how the King would "cut off their cocks and stuff'em in their mouths" when he marched unstopped through "that coxcomb whoremonger Washington and his cronies." He hoped she hadn't heard but the look on her face told proved otherwise.

Phoebe stood staring at Hickey. He stared back. Neither said a word both searching for a sign, a cue.

Hickey did not see anger, nor disgust in Phoebe's eyes

-- those beautiful dark eyes that he had seen in his waking mind and in his sleep each hour of each day since they had been apart. No. There was no hostility. Only pain. Her beautiful face with its coffee and cream hue was wracked with pain. She seemed on the edge of tears. Still she said nothing.

Hickey made the first move. Keeping his eyes locked with hers, he slowly walked to the bars. He pressed his face to the bars and held out his left hand. Phoebe did not move.

She felt the pain. It was cloying. Real. Her heart ached. She had never fully believed Thomas Hickey to be as evil as her father had painted him. That brush never fully covered the Thomas she knew. She had, however, come to feel that, for whatever reason, he had turned against Washington and the cause. Perhaps, there were reasons that she could understand. When word had come from Washington, through her father, that she should visit Hickey, she was torn. She wanted to see him, to talk with him, to ask so many questions. At the same time, she was afraid what she would hear. She was afraid that, perhaps, the Thomas she knew was, indeed, a lie, and that she would come face to face with the madman her father claimed he was. In the end, she knew there was no other answer. She had to see him. She had rehearsed what she would say; how she would touch him. Then, as she came down the corridor, through the foul-smelling jail cells, Hickey's words smote her as surely as if she had been slapped hard across the face. Her cheeks burned. She knew the sound of his voice but she did not know the mad scream of it, nor the venomous tirade. This was a different man; a different creature. It frightened her but it also made her angry, very angry.

Hickey was still standing with his hand stretched through the bars, his eyes pleading for her to come near.

"Phoebe," he stammered, his voice cracking. "Come here. Let me explain..."

Phoebe didn't move. She was staring deeply into his eyes. The flush in her cheeks was ebbing. The anger drained away. Those eyes. They were not the eyes of a madman. They were not murderous, nor seditious. They were gentle, kind, loving eyes. She knew this at this instant like she had never known anything before. Whatever the reasons. Whatever the actions. She knew in her very soul that Thomas Hickey loved her. She knew also that she loved him. She wanted to hold him. She wanted to be with him again.

"Phoebe," Hickey continued, without impatience or demand. "Please." He stretched his hand until his shoulder pressed hard against the iron bars.

Phoebe's fingers twitched imperceptibly and then her right hand rose slowly from her side and extended toward the bars. Their fingertips touched and it was as if lightning had struck the jail and passed through them alone. Their finger tips played with each other and slowly melted into a firm grasp. Hickey gently pulled and there was no resistance. Hickey pressed his face through the bars and Phoebe met his lips. They kissed long and hard like huge draughts from a rare desert well.

The sight of a woman or any stature, let alone one as attractive as Phoebe Fraunces, would normally have met with a symphony of catcalls and derogatory shouts and noises from the other inmates. But, they were so struck by the incongruity of it all, that no one made a sound. Here was this beautiful young girl who had walked up to the cell of a raging bull and was kissing him with passion. And Hickey, the snarling bully, was as tender as a lamb. It was just too odd. Too bizarre to do anything but watch.

Once, for a brief moment, they separated, each drawing in a long breath, looking into each other's eyes, and then kissed again. This kiss lasted several minutes.

Finally, Phoebe spoke.

"Thomas, I'm...I'm sorry. I'm sorry I believed what they ..."

Hickey stopped her.

"No, Phoebe. Please don't. There is nothing for you to

be sorry about. You have done nothing wrong. If I was in your shoes, I would have the same doubts."

"No, Thomas, I do owe you an apology. How could I have ever believed those things my father and brothers and all of the others said about you? When, in my heart, I knew you; knew you as well as I know myself."

"Phoebe, it was quite easy for you to believe those things because many of them were true. Well, at least, I mean, they seemed to be true. But, the reasons why are the most important things. You know me as a soldier in the Guard. But, I am not."

Phoebe cocked her head in puzzlement.

"No, I'm not really. You hear that I have been involved with those plotting against the cause. And I have."

Again, Phoebe pulled back, screwing her face as if Hickey was joking with her.

"But, as I said, the reasons for these actions are what I now want you to know. I did this for us. It was the only way I knew to get enough money so that we could be together. So that we could leave this place and this fight. For our own life. Together."

With that Hickey pulled Phoebe closer and told her everything. He whispered in her ear so that no one else could hear. He told her about his days as a "moon curser," smuggling contraband in and out of Boston. He told her about other special assignments for Hancock and how that had led to his meeting with Washington at the test of the Turtle.

He told her about his spying in New York and the money, the good money, Washington had paid him. He told her how his "appointment" as a sergeant in the Life Guard was only a matter of convenience. He explained how Washington had scores of other 'Hickeys' providing information, some even assigned to spy on the spies.

Hickey carefully explained about the counterfeiting and how it was all part of this double life. He felt hois throat constrict as he described his feeling of helplessness.

Washington, he said, let him go further and further out on the limb. He told Phoebe all about Mary Gibbons and of General Washington's indiscretions with her. His near-death experience in the water engine made Phoeve wince.

He told her everything.

When he was done, he realized that tears were streaming down her face and her mouth quivered in tiny sobs.

"Oh, Thomas. How can you ever forgive me. I have been a girlish little fool."

"No. No, Phoebe. You have been the very high point of my wretched life."

They kissed again and, when they pulled apart, Hickey told her how Washington had said that, if he were to find additional information to help him crush any plot, he would be set free with land in the Ohio Territory -- and, if she still wanted to....

Phoebe's face contorted anew.

"Thomas, I...."

"That's all right, Phoebe," he said, reading this expression as one of doubt. "You don't have to decide now."

"No!" she said firmly. "That's not it. I would go with you this instant. I have no more doubts about my feelings. It's just that...."

"What?" said Hickey gently, holding both of her hands in his, rubbing his thumbs over the smoothness of her skin. "Tell me."

"Thomas, my father sent me here to, well, to give you a message from General Washington."

"A message?"

There was a long moment of silence as Hickey tried to read the fear and sadness in Phoebe's face.

"Thomas," said Phoebe, her voice quavering. "You are to face a Court Martial on Wednesday. The charges are mutiny and sedition."

The look of surprise on Hickey's face made Phoebe burst into tears. She snatched is face in her hands and drew him towards her, caressing him, kissing him.

She kissed him as if it were the last kiss they would ever share. Hickey, too, drank of Phoebe's kisses knowing he had been a fool.

The two older guards arrived, separated them and ushered Phoebe out of the jail.

Chapter Twenty-Three
Washington's Headquarters
Richmond Hill
June 20-24, 1776

10 a.m., Wednesday, June 26
"I hereby call these proceedings to order," said Colonel Samuel Holden Parsons, judge advocate for the tribunal. "Upon direct warrant from His Excellency George Washington, Commander-in-Chief of Colonial Forces, we are here to determine the merit of serious charges brought against Sergeant Thomas Hickey and others. Sergeant Thomas Hickey of the Life Guard, please stand."

Hickey had floated through the day and a half since Phoebe had left his cell. It was all some sort of dream. He would soon awaken with Washington nudging his shoulder: "Thomas, wake up, my boy, you've been working too hard for the cause. I know my sofa is comfortable but you must wake up. I've got the deed to your land all ready for you and I've thrown in a nice wagon. Can't have Phoebe walking now can ..."

"Sergeant Hickey! Please stand!"

Hickey got up on watery legs and stood staring at the panel of three officers.

"Sergeant Thomas Hickey," said Parsons in a nasally monotonous drone, "on warrant of the military commander you are hereby charged with exciting and joining in mutiny

and sedition and of treacherously corresponding with, enlisting among, and receiving pay from the enemies of the
United American Colonies. These offenses being in direct
violation of the fifth and thirtieth articles of the rules and
regulations for the government of the Continental Forces.
How, sergeant, do you plead?"

"I didn't do any of those things," Hickey muttered, bewildered and disoriented

"Are you pleading not guilty?" droned Parsons.

"Uh, yes, I am not guilty of any of this. I was simply
doing what Wash...."

Parsons cut him off in mid-sentence. "There will be time
for your story, Sergeant Hickey. Please be seated."

Hickey sat alone on the narrow oak bench that had been
set down in the middle of what had been the dining room of
the Mortier house. The room had been cleared of its usual
furniture and replaced by the bench for Hickey and two wide
oak tables at which sat Parsons, Lieutenant Colonel John
Longwood, Major Ezra Porter, and Captains Charles Ward
and Patrick Teller. These five would hear the case and make
recommendations to Washington who, presumably with the
counsel of his fellow generals as was always his manner,
would make the final determination. And, while the warrant
from George Washington, listed the proceedings as the court
martial of Thomas Hickey "and others," no others would sit
in the hard, unforgiving oak bench. No "others" would face
this panel.

Parsons rearranged sheets of paper in a sheaf and prepared to begin. He did not like this job. In fact, he hadn't
wanted it but Washington insisted and, if nothing else, he
was dutiful. He would remain so until a few years down his
own personal road when he, too, would face similar charges.
Samuel Holden Parsons of Lyme, Connecticut had just
turned 39. A Harvard graduate he was admitted to the bar in
1759 and had practiced law in his home city for many years.
He had served for more than 18 years as a member of the

Connecticut State Assembly and, in fact, had been generally given credit for suggesting the colonies hold a 'general colonial congress'.

The irony of the muse of history in its dealings with mere mortals can be strangely entertaining. Such was the case with Parsons' selection to head Hickey's court martial. Not too long ago, Parsons, soon to be a general, had been approached by General Israel Putnam to help salvage a special, top secret project. It was Old Put who introduced Parsons to David Bushnell, the inventor of the "Turtle." David's brother, Ezra, who had manned the world's first military submarine, had taken ill with some general camp disorder and was too weak to pilot the Turtle on its soon-to-be-maiden voyage. Parsons recommended his brother-in-law 27-year-old Sergeant Ezra Lee for the job. Parsons had saved the day for the device, which, in a way, had been responsible for Hickey's being drawn in to the service of Washington.

Hickey had no help with his defense. He hadn't even been officially told the charges until this very moment. As he sat listening to Parsons read the dialogue of events and resulting charges against him, Hickey stirred. He shifted on the hard bench and felt life returning to his arms and legs. Like a baby chick, he pecked through the shell of shock and disbelief that had encased him for two days. How could Washington let this happen? Had he, once again, deceived him? Or was this part of the act? As commander-in-chief, Washington couldn't admit to intelligence leaks, philandering or to the extent of conspiratorial sentiment in a New York City precariously balanced between Tory and Whig. Perhaps, Washington had arranged this little charade as the perfect cover. He would expect Hickey to rant and rave and put on a good show; to do all he could to cover their undercover arrangement. Then, regardless of the outcome, Washington would arrange for his exit from the city and the political and military conflict as a whole.

The trance evaporated and Hickey's animal instincts

emerged. He smashed the knuckles of his right hand hard into the oak bench. The resounding bang caused Parson to stop in mid-diatribe.

"Sergeant Hickey! I will have you restrained if there is another such outburst. Respect the command to which you have sworn your allegiance. Will you not?"

"I respect nothing but myself," said Hickey, in what was supposed to be a cover but, in reality, was the truth. He knew it to be true.

Two burly young soldiers, whom Hickey recognized as members of the Life Guard, moved forward to hold Hickey's arms. Hickey shook them off. He sat back down, still but defiant. Parsons, satisfied Hickey would abide his warning for the time being, waved away the guards. The fog that had engulfed Hickey dissipated. He stared directly into Parsons eyes as the judge advocate bombinated on.

"...also that you received a sum of money from one Gilbert Forbes and passed money to other soldiers of the Colonial Army for the purpose of enlisting them into the service of the King and against the American Colonies. Further, that you had arranged for passage of yourself and others to a royal ship of the King's Admiralty to evade your duty as a soldier and to take up with those who stand as enemies to the Colonel Army," said Parsons in the steady, humming voice like a persistent wasp flitting about one's ear on a hot summer day.

When he was done, Parsons ceremoniously replaced the sheets of paper in their original order and looked at Hickey as a teacher looks at a mischievous student.

"Before we call the witnesses against you, Sergeant Hickey, have you anything to say to these charges?"

To the handful of witnesses to the proceedings, Hickey's "defense" was pitiful. In his own mind, however, he was putting on a show worthy of the stage. He was the proper rebellious conspirator espousing innocence in such a blatantly unconvincing manner that he might as well have admitted guilt. The key to appreciating his performance, of course, lay in knowing his special arrangement with Washington; in knowing the months and months of valuable information he had passed for the benefit of, as Parsons kept saying, these United American Colonies. But, no one else in the room had the program for this performance. In such context, the performance was poor indeed.

"I only took money," said Hickey in his roughest dockside manner, "cause I needed it and why not take it from the King? Less he has to use against us. Sure I signed up for a boat ride with the King. Why not? Maybe I'd a blown it up right there in the harbor. Been a real hero. Been treated right. Like I should. Not like this."

"Is that all you have to say?" said Parsons, still droning but with a touch of incredulity that Hickey could offer such a feeble story on his own behalf. This man was facing the death penalty. Did he know that? Congress had specifically approved the death penalty for soldiers convicted of mutiny or sedition.

"If I told you that I had been hired by Hizzoner Gentleman George Washington to do all you have accused me of, would that sit better with ya," Hickey said, amusing himself.

"I warn you, again, Sergeant Hickey, we will have no outbursts. I ask you again, have you anything else to say in your own defense?"

Hickey said nothing. He just smiled that killer smile, the one that had gotten him into scores of beds with scores of women.

"Guards move Sergeant Hickey to the chair there," ordered Parsons, gesturing to a straight-backed chair with no arms at the right side of the room opposite the window.

Isaac Ketcham was called as first witness. A guard stepped through the dining room door and returned with Ketcham. The paper merchant looked straight ahead as he walked to and sat on the oak bench in front of the three officers. Parsons gave him the charge of the court martial and asked his testimony. Ketcham was only too happy to oblige.

"Your honor, I am just ...," Ketcham began but was interrupted by Parsons.

"Colonel Parsons will do," said Parsons.

"Colonel, sir, I am just a paper merchant," said Ketcham, with as sweetly syrupy a spider's voice that ever caught a fly. "I have been separated from my family for weeks now because of a grievous mistake. I had no part in any plan to counterfeit colonial...."

Once again, he was interrupted by Parsons. "We are not here to judge your guilt or innocence, Mr. Ketcham. You have been called to testify as to what you know about said charges against Sergeant Thomas Hickey. Do you understand?"

"Yes, of course. I was just hoping that your honor would help in my plight should I...," seeing that Parsons was getting impatient, Ketcham go to the point. "But, as for Thomas Hickey. Mind you I have no part in his evil schemes but he has taken great delight over the past week or more to tell me of his involvement in, as he put it, 'a glorious plan to snatch General Washington and other generals' and to escape with them to the loving arms of the King's protection."

Ketcham, remembering with the amazingly precise detail that can be had when you are fabricating on the fly, told of lengthy conversations with Hickey in which he revealed details of the plotters, their numbers and secret hideouts.

"Thank you, Mr. Ketcham. You are excused."

Ketcham wanted to make a final plea for his own release but thought better of it. As the guard escorted him back through the dining room door, Hickey said, loud enough for all to hear, "Hope yer arse rots in that cell of yers, Ketcham. Remember, Ketcham, I saved your life. I saved your fucking little life."

Gilbert Forbes was next.

"I am Gilbert Forbes. I am a gunsmith in this city doing

business under the 'Sign of the Sportsman,' opposite Hull's tavern in the Broad Way," began Forbes in an amazingly calm, precise voice. Forbes could afford to be calm. His offer of a deal had been accepted by the Committee of Safety and they had assured him he would escape punishment if he told all he knew. Not even Colonel Parsons was aware of the full extent of this deal. Forbes went into great detail about his involvement. It began, he said, with an order -- a very large order -- for guns. By the time he knew they were going to the King's troops, he was too far in and making too much money.

"I was given one hundred pounds for the purpose of enlisting others into the King's cause," said Forbes coolly. "It was Private William Green, a drummer for General Washington, who first tempted me to approach soldiers. Those so enlisted were to go aboard the King's ships but, if they could not make it there, they were to play out their proper roles right here in the city until the King's forces arrived."

Forbes explained that 'their proper roles' were everything from blowing up powder stores to kidnapping colonial officers.

Asked what Hickey's proper role was, Forbes said: "Sergeant Hickey was given two dollars and signed up. It was thought that he would be valuable in enlisting other soldiers to the King's cause and, in the event he couldn't make it to the ships, he was to lead the other soldiers in kidnapping General Washington. I am Irish myself, you see, and Thomas Hickey said 'Us Old Countrymen have to make our peace, don't we? We have to join together and swear to the King before they arrive and kill us all. And for what?' Sergeant Hickey signed on several other members of the Life Guard."

Colonel Parsons was amazed and baffled by Forbes' calm recital. He had begun to suspect that Forbes had been given some kind of promise. But that was not for him to judge.

"Thank you, Mr. Forbes."

Hickey said nothing as Forbes was escorted out. Hickey knew most of what Forbes had testified to be true. Hickey, too, could see that Forbes was too nonchalant. The prison conversations, he thought, were a set up. Forbes had planned this well and gotten his own reprieve, perhaps not a couple hundred acres in the Ohio wilderness but something as equally valuable to him. He may, thought Hickey, actually be one of Washington's men. Better off to say nothing.

Private Green was called next. This surprised Hickey. What could Green possibly add? Green was a twitchy little drummer with a girlish laugh. His left eye would wander into towards his nose until he blinked to set it straight, which always made Hickey uncomfortable when talking with him.

Green ranted for nearly 10 minutes. He squealed and squawked. He purred. He raged, pointing at Hickey. It was Forbes who had drug him into this whole mess. Hickey was the real leader. He was the one who signed up all the soldiers. He was the one who had threatened Green and bullied him until he got deeper and deeper and couldn't get out.

From time to time, Parsons tried to stop Green to clarify a point. There was no stopping him. At the first sign of interruption, his voice just got louder, faster and more desperate. Finally, he had spent himself and slumped on the bench. He had embellished, exaggerated, overstated and elaborated on Hickey's role in the plot.

Hickey found it laughable. Could anyone believe this pitiful little man?

"Why don't you go suck the general's doodle, Green, you little fuck," said Hickey contemptuously as Green quickly shuffled past, his eyeball dancing wildly in its socket.

The final witness was James Mason.

Mason delivered the coup de grace. The long, heated interrogations had taken their toll on him. Earlier on, alone in his cell, he had hit on Hickey as a way out. Mason coldly relayed "conversations" between himself and Hickey.

"I knew this to be of value, sir," Mason said earnestly to the officers of the court martial. "That is why I made a point of going over and over them until I had them in my memory, pretty much word for word."

If there had been any doubt as to Hickey's guilt in the minds of the five officers, Mason erased the final vestige. He said Hickey had vehemently told him that General Washington was an incompetent officer and that they all would be killed once the King's men arrived. He quoted Hickey as saying 'the King is our only Savior' and 'we have no business talking about independence...a child could sooner break way from his mother'.

Mason had rehearsed very well. His testimony was delivered with seriousness of purpose, deference to the court, and tearful apologies that he had ever been led down this seditious path. Not only did he point the finger at Hickey, he indicted several others including, for the first time in public, Tory Mayor David Matthews, whom Mason said had supplied the cash for all of the enlistments. He wanted the officers to know that he was not as evil a man as he knew Thomas Hickey to be. The thin hair breaks and the dangling sword falls ... into Thomas Hickey's chest.

Hickey was speechless. What was all this? He barely knew Mason. None of this was true. Who was Mason working for? And why? Doubt settled over his mind like chimney smoke on a windless day. Gray and unsettling doubt. Where will this end? He had to believe that Washington would uphold his end of the bargain and, somehow, get him out of this. But who put Mason up to this? Why?

The question echoed in his mind as Parsons had Hickey brought to the wooden bench.

"Sergeant Thomas Hickey you have heard the case and testimony against you. Have you anything else to say in your own defense?"

Hickey thought about the question very carefully. On the one hand, he thought maybe he should let the dam break.

Tell about his spying. Tell about how all of this was for the good of the cause. Sure he made a few dollars but he earned it. But he was not a traitor. A man had to believe in something before he could be a traitor against it. But, he knew he couldn't tell any of this. Who would believe it? Certainly not Parson who was in line to be General Parsons. Certainly no other officer on the board. Then again, he could continue the charade and rely on Washington's good faith. He had learned additional details about the various conspiracy plots. None of these details had come up in this court. He learned that there were at least three separate and distinct groups of conspirators and that one group, in particular was very dangerous. Once Washington made contact, he would tell him this news and then all would be fine. How would Washington accomplish his release? The court had not gone well at all. They would have to find him guilty. Washington might have him removed to custody outside the city. From there he would 'escape' to the west. Parsons had mentioned a death sentence. That, of course, was ludicrous. He had, even by the testimony, not done any more than any of these other conspirators as far as they could tell. Perhaps, Washington would just have him taken to the riverfront and put on a boat. They could say he drowned in an escape attempt.

"I didn't do nothing more than any of these other highwayman," Hickey said belligerently.

"Very well, Sergeant Hickey. This court martial is closed. We will deliberate and you will be called to hear the verdict."

The entire hearing had taken less than two hours. The five officers took less than two minutes to agree on their recommendation. Guilty. Recommended punishment? Hanging.

2:30 p.m., Thursday, June 27, 1776

George Washington sat down at his desk to write the orders for tomorrow. His mind wandered. This was the same desk he had suspected Hickey of prying open and searching.

That memory made him look toward the leather sofa where he had startled Hickey and Sam Fraunces' lovely daughter Phoebe in the midst of carnal pleasure. He looked back to the paper and redipped the quill into the inkwell. Once he had made up his mind, there was no looking back. No remorse. No second guessing himself. This was the only way. There was too much at stake to risk saving Hickey. The dividends from his raids and quick, decisive action in the 'Tory Plot', as it was being called in the news, were already substantial. New Jersey, aghast at the threat from within, had stopped wavering and voted for independence.

Reports were that the King's ship would arrive any day now. What would happen if it were to be made public that, perhaps, the commander-in-chief, selected personally by the Congress, had been responsible for some intelligence leaks? Gen. Lee's protests and others aside, he knew he was the one to lead this revolutionary cause. It just would not do to question his leadership, no matter how trivial the charges.

Besides, soldiers died all the time. That's what soldiers did. They put their life on the line. And, despite his protestations, Hickey was a soldier -- and a very well-paid soldier at that. He had weighed all possible courses of action and all outcomes. This was the only course.

The council of seven generals had only been gone half an hour. They hadn't hesitated based on the evidence, testimony and the recommendation of the court martial. He didn't have to say much at all. He encouraged them to 'decide on the merits'. Of course, he had not told them of Thomas Hickey's service above and beyond the call of the Life Guard. Nor did he mention Mary Gibbons (whose body had been dumped into the sound), nor the scores of other men and women in his employ, hired to gather information and pass on inaccurate information. That was not their concern. A commander had responsibilities for all. Responsibility could be burdensome, indeed.

Within a matter of minutes the council approved of the

verdict and penalty and, with Washington presiding, signed the order.

"Be it known that the prisoner Thomas Hickey shall pay for said crimes by being hanged by the neck till he is dead."

And why put it off? The hanging was set for noon the following day. None of the generals bothered to observe that work on the gallows had begun even before they convened for the afternoon session.

Washington felt a sudden, palpable sadness. Hickey had been very loyal in his own way. He had certainly been less trouble than a dozen others running as spies. It was a difficult thing. It was like whipping a soldier; like any disciplinary action. It was very difficult to make such decisions. But someone had to.

Washington prepared the orders of the day for Friday, June 28, 1776:

"The unhappy fate of Thomas Hickey, executed this day for mutiny, sedition, and treachery, the General hopes will be a warning to every soldier in the Army to avoid those crimes, and all others, so disgraceful to the character of a soldier, and pernicious to his country, whose pay he receives and bread he eats. And in order to avoid those crimes, the most certain method is to keep out of the temptation of them, and particularly to avoid lewd women, who, by the dying confession of this poor criminal, first led him into practices which ended in an untimely and ignominious death."

Chapter Twenty-Four

The Gallows
11:23 a.m., Friday, June 28, 1776

Hickey slowly dragged his hands down from his eyes, drops of sweat soaking into the paper. Had it only been a single year? Had he gone from the moonlit nights on the Charles to this in a single year? He put down the pen, blew on the fresh ink to dry it and the spreading droplets. He folded the paper and on the outside wrote "Miss Phoebe Fraunces." He would give it to the minister on the way to the ... to the end. No. It wasn't the end. Not really. It just wouldn't happen. Washington would have to do something. "The great general of all armies, his worship of Virginia, the Grand and Glorious George Washington, pardons this poor Irish immigrant who knows no better. How great is he who can forgive such a low life as this one. You're right, master. I'm not worth it. I'll just be going now." Then, he'd be gone as quick as a flash of lightning. His horse would drop from under him with exhaustion by the time he reached the Pennsylvania border. His horse. Did anyone know where it was? What would happen to it? No. Nothing would happen. He was going to ride it out of here. With Phoebe clutched tight to his waist. Ride hard and put as many miles between him and this city and its people, all of its people, regardless of persuasion.

Hickey shuddered, despite the heat. It was already near 80 degrees and barely 10 in the morning. It would be a hot one. His spine quivered again. Like the first ill wind of winter, the noise of the crowd shook him into reality. He tried to ignore it but it would not be brushed aside. He tried thinking about Phoebe. But, just as New Yorkers whistled into the November wind, telling themselves it would pass, they knew in their hearts it would not. He knew he couldn't avoid the inevitable. There would be plenty of warm weather again, they lied. Plenty of green grass and sun before that first arctic blast made the earth lifeless and frozen. Yet the snow would come quickly and they would be forced to deal with reality. Harsh. Stark Unforgiving. And, yet once upon them, somehow a relief. The truth was always a relief, no matter how cold. Hickey shivered with the ill wind of the winter of his life. He was aware again of the small holding area in which he sat. He could hear the guards joking outside the door. He could hear the drone of the crowd a mile or so away in the clearing near the Bowery. He wanted to be angry but there was no anger to be found. Just as there was no great reservoir of hope to be tapped. Only reality. He swiped at the sweat falling from his face, ran his fingers over the crease in the note to Phoebe and waited.

A few minutes later, the door opened and four guards led Hickey out into the hot, humid, windless street. They sat him on a wooden box in the back of an open wagon. He faced the rear of the wagon, his hands chained behind him and through an eye bolt in the box. A soldier drove the wagon pulled by a single languid brown horse. He was surprised to watch as 80 men, armed and with fixed bayonets, formed around the wagon for the one-mile trek. The eighty men had been drawn, 20 each, from the brigades of Generals Scott, Spencer, Heath, and, of course, William Alexander who still used his Scottish title Lord Stirling. In addition to the guards, most of the men assigned to the four brigades were lined along the path, several thousand in full uniform.

"Stay close!" shouted a major. "The devil's henchmen may try to spring him."

Hickey smiled as if they were talking about someone else until he realized they thought someone would try to rescue him. Who? Washington?

The wagon jerked forward and Hickey was thrown forward straining the chains. He recovered and sat back staring from side to side. The Artillery Surgeon William Eustis would record later that Hickey had been "unaffected and obstinate to the last." But it was merely that he could clearly see his winter's reality. There was nothing to be done. He had lost to those who had beaten down his father and his father's father. It was inevitable for men like himself. No, there was nothing to be done. He sat calmly, staring into the faces of soldiers and civilians along the route. He could not see the looming gallows until the wagon had come to a stop and he looked over his shoulder.

Executions were great entertainment for eighteenth century Europeans and, with most New Yorkers barely a generation removed from the Old World, the fascination had been carried across the sea. Official records were to record an estimate of more than 20,000 people gathered in the open field to watch the spectacle, very nearly evenly divided between military and civilian populations.

Hickey was unchained from the bolt and yanked from the cart by four burly soldiers. When Hickey's legs failed to respond, they quickly dragged him up the stairs to the gallows platform. Hickey was told to stand at attention. He was, the major conducting the hanging reminded him, still a soldier. He was dressed in his Life Guard uniform, complete with blackened boots and hat. The major, a white-skinned, baby-faced young man with an old man's sneer that seemed quite comical and out of place, stepped forward and, with a knife cut all the buttons off Hickey's coat. He then slashed the red epaulet from his right shoulder.

The crowd erupted in cheers.

One of the two old men who had emerged from the Hog's Head Tavern and pushed their way to the front, yelled: "Use it on his Tory-loving gullet, too, why ye at it!"

His companion cackled. Those near enough to hear gave a great "huzzah" of agreement. The large woman in the brown frock, giggled with glee, her open mouth filled with gaping holes between dark teeth. She again coughed and slapped one of the two girls now pressed close to her skirts and not as willing to sing as they were just a few minutes ago. They stood wide-eyed, fingers playing in their mouths, knowing that what they would soon see would be very scary. The stuff of nightmares for weeks. They pressed closer to the big woman's hips. She crushed them closer to her with her chunky arms.

The major read out the warrant of execution and asked the chaplain to step forward. The chaplain said a few quiet words to Hickey.

"Is there anything you'd like to say to the Lord, my son?"

"No, sir," said Hickey. "What little talking I do to Him, I done already. But I would like you to take the note from my pocket here," he gestured with his chin, "and give it to Phoebe Fraunces, daughter of Sam Fraunces. You know, of Fraunces Tavern? Please."

The chaplain nodded somberly and took the note. As he stepped away, the major quickly snatched the note and stuffed it in to his uniform.

"No!" Hickey snapped. "Not you, you fucking Washington worm. That's not for you. Give it back. I'll cram my boot all the way up yer arse. Give it back to him. You hear me?"

The major smiled smugly as the guards restrained Hickey.

Observers would later say that Hickey had cursed the chaplain "...and God to the very end" remaining unremorseful for his dastardly conduct.

Tears flowed down Hickey's cheeks as he realized the note would never get to Phoebe. Winter had arrived in all of its frigid reality. He realized that there would be no reprieve. Even standing on the platform, he had truly believed this would not happen. Now he knew the truth. He had always known the truth, hadn't he. There was no spring for men like he. Tears turned to sobs as he was led onto the trap door below the gallows crossbar.

The hangman had been standing patiently to the right of the platform, his hands folded in front of him. It took a great deal of will power not to scrape and claw at the black mess with bubbles of sweat flowing through and dripping to his chest. He was a professional. Dignity was to be had. He would do it right. No one in this screaming horde knew just how difficult it was to get this right. The knot, for example. If you didn't place the knot behind the left ear of the victim, it would not do its job. It was the snapping of the knot which knocked the victim unconscious. So there would be little pain. The drop snapped the bones of the neck and spinal cord, pulverizing them and paralyzing the body.

Even then you had to get the length of rope just right. Too long and you'd rip the head right off. Too short and the victim wouldn't be unconscious. No bones would snap. The victim would dance and sputter slowly strangling in a horrible, painful death throe. This could take fifteen minutes or more. He had done this often enough to get it right. He had taken one look at Hickey and knew just how long the rope should be to get it over. And yet, even then, it usually took several minutes before the victim stopped kicking. That's why it was important to tie the ankles together.

He did so with a short cord. He then stepped back and, picking up a black hood, which would be placed over Hickey's face, waited for the signal. The major stepped to the center of the platform and read the words of warning Washington had prepared. When he got to the part about "...avoiding lewd women," Hickey again cried out in a rage. The words were indistinguishable now. Terror had taken hold. He could not think. He tried to think of what he wanted to say but soon settled back into silence. An icy wind blew across his cheeks.

Hickey stared ahead not hearing the jeers of the crowd who were worked to fever pitch now. Just as the hangman was lowering the hood over his face, he saw Phoebe. There in the front. "Phoebe!" he yelled. But only in his mind. No sound. "Phoebe..."

The hangman slipped the noose over the hood, tightened the draw and tugged the knot firmly behind Hickey's left ear.

Phoebe stared, first at the face, and then at the hood. Tears streamed down her cheeks. She, too, heard nothing but knew he had called her name.

The hangman tripped the lever. Hickey dropped four feet until the rope snapped taut. His neck bent at a steep angle and his legs kicked for only a few seconds. Those on and near the gallows caught the horrid stench as Hickey defecated, urinated and ejaculated all at once, the muscle sphincters spasming and going limp. There was a small, weak gasp and he was dead.

The old men slapped each other on the back and nearly bowled over Phoebe as they hastened back to the tavern.

Author's Note

"Moon Cursers" is a work of fiction. While many of the characters did live and breathe during our country's birth, I have never claimed this to be anything other than a historical novel which I hope has been entertaining.

And yet, in my several years of research there were many times when I felt uneasy; as if I were indeed uncovering a bit of secret history.

One of the most disturbing incidents was reported to have taken place early in the 20th Century.

Picture, if you will, an officious woman systematically feeding paper to a small, bonfire contained in a barrel. Page by page, the voracious orange and red flames hungrily devour the dry paper.

Nearly 150 years of dry closets and storage boxes had left the paper more vulnerable than tinder. In an instant, the handwritten inked lines disappeared. Each one of the hundreds, perhaps thousands, of sheets of paper being burned might be worth several thousand dollars to a collector today. That's what a bit of original writing by George Washington is worth, especially the signatures.

The woman was deliberately destroying a healthy chunk of the Washington historical record. What makes the story even more frightening is that she was a librarian. A librarian worse than any of the helmeted book burners of Ray Bradbury's Fahrenheit 451, a professional keeper of the archives purposely destroying part of the historical record.

In so doing, she seems to have made a conscious decision to whitewash the legacy of George Washington.

The account of this grievous attack on primary source historical material was set down by Edward Larocque Tiner in February 1925. Writing for "The Bookman," a literary publication of the time, he reported on an actual interview with the woman. A "New York City library" had acquired an impressive collection of Washington documents and this woman was in charge of the collection. In reading through the material, she found a lot of it "smutty."

Tinker quotes the woman as saying: "I did not want them to become public and destroy the ideal of Washington that had flourished for so long." In what now appears to be unmitigated arrogance, she said: "It was only a question of money. Could we afford to pay the price and then destroy our investment? We could and we did."

Certainly this is not the first time that evidence of a historical figure's humanity has been destroyed to protect some idealized version, which, in time, becomes mythic in proportion. On the other hand, such material is often lost through shear ignorance of the need for its preservation or future value. For example, thousands of letters written by Washington and Thomas Jefferson were simply dumped into the Potomac River on a blustery winter day at the start of the Civil War. Space was needed in the Capitol to quarter troops. The rooms had been used to store government documents. The order went out to clear rooms to make way for soldiers.

Sleigh after sleigh carted tons of what would now be priceless documents to the icy shore of the Potomac where they were dumped. What a tragic loss of historical material not to mention an assault on the environment. Reports say the winter wind blew some of the papers around the city streets where they were picked up and saved by curious passersby. Could someone have picked up Hickey's death statement? Or Washington's accounting of his spy activity?

Most likely, we will never know the complete story of the relationship between George Washington and Thomas Hickey, if indeed it was anything more than general to sergeant. It is a classic tale of the haves and have-nots. The very same muse that bestows a life of power and privilege on a few seems to be at work in sanitizing history. As Robert the Bruce is quoted as saying in the motion picture *Braveheart:* "History is written by those who hang heroes." Or, as Winston Churchill remarked: "History is written by the victors."

George Washington is widely recognized to be one of the greatest spy masters America has known. He ran hundreds of spies known only to himself and whom he paid out of his own pocket. (Later to be reimbursed, of course.) Washington, who kept meticulous financial records, spent $17,000 on what was listed as "reconnaissance." By one popular measure, that's more than half million dollars today.

Consider, for example, the case of John Honeyman of Griggstown, New Jersey. Honeyman, a butcher, was hated by his neighbors. His wife and children were continually abused for Honeyman's Tory sympathies. Honeyman was even arrested by American scouts and taken to Washington's Headquarters just before Christmas 1776. He conveniently escaped but not until he had briefed General Washington on British troop movements. It wasn't until after the war that Washington revealed Honeyman's true contributions. He called him out into the street to publicly thank him for his spy efforts. Honeyman was a Son of Liberty who placed himself and his family in the line of fire for the cause.

Or how about Hercules Mulligan? Mulligan was a popular New York City tailor catering to the Red Coats. He, too, endured the hatred of his neighbors who were certain he was a Tory through and through. Imagine their surprise when General Washington himself came to the tailor's house for breakfast in 1783 after the British had evacuated New York.

Would those New York library papers have talked about Hickey? Would they have mentioned the affair with Mary Gibbons? Would Washington have noted the loveliness of Phoebe Fraunces? Is this the "smut" of which we've been spared?

Google George Washington and you get 682 million hits! We have a state and national capital named for Washington and an impressive monument within the national capital. Seven mountains carry the Washington moniker along with eight streams and 10 lakes. There's the iconic Mount Rushmore. And what city worth its salt does not have a Washington Street? By actual count, there are 33 Washington Counties. Also nine colleges and 121 towns and villages carry the label. The "Father of our Country" is on the workhorse dollar bill and on our 25-cent coins.

It is difficult to separate George Washington from the likes of Odysseus or even Paul Bunyan. Overzealous authors have weeded out the good from the bad and then incinerated the bad. Only recently in what some critics call revisionist history have we come to know the nitty-gritty of many historical figures.

In Washington's case, no one did more damage to the truth or aggrandized the myth more than one Mason Locke Weems, known as 'Parson Weems." Weems wrote "Washington," a fantasized version of a Washington biography, a year after Washington's death. We have him to thank for the cherry tree episode and 'I cannot tell a lie.' The Weems book was a sellout and made him a tidy fortune. And who can really fault him? He admitted he was simply trying to use Washington to teach the young people right from wrong, a modern Aesop. But it was still a fable; a fable that continues to this very day.

History is nothing if not subjective. But, it is interesting how these myths are perpetuated by even the supposedly most learned of historians.

In an article in a national Sunday newspaper supplement several years ago, a widely read historian stated: "With the passing years, his (Washington's) misgivings grew about slavery. He provided for the freeing of his slaves at his wife's death ..."

He says this as if to provide evidence of Washington's magnanimity, of his anti-slavery mentality. Huh? How much of a sacrifice is it to free the slaves not only after you are dead and no longer can use their services but after your spouse has passed as well?

The article makes a case for judging our political leaders on their character as well as their political qualifications. It cites Washington as the perfect example. "He (Washington) informed Congress he required no salary and would accept only reimbursement of expenses." Again, a statement which is, indeed, true. But one can perpetuate a myth by what is not said just as surely as with what is spoken.

What this historian does not mention is that after the war, Washington, who as we have said before was a meticulous bookkeeper, submitted an itemized bill for his expenses over the eight war years that totaled $449,261.51 – plus six-percent interest! Those 1783 dollars would be roughly worth $14 million today.

Who wouldn't be delighted to get six percent today? It would have been cheaper for the fledgling nation to have paid him a handsome salary and covered expenses. Not to mention (as the writer did not), that Washington was spending money that might have been worthless had the British won but was golden with interest if he succeeded.

The object lesson here is not the vilification of historians, nor the crucifixion of heroes. Far from it. It is simply to point out how easy it is to see the glass as either half full or half empty instead of attempting to measure the exact amount of water and report it.

"Moon Cursers" is a work of storytelling but it, too, is guilty of this in a way. For example, the mention of Benjamin Franklin giving counsel to Washington. By this time, Franklin was considered a doddering old fool by the 30- and 40-somethings of Congress. He was mostly ignored and pretty much overruled on all of his suggestions. Washington, possibly the second oldest man there, did well not to say a word.

I also hasten to point out that there is certainly no intent to organize a witch hunt against George Washington. For despite all of his natural human flaws, his place of greatness in history is secured by his insistence on a true constitutional democracy and his absolute rejection of any notion that he be made a monarch of any kind. This is his true legacy, and a magnificent one.

No. "Moon Cursers" is just a tale. It is sometimes easier for the storyteller to paint the picture of good and evil, right and wrong, than the historian, scientist or technician.

And so what of Thomas Hickey and his 'plot?'

Despite the news accounts, which said the gallows would be crowded for months to come, no one else was executed for his or her part in the conspiracy. In fact, no one else was really punished at all. Tory Mayor David Matthews, perhaps the most important of those arrested, walked away from that Connecticut jail. He lived in London to the ripe old age of 74. Dawkins, Ketcham, and the Youngs brothers were all freed.

Not one of the hundreds of other prominent citizens was chastised in any way.

Ironically, Colonel Samuel Holden Parsons who headed up the court martial of Thomas Hickey was himself accused of passing information to Sir Henry Clinton later in the war. He was not hanged. In fact, he went on to serve under Washington in New Jersey and was promoted to Major General. He was appointed by President Washington as first judge of the Northwest Territory in 1789 and retired in

Marietta, Ohio. He lived in the land where Thomas Hickey had dreamed of settling with Phoebe.

After Hickey's execution, Washington insisted that all members of his Life Guard be native-born Americans.

Curiously, no one has yet figured out why Washington made specific reference to 'lewd women' in his statement about Hickey when there was not a single mention of any such sex angle at Hickey's court martial. Some accounts say Hickey complained that it was a woman who caused his demise and Washington was just making reference. There is no proof these words came from Hickey.

Although some accounts indicate Hickey wrote a death row statement (as dramatized in "Moon Cursers"), it seems to have vanished right from the start. While court records freely talk of Mary Gibbons, there is no mention of her after Hickey's death. She simply disappears. Even Phoebe Fraunces seems to have been conveniently eliminated.

During a visit to Fraunces Tavern, still serving as a restaurant in lower Manhattan, I was told by a young attendant: "Oh, we think now that Phoebe was just a myth. There is no proof that Samuel Fraunces had a daughter named Phoebe." Yet several historical texts talk quite comfortably about Phoebe. So, again, who or what to believe?

The political mood changed instantly the minute the noose tightened around the neck of Thomas Hickey.

Here's a report from a history of the Revolutionary War written in 1788:

"This affair (The Hickey Plot) produced a change in the politics of New Jersey. That colony, it was thought, would be among the last to alter its government, whereas now it was to be among the first .... the plot against the general wrought wonders."

Thomas Hickey's death, it seems, brought greater political support for independence. George Washington, always the pragmatist, had perhaps decided to sacrifice a single soldier for the greater good. Or, perhaps, Hickey was exactly as billed: a deserter, opportunist, and traitor. We will never know. It is the duty of the historians to present the facts unfettered. It is the calling of the storyteller to flesh out the bones of history with human emotion. In this context, it is understandable if the fine keepers of Washington's legacy at Mount Vernon, should want to ban such a book as "Moon Cursers." (Not that any such thing has been suggested, mind you.)

However, it is titillating to note that the Washington coat of arms which hangs at Mount Vernon states: "Exitus acta probat." Translated: The end justifies the means.

--JS

About the Author

John Swantek is the author of several books, fiction and non-fiction.

His serialized account of the American Revolution won a Freedom's Foundation at Valley Forge Gold Medal.

It was in researching that project, he learned of Thomas Hickey.

Go to: www.JohnSwantek.com

www.ingramcontent.com/pod-product-compliance
Lightning Source LLC
Chambersburg PA
CBHW070910260626
47162CB00007B/2618